Praise for Linda Winfree's *Uncovered*

"The characters are clearly drawn and distinctive . . . a very
entertaining read . . ."

~ *Mimosa, Long and Short Reviews*

Look for these titles by *Linda Winfree*

Now Available:

What Mattered Most

Uncovered

Linda Winfree

A Samhain Publishing, Ltd. publication.

Samhain Publishing, Ltd.
577 Mulberry Street, Suite 1520
Macon, GA 31201
www.samhainpublishing.com

Uncovered
Copyright © 2010 by Linda Winfree
Print ISBN: 978-1-60504-715-7
Digital ISBN: 978-1-60504-621-1

Editing by Anne Scott
Cover by Anne Cain

First Samhain Publishing, Ltd. electronic publication: July 2009
First Samhain Publishing, Ltd. print publication: May 2010

Dedication

For Jen

Chapter One

She didn't want to go in there.

Madeline Holton paused on the top step before the Chandler County Sheriff's Department, a wicked roll of nerves trembling through her. Going in meant admitting there was no going back, meant facing how far she'd fallen. A piss-ant backwoods department in Middle of Nowhere, Georgia. A pity job extended only because the sheriff was her brother-in-law. God, how had she come to this, anyway?

She really didn't want to acknowledge the answer.

With a deep breath, she squared her shoulders and reached for the door. She wasn't Virgil Holton's daughter for nothing.

Inside, the sharp smell of dust burning off heating coils assaulted her, blending with a fierce odor of stale coffee. The desk officer, phone pressed to his ear, nodded and held up a finger in a silent plea for patience. She tapped a nail on the scarred wooden counter and surveyed the lobby.

The place hadn't changed much since her teen years. A new front door, a fresh coat of paint on the walls, and wax on the industrial tile floors couldn't make the ramshackle concrete-block building more than it was. Like putting red lipstick and cheap perfume on a cheaper whore. Just like she was fairly certain positioning a new sheriff at the helm didn't make it a clean, honorable department.

"May I help you?" The desk jockey graced her with a smile so earnest it hurt.

She straightened her shoulders again. "I'm Madeline Holton. I have an appointment with Sheriff Reed."

Recognition bloomed on his face. "Yes, ma'am. He's in his office, said to send you back when you arrived. Down the hall, through the squad room on your left. Can't miss his office."

The sense of déjà vu deepened as she walked along the narrow corridor. At sixteen, she'd had to call her daddy to come get her from this very station, after she'd wrecked her mama's car. The one she hadn't been given permission to drive. Even now, the memory of his anger made her cringe. Lord help her, she'd never been able to make the old man happy, even when she hadn't been screwing up.

The hallway opened on one side into a grim squad room with mismatched furniture. Someone had painted and waxed here, too, trying to make improvements, but it hadn't worked. Across the space, a door stood partially ajar, a six-pointed star stenciled on its frosted glass insert. Yep, couldn't miss that, could she? Male voices, lifted in irritation, drifted out.

"Are you still pissed?" Heavy exasperation coated Stanton Reed's tone. "Get over it, Tick."

"Hell yeah, I'm still pissed." Tick Calvert. Madeline closed her eyes, any good feelings she had at all about this situation drying up like a pond during a record drought. "You made a personnel decision without consulting me."

"You'd have said no." Stanton's rough exhale dripped with frustration. "We need another investigator, Tick. Cut me some slack here. She's experienced, you've been on sick leave, Chris didn't want to take on a permanent investigations position and it's too much for Cookie to handle alone."

"Bullshit. I've been back full-time over a month now. You can't use that as an excuse. Admit you did an end-run around me, even if it's only to yourself."

"We need her."

"We might need another investigator, but we don't need *her*. She's trouble, Stan, with a capital T. Just wait."

Madeline sucked in a harsh breath. Why was she surprised? She'd harbored no illusions that Tick Calvert would be happy to see her, let alone work with her. At least she knew what she was walking into. She stepped forward and rapped on the door.

"It's open." At Stanton's rumble, she pushed the slab inward and entered the office. Discomfort flashed over her brother-in-law's face. Tick's dark gaze lifted to hers and he grimaced before looking away. Stanton rose. "Madeline, have a seat."

She didn't miss the way Tick, Mr. Southern Raised-Right Manners, failed to rise at her entrance. Yes, working here was going to be fun.

Once she'd taken one of the two worn leather chairs before Stanton's desk, he settled into his chair again. "We were just talking about your taking this position. I know you're looking at it as a temp job, but I have to tell you, it'll help us out while you're here."

At least one member of her family got it. Her mother, Pollyanna-delusional as always, still believed Madeline was home for good, and her sister Autry wanted to indulge in some sisterly bonding kick that involved helping Madeline find a local rental house.

As if she'd be here long-term. Madeline restrained herself from rolling her eyes. No, she was around long enough to begin rebuilding her reputation as a cop, to control the damage from that mess in Jacksonville... Then she was off to a real department in a real city, if the J-ville PD wouldn't take her back. No way was the Chandler County Sheriff's Department, with its history of small-town corruption and male chauvinism, her permanent professional home.

"Let me tell you what I had in mind..."

She listened as Stanton outlined her duties and the plan for her interim employment. Although she didn't look straight at him, she remained aware Tick watched her with ill-tempered resignation and a cynical twist to his mouth. She stiffened her spine. Fine by her. She wasn't any happier about working with him.

"I've got a county commission meeting at ten. Tick will show you around, assign you a unit, make sure you have everything you need." Stanton rose and offered her a hand, his big palm and long fingers engulfing hers. She relaxed a little under his rare, genuine smile. In any case he seemed willing to give her a legitimate chance to redeem herself.

Tick unfolded himself as Stanton left them alone. He gestured toward the squad room and ushered her through the door. "Come on."

Let's get this over with.

The rest of the statement hung in the air.

Madeline cast a surreptitious glance at him. He'd aged well, maturity sharpening the lines of his face, with no silver in his black hair yet, and if pressed, she'd admit he was even better looking as a man in his late thirties than he'd been as a brash nineteen-year-old boy. She dropped her gaze to his mouth, remembering the one and only time she'd kissed him, remembering everything that had happened afterward, and revulsion shivered through her.

Jesus, she wasn't going to make it through this.

"Well?" Irritable, he stood in the middle of the dingy squad room, exasperation darkening his expression. "Holy hell, Madeline, does everything have to be difficult with you?"

Swallowing a retort, she pinned a smartass smirk on her face. "Just waiting for the royal tour, Calvert."

With tight gestures, he pointed out aspects of the area: officer mailboxes, supplies, time clock, baskets for filing reports.

11

"Yours while you're here." He indicated a scarred metal desk, painted a grim pea green. It fronted an identical piece of furniture. Tick jerked his chin toward it. "Cookie's. He's off until Thursday. He's taking the evening shift after that so you can start on days."

Something ugly and a lot like disdain lurked in his words. Madeline bristled. "I suppose you think I should be on nights and I'm getting special treatment because Stanton's married to my sister."

Tick grunted. "I think Stan's the only reason you've got a job here at all."

He continued the department walk-through, showing her the conference room, and downstairs, the jail facilities—or lack thereof, she thought—the employee locker and break rooms, the dispatch office.

The place left a lot to be desired, and she couldn't help comparing it to the sleek modern station she'd worked in during her time in Jacksonville. Again, the sense of loss threatened to swamp her. God, she'd really messed things up.

Upstairs, he pushed open the door to his own office, a room small enough to have been a closet at one time. He dropped into his chair and reached for a leather-bound planner, the fluorescent light glinting off his wide platinum wedding band. "Have a seat and let's take a look at your training schedule."

She remained on her feet, arms crossed over her chest. "I've been in this as long as you have, remember? I don't need 'training'."

His head jerked up, the line of his mouth rigid. "You need to understand how this department works. I'd say that was part of 'training', wouldn't you? Now sit down."

She waited a second before complying, just so he'd understand she did things on her time schedule, not at his command.

With an audible breath, he dropped his gaze to the binder. She flicked a look around the room. Where Stanton's office had been spartan, with only a handful of photos on his shelf and some law enforcement certificates and awards on the walls, Tick's pulsed with his personality. His FBI award shared space with a mounted big mouth bass. An ancient and worn Bible leaned on a shelf next to a variety of training manuals. Snapshots of his family—sisters, brothers, nieces, nephews, his mother—filled any bare areas. More frames took up the corner of his desk, a wedding photo, a casual shot of him and his wife, images of their infant son, all big dark eyes and black hair.

Being here, in this space, looking at the cheerful normalcy of his life, made her edgy. His happiness sparked a long-buried resentment in her. Obviously, he was none the worse for what had happened between them so long ago. His whole life hadn't gone to hell. Why had hers?

Awareness pricked its way down her nape and along her spine. She looked up to catch him watching her with hard eyes. A hot flush ran under her skin, the embarrassment only feeding her anger.

"All right." He scanned the pages before him. "I'll run you through the patrol routes this afternoon. Roger can probably review the dispatch protocol with you in the morning. I'll be your ride-along the next couple of days, and we can turn you loose Thursday. That'll give you Friday through Sunday off, then Monday you can start the three-two-three-two rotation. That work for you—"

The phone at his elbow jangled and he reached for it without excusing himself. "Calvert." He listened, frowning, then lifted his gaze to Madeline's, a mocking twist to his mouth. "Right. Got it covered."

He replaced the receiver and leaned back, still watching her with an expression that sent nerves jangling under her skin. "Well, Holton, you said you didn't need training. Think you're ready to handle a run on your own?"

What could this county throw at her that she couldn't possibly handle? "Sure."

He scrawled directions on a notepad, tore a sheet free and thrust it at her. "The diner's delivery van is down. Prisoner meals need to be picked up and brought back here before noon. Tell Roger in dispatch to give you the keys to unit C-4. It'll be yours for the duration."

A lunch run? He was sending her on a goddamn prisoner lunch run. She stared at the paper trembling in her hand and slowly raised her gaze to his. The fucking asshole. He regarded her with silent, enigmatic challenge. He thought she'd refuse, pitch a fit, make a scene. Jacksonville would see twelve inches of snow before she gave him the satisfaction, even if telling him to shove the duty was her first overriding instinct.

"C-4, you said?" She folded the directions into a neat square and tucked it in her pocket. "I'll be back."

Unit C-4 turned out to be a relatively new, immaculately maintained, unmarked Crown Victoria. This was familiar, sliding behind the wheel, the smooth power of a police package beneath her, the muted crackle of radio traffic filling her being.

God, she'd missed this, hadn't realized how much until now.

The diner wasn't difficult to find and wasn't far from the department, either. Within walking distance. Frowning, Madeline parked in the alley beside the historic brick building. Why hadn't Calvert sent her on foot?

She found the answer inside as the bubbly fresh-out-of-high-school cashier loaded take-out plate after take-out plate in two large cardboard boxes. An unwilling spurt of humor tugged at Madeline's lips. At least Calvert hadn't been a big enough ass to send her after this on foot.

Or maybe it simply hadn't occurred to him.

She juggled one of the awkward boxes into her arms and glared at the second. "I'll be back for that one."

Trying to keep her hands from slipping off, she shoved the door open with one hip and stepped onto the sidewalk. The damn carton was heavier than it looked, and it was farther to the car than she liked. Plus, she'd locked the unit. Her keys were in her pocket; she'd have to set the box down to dig them out.

"Hey, let me help you with that." A smooth drawl filled her ears seconds before strong hands lifted the box easily from her precarious hold.

"Thanks." She rubbed her tingling palms down her hips before tugging the keys from her pocket. She looked up at her rescuer. He was tall, his body tight with the muscles that came from good old-fashioned hard work. He balanced the box easily on one hip. Sunlight glinted off sandy-blond hair, lightened here and there by long hours outside. A denim jacket covered an untucked T-shirt. His faded blue jeans, a hole worn in one pocket, were as disreputable as his scuffed work boots.

Standard farmer attire.

Too bad she'd sworn off farmboys long ago. This one was cute, with a great smile and the prettiest pale green eyes she'd ever seen, glowing in a tanned face, thin lines spreading out beneath long lashes.

He was checking her out, too, his sea-colored gaze roaming from her hair, to her face, over her body and back up to her eyes. He grinned, white teeth flashing against his golden skin. "You're new here."

New? Madeline swallowed a laugh. If he only knew. She wasn't going to explain her convoluted past to a man she'd probably never see again, though. She pointed toward the police car. "I'm parked over here."

He settled the box on the stainless steel backseat and straightened. "Is that all?"

She wavered for a half second. "Actually, there's one more, if you don't mind..."

"I don't." The great smile lit his face again. "Or I wouldn't have asked." He tucked his hands in his pockets as they walked back to the diner. "Good thing I decided to call in a lunch order today, huh?"

She reached for the door and held it. "What do you mean?"

"Might have missed meeting you."

A laugh bubbled in her throat, and she smothered it. The last thing she wanted was a man in her life, and if she was in the market for one, it would be the kind she'd always dated: smooth, polished, interested in sex and no strings.

Not the farmer-type she'd grown up with.

Not even one with a killer body and drop-dead eyes.

He hefted the second box with the same ease and economy of movement. Outside at the car, he tilted his chin toward it. "So you're with the sheriff's department."

"Temporarily."

He tucked his thumbs in his back pockets, the line of his body relaxed. "Maybe I'll see you around then."

Not likely, but she smiled anyway. "Maybe."

He nodded. "You have a good day, now."

Slipping behind the wheel, she watched him amble toward the diner. My, my, he had a nice ass, and the old jeans highlighted it to perfection. Shaking off the purely feminine musings, she shifted into gear and drove back to the station. Any pleasant feelings engendered by the interlude with the good-looking farmer sputtered out as soon as she returned to the sheriff's department. She pulled in and parked beneath the spreading oak trees. The awkward angle of the back door made wrangling the large boxes free difficult. Two deputies exiting the rear entrance came her way.

"Let us get those." The taller of the two spoke first, his voice quiet, his icy blue eyes holding no expression. "I hate when the diner uses these huge-ass boxes. Makes it hard as hell to get them out of the car. Here, Troy Lee."

He passed the carton off to the younger man, who regarded Madeline with blatant curiosity. God help her. There was one in every bunch. She stared him down. The first deputy straightened, balancing the box on his hip much as the farmer had earlier. Sunlight filtering through the leaves glimmered over his nametag: *C. Parker.*

Troy Lee slanted an inquisitive glance in her direction as they walked toward the building. "You're the new investigator?"

People around here truly had no life if they noticed every new face. Guess some things never changed. She nodded. "That would be me."

A third deputy swung the door open for them from inside. "Hey, Troy Lee, Calvert's looking for you. What did you do this time?"

"Hell if I know. He's been pissy lately." Troy Lee shoved the carton onto the counter inside the door. "Man, he's a prick when he's not getting laid."

He trudged up the stairs. Parker began setting meals on the counter. "I have this, Investigator, if there's something else you need to do."

Other than pull her eyelashes out one-by-one because she was stuck working here? Couldn't think of a thing.

Waving an envelope, Troy Lee bounded back down the steps. Parker grinned. "That was fast."

"My training certificate from Tifton is in."

Parker started another row of plates. "Take back what you said about him?"

"No. He's still a prick when he's not getting laid, and lately, he's obviously not."

Ignoring them, Madeline wandered upstairs. In the hallway, she caught a glimpse of the small lobby. Just inside the door, Tick Calvert stood talking with the same tall, good-looking farmer who'd come to her rescue earlier. As she watched, Tick grinned and slapped the other man on the shoulder before he left. The farmer waved on his way out the door.

Madeline shook her head. Well, then. Even if she'd been interested, being Tick's friend put him out of the running. She definitely had enough shit in her life already.

"Holton." Tick's grim voice pulled her from the mini-reverie. "You ready to go run through patrol routes?"

"Sure." She pinned on a patently false enthusiastic smile, and he scowled.

For their first trip out, he put her in the driver's seat but insisted on giving verbal directions as they drove every back road in the county. Finally, her frustration bubbled over. "Damn it, Calvert, I am a local, remember? I don't need you to hold my hand here."

He tapped his fingers on the door panel. "This isn't going to work until two things happen, Madeline. One, you have to do more than go through the motions. Two, you've got to get off that damn high horse of yours."

She scowled at him as she turned left onto a familiar red dirt road. "Like you want it to work."

His brows lowered and a muscle jumped in his cheek. "It's about more than what I want. Stan hired you. He wants you in this position, and I have to make sure my department runs smoothly."

"Your department." She flexed her hands on the wheel. "I thought it was Stanton's house."

He tossed her an infuriated look. "This is hopeless. Pull off up here."

She obeyed without comment, steering the patrol car into the drive of a long-forgotten shack, weathered and forlorn. Tick pushed his door open and exited the car, leaning against the hood, arms over his chest.

After killing the engine, she climbed out and walked to stand at the front of the car. Tick ran a hand through his hair. "Holy hell, I need a cigarette."

With a shrug, she snagged her pack from her jacket pocket and extended it. He stared at the package with mingled longing and repulsion. "Shit, you smoke?"

She shook one free and lit it. "When I feel like it."

His dark gaze trailed the smoke as it curled upward. "I suppose you're going to tell me you're one of those people who can take it or leave it."

She inhaled, letting the tiny bite of nicotine soothe her ragged nerves. "Pretty much."

"Figures."

"Sure you don't want one?"

He snorted. "I want it, believe me. I'm just not taking it. One leads to another with me."

She propped a hip on the hood. "Why, so the great and mighty Tick Calvert does have a weakness after all. How shocking."

"Don't start that crap, Holton."

"Maybe I'm not the only one with a high horse."

He rubbed a hand over his nape, staring into the field beyond the house. "You know what we're going to have to do for this to work, don't you?"

She stiffened, her stomach dropping like she'd just peeked over the edge of some massive abyss.

He turned those dark eyes on her. "We have to deal with what happened."

Chapter Two

He was wiped out.

Out of long-time habit, Tick tossed his keys on the kitchen island and cringed as they clattered against the tile. He tensed, waiting, sure he'd hear Lee's incensed wail. Silence greeted him, and he slowly relaxed.

After flipping through the mail—power bill, insurance renewal notice, junk flyer offering instant riches—he walked to the master bedroom just off the living room. Caitlin sat cross-legged, propped against their headboard, with case files spread over the quilt and their son nursing with blissful single-minded intent.

She looked up from the folder she was reading over Lee's head, her eyes lighting. "Hi."

"Hey." He eased onto the bed and leaned over to kiss her. Her mouth moved under his, and the spice of her shampoo filled his senses.

At his voice, Lee opened his eyes and regarded him for a second before latching on eagerly once more. Tick cradled his son's head, the wisps of black hair soft against his palm. "How was your day?"

"Busy. Guess who decided he wants to nurse every two hours instead of three?"

With his thumb, Tick traced the shape of the baby's ear. Lee opened his eyes again, a slight frown drawing together brows so thin they were almost invisible. "Are you giving Mama a hard time, boy?"

Lee half-smiled at him before shifting his concentration to food again. Tick turned his head to find Caitlin's gaze on his face, the green depths soft with emotion. He dropped his attention to her mouth and leaned in before he checked the movement. Instead, he slid to the side of the bed and toed off his loafers.

"What about your day?" A low note of strain invaded Caitlin's husky voice.

He groaned and pushed up from the mattress. "Don't ask."

All the tension from dealing with Madeline Holton settled in his lower back. She'd made it very—and rather obscenely—plain what he could do with his suggestion that they deal with the past, and the remainder of the day had passed in chilly near-silence, broken only by the radio and any necessary communication between the two of them. He'd been able to feel the waves of resentment coming off her, and it had only made his own worse.

He unbuckled his belt and tugged it off, taking his gear with it. The gun, badge and cuffs went in his nightstand drawer.

"That bad?"

"Yeah." He walked into the bathroom and flipped on the shower. While the water heated, he eyed himself in the mirror. A shadow of stubble darkened his jaw, but he could get by without shaving until the morning. Not like he'd have to worry about leaving Caitlin with beard burn. "What am I cooking tonight?"

"You're not." Paper rustled and Lee snuffled a little, followed by his robust belch. "We're going to Autry and Stanton's, remember?"

Damn. Hands braced on the vanity, he dropped his head. He'd really rather stay in, let being with Caitlin and the baby soothe some of the stress dogging him. However, after a day spent with Lee and those crime scene reports he'd glimpsed, she had to be anticipating getting out. Maybe a couple of hours away from home would take his mind off the fact that it looked like his wife might never make love with him again.

Okay, "never" was a long time and probably an exaggeration. Maybe it looked like by the time they had sex again, Lee would be in high school.

"Tick?" Caitlin spoke from the doorway, baby tucked against her shoulder. Something in her voice told him she'd called him more than once. "We're supposed to be there at seven."

He dragged a hand over his hair and straightened. "Yeah, it just slipped my mind. I'm getting in the shower now."

He stepped under the flow of hot water, letting it ease some of the kinks from his too-tight muscles. Considering the tiled cubicle held some of the hottest memories of his life, it did little for the gnawing sexual tension. He pressed his forehead to the wall and tried to think of things other than having Caitlin's legs wrapped around his waist, water streaming over them as he thrust inside her, his ears filled with her soft moans and the sexy-as-hell way she cried out as he made her come. He groaned. Patient. He simply had to be patient.

The high-risk pregnancy, complete with months of bed rest, and her subsequent emergency delivery had been hard on Caitlin, physically and emotionally. His cancer scare and resulting surgery, coinciding with Lee's nearly eight-weeks-early birth, had put him out of commission when he should have been helping her cope with a hospitalized preemie. Considering Lee had given new meaning to the term "intense personality" since they'd brought him home... No wonder they were out of practice in the bedroom.

Ten months, one week and...he counted, envisioning an imaginary calendar...two days out of practice.

He blew out a long breath and reached for the soap. Patience. A little celibacy had never hurt anyone, and he didn't want Caitlin to feel pressured. He'd just go on, keeping his kisses and touches on the light and casual side, not pushing. He'd wait for her.

Even if it killed him.

"Are you sure there isn't anything I can do to help?" Madeline leaned against the counter and watched her sister bustle about the to-die-for gourmet kitchen.

Autry settled a stack of plates on the island and brushed back a few strands of hair that had escaped her loose knot. "I'm sure. Stanton's putting Gabby down for the night, the lasagna's almost ready, the salad's done. We're good to go."

Madeline tapped her fingernails on the cool granite.

Hands folded over the bulge of her pregnant belly, Autry studied her. "So how was your first day?"

"Okay." With an offhand shrug, Madeline looked away. Autry thought the sun rose and set in Tick Calvert, always had. She didn't know everything that lay between them, and Madeline sure wasn't going to tell her. If she complained about working with him, she'd come off as a whining bitch. The bitch part she was okay with, the whining not so much.

"Just okay?"

"It was all right." Madeline tossed back her hair. Somehow, she liked it better when she and Autry were going at each other's throats. Sisterly bonding could be a bitch too. "God, Autry, it's not like it was the first day of school or my wedding day or... It was an okay day."

Autry lifted her hands in defense, or maybe retreat. "Fine. Forget I asked."

That was better. Autry annoyed, she could handle.

Madeline counted the plates in the short stack, and a sudden sinking sensation grabbed hold of her stomach. "I'm not the only one coming for dinner, am I?"

"Nope." Autry turned away to pull down glasses from a cabinet. "Tick and Caitlin are coming, and Ash Hardison. I don't think you've met him."

Dinner with Tick and the perfect wife? Oh, God. Hadn't the day been enough?

Obviously not. Evidently, she was doomed to pay retribution for the rest of her life for one teenage indiscretion. If she had it to do all over again, she'd never have crawled into bed beside the lousy bastard.

A truck engine rumbled outside.

"That will be Ash," Autry said. "Tick's always late for dinner. It makes Cait crazy."

Footsteps thudded up the steps and across the cedar deck. Single footsteps. Madeline relaxed slightly. She wouldn't have to face Tick, not just yet. A quick rap at the back door echoed in the kitchen.

Autry hefted a pitcher of iced tea from the refrigerator. "It's unlocked." She was still speaking with rueful affection as it swung open and a tall blond man ducked inside. "I don't know why you bother to knock. You're always welcome."

"Because around here, a guy never knows what he'll walk in on." He flashed a wicked grin and hugged Autry. Recognition slammed into Madeline. Gorgeous, flirtatious farmerboy from outside the diner. Gorgeous, flirtatious farmerboy who happened to be Tick Calvert's friend. Oh, just her luck...

"Maddie, this is Ash Hardison. He and Stanton go way back." Autry drew her forward. "Ash, my sister Madeline. She's going to be working with the sheriff's department for a while, as an interim investigator."

"I know." Those perfect white teeth flashed in a genuine smile. Pale green eyes filled with male approval stared down at her. "We met earlier today."

Autry cuffed his arm. "Then why didn't you say anything?"

He ducked playfully. "We weren't formally introduced. I didn't realize she was your sister, just that she was driving one of Stan's squad cars, and I didn't get a chance to ask Tick who she was when I went by the station."

Autry pushed them both toward the living room. "Y'all go get acquainted while I get our drinks ready. Stan should be out in a few minutes."

In the living room, Madeline stood, trying to look everywhere but at Ash and failing. The too-faded jeans and old T-shirt were gone, although he still wore jeans—newer, neatly creased, paired with a white polo that somehow set off his eyes and made the light green even clearer.

He sank onto one end of the big leather couch, his gaze on her face. "So you're Autry's sister."

"So you're Stanton's friend." And Tick's. She needed to remember that. She perched on the edge of an armchair, her stomach fluttering with a blend of nerves and awareness. This was ridiculous. He was good-looking. Whatever. Wasn't like she'd never been exposed to a handsome man.

"Small world."

"Isn't it." She rubbed her hands over her knees. "What do you do?"

An ironic grin played over his mouth. "I'm a farmer."

Like she hadn't guessed that. She brushed back her hair. "Row crops?"

"Some. We truck-farm produce." He chuckled. "Mostly chickens. Alligators. Pecans."

"Alligators?"

"No-waste farming. We feed the dead chickens to them. Turn a pretty good profit off the meat and hides as well." He leaned forward, hands between his knees, warming to his subject. "I wasn't too sure about the gators at first. They were Tick's idea. You know Tick, right? Hell, you have to, y'all would have grown up together."

"Yes, I know him." And wished to God she'd never met the son of a bitch.

"So how long have you been in law enforcement?"

Her stomach clenched. "About eighteen years."

"You must love it."

"I do." Or rather she had, until she'd managed to get her partner killed. The conversation was ripping at her gut, bringing up images and emotions she needed to simply stay buried.

Another engine rumbled, and headlights swept over the front of the house, a big cedar contemporary. Madeline pressed a finger to her forehead, where a low throbbing had commenced. Sitting home and listening to her mother bemoan the fact her little brother was in prison would be more fun.

"I'm blowing this, aren't I?"

"What?" Madeline met Ash's direct gaze. A hint of self-derision twisted his mouth. She laughed, a scoffing puff of air. "There's nothing to blow."

"I beg to differ."

She cast a sideways glance at the kitchen doorway. Beyond, Autry's cheerful voice blended with Tick's deep drawl and another female voice, husky and cultured. Pulling her attention back to Ash, she shrugged. "I'm not in the market for a relationship right now. It's not a good time."

He nodded. "What about a good friend? You in the market for one of those?"

Friends? She didn't do those. Besides, she'd never met a man yet honestly interested in being her *friend*. The image of Tick slapping him on the back flared in her brain. "Don't you have enough friends already? Why bother with me?"

Surprise flashed in his eyes, but he didn't look away. He rubbed a finger over his chin. "I find you intriguing. I'd like to know you."

He found her intriguing? Um, yeah. Like a train wreck, maybe. "I—"

"Looks like everyone's here." Autry ushered Tick and his wife into the room. Tick settled a car seat bearing a sleeping infant on the coffee table. His dark gaze clashed with Madeline's, and his chin lifted to a familiar, damning angle.

"I hope y'all are hungry." A pretty smile lit Autry's face. "I made two pans of lasagna, and Stan hates leftovers."

"Well, I'm starved." Ash pushed to his feet. He was tall—probably six-four at least. She liked tall men, liked the way having to gaze up at someone made her feel fluttery and feminine and...she needed to remember she wasn't seeking any man, tall, green eyed, muscular, or not.

Indulgence colored Autry's laugh. "You're always hungry."

"I work hard."

"Madeline, have you met Tick's wife?" Autry gestured at the slender brunette at Tick's side. Madeline's eyes narrowed on the other woman's face. She was familiar, like they'd met before, and not because Madeline had seen her photos in Tick's office. "Caitlin, this is my sister, Maddie—"

"We've met." Madeline cringed a little at the cold note in her voice. She had met Caitlin once, years before. So Tick's wife was the Fed who'd informed her of her father's death. It really was a small world.

Caitlin extended a hand, her bottle-green eyes cool and watchful. "A pleasure to see you again, Ms. Holton."

"Madeline, please." She took the proffered hand, studying the details of Caitlin's face. She was a beauty but appeared tired, a little drawn, the line of her mouth tight.

Autry rubbed a hand across her belly. "Maddie is Stanton's new interim investigator."

"Really." Caitlin arched a brow. Some indefinable unspoken communication passed between Tick and her, and he scowled.

"Looks like he's grown." Ash leaned over the drowsing baby and touched a finger to his cheek. He stirred and Caitlin stiffened.

"Ash, wait, please don't—"

A plaintive wail rent the air, and Caitlin cringed. Tick's lashes fell, his shoulders slumping with his muttered "hell".

"Lee's here." Stanton strode into the room, chuckling, as the baby's coughing cries grew louder. Tick slanted a killing scowl in Stanton's direction.

Caitlin leaned down and made quick work of the straps holding the squalling baby in the seat. She lifted him against her chest, murmuring soothing nothings. Ash grimaced. "I didn't mean to—"

"It's okay." Tick waved off the apology. "He's just grumpy. If you hadn't set him off, something else would."

"He was born grouchy." Stanton slapped Tick on the back. "Don't know where he gets that from."

Against Caitlin's chest, the baby scrunched into a stiff ball and howled while she dug in the diaper bag. Madeline's throbbing pulsed harder. Did all babies do that? Maybe she hadn't missed out on anything by not becoming a mother, after all.

With a pacifier and some patient comforting, the baby soon rested, half-dozing, in his mother's arms. After a few minutes, Caitlin tucked him back into his carrier. Autry hustled them all to the table, and Madeline found herself sitting at Ash's side and directly across the table from Tick.

Great. Just wonderful.

The busyness of passing food and filling plates blessed her with a few moments of distraction. Under the table, Ash's knee nudged hers. She glanced at him quickly, only to find him turned away to pass the salad bowl in Stanton's direction. She resisted an overwhelming need to shift sideways.

"Madeline, you're here only temporarily?" Caitlin's quiet question startled her.

"Yes." She studied the other woman. No guile or malice gleamed in her gaze; the question seemed posed out of mere politeness or curiosity. "For the next six weeks."

In the process of sprinkling parmesan atop his lasagna, Tick made a nondescript noise in his throat. Caitlin's gaze flicked to him, then back to Madeline. "So you're on leave from your department?"

"That's right." Awareness of Ash's regard trickled down her spine, swirling into the tension caused by Caitlin's questions. Something about that easy inquiry set her teeth on edge. She narrowed her eyes at Caitlin. Two could play the oh-so-polite interrogation game. "You're FBI. Which branch? Organized crime?"

"Behavioral science. I'm a criminal profiler."

Well, didn't that beat all. Those innocent questions suddenly made a lot more sense. Madeline forced a smile to her lips. "Sounds interesting."

"It can be." Caitlin brushed her hair behind her ear. "If I remember correctly, you're with Jacksonville's PD."

"Yep." Her stomach knotted and she choked down the bite she'd just taken of her sister's luscious vegetable lasagna. "Homicide."

Caitlin's gaze lingered on her a second before she turned to ask Autry about her latest obstetrician visit. With attention finally off her, Madeline let herself relax, only to look up and find Tick's hard gaze on her. Her appetite decimated, she picked at a piece of crusty garlic bread and pushed her salad around its plate.

As much as she hated to admit it, maybe Tick was right. Maybe they just needed to deal with what had happened that long-ago night and in the days that followed. Whether she liked it or not, she would have to work with him, at least for the six weeks she'd promised Stanton when he'd offered her the temp position.

Dealing with the past wasn't an option tonight, though. She glanced at Caitlin, then at Ash. Definitely not tonight.

Maybe tomorrow, when Madeline was once more trapped in a squad car with the one man who truly despised her.

Damn, he was headed for deep trouble. While he helped Stanton and Tick clear the table, Ash studied Madeline Holton once more as Autry moved the women outside to take advantage of an unseasonably warm evening. She had to be one of the most beautiful women he'd ever seen with her long dark hair, big hazel eyes, full mouth.

She was also, from his experience, the most dangerous type of woman a man could encounter. First impressions could definitely deceive a guy. That afternoon, outside the diner, he'd seen a brashly confident woman, sure of herself, the kind of woman who met a man on equal footing. She looked anything but confident now, choosing a chair near the edge of the deck, as far from Autry and Caitlin as she could get. Her body stiff, she folded her arms over her chest and stared into the yard.

Removed. Isolated. Not what he'd seen in her that afternoon. He almost smiled. One thing was for sure—she was a dichotomy. A challenge to figure out.

Hell, he knew how dangerous those were as well.

His second impression had surely been tainted by what little Stanton and Autry had said about Madeline—quick-tempered, stubborn, demanding, always wanting to take the hard way anywhere. As he'd talked with her earlier, he'd caught glimpses of the woman he'd thought she was first, tempting him to forget his hard-won common sense. He'd been willing to overlook that, give in to the temptation to get to know her better.

Until Tick walked in the room.

Over dinner, his third impression had cemented his conviction that Madeline Holton was a woman to be avoided. She was distinctly uncomfortable, her posture rigid and aloof, a sure sign that she didn't feel she belonged. Even more obviously, she had some type of hang-up where Tick was concerned. She darted secret looks in his direction, and with each one, her expression grew more and more unhappy, the line of her shoulders grew more and more taut.

Therefore, despite being the most intriguing female he'd met in a long time, Madeline was off limits. He'd already had one high-maintenance woman with a hankering for another man try to ruin him. He didn't need another one.

Shrugging off the musings, he passed a stack of silverware to Tick, who was loading the dishwasher while Stanton wiped down the kitchen. He squinted at Tick's drawn features. "You look wasted."

"I am." Tick dropped the forks in the basket. "Tired as hell."

"See?" Stanton swiped a sponge over the island. "Having Madeline on hand will take a load off you, too."

Straightening, Tick fixed him with a deadpan stare. "Right. Having her around is going to really help things at work. This is the same woman who blamed you for her father's death. For your daughter's death. Remember?"

"Her father had just died, suddenly and violently. People do odd things under those circumstances."

"Yeah."

"Tick—"

"I'm going to remind you of this conversation when we're cleaning up whatever mess she causes before she skips out again."

Curious, Ash leaned on the counter, cast a quick glance out the window at the women on the deck then shifted his attention to Tick. "You don't like her?"

"I don't trust her." After adding detergent to the dishwasher, Tick closed the door a little harder than necessary. "She's a conniving liar."

"Damn it, Tick." Stanton looked toward the kitchen door, which led to the deck. "Keep your voice down."

"Trust me, she knows how I feel."

Stanton studied Tick, frowning. "Autry's never said anything—"

"Autry doesn't know." Tick passed a hand over his jaw. "Look, just drop it, okay? You hired her, she'll only be here six weeks—if I'm lucky—and I can handle it that long."

"What did she do?" At Ash's quiet question, both Stanton and Tick turned surprised expressions in his direction. He shrugged. Yeah, asking was out of character for him, but he hadn't been able to help himself.

Tick's dark gaze flitted from Ash to Stanton. "I can't say."

"What? First, you're bitching because I hired her, then you insinuate she's less than ethical, and now you can't explain. Shit, Tick."

"I promised Virgil I wouldn't." Tick's shoulders moved in an uncomfortable roll. "He didn't want her mother or...anyway, I gave him my word."

Stanton pinched the bridge of his nose. "Well, that's just great."

Tick shrugged. "I'll stick close to her, Stan, keep an eye on her, all right? We'll find a way to make it work. It's only six weeks. How much damage can she do in a month and a half?"

Who was Tick trying harder to convince—Stanton or himself?

"I'm going to see if Cait's ready to go." Tick jerked a thumb toward the back door.

Once it closed behind him, Ash slanted a sideways glance at Stanton. "He's wound pretty tight."

Stanton huffed a humorless laugh. "No kidding. I thought having Madeline here, taking some of the pressure off him would help. Guess I was wrong."

"He'll be fine. He always is." Ash rested both hands on the counter's edge and let his gaze travel to the window once more. On the deck, Tick leaned down to lift the baby from Caitlin's arms and waved Autry to stay seated. Madeline darted another of those secretive looks at him. Ash frowned. Something was...off...there, something he didn't get.

Was that attraction or dislike that kept her so focused on Tick?

"He'd better be fine. I need him back on his game." Stanton came to stand beside him. Madeline unfolded from her chair, and as Caitlin and Tick came in the back door, her voice carried in with them.

"I think I'm going to head out as well." That indefinable strain

27

tightened her words. "Thanks for dinner."

"You don't have to go yet." Autry followed her sister into the room. "It feels like you just got here."

"It's been a long day." Irony laced Madeline's voice. Tick looked up from placing the baby in his carrier. Palpable tension vibrated between them before he dropped his gaze.

He hefted the infant seat. "Cait? You ready?"

At her nod, they exited in a small flurry of thank-yous and good-nights. Autry turned to Madeline. "I wish you'd stay a little longer."

She shrugged into her jacket. "I have an early day tomorrow."

"I'll walk out with you." Ash pulled his keys from his pocket and leaned down to kiss Autry's cheek. "Dinner was awesome."

Madeline eyed him, wariness coloring her features. "You don't have to."

He put on an easy grin. "You're not the only one with an early day ahead of you."

Outside, a hint of cool air kissed the unseasonable warmth. His truck waited beside her compact sedan and the gravel walk crunched under their feet as they walked toward the vehicles. She glanced back once at the house, a strange hurt flickering over her features before she straightened her shoulders to a near-impossible angle. Unhappiness hung around her like a pall, a loneliness that stopped him from cutting his losses, especially after everything Tick had said, and walking straight to his driver's side door.

He leaned against the truck's hood while she unlocked her car. "What do you like to do during your free time?"

With the door partially open, she froze and confusion glinted in her hazel gaze before disappearing beneath shuttered contempt. "You don't give up, do you?"

"What are you so afraid of?" He spread his elbows to a more comfortable position.

She slammed the door and came to stand before him. Outrage rolled off her in waves. "I'm not afraid of anything. I've told you I'm not interested and you won't back off. End of story."

Bravado. Lots of ballsy bravado that still didn't quite cover the soul-deep isolation that shrouded her and called to him. Pushing wouldn't work with her, though. "If that's the way you want it."

"It is." Her chin lifted to a challenging angle, daring him to dispute her statement.

"Good night, then." He inclined his head and stepped away from the truck. She backed up, stumbling a bit in her haste. He didn't reach to steady her, but let her regain her footing alone. "It was a pleasure meeting you, Madeline."

She snorted. "Sure it was."

He lifted a hand and strode around to the driver's side. The old Ford rumbled to life, reliable as ever, and while the cold-natured engine warmed, he patted the gas pedal a couple of times. His wrist draped over the wheel, he watched in the rearview as Madeline reversed hard and flew down the drive. He shook his head and reached for the gearshift.

Confident and breezy, then prickly and wary. Obsessed? Lonely and afraid of connecting.

Like he could walk away from that puzzle without a second thought.

"You didn't tell me Autry's sister was your new investigator." Caitlin shifted her fingers over Lee's soft hair. His eyes drooped sleepily, mouth relaxing, and Caitlin eased him away from her breast and slid her chemise strap into place before lifting him to her shoulder and rubbing his back.

"Mmpf." Clad in a pair of navy sleep pants, Tick sprawled on their bed, face turned into his pillow. "Been trying to forget."

Lee burped softly against her neck. Caitlin rose from the rocker, her gaze trailing over Tick's strong back. "You seemed edgy tonight."

"Yeah." With his foot, Tick pushed the quilt toward the end of the bed. He curled both arms under the pillow and pulled it closer. "A little."

"I'm putting the baby down. I'll be right back."

Tick's only reply was a noncommittal grunt. She paused in the doorway and watched him a moment before taking the baby upstairs.

Getting Lee settled didn't take long, but Caitlin lingered over him. She didn't know which was worse—that her husband only seemed to touch her when he had to or that he'd stopped talking to her. She stroked the soft back of Lee's little hand. His fingers curled and flexed.

She had no doubt that Tick was in full protective-male mode where she was concerned. While she loved the trait in the right time and place, at the moment, protection was the last thing she wanted from him. She wanted her husband back, all of him, from the man who confided in her and talked about everything with her, to the sweet, playful, often demanding lover who shared her nights. Since she'd always been a take-charge kind of personality...maybe it was time to take him back.

Maybe once she forged that physical connection between them she could get him to open up about why Madeline Holton seemed to put him so on edge.

Leaning down, she whispered a kiss over Lee's brow. If she was lucky, this would be one of the nights when he chose to sleep through his middle-of-the-night feeding. She had distinctly naughty plans for his father.

Downstairs, she cut off all the lights except the one over the kitchen sink. In the bedroom, the lamp glimmered on Tick's bare skin. He remained where she'd left him, eyes closed, lashes fanned over his cheekbones. With a tug of desire kicking off within her, she pulled off the boot socks she always filched from him when winter made the hardwood floors too cool for comfort.

"Tick." She placed a knee on the mattress, swept her fingers across the small of his back, dipped them into the dimples at the base of his spine.

"Mmm?" Sleep husked his voice, making the drawl a deep purr she felt all the way through her body. She shivered. God, she loved that voice, loved the way his murmur, before he even touched her, could make her ready and wet.

"Tired?" She straddled his thighs, rubbing her thumbs along his spine, working the kinks out of the muscles. The warm resiliency of his flesh under her fingers shot tingles of awareness along her nerve endings.

"Yeah." He turned his head, resting his cheek on his arm, and a heavy sigh rumbled from him. She moved higher, stroking and massaging the tension from his body. "Lord, that feels good. Love your hands on me. Don't stop."

"Don't worry." With her knees, she hugged his hips, the simple act of touching him sending sparky flashes of wanting through her. She ached, a heavy yearning settling low in her belly, flowing between her legs. It had been too long. "I won't."

Under her touch, she felt the strain leave his long, lean frame. Memories cascaded through her mind, other nights when she'd done this, leaving him boneless and satisfied, until he turned into her, and they came together in a slow, easy coupling.

Bending forward, she feathered her lips over his shoulder, his nape. His clean male scent infiltrated her senses, heightening the coiling desire building in her. She nuzzled his shoulder blade, smiling.

"Tick." She stroked her fingers down his rib cage, loving the texture and heat of his skin.

A soft snore grumbled from his throat. Caitlin stilled, the desire dying a swift, hard death. She studied his face, relaxed in lines of deep slumber. With a strangled sigh, she straightened and slipped to his side. On her back, she stared at the ceiling, frustration curling through her. Another quiet snore and she dug her nails into the sheet.

Damn it.

Chapter Three

With her faded Springsteen T-shirt sticking to her torso, Madeline jogged up the back steps. Red clay dust clung to her favorite old running shoes, and she stopped to knock it off before opening the kitchen door.

Too-dry warmth washed over, thanks to her mother's tendency to keep the furnace going full blast once the temperature dropped past forty. The rich smells of coffee and fried eggs wrapped around her. Her mother sat at the table, sipping coffee and reading the local newspaper. Madison dropped a kiss on her hair and crossed to pull a bottled water from the fridge.

"Morning, Mama." She tilted the container up and let the icy liquid trail down her parched throat.

"Good morning, baby." Mama didn't look up from the paper. "Your eggs are in the microwave."

Madeline restrained herself from rolling her eyes. Mama should know by now she didn't eat fried food in the morning. Why did she keep trying to push the damn eggs on her?

With a sigh, Madeline pulled the plate from the microwave. The congealed eggs stared up at her with jiggly yellow centers, and her stomach turned. God, she would have to choke down a couple of bites just to please her mother.

She grabbed a fork and leaned against the counter. "Mama, what is that in the north pasture?"

The large metal buildings had gleamed dully in the early light. A weird, rank smell had hovered around them with the misty morning air.

Her mother turned a page. "Alligator houses."

"Alligator—" Her conversation with Ash Hardison came back, slamming reality into her brain. "Why are they on our land?"

She didn't miss the slight way her mother's hand trembled as she settled her coffee cup on the saucer. "It's not our land anymore, honey."

"What?"

Mama lifted her carefully composed face to Madeline's. "I sold everything north of the creek to Tick and Ash."

Hot anger scalded Madeline, singeing her nerve endings. Everything north of the creek left only the house and five acres or so surrounding it. The Holtons had been centennial farmers, even though her daddy had been more of a "gentleman farmer". Now all that was gone? In Tick Calvert's hands.

Madeline sucked in a harsh breath. "Mama, when did you do this?"

"The summer after your daddy died." Unless she'd been listening so carefully for it, Madeline would have missed the tiny tremor in her mother's voice. The anger flashed into fury. That slimy... Taking advantage of her mother's grief.

So Tick wanted to deal with the past, did he? Well, first she had some more recent events for him to face.

The damn water was colder than a well digger's ass. Even through the rubber boots, Ash could sense the chill seeping in. At least it made the gators sluggish. He preferred them this way, a little disoriented and a lot slower than they were during the warmer months.

"Hell." Water sloshed. Tick swore again while he grabbed for another of the three-foot reptiles. He stumbled, and Ash muffled a laugh. They'd been at this since just after four a.m., and Tick was wearing down. "Slippery son of a gun."

"Maybe you're just getting old and slow."

"Younger than you are." Tick sent him a mock glare as he flipped the alligator onto its back atop the long table in the middle of the room. With one hand, he kept the gator's mouth closed; with the other, he rubbed down the scaly abdomen. The whole body went limp. While Tick held the animal, Ash slid two gloved fingers inside the orifice just above the tail, feeling for the telltale nub.

"Male." He added a mark to the tally sheet.

Still clasping the alligator's mouth, Tick spun it over.

"You bastard." Madeline Holton's infuriated voice echoed through the high-ceilinged room. Ash jerked in response, aware Tick startled next to him as well. Too late, Ash saw Tick's hand slip on the gator, saw the tail whip a second before the reptile bent itself into a u-shape and snapped at his own gloved hand. Ash yanked back but not before the alligator got a good chomp at the fleshy part of his hand below his pinky.

"Fuck." Blood spurted from the wound, and he grabbed it with his other palm. Tick grasped Ash's wrist and pushed it over his head. The alligator slid from the table back into the water. Ash smothered a groan. Now their counts would be one off. "Shit."

"Come on." Tick nudged him toward the horizontal opening to the corridor, where Madeline waited, her face flushed with ire. "Let's see how bad it is."

They climbed through the passageway, Ash almost toppling over since he had to balance with only one hand. Eyes narrowed, Madeline watched them, her attention focused on Tick. Ash grimaced at the pain shooting from his hand down his arm. What was she doing here, anyway?

Tick's gaze flared, and he glowered at Madeline. He pointed down the covered walkway. "Office. Now."

In the cramped room they jokingly called the office, Tick pushed Ash toward the chair and dug in the dented file cabinet. He glared at Madeline. "What the hell is your problem?"

Ash rested his elbow on the desk blotter. A thin trickle of blood ran over his fingers, an ache pulsing in his hand. He glanced from his friend to the irate woman and back.

"My problem is you, you son of a bitch." Madeline's chest heaved with a harsh breath. Her gaze darted to Ash's, and her face darkened further. "Actually it's both of you. How could you do this to her?"

"Do what?" Ash deliberately kept his voice quiet, pulling up the tone he'd always used around a skittish horse.

Madeline threw out her hands. "Take advantage of my mother to get your hands on this land. My God, I suppose I should be grateful you waited until Daddy was cold in the ground before you moved in on her."

Tick closed the file cabinet with a soft click. "How did you ever make it in investigations?"

She planted her hands on her hips. "What are you talking about?"

"The way you jump to conclusions and go from point A to point R without thinking. Goddamn, it's a wonder you ever closed a case."

"Tick." Ash leaned back in the chair, removing his arm from the desk.

"You're not even going to deny it, are you?" Madeline shook her head, the thick mass of her shining brown hair escaping a loose knot to spill about her shoulders. "You can't."

"There's nothing to deny. You're so off base it's not funny—"

"Tick." Ash raised his voice, finally bringing Tick's frustrated gaze in his direction. "I'm bleeding profusely over here. Find the medical kit, would you?"

Muttering a foul curse, Tick yanked open the next drawer. Ash examined Madeline's furious expression as she scowled in Tick's direction. He'd been wrong the night before. He'd assumed her obsession with Tick stemmed from a thwarted attraction. But no desire or wanting lurked under her anger. No, that was something very different, a heavy dislike, something close to hatred. Something very much like revulsion.

Tick set the first aid kit on the desk. While he tended to the wound on Ash's hand, Ash watched Madeline. She was still so furious she was almost shaking, a fine tremor running through her. Face pale, she glanced around the office, nostrils flaring slightly, chest moving with uneven breaths.

"Madeline." Ash called her name as gently and calmly as he could, considering Tick had just poured disinfectant over his hand, the raw sting threatening to take his breath. Arms crossed over her midriff, she slid that glittering hazel gaze in his direction. "It's obvious you're upset."

"Upset?" Her laugh was a harsh, ugly sound. "Upset doesn't begin to cover it."

"Did you bother to ask your mother *why* she sold us the land?" Tick pulled the edges of the wound together and began placing butterfly bandages along the seam. "No, wait, that would have taken an open mind and foresight."

"I didn't have to ask." Madeline seemed to spit the words at him. "All I had to hear was you were involved."

Ash winced, both at the venom in her tone and the way his hand throbbed under Tick's capable but less-than-gentle ministrations. "She came to us, you know. We were going to buy up the road, closer to the highway."

"Why would she come to you?" Madeline stabbed a trembling finger at the floor. "This land has been in my family for over a hundred years. She knew how important that was to my father. No way would she have—"

"Because of Nate." Tick straightened with a weary sigh.

"What do you mean, because of Nate? What does he have to do with this?"

Tick snapped the first aid kit closed. "The truck he was driving when he busted that stop sign and killed Amanda Harrell? Your parents had taken out the note on it. The title was still in their name. That made your mama liable for the accident and Lord knows the substandard insurance your brother had wasn't going to pay out on the lawsuit."

"Selling the land to us meant she didn't have to maintain it and allowed her to keep the house, which she might have had to sell if she hadn't found a way to settle that lawsuit." Ash flexed his fingers experimentally and reached for the bottle of acetaminophen on the desk. "And according to the terms of the sale, if we ever want to sell out, you and your sister have the first right of refusal, so the land would go back into your family."

Madeline blinked hard, opened her mouth and closed it again in a firm, tight line. The color in her cheeks could have been anger or embarrassment.

Ash held her gaze. "Talk to your mother. Let her be the one to explain."

She didn't speak again, only turned and strode out of the office, letting the door close quietly behind her.

In her car, Madeline rested her forehead on the steering wheel. The adrenaline crash rolled through her, leaving a sick nausea trembling in her throat. Why did she just *know* the two men were having a good laugh right this second?

At her expense. She wanted to hold on to her anger, but her detective's instincts whispered that Ash had seemed sincere in his explanation. Talk to her mother.

Talk to her mother, when Madeline knew sometimes her mama would produce a half-complete version of events. She preferred living in a reality of her own making, rather than deal with the hard stuff. Look how she'd ignored Nate's problems for years. Look how she'd ignored the brewing tension between Madeline and her father so long ago.

She smacked her open palm against the steering wheel lightly. Damn it, why hadn't she remembered that before she went looking for Tick with both barrels loaded? She'd made things worse and now she had to spend the entire day with him.

And Lord knew, he could be an ass when he was in a mood.

Eyes dry, she lifted her head and gazed at the neat farming operation. Talking to her mother was out of the question. She needed someone who would be relatively objective, someone who would still have access to the inside facts. She glanced at her watch and fired the engine. She had time to go by Stanton and Autry's before she had to be on duty.

A few minutes later, nerves twisting through her, she knocked on her sister's back door. Authoritative footsteps thudded on hardwood floors and Stanton swung open the door. Madeline forced herself to smile up at him. At six-six, he nearly towered over her; obviously, her sister liked tall men as well. Weird, having something in common with the sister she barely knew.

He nodded, his greenish-gold gaze wary and a little distant. "Morning, Madeline."

"Hey." She tucked her hands in the back pockets of her khaki slacks. "I was wondering if I could talk to you and Autry a few minutes?"

He stepped back, but the wariness in his eyes didn't diminish. "She's getting dressed but come on in. You're up early. You don't have to be on duty until nine today, right?"

"I went for a run." And more than likely, made a complete and utter fool of herself. Damn but she was good at that. An image of Ash's pained grimace, the blood trickling down his wrist rose to torment her. That had been her fault too.

Stanton returned to the kitchen island, where he'd been preparing a cup of coffee. He held the carafe aloft. "Want some?"

"No thanks." The universal cop's caffeinated drink of choice had never really been her thing.

"Juice? Milk?"

"I'm good." She leaned on the counter, her stomach tied in knots. "Stanton, what do you know about Mama selling the farm to Tick and Ash?"

He stopped with his mug halfway to his mouth and darted a quick look at her. "She didn't tell you?"

Madeline made a moue. "Mama doesn't deal real well with harsh-reality conversation. I'd never get the whole story out of her."

"The Harrell family sued after the accident." Stanton ran a hand over his jaw. "Because your mama legally owned the truck, their lawyer went after her, since it was obvious Nate didn't have anything to take. Ash and Tick were looking for a place to put that alligator operation of theirs. It seemed like a good solution, especially since it would allow her to offer the Harrells a settlement."

Madeline closed her eyes. Why couldn't her mama have simply told her that? And why hadn't she stopped to question further before going off on Tick and Ash?

That would have taken an open mind and foresight.

Tick's censure echoed in her mind. Ah, damn it all, why did she consistently let her anger get the better of her? She was always making a mess of everything.

"Madeline?"

At Stanton's quiet voice, she lifted her lashes. He watched her with steady concern and she made herself produce a nonchalant smile. "Thanks for telling me. I should be going—"

"Is there anything I should know?"

Other than the fact she'd stepped in it royally once more and working with Tick for the next six weeks would be even harder? Probably not. "No, I was just curious. Thanks again and tell Autry I said hello."

He followed her to the door. "I will. Have a good day, all right?"

A good day. Like there was ever such a thing in her life.

Tick remembered at the last second not to slam the back door. Simmering anger pulsed under his skin. Damn Madeline Holton for her hard-headedness and inability to think before she spoke. Damn Stanton for hiring her in the first place. Damn Ash, too, for being so freakin' calm about the whole mess. Even as he'd planned to go into town for a tetanus shot as soon as the doctor's office opened, he'd already been excusing Madeline's behavior.

That was the problem. Tick tossed his damp socks in the laundry room and strode toward the bedroom. No one had ever made Madeline face up to anything she'd ever done. Not even himself. Maybe if he'd refused to go along with Virgil all those years ago, maybe if he'd been stronger...

Maybe nothing. Living in the past was a sure way to go crazy. He planned to go to work, do his job, deal with her the best he could. It was only six weeks. Correction, five weeks and six days. He could deal that long.

The shower was running, steam curling under the bathroom door. He stripped his shirt over his head, muscles protesting the work he'd put in already that morning. He'd be stiff later, after sitting in a patrol car all day. Memories of Caitlin rubbing the tension away the night before, putting him into the best sleep he'd had in weeks, sifted through his head and a grin quirked at his mouth. Maybe he could convince her to do that all over again.

Maybe he'd actually stay awake long enough to convince her to let him seduce her when she was done. Some of his ill temper evaporated. Even if they weren't making love, he'd enjoyed having her touch him with a sense of affection and intimacy once more. Maybe the whole patience thing was paying off.

He shoved off his jeans and was considering joining her in the shower, as he'd done too many times to count in the past, when the water stopped. He shrugged off the lost opportunity. He'd be ready for a long soak in the clawfoot tub when he returned home. If Lee was in a cooperative mood, perhaps Tick could entice Caitlin into joining him.

The bathroom door opened and Caitlin emerged, damp hair pinned in a knot, a large bath sheet wrapped around her sarong-style. Relaxing further, he resisted the urge to pull her against him and settled for brushing a quick kiss over her cheek. He smelled of alligator funk and she wouldn't want him all over her after her shower.

"Hey. I'm gonna get cleaned up." Without waiting for her reply, he headed for the shower. Minutes later he surfaced, feeling cleaner and more human. The bedroom was empty, the quiet noises of Caitlin setting up her files and laptop in the living area filtering in. Whistling an off-key version of an old REM tune, he tugged on khakis and his uniform polo and added his gear: badge, holster, cuffs, keys. Maybe Mama would watch the baby for a couple of hours that evening. Much as he loved his son, he was jonesing for some one-to-one time with Caitlin, even if it was only coffee and a walk, or a quick dinner at Wutherby's.

He grabbed his duty jacket from the closet and strode through to the living room. Caitlin laid out photos on the dining room table, frowning in concentration.

"I'm going to be late if I don't get a move on." Laying the jacket over the back of a chair, he stopped behind his wife and wrapped his arms about her. At the first touch of his hands, her entire body stiffened. The nonverbal rejection slammed him in the gut, and his question about wanting to do something together later died on his lips.

He stepped back, eyeing the tight line of her posture. She'd been fine last night, but now she was wound tighter than a two-dollar watch. "Cait? What's wrong?"

She didn't look at him, merely moved a crime scene photo to a different place in the array. "Nothing."

Oh, holy hell. He knew that "nothing" well enough. During the frustrating roller coaster of trying to conceive, she'd taken hormone injections daily, and they'd suffered through her resulting wicked mood swings together. That "nothing" meant anything but. He sighed. "Cait—"

"Tick, not now. I've got to get this done before the baby wakes up. It's impossible to think about patterns once he gets going." She shifted another picture with tense, edgy movements. "Besides, didn't you say you were going to be late?"

"Yeah." He jerked a hand through his hair and reached for his jacket. They didn't normally part without even the quickest of kisses, but he wasn't sure he wanted to risk it right now. He'd leave this particular move up to her. If she turned into him, then he'd know it was all right to lean in. "I'll see you tonight. I shouldn't be too late. Call me if you need anything."

She didn't look around at him. "Sure."

With all the tension from the morning back in full force and frustration stinging him, he pulled on his jacket and strode out to his truck.

Somehow, he just knew this day was going to get worse.

Chapter Four

Silence coated the patrol car like smothering molasses. A tension knot at the base of Madeline's neck pulsed. She should apologize, she really should, and take Tick up on his suggestion from yesterday that they just deal with the past.

She should. But she couldn't. The words wouldn't come and Tick's brooding presence did nothing to coax them forward.

As she steered into a left-hand turn onto Scott Street, she cast a surreptitious glance at him. He slumped in the passenger seat, thumping his thumb on his knee and glaring out the window. Bad humor emanated from him in rolling waves.

Yes, that was going to induce her to talk to him.

"Stop here." He flicked a finger at the small parking lot between the old fire station and an ancient row of shops. Madeline obeyed without comment. While she'd been away, the fire station had been updated into a physician's office and the little set of shops held an insurance agency, a trendy gift shop and a beautician's parlor.

She idled to a halt along the sidewalk. A quick glance told her why he wanted to stop. Ash stood on the grass beside the doctor's office, talking with a tall dark-haired man. She narrowed her eyes. A familiar tall, dark-haired man. That had to be one of Tick's brothers, the family resemblance too strong to miss.

Tick swung out of the car and she followed more slowly. Ash held one neatly bandaged hand aloft and made a chomping motion with his other. She cringed as guilt crashed through her. At least he was grinning about it, his white teeth flashing.

He greeted Tick, his gaze sliding to Madeline as she joined them. She cast a quick glance at Ash's companion. Yes, definitely a Calvert male. Tick's brother Del, younger by a year, and always the quietest of the Calvert sons.

Tick jerked his chin at Ash's hand. "How is it?"

"Not as bad as it looks, Layla says. She stitched it up, gave me some antibiotics. Said to tell you to stick to arresting people and let her do the medic stuff."

Tick's reply was a noncommittal grunt. Del clasped his brother on the shoulder. "Glad you stopped. Have you got a minute? You need to sign the riders to that new policy."

"Yeah." Tick shrugged and glanced at Madeline. "I'll be right back."

They strolled to the insurance agency, leaving Madeline and Ash alone. She looked at his injured hand before meeting his gaze. The pale green of his eyes seemed to glow against his tan. Concern glinted in those eyes, and remorse curled through her again. The guy had been nothing but nice to her from the beginning. "I'm really sorry about this morning."

"It's okay."

"No, it's not. I was a bitch and you didn't deserve that." She waved at his hand. "Plus I got you hurt. Coming in to town probably messed up your whole routine today and—"

"Mad, stop. Please." He chuckled, a rich sound that seemed to roll through her and set off flutters in her belly. "Injuries are part and parcel of farming. Believe me, I've had worse than this. It could have happened even if you weren't there. Besides, I needed to make a run by Twitty Feed and Seed anyway, so coming into town wasn't a major hardship."

She narrowed her eyes at him. "You're too good to be true."

"See what you missed out on by not wanting to be friends?"

"Can women and men really be friends?"

He laughed, a deeper rumble that only intensified the flicker of attraction. "So did you talk to your mom?"

"Stanton." She grimaced. "Mama can be... Well, I figured Stanton would be more objective."

"Yeah, he's pretty steady and straightforward." He rested his hands at his hips and winced, lifting the injured one.

Guilt stabbed at her once more. "I am so—"

"Don't say it. It's over and done with, all right? An accident, pure and simple." A gleam lit his pale eyes. "But if you're hung up on it, maybe I'll let you make it up to me."

"Really." She tilted her head. "And how is that?"

"Let me cook you dinner."

"I think you have that backward. I should be the one cooking for you."

"Yeah, but Autry let slip that you couldn't boil water." His bright grin flashed, warming her all the way through.

"Yeah, and I told you I wasn't in the market for a man right now."

"Which is why we agreed to be friends, remember?"

She'd done anything but agree to that, but she didn't demur. Instead, she gave in to the smile tugging at her lips and glanced away. Farmerboy or not, he was a smooth charmer, that was for damn sure. She could like him, if situations were different.

"Dinner, huh?"

"Yeah. We're going to be friends, and friends do those kinds of things—have coffee together, dinner, movies. Come on, what do you say?"

Anticipation licked through her, the first positive emotion she'd felt in what had to be forever. "All right."

"Great. Seven work for you?"

"Seven is perfect."

He rattled off directions to his home and she recognized the location as what had been a long-abandoned farmhouse. Remembering the fallen-down state of the home before, she couldn't wait to see what a bachelor's touch looked like on it.

"Well, I've got to go. I still have a lot to do today." He gazed down at her. "I'll see you tonight."

"I can't wait."

And she couldn't. Suddenly, Tick's ill-temper and all the junk of their past didn't weigh quite so heavily. She watched Ash walk away toward the battered pea-green Ford that listed to one side a little forlornly.

Her day was definitely looking up.

Tick's gloomy disposition couldn't dim her newfound optimism. Somehow, Ash's easy acceptance loosened the knot in her throat. When she and Tick stopped at a convenience store for something to drink, she didn't fire the engine immediately. She couldn't look at him but gazed instead across the dusty gravel parking lot and cleared her throat.

"I'm sorry, about this morning." Pushing the words out hurt, her pride stinging.

"Yeah."

She wrapped her fingers around the steering wheel until her knuckles ached. She wouldn't give in to her normal response to his animosity. No matter how badly her temper itched to be turned loose, she would hold it.

"I think you were right yesterday." Those words tried to stick in her throat. "For this to work, we've got to deal with the past."

"Really."

"Tick." She darted a glance at him. He gazed out the passenger window, a cup of coffee balanced on his knee. "I'm not proud of it, you know. What I did."

"I imagine not."

Her anger flared and she swallowed. "Do you have to make this so damn hard?"

He turned his head, a banked irritation burning in his dark eyes. "What do you want me to do, Madeline? Say it's all right? Let you off the hook as easily as Ash did this morning?"

"I can't believe you're still holding a grudge this big. Aren't you the one in the church pew every Sunday morning? I thought there was this whole thing about forgiveness in the Bible."

"It's not a grudge. I forgave what you did a long time ago, Madeline. Forgetting is something else entirely." He lifted his cup for a cautious sip. "You can damn sure bet after this morning, Ash and I both will be more careful around those alligators. Know why?"

A sick feeling settled in her stomach. "Why?"

"Because if the gator bites one of us once, that's the gator's fault. If we let it happen a second time, that one's on us. Alligator behavior doesn't change much. Ours should."

"You're comparing me to an aggressive reptile with a brain the size of a walnut."

"No, I'm saying your behavior hasn't changed in the last eighteen years. You still act and speak without thinking about the consequences. You're still focused on how everything affects you and the hell with everyone else. You're dangerous, Madeline, and I'm not going to sit here and lie and say being in this car with you on patrol, having you work in my department doesn't scare the shit out of me. Because your traits are the ones that get other cops killed."

He paused a second and the sick churning in her gut worsened. His mouth tight, he met her gaze.

"But you already know that, don't you?"

The words slammed into her and the nausea threatened to overwhelm her. It was one thing to have the guilt in her head...quite another to have Tick Calvert throwing it in her face. She knew what she'd done, that Jack had paid for her impulsivity, and she sure as hell didn't need Tick's reminder. She flexed her hands on the wheel and swallowed hard, her vision blurring. She blinked, hard.

"You bastard."

"Yeah, we already covered that one today." He sounded bored. He lifted the cup to his mouth again, and she fought the urge to knock it out of his hand, to scream at him, make him take back those awful, damning words. She sucked in a deep breath, trying to get herself under control, trying to smother the sob that wanted to be set free.

"Let's get one more thing out in the open, Madeline." He leaned to set the cup in the holder. "I have no intention of letting your impulsivity and lack of foresight get me killed. I have a boy at home, and I'll be damned if he grows up without me because you did something stupid. If it comes down to me or you, I have no problem telling you that I'm the one walking away. So don't get any delusions that we're partners or anything more than what we are—two cops with distinctly separate agendas. Don't think I'll ever make the mistake of trusting you again."

Without reply, she turned the key in the ignition, her hands shaking. She'd barely pulled onto the highway when the radio crackled. "Chandler to C-2."

He reached for the mike. "Go ahead, Chandler."

"We have a possible 10-109D, 183 Miller Court." At the ten code for a death, Madeline's ears pricked up.

"Affirmative, Chandler. C-2, C-4, en route." He replaced the microphone and gestured toward the intersection ahead. "Turn left—"

"I know where it is."

She flipped the lights on but left the siren silent, and increased her speed, taking the turns smoothly. Anticipation of a different sort flickered through her. She was a homicide detective, after all. This was what she lived for.

The small ranch house at 183 Miller had been the town's rental whore as long as Madeline could remember. No one lived there permanently—people moved in, stayed weeks or months, and moved on. The result was the little house's forlorn air, as though it was always waiting to be abandoned once more.

Damn, it was sad when she could relate to an inanimate building.

Shaking off the depressing musings, she shifted into park at the curb and swung out of the car to join Tick on the walk. Moving boxes sat stacked next to a large rolling trashcan. Tick approached slowly, one hand on his unsnapped holster, his gaze flicking over the front of the house.

The front door swung open, and Madeline tensed, reaching for her own gun. Something familiar about the woman who stepped onto the porch tugged at Madeline's remembrance, and she frowned. That wasn't...it couldn't be.

No fucking way.

The cosmos couldn't be out to get her *that* much.

Sunlight glimmered off bottled-blonde hair that needed a root touch-up. The woman's big blue eyes locked onto Tick with the speed of a homing missile and Madeline stiffened further. Shit damn *fuck*.

Obviously, the cosmos wasn't through with its weird joke on her yet.

The blonde stopped on the top step, a hand over her heart. "Oh my Lord, Tick Calvert. I am so glad to see it's you. There is a skeleton under my house."

Fucking hell, it was her. From the sudden tightening of Tick's posture, Madeline was sure he'd recognized her as well. Madeline sucked in a deep breath. This was not going to be pretty.

Tick stopped, one hand still resting on his holster, one foot on the bottom step. "Allison?"

She nodded, a wild blend of emotions passing over her face—fear, surprise, reminiscence, attraction, longing. "Yes, I just moved back a few days ago to take a job at McGee's." She waved a hand behind her. "I'm renting until I find something permanent and I went into the crawlspace to look at the pipes—I was afraid there was a leak—and there is a *body* under there."

"You mentioned a skeleton?" At Madeline's question, Allison Barnett turned her attention on her. Madeline squared her shoulders under the rabid hatred that filled the woman's blue gaze as soon as recognition sank in.

"Yes." Allison shifted her gaze back to Tick, dismissing Madeline as something beneath her notice. Madeline rolled her eyes. No surprise there. Allison's voice took on the breathy quality that had half the senior boys panting after her when they'd been in high school. Even then, though, she'd been fixated on Tick Calvert. "There are bones and a pair of shoes, some fabric too."

Tick slanted a look at Madeline and shrugged. "Might be animal. A dog or raccoon or something that got under there and died."

Madeline nodded, examining the foundation. From this point, she didn't see any holes for an animal to enter through, but that didn't mean there wasn't one in the back.

"Let's check it out." Tick lifted his gaze. "Can you show us, Allison?"

"Of course." She gestured toward the door and fell into step with Tick as they entered the house, gazing up at him while she led them through a small living room overflowing with kitschy home décor items and into the adjoined eat-in kitchen.

The access panel to the crawlspace stood open, resting against the avocado refrigerator. Tick and Madeline knelt on either side and he shone the bright beam of his small Maglite down into the darkness. Allison leaned on the counter, arms crossed over her chest. Madeline sensed the waves of malevolence rolling off the woman.

Tick might have forgiven, but Allison Barnett sure as hell hadn't.

"I don't think you can see it from there," Allison said. "It's farther down, like where the sink and the stove meet. I could see the wiring for the stove when I was down there."

Nodding, Tick rested his hands on his knees. "We don't both need to go. If it's human and there's forensics of any kind—"

"We don't want to further contaminate it," Madeline finished for him. Excitement spiked along her nerve endings once more. "I'll go. I'm smaller."

She pulled her own flashlight free and slid awkwardly into the short, narrow space. Spider webs hung in long strings from the joists and a damp, moldy smell lingered in the air. Holding the light between her teeth and using Tick's bouncing beam as added illumination, she crawled forward. Water dripped from a gray pipe to her right. There was the heavy electrical wiring for a big appliance.

The remnants of a shoe lay before her. Extending from the ground next to it was a long, yellowish bone. It disappeared under the dusty soil. But above that, protruding from the dirt was a small, distinctive bone fragment. A metacarpal.

A human finger.

"Calvert," she called over her shoulder and began the painstaking process of backing up the way she'd come, trying not to further disturb the scene.

"Yeah?"

"Call the coroner and the crime scene unit."

While they waited for the forensics team to arrive from the GBI office in Moultrie, Madeline examined the outside of the house. Allison seemed distraught that there'd been an actual dead body under the house she'd lived in for all of six days, and Tick's focus ended up being directed at calming her down and helping her make arrangements for somewhere else to stay. Allison was eating up being reconnected with him, and her pleasure at the turn of events made Madeline sick.

If she'd ever forgotten why she disliked Allison Barnett so much, here it was in all its clarity—the girl had always been a tad off, a tad obsessive, when it came to Tick, almost as if she lost some part of herself in his presence.

Madeline had to give him this, though, as she rounded the corner of the house and walked to where the pair stood talking at the porch—

he was nothing more than consummately professional with Allison. As Madeline joined them, he snapped his cell shut and returned it to the clip on his belt. "Tori will be here shortly. She'll help you get settled somewhere tonight. I'm afraid until the initial scene investigation at least is finished, you can't stay here."

"Thank you so much, for everything." Allison touched his forearm lightly. "You don't know how I appreciate this."

"Madeline." He stepped to the side, jerking his chin toward the street. "Crime scene van is here."

Madeline avoided Allison's eyes, concentrating instead on Tick's professional mask. "The foundation is sealed all the way down to the concrete apron. There are a couple of really small vents but it looks like the only access is through the panel in the kitchen."

The arriving crime scene technicians and Georgia Bureau of Investigation agents stopped to greet them.

"We'll walk you through." Tick signaled for the young deputy who'd arrived also. "Allison, Deputy Farr will stay with you until Tori arrives and then you can get what you need from the house."

During the hours that followed, as the crime scene unit removed the skeletal remains and made a painstaking record of the area and all possible evidence recovered, Tick surprised her by not only listening attentively to her theories but allowing her to take an active role in the investigation. She'd not expected that from him, certainly not after his statements earlier that day. Some of her tension and apprehension drained away, leaving her focused on the intricate puzzle inherent in the remains and their location.

Once the skeleton, remarkably complete, lay arranged neatly in the body bag, Madeline and Tick hunkered on either side of it. He sketched a finger over the pelvic area. "Female?"

"Looks like it." She kept her voice pitched low, out of the sense of reverence the dead always inspired in her. No gallows humor so popular with other detectives for her. Each victim was a real person, one who deserved respect and justice. "She's been here a long time too. At least five years, as dry and clean as those bones are. Decomposition is complete."

"Don't think the shoe down there is hers, though. It's a man's shoe, size ten." He glanced at the tape measure stretched alongside the body bag, indicating the skeleton had a height of approximately five and a half feet. "She's too small for that."

"It could be related, if we can date it. Maybe it's been with her whole time."

"We can definitely work that angle, especially if there's anything to help us place her within a time period. Ford did that for us with a body we had a couple of years ago. The guy had a metal screw in his leg that wasn't used medically anymore, helped us narrow the time period."

"Then we can contact the rental agency, get a list of their tenants."

"Shit, that list will be huge. But you're right. It sounds like the smartest place to start." He looked up at her. "I'll start going through old missing-persons reports too, but the records from Hollowell's time in office are a mess. Not sure if we even have everything—"

"Investigator Calvert?" A GBI crime scene tech appeared in the doorway. "Could I speak to you a second?"

"Excuse me." He rose and followed the agent from the room.

With him gone and only the soft buzz of the technicians talking, Madeline studied the remains, the skull grinning at her as though keeping a gruesome secret.

"Who are you, sweetheart?" she whispered. "What happened to you? And why the hell are you here?"

Chapter Five

Tick was late, after he'd promised Caitlin he wouldn't be. To top that off, he'd tried calling her and kept getting the voice mail, both on their landline and her cell. He was pretty sure if they'd had a dog, he'd have been sharing its house.

The sound of her voice trailed down the stairs, and he took them two treads at a time.

He found them in the upstairs bathroom, painted blue and white and decorated with prints of old sailing ships, Caitlin kneeling by the tub, Lee chortling and cooing while kicking water everywhere. Warmth and home and love curled through him. Even if she was pissed at him, he couldn't think of anywhere he'd rather be.

"Hey." Dropping to the braided rug, he joined them. He tickled Lee's pudgy tummy and earned a big toothless grin in return.

"I thought I heard you come in." One hand supporting the baby's head, she leaned sideways to brush her lips across his. "I owe you an apology for this morning. I was horrible to you. I was frustrated and I didn't mean—"

He caught the words with his swift kiss and reached to take the baby wash from her. "It's all right."

Scooping warm water over the baby, he lathered the small, wriggly body. "Shoot, son, you're as slippery as Daddy's alligators."

"He's usually as grouchy as one of them too," Caitlin said softly and moved to help rinse. She lifted the dripping baby from the tub and Tick wrapped a soft towel around him before gathering him close. With a smile, Caitlin feathered her fingers over Lee's head. "But he's been in a good mood today."

"I hate I missed that." Tick kissed his temple, inhaling the clean baby scent. "Has he eaten?"

A sweet smile flirted with Caitlin's lips. "Just before his bath. He's getting sleepy."

Sure enough, when Tick shifted Lee in his arms, the little lids were already drooping. "Come on, Leebo," he whispered into the wispy hair atop the warm little head, "Daddy'll put you to bed."

He carried his son through to the nursery, keeping up a steady stream of talk while he diapered, lotioned and dressed him. The quiet sounds of Caitlin clearing things away in the bathroom filtered down the hall, and she appeared in the doorway as Tick tucked a thin blanket around the baby.

"He's almost out." Tick slanted a smile at Caitlin. Water spots dappled the fitted white T-shirt she wore over pink yoga pants. She didn't return his smile, but watched him with a soft, serious gaze, and his stomach dropped. Hell, maybe he was in the doghouse after all.

He joined her at the doorway and she stepped backward into the dim hall, her eyes glittering.

A frown pulled at his brows. "What is it, Cait?"

She leaned against the opposite wall. "I miss you."

Her fierce whisper sank into his consciousness, and his lashes fell, relief crashing through him. A low, rough laugh escaped him.

"It's not funny, Tick." Her husky murmur caught on his name. "You're either pulling extra hours with the department, filling in, or you're on that damn farm. When you are here, you're not *here*. You don't talk to me, you go out of your way not to touch me, and do you know how long it's been since we made love? I miss you and I want you back, damn it."

He crossed the hall, grasped her chin and kissed her. Hard. Fully. Completely. The way he'd wanted to for weeks.

"Want an exact count on how long it's been?" he murmured against her mouth. "I can give you one."

"No." She gently sucked his lower lip between her own and he groaned. "I want you."

"You realize it'll be fast the first time, right?"

"Who cares?" She wound her arms around his neck and pressed closer. "Fast is good. We can be slow the second time."

"And the third." Bending to slip an arm beneath her knees, he swung her into his arms and headed for the stairs. "Maybe the fourth."

"Confident there, aren't you, Lamar Eugene?" She laughed into his throat. "Oh my God, I love when you do the Rhett Butler thing."

"Yeah?" He almost missed a step as she nibbled the side of his neck. Laughter and arousal warred in him. "Keep doing that, precious, and we won't make it to the bed."

"You say that like it's a bad thing."

"Considering how long I've waited to make love to you again, I'd like to do it right." He skirted Lee's baby swing in the living room and narrowly avoided tripping over the car seat.

"I've never known you to do it wrong, Calvert."

"You're good for my ego, Falconetti." He dropped her on their bed and knelt over her, staring into eyes dark with desire. "Lord, I love you."

She touched a fingertip to the middle of his bottom lip and trailed it along the line of his throat. "I love you too." An impish smile curved her mouth. "Now get naked and ravish me before your son wakes up."

"Gladly." He pulled his shirt over his head before he reached for hers. Leaning forward, he kissed her, delving into the silky moistness of her mouth. He palmed the outer curves of her breasts, a little fuller and lusher now that she nursed their child. "You're beautiful."

Her fingers were all over him, from his shoulders to his pecs, down his abdomen and up his spine. He groaned and skimmed the loose pants from her hips, taking her brief panties with them.

She reached for his belt. "You haven't even taken your gear off."

"Don't care. Get it later." He dipped a hand between her legs, her sudden gasp kicking his own arousal up a notch. He slipped one, then a second finger inside her. "Holy hell, you're wet."

"You do that to me. Hurry, Tick." She shoved his khakis and boxer-briefs down his thighs. Cuffs rattled, keys jingled and his holster thudded on the floor as he kicked free of the pants. He lowered his head to nuzzle at the side of her neck, just below her ear at the sensitive spot he knew set her on fire every time, and circled his fingers, brushing his thumb across her clitoris. On a muffled moan, she parted her thighs and pulled him down, arching into him. "Please."

The phone rang, its shrill tone tearing through the thick desire in the room. She tensed beneath him.

"We're not answering that," he said, slumping, the mood already slipping away. He rested his elbows on the bed, his brow pressed to her sternum.

"We have to. You're on call, remember?" She stretched to grab the offending object from the nightstand. Tick rolled away to stare at the ceiling. Whatever it was, it had better be damned good. "Hello? Yes. He's here. Hold, please."

One hand over the receiver, she met his gaze. "It's for you. An Allison Barnett."

He bit off an oath and reached for the phone. What the hell did Allison want, anyway? He cleared his throat and tried to make sure his voice was even. "Hello?"

"Tick, hey, I'm so sorry to bother you at home." Remorse coated her breathy voice, and he closed his eyes, a pang of regret over his anger pricking at him. The woman had come face to face with a skeleton under her house. Being freaked out was probably normal under those circumstances.

"It's okay." He sat up and caught Caitlin's lifted eyebrow at his words. He shook his head and mouthed "work" at her. "What can I do for you?"

"I really hate to ask but I need to get in the house. Some of Willow's school stuff is in her room and I don't want her to be without it. She's still adjusting to being in a new school and she's so conscientious. Not having her books would be terrible for her." She paused a half second and he swallowed a curse. "Is there any way you could..."

"I'll meet you there in about fifteen minutes."

"That's fabulous. Thank you so much. I'll see you in a little while."

The phone went dead.

"Damn it." He dropped it on the bed and bent to gather his clothes. "I won't be gone long. I promise."

"Who was that?" Caitlin reached for her T-shirt, and he tugged it out of her hands.

"No way. You stay here, just like you are and wait for me to get back."

She pulled the garment free. He sighed as she slid it on. "So where are you going?"

"Her house is a closed crime scene, and she needs her daughter's school books. I have the damn keys to the house." He stepped into his slacks and tucked his shirt in.

"Allison Barnett?" Caitlin frowned as she slipped on her yoga pants again. "I've heard that name before."

Foreboding slithered down his spine. "I doubt it. She's been gone from here forever."

Caitlin pulled up one knee and rested her chin on it, her brow pursed in concentration. Tick swallowed a groan. As good as she was with making connections, he was screwed.

"Allison...oh my God." A note of glee entered her voice, and he cringed. She covered her mouth and stared at him, her eyes sparkling. "She's the cheerleader, isn't she?"

He tried to head it off. "Cait—"

"She is. This is the one you lost your virginity with." She laughed, the hand over her mouth doing little to muffle the sound. "In the football equipment room."

He was going to kill Del. As his brother was the only other person who knew about that teenage indiscretion besides him and Allison, Del was the only way Caitlin would have known.

Hands at his hips, Tick gazed down at his wife. An answering smile tugged at his own mouth. "Are you finished?"

"You're leaving me to meet the woman who took your innocence." Caitlin lay back on their bed, a hand over her chest as she tried to control the giggles. "Should I be threatened?"

He grasped one gorgeous ankle and tugged her toward him before leaning down to kiss her. "No. Not in the least."

Unable to resist the dark sweetness of her mouth, he deepened the kiss until she moaned into his. He pulled away with a grin. "Now hold that thought until I get back. I won't be long."

Twelve minutes later he stood in front of the house on Miller Court, hands in his jacket pockets, waiting on Allison. Damn, it was cold tonight. The weather had been on a typical southwest Georgia roller coaster lately—unseasonably warm for a day or so, then dipping witch's-titty low just to bounce back up.

He could think of things he'd rather be doing than standing around in the cold in what had always been one of the less favorable areas of town. The small brick ranch houses sat close together with cramped postage-stamp yards. How had that girl rotted beneath this house without anyone noticing the smell?

And who was she? The familiar need to track down the answers took root in him again. He didn't like unfinished business or unanswered questions, never had.

Headlights swept the houses as a small car turned onto the narrow street. The Honda braked with a soft metallic whine behind his truck. The interior light bounced off Allison's blonde hair. She hurried up the walk, pulling her thin sweater about her.

"Hi." She smiled as she reached him, laying a light hand on his biceps. "Thank you so much for doing this."

"No problem." He would have to repent for that lie later. Jingling the house keys, he bounded up the steps. The sooner he took care of this, the sooner he could be back at home, back in bed, wrapped up in Caitlin.

The lock stuck and he jiggled the key, pulling the door toward him as did so. "How old is your daughter?"

"She's thirteen."

"Thirteen?" He glanced over his shoulder at her as the door swung inward. "Lord, I can't imagine you with a teenager."

She laughed, the airy sound from their youth a little drier and harsher now. "Willow is my baby. Tick, my oldest is seventeen."

"Wow." He shook his head and stepped back to let her precede him. "That's wild."

"Yeah." Some indefinable sadness filtered into her voice and she stopped in the hallway, shivering, moving a step closer to him. "The house feels different now."

He could understand that. Finding a corpse, even one long dead, under her home had to be a bitch.

"It shouldn't take me but a couple of minutes to get Willow's things." She pressed the light switch near the hallway door. Nothing happened. She flipped it a couple more times, frustration drawing her mouth into a tight line. "Darn it. The wiring in this place is a mess. I bet the fuses are blowing again. I kept having to stumble to the electrical box in the utility room all last week."

He pulled his Maglite from its pouch and shone the bright beam down the narrow hall. "Better?"

She flashed a smile in his direction. "Thanks."

Holding the sturdy flashlight aloft, he followed her. In the back bedroom, she gathered an armful of textbooks and added a navy fleece and stuffed unicorn to the mix. Edgy impatience crawled down his spine. Sweet Jesus, she was taking her sweet time, picking up the kid's stuff.

Catching his eye, she shrugged. "She's had it forever and she's lost without it."

"Anything else you need while we're here?" His phone buzzed against his waist, and he pulled it free, flipped it open to read the naughty little text message from his wife.

Holy...

Allison had to hurry it up.

"I think this is...oh, wait." Juggling the books, she pointed back down the hall. "I can't remember if I grabbed pajamas earlier. Would you mind pulling some from my top drawer?"

Impatience burned under his skin, and he smothered it. This mess wasn't her fault, and the discovery of the remains had thrown her life into uproar enough. The light filtering in from the mercury lamp over the backyard kept him from stubbing his toes on the massive cannonball bed that dominated the room. He pulled the dresser drawer open and snagged the sleep set lying on top.

She waited at the doorway and he reached for some of what she held. "Here, let me take the books."

"Thanks." She handed them over. With her arms full, they got a little tangled, and it took him a second to extricate his wrist from her hand.

He opened his mouth to ask if there were any more needed items and closed it. He was ready to get home, damn it.

His phone vibrated along his belt again. He tilted his head toward the front door. "It's getting late. Let's get you out of here."

Her laugh trilled as she picked her way through the dark living room. "It's barely eight thirty."

Shit. They'd put Lee down at…aw, he was screwed. Or rather, he wouldn't be if he didn't get Allison the hell out of here, fast.

"I should really buy you a coffee or something." Allison stopped at the bottom of the steps while he secured the house. "I think this counts as above and beyond the call of duty."

She had no freakin' idea.

He had to wait for her to unlock the damn car before he could settle the textbooks on the backseat. She tossed the other items on the cluttered passenger seat and turned to look at him, her arm resting along the open door.

"Well, thank you again. You'll call me, won't you, when we can come back?"

"Sure." He flipped through his keys. "Good night."

"Good night, Tick."

He made sure her car started and she pulled away before he headed in the other direction. Luckily, he caught all the traffic lights on green and ten minutes later pulled to a stop in the driveway. The back door opened as he climbed from the truck. Caitlin leaned against the porch column.

Tick strode up the brick walkway. "Tell me he's still asleep."

"Out like a light." She shook her head, shivering a little in the cold air. "What took you so long?"

"You don't want to know." He bounded up the steps, pausing just long enough to sweep her up into his arms. Inside, he pushed the door closed with his foot.

On a soft laugh, she wrapped her arms around his neck and pressed closer. "Well hello, Rhett."

An answering chuckle rumbled in his chest as he carried her through to their bed. "Come on, Scarlett, and I'll show you just how much I do give a damn."

Madeline parked next to Ash's decrepit Ford, nerves she hadn't felt since she was a fifteen-year-old girl fluttering low in her belly. She was late—the crime scene investigation had dragged way past the end of her shift. She'd called Ash to cancel dinner with a distinct sense of regret. He'd surprised her by telling her to come when she was ready;

dinner would wait.

She couldn't remember the last time a man had been so understanding about the demands of her career.

Um, probably because that had been never?

Sucking in a deep breath, she swung out of the car. It was cold, her exhale coming in a puff of steam, and she tightened her blazer about her as she approached the porch.

With a coat of fresh paint, the old saltbox-style farmhouse gleamed under the bluish mercury light. A couple of rockers sat on the wide porch, a lamp shaped like a lantern shining brightly by the front door. The impression was clean, neat and masculine.

She knocked, shivering a little as a chill wind blew across the yard, slipping in beneath her jacket. Moments passed with no answer, and she lifted her hand to rap again.

The door swung open, and Ash grinned an apology at her. "I'm sorry. Should have told you to come round to the kitchen door."

He stepped back to let her enter and inside heat wrapped about her.

"Let me get your jacket." Warm hands descended on her shoulders and she shrugged out of the military-style blazer, glancing around at an equally neat living room. The hardwood floors shone, a couple of couches and a big pine trunk sharing space before the fireplace.

"Nice place. You've done a lot with it."

"Pretty bare, isn't it?" His rich voice tickled her ears.

"I wouldn't say bare." Books packed floor-to-ceiling built-ins. True, the room held little clutter or knick-knacks, but what there was—some pottery pieces, a well-worn guitar leaning against the wall, framed photos and a couple of paintings—hinted at the personality of the man behind her.

And she'd never been able to resist a good mystery.

She glanced over her shoulder at him, finding his pale eyes resting on her and glowing with humor and good old-fashioned male attraction. The tiny flutters took up residence in her belly once more. My God, the man was handsome.

"Something smells good." She stepped back, aware now of spicy aromas flowing through the house. Beneath her lashes, she swept a look over him. Casual looked good on him—jeans, a bark-brown buttondown shirt that made his eyes seem brighter, loafers.

"Seafood étouffée." A brash grin lit his face, the awareness she was checking him out passing and crackling between them. "Hungry?"

"Considering lunch was a pack of crackers and a Coke? Yes."

Laughter glimmered in his gaze and he reached for her hand. "Come on and let's get you fed, then."

Her palm tingled at the warm contact of his skin on hers. The sensation moved up her arm in a pleasant wave as he led her through to the large eat-in kitchen.

Like the living room, this area was clean and neat, but bore the unmistakable stamp of a strong male personality and that of someone who liked to cook—bold reds and browns against white subway tiles, gleaming copper and stainless-steel cookware.

A scarred antique table set for two waited by the large window at the end of the room. The spicy smells of tomatoes, onions and peppers filled the air. Her stomach gave a tiny rumble and gnawed on itself. That lunch of peanut butter crackers was seriously a long way behind her.

He pulled out her chair. "I'd planned on opening a bottle of wine, but if you'd rather have something else—"

"Wine sounds heavenly." She didn't indulge often, but one glass shouldn't hurt. She spread her napkin in her lap. Aromatic steam drifted from the rich seafood stew over its bed of rice. "This looks fabulous."

"Go ahead and start." He moved to the counter, and she took him at his word. Savoring a bite of the wickedly savory concoction, she watched the muscles move in his back and arms as he uncorked a bottle of wine and poured two glasses. Graceful, not awkward as many tall men were. Nice hands, strong with tapered fingers and short, clean nails. Hardworking hands, the bandage a stark white against the tanned skin of his left, a few nicks on the knuckles and a thin white scar on the back of the right.

A picture of those hands sliding over her breasts, cupping and molding, flitted through her mind, and she shifted, tiny darts of desire shooting through her.

He set a glass of wine before her and sank into the chair opposite.

"Good?" He gestured at her bowl.

God, she was fixated on his hands now. She reached for her fork again. "Very."

They talked over the meal. Madeline found he drew her out easily, asking uncomplicated questions about her day, her time back in Chandler County, without hitting anything that disturbed her slow slide into relaxation. He answered her questions about the farm and what he'd done with the house, making her laugh with stories of his misadventures in renovating.

Afterward, he refused to let her help him clean up, but she

lingered in the kitchen as he loaded the dishwasher and stowed the leftovers. He was more than good-looking—nice, smart, funny—and she liked him way too much already.

Being attracted to him was one thing.

Liking him? That was a whole other ballgame.

He dried his hands on a striped towel and picked up his half-full glass. "Why don't we go in the living room?"

"Ash, I really should go." Regret pulsed in her at the words. Oh, yes, being with this guy was dangerous on all sorts of levels. "Dinner was wonderful but—"

"But friends spend time getting acquainted." Another of those engaging smiles lit his face. "And I want to get to know you, Madeline. Half an hour. Deal?"

"All right."

In the other room, she glanced at the books on the shelves and the photos on the walls while he turned on quiet music. She smiled at the mishmash of titles and genres, everything from classic Fitzgerald and the complete works of Marlowe and Shakespeare to Crichton, Grisham and a plethora of nonfiction books. Images of his life peeked from frames, what looked like a West Point graduation, a group of young men in army fatigues, Ash and Stanton, both several years younger, on a fishing boat with two preteen boys, a lovely young woman with the same pale green eyes as he, and a more recent snapshot of Ash and Tick leaning against an old Massey Ferguson tractor.

Loss shivered through her. She didn't have photos like this. Somewhere, she had some snapshots from high school shoved in a box, but her life revolved more around crime scene photos than Kodak moments.

She squared her shoulders. There was nothing wrong with that. She simply lived her life with purpose. If being dedicated meant going without a few photographs, big deal. It wasn't like she'd missed anything major.

On the shelf below, a frame held one of Stanton and Autry's wedding photos, another one of Gabby's studio portraits, her funny little chestnut curls fluffing out from her head. Madeline smiled and touched a finger to the toothless grin. At nineteen months, her niece was a character already. Leaning next to the frame was another snapshot, slightly unfocused, one someone had obviously taken on impulse—Caitlin Falconetti seated in a rocking chair and holding her baby but smiling up at Tick as he leaned over them. The baby's face scrunched as if a wail was imminent.

"That's right after they brought him home." Ash tapped the glossy paper. "I was trying to figure out how to use the damn camera."

He stood close enough that she could see the brown flecks that hovered around his pupils, but not so close that she felt invaded. His clean smell filled her nose—soap and something elusive.

"It's a nice photo." It was, the joy and emotion palpable despite the soft fuzziness. She took a step back, putting a little distance between them. "Obviously, you like pictures. And books."

A self-deprecating sound rumbled from his throat. "I'm not much for television. Give me a book any day. Think it comes from my time in the army, sitting around with nothing to do for hours on end."

"So you traveled a lot."

"Yeah." He bent down and tugged a memory album from a lower shelf. "Come sit down and I'll show you the worst pictures of Europe ever taken."

She joined him on the couch, knee bumping his as they paged through the book. She sipped at her wine, laughing softly at his comments on military life when he reached a spread of photographs depicting tents in the sands of Kuwait.

"Talk about sitting around and waiting." He rapped one of the photographs. "I read *War and Peace* sitting out there, then started on *Anna Karenina*."

Setting her empty glass aside, she shook back her hair. "How on earth did you end up here, in Chandler County, Georgia of all places?"

"Stanton and Tick." He flipped the album closed and took the last swallow of his wine. "Stan and I were in the army together. We stayed friends after he went to the FBI. When I got out of the service, I wasn't really sure what I wanted to do. I thought about ranching, back home in Texas, but Tick kept going on about investing in no-waste farming. I came down here with him to look at a couple of operations, and somehow, ended up a chicken farmer."

"You sound like you love it."

"I do." He half-turned, resting an arm along the back of the couch, his gaze on her face. "It's a challenge and I never could resist one of those."

"Really." She needed to look away from those glittering eyes and at the same time needed to keep staring into them, needed to be drawn into the blatant desire suddenly blazing there. She leaned forward, simply to get a closer look at the mesmerizing depths, as clear and green as Lake Blackshear on a quiet spring day.

"Really." He moved, bending down to cover her mouth with his own. The heat of supple lips warmed hers. A hint of wine lingered on his breath and skin, lending a rich layer to the kiss. Madeline parted her lips just enough to mingle her breath with his and allow her to suck a little at his upper lip. He lifted his mouth, brushed his lips across hers, lowered so they meshed once more.

Madeline folded her arms about his neck and tilted closer. Sparkling pleasure spread through her, fizzing in her bloodstream. A sweet ardency curled between them, fueled by a series of nipping little kisses, mouths exploring, parting, coming together again. She curved a hand around his nape, his short tobacco-gold hair crisp and soft under her fingers.

"Do you kiss all your friends like this?" she murmured against his mouth.

"No." He rubbed the palm of his uninjured hand over her shoulder, the soft timbre of his words vibrating through her. "I can honestly say I've never done this with Stan or Tick."

She giggled, wanting to press into his touch. "Well, that's a relief."

His other arm came around her waist, and he tugged her closer. She went willingly, opening her mouth to him, taking everything he offered as his tongue swept between her lips, giving him in return her own passion.

He traced the back of one knuckle down the edge of her blouse, leaving behind a trail of sensation. At the top button, he paused, as though asking tacit permission.

Still kissing him, she slid her hands down to front of his shirt, popping first one button, then another and another free, allowing her access to hot, naked skin.

For a moment, he toyed with the tiny pearl closure before he slowly pushed it through the opening and caressed the inch or so of skin revealed. In a painstaking procession, he undid her shirt, parting the fabric long after Madeline had dispatched his own.

He eased the garment from her shoulders, leaving it draped down her arms, and finally abandoned her lips to suckle lightly at the curve of her shoulder.

"Gorgeous," he murmured against her skin, and she let her head fall back on a stolen breath, the desire trembling through her lower belly and settling into a fiery agitation between her thighs.

Lifting his head, he trailed one finger down the thin strap of her bra. She stared at his face, the unvarnished wanting tightening his features only intensifying the slow burn in her body. He looked at her like she was some fabulous surprise he wanted to unwrap layer by layer.

She wanted to let him, wanted to go on touching him and being touched, wanted to forget everything but how being kissed by him was so absolutely damn incredible.

"This is not smart," she breathed.

"I know." That fingertip moved lower, stopped at the swell of her breast, touching, yet not.

"We barely know one another."

"You're right." His hand tightened on her waist, the bandage a light scrape on bare skin.

"I'm not staying here. I'm going back to Florida in a few weeks."

"Yes." He dipped his head, resting his lips on her shoulder again. The movement brought her torso into closer contact with his. The heat and warmth slammed through her.

"Ash..."

"Hmm?" His mouth moved.

"I want you."

He straightened to look at her, devilry dancing in his stormy green eyes. "Thank God."

She rubbed her knuckles down his smooth jaw and nodded once, a sharp jerk of her chin. "Take me to bed."

"Come on."

He rose and pulled her with him, through a formal dining room and down a dim hall, to a darkened room at the rear of the house.

Chapter Six

Ash flicked on the small lamp sitting atop his dresser. In the soft light, he gazed down at Madeline, a quiet surge of need pulsing in him. She stepped forward and laid her palms on his bare chest. Sensation spread out from her hot hands and he shivered.

He'd been right the first time. She was dangerous. Doing this, taking her to his bed, probably ranked as one of his less-than-smart decisions, but he was going to do it anyway, consequences be damned and consigned to be dealt with later.

Because he simply couldn't make himself walk away.

He slipped a finger beneath one thin bra strap and slid the knuckle down her chest, her skin smooth and heated under his easy touch. She watched him, hazel eyes slumberous and dark, and she took another step toward him, gliding her hands up his pecs to his shoulders, fingers exploring the dips and rises of his muscles.

Sensual mischief curled her lips and glinted in the depths of her eyes. "Nice."

Chuckling, he lowered his head to kiss her. She didn't hold anything back, but opened her mouth beneath his, stroking her tongue between his teeth with teasing little curls. Oh yeah, she was dangerous, but he couldn't remember the last time he'd felt this overpowering urge to get closer, to strip everything away until there were only the two of them and the building desire. He sure as hell hadn't felt this way with Angie or Layla or any of the safe women he'd dated the last few years.

"Madeline," he mumbled against her lips and stroked his hands over her curves to rest at her hips. He dipped his fingers beneath the waistband of her low-rise jeans. The skin there was soft and hot too. God, she was hot all over. He couldn't wait to have her all over him.

She purred and tilted her hips into his. Wanting spread through him, firing through his groin, his dick growing heavier, harder, with her nearness. She rubbed against him, a slow, naughty movement. "Very nice."

Leaning back, she grasped his belt and went to work on the buckle. His mouth went dry and she held his gaze while she wrestled the buckle free and popped the button loose before lowering his zipper.

She wrapped her fingers around the waistband of his boxer briefs, brushing his stomach. Every muscle in the vicinity jumped. Shit, the woman wasn't dangerous...she was deadly. She'd taken him from half-ready to damn-if-she-touched-him-he'd-lose-it in a few short moments. Was this Madeline, confident and utterly sexual, the real one? The wary, isolated Madeline had disappeared as soon as they walked through his bedroom door.

Head tilted back, she lifted her eyebrows. "Can't wait to find out if you look as nice as you feel."

He had to force air into his lungs, and his laugh came out shakier than he would have liked. "Damn, I like a woman who isn't shy."

The woman actually laughed. She shoved his jeans and briefs down a few scant inches, not quite exposing him. "Then you should love me."

He opened his mouth, intending to parry with some smartass comment. Her hand cupping, squeezing, his pulsing erection through his jeans sent every coherent reply out of reach. Instead, he attempted to catch his breath and stiffened his knees so he wouldn't end up on the floor.

She eased jeans and underwear down, his happy-to-see-her anatomy bobbing free. Slipping his shoes from his feet, she tossed them behind her and nudged him into stepping out of the denim and cotton garments. Kneeling before him, she slid those hot palms up both thighs. His belly tightened with an unbearable anticipation.

"Very, very nice." She curved her fingers around him, tracing the vein running from base to tip. Holding him firmly, she swirled her tongue around the head. Sparks shot along his veins, and he groaned. Hell, he was gonna end up on the floor for sure, and God, if she kept that up, he was gonna cry.

Still fisting him, she took him into her mouth. Heat and moisture surrounded him, enveloped him. Head thrown back, he let his eyes slide closed.

Oh, yee-ha.

He tangled his uninjured hand in her hair. "Hell yeah, baby, that's good."

With a quick pinch on his thigh, she let him go. "I'm not your baby. Find another endearment."

Humor spiked in him, tempering the raging need somewhat. "Honey, sweetheart, sugar...whatever you like."

"I'm not much for love names, period, Hardison." She twirled her tongue about him once more, like he was a melting ice cream cone on a hot day. "Although I like the way honey drips off your...lips."

He laughed, and she chose that moment to take him to the back of her throat.

"Madeline," he gasped, barely controlling the urge to lunge forward. His fingers tightened in her thick tresses, pulling.

She pinched him again. "Careful," she mumbled around the head of his dick.

"Bossy, aren't you?" The words came out on a strangled moan. Hell, she was killing him, with that slow spin of her tongue, the playful scrape of teeth, the way she took him deep then sucked the head, making him hurt with need, then slowing him down so he buzzed with a simmer of wanting.

"Mm-hmm." She slowed on him, nails a light abrasion on his balls. Under her easy teasing, they tightened, desire rippling up into his belly and out to his bloodstream. If she didn't stop that...

"Damn, honey, you're dangerous." He eased away and tugged her up, covering her lips with his. Dipping his tongue into her mouth, he skimmed the straps down her arms and fumbled with the back until the clasp sprang free. The silky little bit of nothing fell to the floor. He cupped her breasts, the rounded flesh filling his palms, and flicked his thumbs over hardened nipples.

"Oh, that's nice too," she murmured. She moved, shimmying out of jeans, until she was naked and pressed against him, belly nudging his erection while he toyed and played with the stiff peaks, tugging, kneading, pulling.

One arm wrapped around her waist, he caught a reddened nipple between his lips, nibbling, sucking. She arched, rubbing against him. "Yes, like that. Just like that."

With a groan of approval, he lifted her against him and took the two long steps to the bed, stretching her across it, never taking his mouth from her breast. She dug her hands into his hair and shifted beneath him, panting.

"You're strong. I like that." She bowed into him, damp curls sliding along his belly. "Fuck me."

Yeah, she was bossy. He liked that too. But she probably needed to know up front that he'd followed all the orders he was going to back during his military days. "Not yet."

"Ash—"

"I said not yet." He pressed open kisses down her belly, holding her hips and ignoring the throbbing at his stitches.

"I mean it." Her thighs fell open and she gripped his hair, trying to pull him back up. "Fuck me now, hard."

"Not..." he nipped the inside of her thigh, spreading her vulva and sliding his thumb along her wet folds, "...yet."

He dropped his head, tasting her, and she moaned, twisting beneath him. He held her hips, keeping her still while he toyed with her clit with his teeth, sank his tongue inside her, savoring her. She pulled his hair, and he winced, tapped her hip.

"Not so hard, honey."

"Very hard." She pulled again, gasping and pushing into him. "Get up here. I want you inside me."

He fumbled in the nightstand and readied himself in record time. She watched, the hunger in her face making his hands shake. He leaned over her, and she pulled her knees higher, spreading herself, opening herself further for him.

"Goddamn, that's sexy." Positioning himself, he drove forward. Slick flesh enveloped him, hot even through the thin latex, and he groaned, gritting his teeth against the intensity.

"Oh, yes." She bucked up to meet his next thrust. "Do it harder. Do *me* harder."

"Happy to oblige." He pushed the words out, slamming into her. Strong muscles pulled at him, tightening, stroking. His arm buckled, and he rested on his elbow, sweat breaking on his brow. Good Lord, he hoped she was close because after her little oral performance on him earlier, he wasn't sure how long he'd hold out.

Four thrusts later, the heat intensified, and she tightened around him, a raw scream breaking from her throat. The rapid spasm of her body around his shoved him over the edge, the force of sudden orgasm rushing through him. He drove deeper, holding himself still as the intensity drained him.

He slumped, forehead on her shoulder. She rubbed at his arms, tiny puffs of laughter escaping her. "Very, very nice."

Chuckling, he rolled his brow against her skin and tried to gather his strength to move. The woman wasn't dangerous. She was downright lethal. But at least he'd die a happy man.

She nudged him. "Have you lost the power of speech, Hardison?"

"One word for you, honey." He was so out of breath that the laugh she dragged from him hurt. He lifted his head to grin down at her. "Yee-ha."

Madeline rolled over and flung an arm across the bed where Ash should be. Her questing palm met cool sheets instead of warm male chest. She opened her eyes. The room lay shrouded in shadows, the kitchen light filtering down the hall but only alleviating the darkness so much.

She sat up, pushing her hair back and glancing at his bedside clock. Just after five. She'd stayed longer than she'd intended. Actually, she'd tried to slip away after the second time, when she'd shoved him back against the pillows and rode him in sweet retaliation of that whole "yee-ha" business of his.

An evil smile pulled at her mouth. She'd made him yell, too, and it hadn't been "yee-ha". Actually, she'd rather enjoyed hearing him call her name there at the end. None of the "baby" or "honey" mess, either. Simply two people who clicked in bed.

Which made his whole insistence that she stay a while afterward silly. Yes, she'd fallen asleep despite her best intentions, but he'd made it damn hard not to, with his big hands stroking her back while he held her and whispered in the dark.

She buried her face in her hands and blew out a long breath. Her mama was going to have a fit, even though Madeline had specifically told her she wasn't sure when she'd be in. Living at home with those expectations again was even harder than she'd thought it would be.

Naked, she slid from the bed, the wood floor a chilly shock to her bare feet. She flicked on the lamp and prepared to gather her clothes.

Instead, she found them neatly folded and waiting on a straightback chair by the door. His small thoughtfulness brought a smile to her lips. He was decent. She liked that.

The warm smells of coffee and biscuits drifted from the kitchen. Dressed, she headed that way, only to find the room empty, save for a pan of buttermilk biscuits covered in foil and warming on the stove. Unable to resist, she grabbed one of the flaky delights and scavenged in a spotless refrigerator for a glass of milk.

A copy of *Farmer's Report* lay on the counter next to a small stack of mail, and she flipped it open idly. He was obviously already up and working. She'd forgotten how early a farm day could begin. Silly of her to hover on disappointed because he wasn't there to wake up with her. And if she was disappointed? It was only because the man was damn good in bed. The pulsing ache between her legs was testament to that.

Male voices flowed from the yard near the back porch. Glass halfway to her lips, Madeline stilled. Ash's voice. And Tick's.

Ah, *shit*.

Bet she could just imagine Tick's reaction to her being here and

67

there was no way he could miss her car with its Florida tags in Ash's driveway. She steeled herself, putting on the bitch like a cloak.

One set of footsteps thudded on the stoop. "You just don't get it, Tick."

"I don't want to get it."

Oh yeah, they were talking about last night for sure. Anger curled through Madeline with poisonous tendrils. Just like Tick to be pissed off because she wasn't good enough for his friend—

"It's a simple system." Annoyance tinged Ash's voice.

"It's simple to you. No one else can begin to comprehend it." Tick laughed. "Ash, man, our accountant quit because he didn't get your system. We've got to redo it, or it's going to end up costing us money."

They were talking about the farm's books? Madeline cringed. Her anger drained, leaving the familiar shame and embarrassment. At least they hadn't been present this time. She should be grateful for that much, that she hadn't had the opportunity to jump down Tick's throat like she had yesterday.

She dumped out her milk and rinsed the glass, her appetite gone, swamped in the curdling self-disgust. Why couldn't she just apply the same critical thinking and reasoning she used in her job to her personal life?

Except she didn't always apply it professionally, did she?

But you already know that, don't you?

Tick's voice, those damning words, pounding in her head.

Goddamn, she didn't want him to be right. If he was right, then that meant she really was the horrible person he'd always believed her to be.

A truck rumbled to life outside, and boots thumped across the porch. She glanced around. Where was her purse? She needed to be out of here. The back door opened, a gust of icy wind coming with it, and Ash stepped inside, rubbing his gloved hands together, his sock-clad feet quiet on the floor.

"Damn, it's cold out there." He flashed that great grin at her. "Good morning."

"Hey." She looked everywhere but his face. "Thanks for putting my clothes together. Where's my purse?"

"In the living room." He was staring at her, she could feel it. "What's wrong?"

"Nothing." She walked through the dining room to the living area. "I need to go."

"Madeline." His large hand closed on her shoulder, and he turned her to face him. Concern and confusion glinted in his pale eyes.

"Don't." She held up her hands and backed up a step. She shook her head, trying to put all the conflicting thoughts jumbling around in her head together. "I shouldn't have...this was not a good idea."

Still eyeing her, still frowning, he rested his hands at his hips. "Do I get to disagree?"

"I told you I wasn't looking for..." She waved between them. "I can't do this."

"Do what? Be my friend?"

"That"—she pointed down the hallway—"wasn't friendship."

"Madeline." His voice firmed. "Stop prevaricating and tell me why you're so ready to run this morning. This is not the same woman who blew my mind last night."

Because that woman wasn't real. That woman was nothing more than the confident façade she'd been putting on for years, the one who was good at fucking and used it as a shield. No way would he want the one who lived underneath that front. That one was a mess, and she didn't make anyone a good friend.

That one didn't make a good anything for anyone.

"Mad."

The diminutive hit her, hard. She stepped farther backward. "Don't call me that, please."

"Okay." His hands were up now, his voice quiet, his eyes watchful. The posture was familiar. She'd seen it on dozens of cops over the years, had even used it herself. That was the dealing-with-the-crazy-unpredictable-person stance. "Can you calm down and tell me what's up?"

"I am calm." She was, icily so, a shiver moving over her cold skin. "And I need to get out of here. I have to get ready for work."

"All right." He nodded, a slow, even movement. "So how about dinner tonight and we'll talk then?"

Dinner tonight and she'd fuck him again, he meant. She'd let enough men use her over the years to not get that implication. She threw back her shoulders. "I don't think so."

"Madeline—"

"I said no. You've had your one free ride, Hardison."

His face went white, eyes burning at the insult. His mouth tightened, and she could literally feel the way he was biting back words. She narrowed her eyes, willing him to spit them out, to give her a reason to leave in anger and not look back.

She was good at that.

"Okay." His curt tone didn't quite cover the sizzling anger underneath. "Call me if you change your mind."

"Yeah." She snagged her purse and moved toward the door. "Goodbye, Hardison."

The woman was crazy.

From the back of his truck, Ash tossed another bag of fertilizer on the stack in the barn. Absolutely-fucking-insane. Awful close to ex-wife nuts, except he'd never met anyone who really approached Suzanne's level of sheer malevolent lunacy.

He paused and pushed his cap back, rubbed his wrist over his forehead. As wild as Madeline's behavior and mood swings were, he couldn't call her crazy, not really.

Hurting and desperate, maybe.

Hell, he knew what that felt like, when everything, including his actions and emotions, had been scarily out of control. Thank God for Stanton, who'd been steady and on-hand, pulling him back from the edge of self-destruction.

Who was going to pull Madeline back?

"Not you." He spoke aloud. His hand pulsed with needles of pain, and he shook it lightly. "You're not in the fixing-people business, remember?"

The barn cat looked up from her lazy self-bathing and eyed him like he'd gone over the deep end. He jumped down from the truck bed and pulled the last bag, hefted it to his shoulder, carried it to the neat stack. Along the way, he addressed the cat again.

"That's right. I'm not getting involved, or I'll be crazy too."

The cat yawned and held up one paw for a good lick.

"Exactly. Like the lady said, she doesn't want a man in her life right now. Not even as a friend."

Which was probably what she needed more than anything. Hadn't he sensed the loneliness that hung around her?

The cat extended in a drowsy motion and curled around to groom her back.

"I'm done." Ash tucked his gloves in his pocket and propped his hands on his hips. The cat ignored him. "She doesn't want to tell me what's going on, that's fine. I don't need to know anyway, right? Because there's nothing between us."

Rising into an arched stretch, the car meowed once and slinked off into the shadows.

"Right." Ash sighed, defeat heavy in him. He reached for the cell phone clipped to his belt. Maybe Tick was free for lunch.

Madeline gnawed the inside of her bottom lip until it hurt. Nearly twenty years later, she could still navigate the back roads to Moultrie with her eyes closed. The thirty-minute drive to the crime lab gave her too much time to think and she really wished Tick would pick a fight, so she'd have an excuse not to reflect. Instead, he sat silent in the passenger seat, reading through a fat file of ancient missing-person reports.

She flicked a sideways glance at him. "Reading in the car doesn't make you carsick?"

He didn't look up. "No."

Nerves jumping in her gut, she rubbed her palm along the steering wheel. "Find anything?"

"No."

"Did you contact the rental company yet?"

"No." On a harsh sigh, he lifted his head and smacked the folder shut.

Slowing as they came into Doerun and the speed limit dropped, she slanted a look at him. He regarded her with barely concealed annoyance, and she shrugged. "What?"

"I'm trying to read but you obviously want to have a conversation. You tell me what."

"What makes you think I want to have a conversation with you, of all people?" She braked for a stop sign.

"Experience." Irony lurked in his tone, a private joke she didn't get. Irritation spiked in her.

"All I did was ask questions about a shared case, Calvert." She waited for a semi to rumble past before turning right onto the Moultrie highway.

"Sure and—" A Gary Allan tune rent the air, and he tugged his cell from his belt. "Calvert. On my way to Moultrie, why? Um, yeah—" He rotated his wrist to look at his watch. "I can probably do that. Call me first before you head out though. Later, man."

An indefinable surety that Ash was on the other end of the connection shivered over her. She blinked, hard. She'd made a mess of that this morning, as well.

What a surprise.

"I'll call the real estate office when we get back." Tick clipped his phone into place. "I'm really hoping Ford can narrow the timeline down for us."

"You said that yesterday."

He glowered, mouth closed in a taut line. Just like Ash. What was it with them? They couldn't call a bitch a bitch when she was right in front of them?

His audible exhale filled the tense space. "You know, when I was at the Miller Court house last night, I was thinking it would be strange for that body to be decomposing and nobody smell anything. If Ford can't give us a timeline, talking to the people who live around there, or who have lived there in the past, might turn up a lead."

The semi slowed for a left-hand turn and she braked. "You went back last night? What for?"

"Allison called. She needed some of her kid's stuff."

Yeah. Sure she did. Madeline shook her head. Men were so dense.

The two-lane rural highway opened up into four lanes as they approached the Moultrie bypass. Gosh, now this area had changed for real. Where there'd been one lone gas station and a couple of fast food joints, there were now hotels and swankier, trendy restaurants, joined by a small technical college.

The small brick building that housed the GBI crime lab sat next to the sprawling Colquitt County Jail. A brisk wind tossed stray leaves across the parking lot, and as they exited the car, Madeline pulled her blazer tighter. Hell, she hated cold weather, especially the damp chill of a southwest Georgia winter. She should have brought her scarf and gloves.

Inside the cool autopsy lab, two medical examiners—one male, one female—worked over stainless steel tables. Tick jerked his chin at the male agent bent over an elderly man's nude body and crossed to the second table, where the female agent had their skeletal remains laid out.

"Morning, Ford." He motioned in Madeline's direction and made quick introductions. Ford was petite, her small frame swamped in green scrubs, her mask and head cover leaving only her vivid blue eyes visible, sparkling with intelligence and good humor. "Can you tell us anything yet?"

His voice sounded funny, emerging strained and hoarse. Madeline glanced at him, curious. He'd covered his nose and mouth with one hand, and his skin had taken on a definite pasty tone. Humor spurted through her. The high and mighty Tick Calvert couldn't handle an autopsy lab. It was too good to believe.

Ford gestured at the bones. "Caucasian female, fifteen to eighteen. Never had a child."

Madeline jotted a note in her pocket pad. "What about the cause of death?"

Behind her a saw whirred to life, followed by the crunching of bone. If anything, Tick paled further. Ford looked at him. "Are you okay?"

"Shit, no." Hand still over his face, he bolted. The door swished closed behind him. Madeline smothered a laugh.

Ford pinned the other tech with a frown. "You know he can't handle that, Young. You did that on purpose."

Young continued to cut. "Hey, I'm just clearing the backlog."

Madeline suppressed her humor and caught Ford's gaze. "Cause of death?"

She didn't hold out much hope for an answer. They hadn't found any bullets in the dirt under the house, so Madeline was pretty sure she hadn't been a shooting victim. If the girl had been strangled or beaten, the evidence of that would have been lost as the flesh decayed.

The door swung open, Tick's long strides quiet on the tile floor. He stopped beside her, a strong odor of peppermint clinging to him. A smile curved her mouth. So he was trying to cut the autopsy smell by popping mints, but what was he going to do about the sights and sounds?

Ford flicked a glance at him. "Better now?"

"Yeah." He crossed his arms over his chest.

"You have your choice of two possible causes of death." Ford touched the skull with a gloved hand. "The fracture line here indicates massive blunt-force trauma. Enough to cause cerebral hemorrhage, which would have led to death without medical intervention."

"You said we have a choice?" Madeline scribbled another note.

Ford pointed to the ribs laid out in meticulous order. "See these marks?"

Faint lines marred the yellowed bones, jagged lighter areas. Tick's expression tightened. "She was stabbed."

"Multiple times. So...she could have bled out from that."

Madeline rolled her shoulders, trying to relieve the tightness there. "Anything that might give us an idea how long she's been down there?"

"The bones are clean, so we're talking at least five years. But you didn't find any remnants of female clothing with her, which means she was probably buried nude. No jewelry or other objects which might help us place her in a specific time."

Tick heaved a sigh. "Great."

"Listen," Ford said, "if I come up with something else, I'll give you a call. But don't count on it. If you come up with dental records from a missing-person file, send them over, and I'll do a comparison."

"Thanks, Ford."

Outside, Tick dragged in audible gulps of air. Madeline took the high road and refrained from ragging his ass about the fact he'd basically gotten grossed out and tossed his cookies. She'd save that button to push later when he was *being* an ass.

She unlocked the patrol car. "This case is going to be a bitch."

Tick grimaced at her over the roof. "What do you care? You're not going to be here."

Anger trembled to life in her, and she opened her mouth to tell him where he could go.

Instead, she snapped it shut. Of course, he was right. Cold cases could take weeks, months to solve. She wouldn't be here that long.

Why that thought sent a pang through her was beyond comprehension.

Chandler County was the last place she wanted to be, wasn't it?

Chapter Seven

Ash leaned against the hood of his truck and glanced at his watch again. He was early, but Tick needed to get a move on. It was icy cold, a sharp wind blowing beneath low, angry clouds, and the lunch rush was about to be in full swing. A familiar rumble caught his ear, and he levered away from the truck. Tick was on time for once. Maybe that explained the sudden cold weather—hell had finally frozen over.

Tick maneuvered his white 4x4 into a slot near the end of the pecan grove that served as the Hickory House's parking lot. Ash met him at the edge of the gravel driveway. Dark hair ruffled by the wind, Tick ducked his head and flipped the collar up on his black duty jacket. "Hey."

Ash nodded. "Thanks for coming."

Tick shoved his hands in his coat pockets as they walked toward the front door. "What's up?"

With a glance around at the patrons already in line, Ash pitched his voice low. "I need to ask you about Madeline."

"Ah, holy hell." Tick's words emerged on a muffled groan.

"I know you don't like her, but—"

"Ask Stanton. Or Autry."

They paused in front of the cashier. Tick stared up at the menu he knew by heart, his face tense.

"I just want to ask you a couple of questions."

"You're going to make me break the rule."

Ash swallowed a laugh at Tick's disgruntled tone. His baby sister wasn't the only one who could sulk. "What rule?"

"The one where I don't interfere in my friends' relationships with women." He rolled his shoulders. "I don't want to get into this...thing...with you and her."

The blonde cashier pinned them with a look. "Boys, are you going to order or just stand here all day?"

"Sorry, Gayle." Ash pulled out his wallet while Tick reached for his. "Let me get a turkey platter and a sweet tea."

"Pork sandwich and coffee."

Gayle nodded and handed Ash his change. The door tinkled open behind them.

"How's the baby?" she asked, preparing to ring up Tick's order.

"Good. He's—"

"I've got his, Gayle." A thin female hand with bright pink nails closed on Tick's as he went to hand Gayle a ten. Tick stiffened visibly, and startled, Ash glanced down at the blonde who'd stopped by them. She was pretty enough, delicate features, big blue eyes, but still a little rough around the edges—lines fanning out from her eyes, the blonde a little too bright.

Those blue eyes were pinned on Tick, and she shook her head, still holding his hand as he opened his mouth to protest. "Don't say no. I owe you for rescuing me last night."

"No rescue to it." Tick tried to extricate his hand, and Ash covered a grin. Tick glowered in his direction. "I didn't do much."

"Listen, the way Willow was smiling this morning, you're the equivalent of Santa and Mother Teresa rolled into one." She fixed Gayle, who was watching avidly, with a bright smile. "I'm paying for his lunch. Can you add on a chef salad and a diet Coke too?"

"Sure thing." Gayle glanced between them, obviously waiting for Tick to protest again. He eyed the line forming behind them, and Ash could see him give in. He returned his wallet to his back pocket, and the blonde beamed in triumph.

"Thanks." Tick's smile was a shade too tight, but Ash doubted the woman noticed.

With a wave, she disappeared into the restroom on the pretext of washing up.

"Who was that?" Ash led the way toward their usual table in the far corner of the back dining room. The heater was turned up, blasting hot, dry air into the room.

"Tell you later." Tick didn't look back. "Gayle on the phone yet?"

Ash tossed a casual check over his shoulder. "Yep."

"Damn it." Tick jerked out his chair and shrugged out of his jacket in terse movements. He draped it over the back. "It'll be all over the county before suppertime tonight."

Humor quirked at Ash's mouth. "Oh, yeah. Cait's gonna give you hell too."

"She's already playing this one for all it's worth, believe me." Tick unrolled his silverware. "At least the rumor mill will have something new to talk about for a few days."

Ash nodded at the waitress as she set their drinks before them. Steam drifted lazily from Tick's coffee. Tick frowned at the bubbling cola the girl placed at his elbow. "Wait, this one's—"

"Do y'all mind if I join you? My coworker just called, and she can't make it." The blonde slipped adroitly into the chair next to Tick's. She touched his forearm with a light hand. "It would be so fun to catch up."

She graced Ash with one of those high-wattage beams, obviously waiting to be introduced. Tick met Ash's gaze with an apparent how-do-I-get-out-of-this-one expression. Ash half-lifted his brows, resigned to not getting the answers he'd wanted about Madeline. Not at this meal, anyway.

He extended his hand. "Ash Hardison."

"Allison Barnett. Nice to meet you." She'd tilted her chair so she was half-facing Tick. With an impish twinkle in her eyes, she gestured between her shoulder and his. "We were high school sweethearts."

"Really?" Ash muffled a guffaw. Yeah, he could see Caitlin giving Tick a fit with this scenario. Hell, he planned on giving the guy as much guff as possible later over it. Tick knew it too, eyeing him with a killing, doleful look. "I can't wait to hear more."

Allison scooted her chair closer to Tick's. "Oh, this is going to be so much fun."

Tick shifted and Ash moved his ankle before his friend could kick him under the table. Ash covered another grin with his injured hand, some of the tension he'd carried with him since that scene with Madeline finally falling away. Miss High School Sweetheart was right. This was going to be a blast.

"Madeline?"

At the door to the Bistro, where she was supposed to meet Autry for lunch, Madeline turned. Caitlin Falconetti approached, baby carrier on one arm.

"Hi." She smiled, a relatively genuine curve of her lips. "I'm supposed to waylay you, grab us a table and let you know Autry's been delayed but will be here soon."

"Thanks." Madeline lifted an eyebrow and swung the door open. She hadn't been aware this was a group lunch. Not that she should be surprised. Sisterly bonding had never been high on her and Autry's list of things to do.

Madeline glanced in the baby carrier as she held the door for

Caitlin's entrance. Warmly bundled, Lee dozed in utter peace, his little lips pursed. He didn't flinch at the steady buzz of conversation inside the high-ceilinged Bistro, Coney's trendiest restaurant, in what had once been the Chevrolet dealership. The concrete floors, now polished, sported a marbled faux finish and black paint covered the walls. Huge plate-glass windows afforded patrons a panoramic view of downtown Coney.

She followed Caitlin to a table in the far left corner. Caitlin settled Lee's carrier in a chair, turning him and lifting a plaid canopy so the streaming sunlight didn't hit his face.

Madeline took the seat opposite and fiddled with the laminated menu. "Figured if you were in town, you'd have lunch with Tick."

"That was my plan, actually." Caitlin tucked the blanket more firmly about the baby. "But when I called, he already had plans with Ash."

Madeline's stomach dropped. She covered it by shaking out her linen napkin and perusing the menu, although none of the offerings registered. When the smiling hostess approached, gratitude speared through Madeline as Caitlin asked for a few minutes before their other party arrived. With a nod and their drink orders, the redhead walked away again.

The baby settled, Caitlin crossed one leg over the other and rested her hands on her knee. "So have your first couple of days gone well?"

Oh yeah, riding around trapped with your son-of-a-bitch husband has been just peachy.

One of Caitlin's neat brows arched, and for a second Madeline thought maybe the thought had come out aloud. She pulled in a sharp breath.

"Asinine question, right?" Caitlin leaned back, her dark green gaze steady on Madeline's face. "The way you feel about this place, none of your days here can be good."

The inhale she'd just taken whooshed out in surprise. That level of directness simply didn't exist in this town, where everyone danced around the truth or outright buried it.

She started to dispute the statement but swallowed the words. No, none of the days since she'd arrived home—*here*—had been good. Memories of being in Ash's bed, his arms about her, his deep voice whispering in the dark, curled about her, and she shoved them down. That was nothing, and even if it had been something, it lay ruined now.

Caitlin tilted her head, a winsome expression lifting the corner of her mouth. "I've left you speechless. Guess I shouldn't ask you why you came here, if you hate it so badly."

"Lady, you don't belong." Madeline reached for the unsweetened ice tea the hostess had brought. She choked down a couple of swallows. "What the hell are you doing here? And don't say it's obvious. Because I don't get what the hell you're doing with him, either."

Caitlin's husky laugh held real humor. "You really don't hold back, do you?"

"Neither do you."

"What am I doing here?" Caitlin lifted one shoulder in a graceful shrug. "This was more important to Tick than Virginia was to me. I can profile from anywhere. He offered to go back to the Bureau, but I wouldn't ask that of him. He loves this place, loves what he does."

Madeline glanced away, watching the traffic and a couple of young mothers in the park across the street. Anything she would say in response to that would come out rude.

And probably hateful.

She was going to learn to control her damn mouth when she was here if it killed her.

"Stop overthinking." The cat-and-mouse smile appeared once more. "You're not going to offend me, Madeline. Believe me."

"Stop profiling me."

"I can't help it." Caitlin shrugged again. "Second nature when someone intrigues me."

Nerves trilled along under Madeline's skin. "We haven't known one another long enough for me to intrigue you."

"Doesn't matter. The way Tick tenses up when you walk in or someone mentions your name? Trust me, I'm going to be all over that."

"You don't have to worry that your husband and I are into each other." Madeline reached for her tea once more. This conversation struck way too close.

"I'm not. It's not sexual tension. It's..." Caitlin shook her head. "If I say it, then I'll be offending you."

Oh, great. "Go for it, Falconetti."

"Remember you asked for it, Holton. All right. What I read in Tick when you're around?" Caitlin leaned forward, her eyes intense. "It's the same tension I feel in him when someone brings up Billy Reese or Jeffrey Schaefer or Benjamin Fuller. I can't help wondering what puts you in the same category in his head."

Madeline didn't have a clue who Benjamin Fuller was, but Reese and Schaefer? She was on level with a rapist and a serial killer. That shouldn't hurt. It shouldn't matter, but shit damn *fuck*, it did.

Because even if Caitlin couldn't make the connection, Madeline could. Being in that elite company made her someone who destroyed lives. Sweat beaded on her upper lip and she set the glass down before she dropped it. God, that's who she was too. It didn't matter if she left Chandler County or went back to Jacksonville or moved on somewhere else. Where she was didn't matter because she couldn't change *who* she was.

Or what she'd done.

"Madeline." Something about the soft way Caitlin spoke her name pulled her back to the awareness that Caitlin had probably called her more than once. Caitlin's quiet watchfulness held a note of concern now, and Madeline looked away from that inscrutable gaze that saw too much. Caitlin touched the back of her hand quickly and withdrew. "It's going to be all right. You get through it."

"Don't say that to me. You have *no clue*. You don't know me or anything about me. You know jack shit, Agent, so don't go blowing sunshine up my ass about how I'm going to survive this. You don't know what *this* is, so you can't get that there is no—"

Horrified, she shut her mouth. Tears burned her eyes, and she blinked, turning away.

"That's right. I don't know. I can't." Intensity vibrated in Caitlin's husky tone. "But I know what it's like to be dead-bottom, where there's absolutely nothing left and nowhere to go."

"No, you don't." Madeline shook back her hair and tipped up her chin, put on her best fuck-the-world persona, narrowed her eyes at the calm woman looking back at her. "People like you never get it."

"People like me." Irony shimmered in the words, and Caitlin turned her gaze away, leaving Madeline with the same sensation she'd felt with Tick earlier—that there was a private joke she wasn't privy to. "What are you doing here, Madeline?"

Pulled together again, Madeline glared. "What are you talking about?"

"You don't have to be *here*. There are a thousand other places you could have gone." Caitlin leaned forward. "You're here, because on some level, you want—or need—to be."

"Knock off the profiling bit, Falconetti." Mirroring Caitin's posture, Madeline dropped her tone to the one she used when questioning an uncooperative suspect. "You know nothing about me."

"You might be surprised." Caitlin flicked a negligent gesture toward the front window. "There's your sister. And Tori."

Fuuuuck. Not sparkly, perky little Tori Calvert. Not in conjunction with smooth, polite, perfect Autry. She remembered her grandmother's warnings about people struck down instantly by the wrath of God.

What did she have to do to arrange that?

Aware of Caitlin's steady gaze, Madeline endured the next few minutes as her sister kissed her, Tori bestowed one of her trademark hugs, and both women cooed quietly over the still-sleeping baby.

Tori was her normal Homecoming-Queen-on-speed self, smiling and bubbling over with conversation. Just being in her vicinity made Madeline tired. The younger woman shook out her napkin and placed it in her lap before leaning forward, her big dark eyes sparkling. "Well, the gossip mill is at work extra hard today. Guess who's in the middle of it again?"

"Tick, I'm sure." Caitlin rested her chin on her hand. "What now?"

"Honey, you better watch out." Autry actually giggled, her blue eyes brimming with mirthful teasing. "You have competition."

The rock of foreboding settled in Madeline's chest.

Caitlin looked between her sister-in-law and Madeline's sister with an indulgent, exasperated expression. "What are you talking about?"

"Well, the word from the Tank and Tummy is that an old flame just bought him lunch over at the Hickory House."

"He went to lunch there with Ash." Caitlin lifted her water. "What's this about an old flame...wait. Not Allison Barnett?"

Autry stared. "How did you know that?"

"She called him at home last night to open up her house, which is a closed crime scene." Caitlin waved a dismissive hand. "Makes sense she'd do something as a thank-you."

Heat, followed by a chill, flashed over Madeline's body. Nothing Allison had ever done made sense.

"Well, he should have better sense than to let her sit at the table with him and Ash, even if he did let her pay." Tori sprinkled sugar into her tea. "He knows how Gayle is and once Jeannette at the Tank and Tummy got a hold of it... Lord, someone will call Aunt Maureen, who'll tell Mama and she never liked Allison anyway. Next thing you know, the story will be he's having some wild affair."

"Oh, that's a given." Autry nudged Caitlin's foot with her own. "Because it's common knowledge around town that you're not—and I quote—'giving him any'."

Caitlin touched her fingers to her forehead on a rueful laugh. "This is the oddest town ever."

"I know a good divorce attorney when you're ready," Autry deadpanned, but Madeline couldn't force a chuckle. It simply wasn't funny. Autry turned to Tori. "Why didn't your mama like Allison?"

"Who knows?" Tori shrugged. "I didn't like her, but I was eight. She pinched me because I touched her sacred, precious prom dress."

"I wouldn't like her either." Caitlin smiled, a finger pressed to the corner of her mouth.

"I remember being thrilled when they broke up because she hated having me around," Tori continued. "That was pretty soon after Daddy died, so Tick would have been at UGA then."

Nausea trembled in Madeline's throat. She curled her nails into her palms. Destroyed lives. Except that Tick's wasn't. And Allison...she'd obviously married, had children. Madeline's daddy had survived with her gone after it was all over. Their lives had gone on.

Madeline's life was the one that ended in ruins.

"Maddie?" Autry's gentle touch at her knee brought her back to the conversation. "Weren't you and Allison friends in school?"

"Not friends, not really." She swallowed and forced her voice to sound normal. "We ran in the same crowd, though."

The conversation turned to other directions, and Madeline, grateful, tried to relax. Instead, the guilt and apprehension grew, twining together into a knot that sat in her throat and threatened to choke her. Lee woke and Caitlin lifted him to her lap, soothing him, smiling over his dark head at something Autry said.

No, Caitlin Falconetti didn't have to worry about Madeline interfering in her marriage.

But Allison? If she still had her ability to find a weakness and worm her way through it...

Then Caitlin might need to worry about her. Because Madeline sure as hell wasn't the only one with a history of destroying other people's lives.

After lunch, Madeline filched the thick folder of missing-person reports from Tick's office and settled in at the scarred metal desk designated as hers. A fresh manila file lay on the scratched top. Inside, she'd tucked a copy of Tick's original report from the Miller Court house along with his notes on the quick witness interview he'd done with Allison. After finally managing to get her laptop connected to the less-than-reliable wireless server, she had crime scene photos slowly spitting out of the shared printer.

She flipped to the next missing-person report. Tick was right—this case could take forever to solve, if they ever did. She wouldn't even be here for the outcome, so why was she getting so wrapped up in this unknown girl?

One of the deputies she'd met the first day wandered through, dropped a couple of reports in the basket on the counter, but didn't speak. Parker, the quiet one. At least it wasn't Troy Lee, who she'd already figured out liked the sound of his own voice, because he never stopped talking. With him around, she'd never get anything done. Now-familiar footsteps sounded down the hall. A door opened, closed, opened again.

Madeline frowned at one report and jotted a note on the pad at her elbow. The missing mother of two had been almost twenty-seven, too old for their victim. Another dead end.

"Madeline, did you take..." Tick sighed behind her. "Listen, would you ask before you take something off my desk?"

She didn't reply and ignored his near-silent huff of exasperation. Without looking she knew he was scowling.

He pulled the straight chair from beside her desk and spun it around to straddle it. He gestured toward the file and her notes. "Anything?"

"No." She tapped her pen on the paper. Propping her elbows on the desk, she rested her forehead on her hands. "How long ago was that house built?"

"Twenty-five, maybe thirty years?"

"We're both old enough to remember. Any girls this age who went missing in that time frame?"

Frowning, he spun his wedding band around his finger before shaking his head. "None I can think of. But she could be from anywhere, someone who was passing through. We had a Jane Doe victim three years ago that we never identified. She didn't match to any missing-person reports in the national database. The closest we could figure, she was a runaway who'd slipped through."

"Yeah." Madeline rubbed her eyes and lifted her head. She thumped the file folder. "This is probably a waste of time. I'll enter our stats into the national database and see what comes up."

"Sounds good." He stood and returned the chair to its spot. "I've got paperwork to finish today. Come get me if you need me."

"Sure." If at all possible, she wouldn't "need" him for anything. An irresistible urge gripped her before he made it beyond the doorway. "Hey, Calvert?"

He turned at the door. "Yeah?"

"I know how you feel about me, that you have no reason to trust me or listen to me, but you should really be careful with Allison. I'm serious. Just...remember that."

His brows dipping into a frown, he nodded once before disappearing into his office.

The door closed softly behind him.

Chapter Eight

The Cue Club wasn't much different from when Madeline had been seventeen, sneaking in and trying to smile and flirt her way around the fact the bartender knew she was underage, knew she was Virgil Holton's daughter. A touch of humor curved her mouth. She'd always suspected the continuous battle of wills was as much fun for him as it had been for her.

Even if she'd lost. Every. Single. Time.

In the intervening years, the furniture had been moved around, the pool tables replaced with newer models and a few more framed sports articles graced the walls. But the couple swaying together on the tiny dance floor, the country music tinkling from the jukebox...all that remained the same. The bartender was new, a pretty little blonde who worked the customers lining the polished counter like a pro.

"Maddie!" Across the room, a familiar redhead waved and recognition jolted Madeline, much as it had when she'd heard Donna's voice on the phone. Being intimately acquainted with Madeline's hatred for Chandler County, Donna had sarcastically welcomed her home and invited her to "come out and play" for old time's sake. Obviously, enough of the desperate-to-belong Madeline of old existed because she hadn't been able to resist.

"Hey, hey, Maddie Rae! Look, the whole gang is here." Donna patted the empty seat beside her. Madeline glanced at the other side of the shadowy booth, shock running over her.

Allison Barnett bared her teeth in a semblance of a smile. The old hatred sparkled in her eyes.

"Hey." Despite the better judgment screaming at her to go, Madeline slipped in beside Donna. Next to Allison was Stacy Cheek, another of the girls who'd made up their loose clique in high school. All they needed was Lori and Kelly to round things out. Only Lori was gone, killed in a freak car accident on the Panama City strip during her sophomore year of college. And Kelly...Kelly had taken off on them so long ago.

Stacy leaned forward to grasp Madeline's hands as Donna wrapped a fierce hug around her shoulders. "Gosh, it's so good to see you."

And this was too much too soon. This wasn't high school; they weren't seventeen and eighteen anymore. Madeline eased free of Donna's hold, the heavy smell of beer and tequila choking her. "You too."

"I can't believe you're back," Donna said as the waitress arrived to take new drink orders. Madeline ignored Allison's mocking smirk when she ordered a red wine. "You got *out*, baby. All three of you—Kelly, Allison, you. I always envied you that."

"It's temporary." Madeline reached for one of the roasted peanuts in the bucket on the table. "I'm only going to be here a few weeks."

"That's what I said," Stacy said, her expression glum. "And here I am, still working in the office at McGee's, trying to make ends meet since Scott couldn't make a child-support payment on time if his life depended on it."

Donna smiled and reached for Stacy's hand. "But we're all in it together, honey." She waved a hand around the table. "All three of us work at the plant now, Mad. Hey, I hear there's an opening for a security manager. You could join us over there."

Sure. Right after she cut out her own heart. She shuddered. What if the Jacksonville PD didn't take her back or she couldn't get another major department to hire her? What then? Working security at the chicken plant actually made Chandler County's backwoods sheriff's department look good.

Desperate to change the subject, she faked a smile for Stacy. "I'm sorry to hear you and Scott split up."

"I'm not." Stacy's brittle laugh cut through the air and drew the attention of several patrons near them. "Son of a bitch wouldn't know a clit if it walked up and bit him on the ass."

"Could be worse." Donna reached for her beer and slugged half of it down. "He could have been like Joey. On a mission to conquer every strange pussy in the county."

The crudity grated and Madeline gratefully accepted her wine from the server, giving her watch a surreptitious check. Fifteen minutes. She'd hold out fifteen minutes then escape. Listening to Mama bitch about Nate's being in jail and Madeline's failures was preferable to this. Hell, being trapped with Tick was preferable to this. At least he possessed a modicum of common decency.

"Allison, you can hop in anytime." Stacy nudged Allison's side. "Give us the down and dirty on your divorce."

Allison shook back her shining hair and spun her beer in a slow circle. "He just wasn't the right man for me."

She swung her gaze slowly to Madeline's, and once again, the animosity glittered in the blue depths. Madeline exhaled. Maybe ten minutes. That look in Allison's eyes had never been a good thing. Suddenly, that malevolent light changed, shifted, morphing into an avaricious hunger, her entire face lit with it, and Madeline didn't even have to turn her head to know who had walked through the door.

"Oh, yum." Stacy licked her bottom lip. "Ride 'em, cowboy."

Donna stared toward the entrance as well. "No, honey, you got it wrong. That right there is definitely ride *me*, cowboy."

Cowboy? Maybe it wasn't Tick. Lifting her glass, Madeline slid a shuttered glance in that direction. She barely managed to not sputter on the sip of pinot noir she'd just taken.

Holy fuck, it was Tick.

And Ash.

She drank in the details of his appearance as the two men approached the bar. He did have on cowboy boots, expensive but well worn, and on him it looked good, natural. His jeans were equally faded and frayed, molding strong thighs and that fantastic ass of his. A cotton shirt stretched over muscular shoulders and arms, the sleeves turned back a couple of times to reveal tanned skin.

A memory flashed over her, that tall powerful body between her thighs, pounding into her, making her come, breaking her into a thousand little splinters of pleasure.

Another memory, those big hands stroking her hair, his rich murmur soothing her to sleep.

Donna jabbed her in the side. "That's Ash Hardison. He's new here, owns one of the local chicken farms. Big buddies with your brother-in-law."

"That has to be the finest ass known to woman. God, I love when he comes in the office." Stacy wriggled on the vinyl seat. "It's all I can do not to cream my panties, right there."

The look Donna slid in Stacy's direction was pure evil. "Too bad he doesn't share your interest. Turned you down flat when you threw yourself at him, didn't he?"

Stacy glared. Madeline tensed. She'd seen that look before too, usually right before Stacy slapped someone hard enough her mama felt it. Stacy leaned forward, eyes trained on Donna's.

"Bitch."

"Whore." Donna smirked and leaned back.

Madeline rolled her eyes. The maturity was staggering.

"He's with your 'right man', Allison." That was Donna, stirring up trouble, just like always. Why the *hell* had Madeline thought this would be fun, delving back into the good old days? There hadn't been any such thing and this sure as hell wasn't her idea of fun.

Had she really been this kind of person? Surely not. And surely, if she had been, she wasn't now.

Allison didn't say anything, her gaze trained on Tick as he and Ash took their beers and wound through the small crowd to an empty pool table. Madeline studied them. They were obviously engaged in a heavy conversation, both bearing serious expressions, Tick talking with his hands as he often did. The light over the billiard table glinted off his wedding ring. He'd changed from his investigator's uniform, wearing jeans and a buttondown shirt like Ash now.

"You should make a play for him, Allie." Stacy sipped at her beer. "You steered him away from Kelly way back when, and it would be nice to see someone steal him from that stuck-up bitch he married."

"The scuttle is she's not giving him any, and that baby of theirs is four months old now," Donna added. "You know that has to be one hungry man."

The vitriolic words took Madeline's breath. She smacked her glass on the table, afraid for a second that she'd break the stem. "Do you hear what you're saying?"

"What?" Stacy spread her hands.

"Have you even met her?" Madeline shook her head, disgust filling her throat. "You don't even know her, do you, and you're calling her a bitch, saying someone needs to steal her husband."

"God, Madeline, what is your problem?" Donna flipped back her too-red hair.

Madeline reached for her purse. "I'm not the one with a problem here."

Stacy hissed in a breath. "You—"

"Bitch." Madeline waved off the insult. "Yeah, yeah, I know."

"You've changed, Mad." Donna huffed the words. She tilted her beer to her lips.

"Thank God," Madeline murmured beneath her breath, the pressure in her chest lightening somewhat. "Good night, girls. Wish I could say it's been fun."

On her way to the side entrance, she dropped a bill off with the bartender. Before slipping outside into the frigid night, she looked back. Ash leaned on his pool cue, a grin lighting his face as Tick missed a shot. Drawing her jacket more closely around her, Madeline turned away and stepped into the chilly, damp air.

"You've already slept with her, so why are you asking questions now?" Tick missed his shot and Ash chuckled. That ten bucks would be his for sure. Tick sucked at pool almost as bad as he did at golf. "Isn't it supposed to be the other way around?"

Tick stepped back and Ash stepped forward to line up his shot. "Maybe not all of us are as slow to start as you are. It took you, what? Nine years to get in Cait's bed?"

"You're funny. A regular Jay Leno." Tick rested his hips against the empty table behind them. "At least I know I'm in the right bed. There's something to be said for getting to know a woman *before* you sleep with her. You know that, right? Or wasn't Suzanne a big-enough lesson for you?"

Ash smacked the cue into the ball too hard, totally screwing his plan to end the game in four moves. He cast a narrow-eyed look at his friend. "Bringing the crazy ex-wife into this isn't nice, Lamar."

Holding his stick out to one side, Tick gave him a long-suffering look. "Did you sleep with Suzanne on the first date?"

The back of his neck heated. "Yeah."

Tick lifted his brows in the "I rest my case" expression Ash hated.

"See, you let your dick lead you into things before your head has a chance to catch up." Tick actually managed to put the six ball in the corner pocket. "And it's attracted to dangerous women. Your head likes the safe ones. But you don't listen to it and then you end up married to some crazy bitch who seduces your brother, runs over your dog and tries to kill your father."

"She did not try to kill my father."

Tick sank the three. "She put ground-up azalea leaves in his tea. Those things are poisonous. I think that falls under the umbrella of 'trying to kill someone'. I'll have to check the criminal code, though."

"Now who's the comedian?"

The eight ball made the side pocket. Tick straightened. "You owe me ten bucks."

"I'll make it twenty if you'll answer my questions without further commentary on my choices in women."

Tick rolled his dark eyes heavenward. "Keep your money. I'll answer your damn questions. First, tell me this, because I just don't get it—why are you interested in her?"

"Stanton didn't get you and Cait either."

"That is so different, it's not in the same zip code." Tick propped on the corner of the table. "You didn't answer the question."

"I don't know. She's...she's different." Ash scrubbed a hand over his nape. "Ever been in a room full of people and been completely alone, all at the same time?"

"I've been there."

"Me too." He leaned against the other table and surveyed the area around them, then lowered his voice. "I think she's there all the time."

"And you just have to rescue her, right? Even if it ends up kicking you in the balls. Shit." Shaking his head, Tick pushed to his feet and laid his cue aside. "What do you want to know?"

Ash frowned. How to articulate what he needed to understand, the one thing that bothered him most, the way she refused to let him in at all. He blew out a breath. "What made her so hard, so damn scared of letting anybody close?"

"I've barely seen the woman in eighteen years, except for from a distance at her daddy's funeral. How the hell am I supposed to know?"

"Because I think it happened here." Ash tossed his cue on the table and folded his arms over his chest. "And I think it had something to do with you."

Tick glanced away, muttering a word Ash knew he used with utmost rarity.

"You're going to pull that 'I gave my word' bullshit on me, aren't you?"

"I did."

"The man you gave it to is dead, Tick. What is it going to hurt to tell me?"

"Because it's my word, Ash. Hell, you should get that."

"Yeah, and Caitlin made her brother give his word that he wouldn't tell you what happened while you were in Mississippi, too. How bad do you wish he'd have broken that?"

"That's dirty, Hardison."

"Well?"

"Hell, yeah, I wish he'd said something. But that's different, Ash. That affected both of us, me and Cait, directly. This doesn't...it doesn't concern you."

"Yeah, it does. She needs help."

"Which is exactly why you should stay away from her." Tick's shoulders slumped. "See? I'm doing it already. You're making me break the rule."

"Tick."

"If you want to know so bad, why don't you ask her?"

Like she'd tell him anything. Arms still crossed over his chest, Ash regarded Tick with a steady stare.

"You're obsessed." Tick racked the balls. "Good damn thing you don't have a dog this time."

"Tick. She's not going to run over my dog. I'm pretty sure my dad is safe, and after the last time, my brother won't look twice at a woman I'm interested in. Now spit it out."

"You really don't want to know this, Ash. It's ugly."

"Yes, I do."

Tick gazed at him a long moment, mouth set in a tight line. "Fine. Just remember later, you asked for this."

"I will."

"Let's go, then."

"Go where?" Ash frowned and waved at a booth. "What's wrong with right here?"

"Home. Because if I tell you, that pretty much means I have to tell Cait, and I'd just as soon relate it one time only. The whole damn thing still makes my skin crawl."

Madeline let herself in the back door and eased across the kitchen floor. The television played softly in the living room. Yeah, even this felt familiar—sneaking in after a night with her little girl clique, a hint of wine on her breath, sure of what she'd find in the other room. Except her daddy wasn't waiting for her, with judgment and swift retribution. She'd never figured out why he didn't see that grounding her only made the urge to sneak out that much stronger.

In the big room with the tall windows, a blue glow flickered from the television. Her mother's favorite nighttime drama. The table lamp cast a muted glow in the room, and Mama dozed in the wing chair before the television.

Madeline bent to tuck the afghan around her legs and eased the empty bottle from her fingers. It was one of the small ones her mother favored, the ones Madeline knew she'd find empty and full, tucked all over the house. Once, when she was about thirteen, she'd tried to find them all, to get rid of them.

The bottles were like the heads of the Hydra—cut one off, more grew back in its spot.

Sure her mother was sleeping and not passed out—that looked different—Madeline trudged upstairs. In her bedroom, still decorated in the girlish pink she'd always hated, she shed her clothes. Too bad she couldn't slough off the past so easily, but at least she could wash away some of the tension. In the shower, she turned her face up to the lukewarm spray.

She wasn't one of those girls anymore. She wasn't. No matter what Tick Calvert believed about her, no matter how easily she'd fallen into Ash Hardison's bed. She was not the same Madeline Rachel Holton she'd been at eighteen, the one who'd selfishly stolen Trevor Dailey away from Donna. The one who'd skipped classes and given Bobby Wentworth a blowjob behind the weight gym.

The one who got drunk on Saturday night and refused to sit in church like a good girl on Sunday morning, who broke her daddy's heart.

The one who'd helped Allison Barnett crack Kelly Coker's dreams wide open.

The one who'd tried to make everything right by getting back at Allison later, the one who'd ruined *everything*.

Madeline bowed her head, letting the warm water rush over her hair. Memories pulsed in her brain, Kelly's big eyes full of tears and anguish, not over Tick Calvert, not really, but over Madeline and Allison's betrayal. Because they were supposed to have been her friends. Kelly, a little innocent beneath the bravado, a little lost because of the way it was at home, had never really gotten that girls like that didn't have friends. They merely kept their enemies close.

No wonder Kelly had run away.

A runaway. A runaway who'd slipped through.

Tick's voice, whispering through Madeline's mind. She reached for her shampoo, working the lather into her hair. No, it couldn't be. Kelly had run *away* from Chandler County. Madeline had even received a postcard from her, from Panama City Beach. She'd taken it out to Kelly's mama, who'd looked at it with grief-bleary eyes and never really said a word.

Kelly's mama, who never filed a missing-person report on her daughter as far as Madeline knew. Mrs. Coker had always seemed to just assume Kelly would come home, when and if she was ready.

What if she had come home to Chandler County?

What if somehow, she'd ended up under that house on Miller Court?

Rinsing quickly, Madeline grabbed a towel, wrapped it around her wet hair and stepped onto the rug. She slipped into her terry robe, the weird blend of excitement and anticipation that heralded a possible lead pumping through her.

She padded through to the bedroom and threw open the closet door, scanning the shelves. Where...

There.

Reaching up, she pulled down the dusty navy-and-white striped memory box. She settled on the bed with it, her stomach churning as she lifted the lid and set it aside. No corsages or dance photos, no spirit ribbons or girlish notes here.

A couple of beer bottle caps, which she laid aside with a plastic wristband from the state fair. A Gold Circle condom, still in the wrapper. A lock of dark hair, caught with a brittle rubber band.

The postcard lay at the bottom of the box with a small set of snapshots. She lifted the card, frowning over the smudged postmark. Yes, mailed from Panama City, a few weeks after Kelly had run away. Before that last night, when Madeline had gone after Allison with a vengeance.

Setting the postcard aside, she studied the photo below it. The six of them at the lake. Kelly a little shorter than the others, her petite curvy frame clad in a bright blue bikini.

She was the right height. She'd been missing, presumed a runaway, long enough for that clean set of bones to be hers. It could be her. That body could be Kelly's.

Slipping from the bed, Madeline pulled jeans and a sweater from her still-packed suitcase. She wanted to run this by Tick, and she wasn't waiting for morning to do so.

Ash settled on the couch in Tick's living room and tried to quell the hum of impatience. He probably should feel bad for pushing Tick to spill this when he quite obviously didn't want to, but he couldn't. Somehow, finding out what drove Madeline, what made her react and attack, was more important.

That should have scared him. He didn't understand the need yet, but he acknowledged it. He was no longer the twenty-year-old kid who'd fallen under Suzanne's spell and married her, and Madeline wasn't Suzanne.

"Ash, are you sure you don't want anything?" Caitlin set Tick's mug on the pine coffee table before placing her own glass of milk on the low table by the leather chair.

"I'm fine." He wanted Tick to stop prevaricating by fussing with Lee, bouncing the grumbling baby against his chest and rubbing the little back, but he couldn't very well say that to Caitlin. Besides, he knew from experience that attempting to push Tick into anything led to nothing but frustration. He'd simply dig in and refuse to budge.

"Give him to me." Caitlin nudged Tick's shoulder as she sank into the chair.

He shifted on the ottoman to give her room to stretch out her legs.

"He's okay."

Caitlin pinned him with a look. "He's hungry and you're using him as an avoidance tactic. Hand him over."

Tick's lean frame heaved with a sigh, but he passed the agitated infant into her arms, the small legs pumping in protest as he screwed his face up to cry. Caitlin settled the baby at her breast with sure hands, an artfully draped receiving blanket offering a sense of privacy. She poked Tick's side with her bare toe. "Now talk."

He dropped his head, elbows on his thighs, hands between his knees. With thumb and forefinger, he spun his wedding band in a slow circle that made Ash crazy.

"Madeline and I grew up together. Mama and Miss Miranda were friends, Daddy and Virgil were big buddies. She was only a year behind me in school. So Sunday School, youth group, that kind of stuff—we were always together." Tick didn't look up. "We never did get along. Daddy always said it was because she was as stubborn as I was."

A winsome smile curved Caitlin's mouth. "Now that's a frightening thought."

A deep breath lifted his chest. "Anyway, the older we got, the less I had to do with her. We moved in different circles, at least until I started going with Allison. That was the end of my senior year. We dated for about a year once I went off to UGA."

"You dated her for a year?" Now that was a surprise. Although the little blonde had giggled and referred to Tick and herself as "high school sweethearts" during lunch, Ash had taken it for a short-term relationship. She simply didn't seem like Tick's type.

Of course, Suzanne had been exactly Ash's type when he was that young, so maybe it was true a guy's tastes changed as he matured.

Tick shrugged. "Off and on."

Behind him, Caitlin adjusted the baby's position. Tick straightened and moved to place her feet on his thighs. His gaze on the floor, he began a slow massage of one trim foot.

"Then Daddy died that summer after Madeline and Allison graduated. Allison and I had had this big blowout a couple weeks before, but she made this big point about 'being there' for me after Daddy was killed."

Caitlin made a small, disparaging noise in her throat. When both Ash and Tick looked at her, she waved in dismissal. "Never mind. Go on."

"We buried Daddy on a Tuesday. So Saturday night, she's wanting to get me out of the house, insists we go to this party. By that time, I was too damn tired to fight, so I went." He rested the sole of Caitlin's foot against his thigh and lifted her other. "It was a drunk party and those things were never really my scene. I was pissed with Allison by then for dragging me there, and we were fussing. I'd, um, not been sleeping because I kept seeing that plane burn when I did, and I was irritable as all get-out. I had a couple of beers before I realized I wasn't in the shape for that. Decided I'd sleep it off a while before I tried to drive home."

He cleared his throat.

"Anyway, I went up to Trev's bedroom—he was the guy throwing the party—to crash. I did too. Must have been out in a couple of minutes." He rested Caitlin's other foot against his thigh and rubbed an absent circle on her ankle. "So I wake up Lord knows how long later and I'm...well, I'm not alone in the bed."

Shit. Ash got a picture of where this particular story was going, and he didn't like what was coming into focus. Caitlin was putting it together, too—he could tell from the way her elegant brows dipped together in a slight vee.

Ash leaned forward, his posture mirroring Tick's from earlier, elbows digging into his legs, hands clasped loosely, his stitches pulling, but his attention focused on Tick's uncomfortable expression. "It wasn't Miss High School Sweetheart, was it?"

His voice came out like ground glass. Tick's mouth tightened.

"No." Tick met his gaze dead on. "It was Madeline."

Oh, *fuck*. Ash pinched the bridge of his nose. Yeah, he got where this was going. He'd been there before—him and Robbie and Suzanne.

"I didn't react real well."

"Knowing you, I imagine not." Caitlin's wry tone held very little real humor. She moved, handing Lee and a fish-emblazoned burp cloth to Tick, adjusting her shirt, her gaze on Tick's face.

Holding the baby in a seated position on his lap, Tick rubbed his back with a gentle hand, coaxing forth a series of small belches. "Allison didn't either when she walked in about thirty seconds later, and it just went downhill from there. Allison's screaming and Madeline's taunting her and my half-drunk ass is still trying to figure out exactly what happened."

Caitlin lifted an eyebrow at him. "Which is what?"

"Not what you're thinking." He rested Lee against his abdomen, one hand holding him in place. "You know, I never really got what Madeline's intent was. I mean, it was pretty obvious what her intent was considering what she was doing when I woke up, but not her purpose, because she sure as hell didn't have a thing for me personally and she never did anything without a reason. They might be twisted reasons, like making her daddy crazy, but she always had them."

"So that's it?" Ash scowled. Something didn't add up here. "That's what all the tension between y'all is about?"

Caitlin's dark green gaze flicked in his direction. "Don't feel bad. I'm not getting it either."

"That's because that's not all." Tick leaned down to snag an orange and blue octopus from the floor and dangle it before Lee a moment. The baby, in a rare good mood, chortled and Tick danced the toy over the pudgy tummy with a tickling motion. "You know, if it had stopped there, when Allison cussed me out and walked out after slapping Madeline and calling her every ugly name in the book, everything would be fine. But Madeline wasn't satisfied with that."

A lurking bitterness tainted his voice. Unease tiptoed down Ash's spine with hobnailed boots.

Caitlin leaned forward and lifted Lee into her easy hold. He gummed a vinyl pad attached to one octopus tentacle. "Tick?"

Jaw tight, he met Ash's gaze.

Just remember later, you asked for this.

The warning hung between them. Tick cleared his throat once more, a raw, grating sound. "I called Del to come get me because Allison had taken my truck. He made me go to the diner for coffee, to sober up a little before we went home, in case Mama was up." He paused, rubbed a hand over his mouth. "So Madeline, drunk or mad or whatever the hell it is that gets into her, I guess decides it's all my fault. When Del and I get home, about four in the morning, all the downstairs lights are on, and Virgil Holton's truck is there.

"I could hear Madeline screaming and hollering from the driveway. Seems Madeline had shown up on our doorstep, all full of righteous indignation and ruined innocence, because I'd had sex with her, possibly forced myself on her, and hell, now she might be pregnant. When Mama couldn't calm her down, she called Virgil."

"She said this to your mother?" Caitlin's husky voice held hushed resignation. Ash got that too. Shit, what had that younger Madeline been thinking? Unless Tick was right and she'd been out to get him—and hurting his mother was the way to go to do that.

"Yeah." Tick's jaw was so taut now it might have been carved from the same granite that made up Stone Mountain. "Four days after she put Daddy in the ground."

"My God," Caitlin breathed, sympathy darkening her eyes, "what she must have been going through."

"Yeah." Tick's chin jerked in a sharp nod. "And like she needed Madeline's bullshit—"

"Tick, sweet thing, I meant Madeline, not your mother."

His head whipped in her direction. "What the hell? Did you hear anything I just said—"

"I heard everything. I feel for your mother, I do, but I also know she's one of the strongest people I've ever met, and somehow, I think the event had more of an impact on you than it did on her."

"And an even bigger impact on Madeline," Ash said quietly.

Caitlin's gaze flickered to his again. "Yes."

Tick lifted his hands and glanced toward the ceiling. "I don't believe this."

"Tick." As best she could with Lee, gumming the octopus, tucked in one arm, she leaned to touch his thigh. Ash didn't miss the way he flinched and tightened under that easy contact. "You're still looking at this like a nineteen-year-old boy who'd just suffered a horrific loss—"

"Holy hell, now you're going to do it too." Incredulity darkened his eyes. "You're going to make excuses for her."

"No, I'm not. What she did was wrong. But I can't overlook that what you're describing are the actions of a deeply troubled teenage girl, one with a domineering, demanding father and an alcoholic mother—"

"What?" Tick's voice cracked with disbelief. "Shit, Cait, what are you talking about? Yeah, Virgil was heavy-handed with them and he expected a lot, but Miranda Holton is not an alcoholic."

"Well, according to your mother, she is," Caitlin retorted, completely unruffled.

Tick stared at his wife, and despite the seriousness of the situation and the topic at hand, Ash swallowed a laugh. The little taste of humor was welcome, freeing him for a brief moment from the painful empathy that had gripped him with Caitlin's words. If Madeline had been troubled as a girl, she was equally more so now, merely on a different level.

Shit, he knew how to pick 'em, didn't he?

"How..." Tick shook his head. "When...?"

Caitlin laughed. "What do you think I'm doing while you're playing football with your brothers on Sunday afternoons? The only way to survive living in this place is knowing everything about everyone else, and your mom is a boundless source of discreet information."

"I still think you're making excuses for her."

"No, I'm trying to get you to look at it from a different perspective. Try the wickedly brilliant thirty-seven-year-old sheriff's investigator one. Use your objectivity."

"Cait—"

"So what happened?" Ash rubbed a thumb over his bandage. They could fight the perspective issue out later, and Tick could lose that argument too. He'd started this by asking Tick for the truth, and he intended to finish it. Maybe then he could figure out whether to move forward with Madeline or walk away.

Tick shrugged. "Virgil told Mama it was just Madeline's craziness, as usual. Trust me, Mama had been privy to plenty of it before. She and Del went to bed, and somehow Virgil got Madeline calmed down and in his truck. He didn't want Miss Miranda to know, said he'd handle it, make sure nothing else was said to upset Mama. Asked me to keep it quiet. I gave him my word."

"Manipulative bastard." Caitlin brushed her lips over Lee's head. Tick's eyebrows rose, and she shook her head at him. "What? He was. Let me reiterate—you were only nineteen. You'd just lost your father, whom everyone knows you adored, and he used your loyalty to your mother to keep you quiet. Excuse me if I find that a tad repulsive."

Tick opened his mouth. Ash waved a hand at him. "Give it up, man. She's going to win anyway. Just finish it."

"That's it. I went back to school, Madeline headed off to Mercer but didn't finish the quarter. Dropped out and ran off to Florida. Never looked back."

"Oh, I'm pretty sure she looked back," Caitlin murmured. "Probably every damn day of her life."

"Yeah—" Ash stopped as headlights swept over the windows.

Caitlin reached for Tick's wrist and rotated it to read his watch. "Who is that this late?"

"I don't know." Tick rose and headed for the door, one hand brushing over the place where his holster normally was. Ash shook his head. The cop habits he just didn't get. At the glass-paned kitchen door, Tick stopped and groaned. "Shit, why am I not surprised?"

Anticipation tinged with dread skittered down Ash's spine. Only one person inspired that tension in Tick.

"Who is it?" Caitlin shifted a nearly drowsing Lee to her shoulder.

Tick shot her an ironic look and swung the door open. "Madeline. Fancy seeing you this time of night."

Chapter Nine

"Hey, I'm so glad you're still up. Listen, I need to show you something." Madeline knew she was babbling, but the excitement of a possible lead to a piece of the puzzle was irresistible.

"What are you talking about?" Tick stepped back to allow her entrance.

She waved the photo as she stepped inside, warmth curving around her after the chill of being outside. "I might, just might, have an idea on our Jane Doe—"

The words died as her gaze clashed with Ash's. He looked back, eyes grayish green, storm tossed. A weird tension hung in the room. Caitlin glanced at her once, sympathy flashing over her face before she focused on Lee, who was beginning to fuss.

Unease cascaded over Madeline in a harsh flow. Something strange was up here. Why did she just know that something involved her?

Knowledge glimmered in Ash's eyes, and dread settled deep in Madeline.

Shit damn *fuck*. She didn't want to know what was going on. She'd talk to Tick and get out, as soon as humanly possible.

She brushed her tousled hair behind her ear and folded her arms over her midriff as Tick shut the door. "I'm sorry. I didn't mean to interrupt."

"You didn't. We were just talking." Tick reached for the photo. "What do you have?"

Her focus was gone, like a shimmering mirage disappearing the closer one got. How did simply being in the room with Ash Hardison do that to her? Never before had she let a man get under her skin like this.

"Madeline." The same old frustration returned to Tick's voice, and heat rose under her skin, her cheeks burning.

"I..." She made herself look at him, meeting those dark censure-filled eyes. Jesus, he looked at her like it had just happened *yesterday*. Drawing up her shoulders, she shook back her hair. "I have an idea on our Jane Doe."

He squinted at the picture. "This is you."

Leaning forward, Madeline tapped Kelly's smiling face, half-hidden by his fingertip. "Kelly Coker."

"You're going to have to explain this to me." Tick frowned and looked over his shoulder at his wife and Ash in the living area. "Let's go in the study. Y'all excuse us a minute."

Without taking another glance at Ash, she followed Tick down a short hallway. The room he called the study lay behind the formal dining room. A lamp glowed on a pine table by the leather couch, a reading lamp cast a pool of light on the desk. Framed photos and a couple of wildlife prints—sporting fish—graced the walls and an eclectic collection of books packed the floor-to-ceiling shelves. The room was warm, welcoming and intimate, and something about it whispered to Madeline that Tick hadn't decorated it, but rather that this was the result of the hand of someone who loved him and knew him well.

Being in here made her skin crawl.

"What have you got?" He propped on the edge of the big pine desk and reached for the photo.

She pointed at Kelly's face once more. "It might be a long shot, but Kelly ran away from home my senior year. We all thought she ended up in Florida, and her mama never reported her missing that I know of. What if she came back? What if she somehow ended up under that house?"

His brows lowered in a frown of concentration. "It's a possibility. We can try to locate her dental records, start running down her whereabouts. Right now, anything's a lead."

She nodded and looked around the room, anywhere but at him. A different wedding photo sat on his desk, more snapshots of Lee's infancy. All the trappings of a happy marriage, a good life.

A quick swallow cleared the lump from her throat. "I should go and let you get back to... I shouldn't have just shown up on your doorstep. Sometimes, when a lead or an idea pops up, I get a little impulsive. It used to drive—"

She cut the sentence off, the familiar nausea settling in her upper chest. Of all people with whom to bring up Jack, she had to pick Tick Calvert. Why the hell had she come here anyway? All she had to do was pick up the phone. No, she jumped in her car, to go tearing over here to show him in person.

The same kind of sheer impulsivity that had gotten Jack killed, that had effectively ended her career.

Maybe Tick had been right when he'd said she knew all about getting other cops killed. She shied from the dart of pain the idea brought with it.

"I'm just going to head out now." She reached for the photo Tick still held, avoiding his suddenly narrowed gaze. He let her take the glossy paper but straightened from his negligent posture at the desk.

"Madeline—"

"I'm sorry again for interrupting." She slipped from the room before he had a chance to reply. When she reached the large keeping room that held the kitchen and living area, Caitlin had disappeared, and Ash stood before the bank of windows overlooking the porch.

At the sound of her shoes on the hardwoods, he looked over his shoulder. "Finished?"

"Yes." She didn't elaborate, didn't stop for chitchat. She was out of here, away from the weirdness, away from the fear that he *knew*. "Good night."

The doorknob slipped under her damp palms, but she managed to get the door open. Outside, she dragged in a deep breath and almost ran down the steps. What had she been thinking coming over here?

That was the problem—she never thought first when it was vital. God knows, she'd not thought that night she'd crawled into bed with Tick; she hadn't thought the day Jack died and look what had happened then.

What was wrong with her?

"Madeline, wait." Footsteps clattered on the steps behind her.

"He told you, didn't he?" She didn't slow, reaction and a trembling blend of anger and fear swirling through her. Fear? No, that was crazy. She didn't have anything to be afraid of. She was mad, furious, at Tick Calvert, that was all. How dare he tell Ash?

"I said wait." A strong hand closed on her arm, swung her around to face him. In the dim blue illumination of the mercury light, his eyes glittered. His breath puffed into the air and disappeared.

She stepped back, knocking his hand away. "Don't touch me."

Her heel went off the walkway, sank into soft dirt, and her balance disappeared. She flailed a second. Oh God, no, she was going to fall on her butt in front of him...

He caught her, warm fingers cupping her shoulders, lifting her, pulling her closer to him.

Stomach to hard belly, soft curves to firm chest, they stared at one another.

"You know, don't you?"

"Yeah." His hold tightened. "I know."

Bile crowded her throat. Damn it all.

"Madeline," he whispered, "it's okay."

"No, it's not." She shook her head, closed her eyes. "It's not okay. He shouldn't have—"

"I made him. I asked him."

She lifted her lashes at that, a knot of pain burning in her chest. "Why?"

"Because I needed to know." Confusion glinted in his eyes. "Don't ask me why. I can't explain it. All I know is it was standing between us and I needed to understand. It's not like you were going to tell me if I asked."

Of course she wouldn't. She'd buried that secret shame so far away, kept it hidden, even from herself when possible. She'd never told anyone, not even Jack, who knew almost everything about her. Why would she have wanted Ash of all people privy to all the sordid details?

"You didn't need to understand anything." She pushed the anger into her voice, trying to smother the hurt. "It's none of your business, Hardison. And what do you mean, standing between us? There is no *us*. I've known you two fucking days."

"There's an us, Mad, whether you want to admit it or not."

"I told you not to call me that."

"Stop dodging the issue."

"I'm not dodging anything. *You're* not anything. Got that, Ash? You're not *anything* to me."

He remained silent, merely staring at her, and the resentment and hurt flared into desperation.

"Did you hear me? I said you weren't anything."

"I heard you." He inclined his head once. "So you're saying it doesn't matter if I turn around and walk back inside, and that's it between us."

The image flashed in her head, of his doing just that, of being left cold and alone once more. She drew herself up, the vulnerability of needing him in any way making her even angrier, even more desperate.

Too much too soon.

The laugh she pushed from between her lips dripped derision. "Well, I'd hate to see that happen. You are a good lay."

"That's easy for you, isn't it? Putting me into that little slot."

Infuriated, she shoved at his chest. He didn't budge.

Since she couldn't move him, she poked a finger into his chest, hard. "It's the only slot I want you in, Hardison. I told you, I'm not in—"

"The market for a man right now. Yeah, yeah, I know. You've told me, and I've told you—"

"I don't want to be your friend."

"That's the problem. I don't think we can be 'just friends', Madeline. I may not like it, I may not understand it, or be sure I'm doing the right thing, but there it is. Whether you want to admit it or not, there's *something* between us."

She'd show him what was between them—pure sex.

Grasping his jacket lapels, she took his mouth. He opened immediately, allowing her to devour him. The kiss was carnal, raw, an approximation of what she wanted with him, and heated energy speared all the way through her, down her legs, tingling to her toes.

She wrapped an arm around his neck and surged closer, taking his tongue deeper in her mouth, mewling in pleasure as his hold on her tightened. Yes, they had something between them—raw passion, plain old-fashioned desire.

That was all. The sooner he understood, the better.

One big hand moved up to cradle her nape, the other stroked soothing ellipses over her spine. The tone of his kiss changed, from ravaging and marauding to worshipping and gentling. Rather than thrusting, he swept the tip of his tongue over her lips, taking little sips of her, nipping at times, then calming the burn with an easy caress.

Madeline curled closer, one arm wrapped across his shoulders, the other trapped between them, still clutching his lapel. The force of the desire remained but channeled differently, a warm vigor that spread throughout her being, drawing her nearer and nearer to him, deeper and deeper into the circle of him. He lifted his mouth a millimeter.

"Tell me I'm not anything, Mad," he whispered. "I don't believe it."

Stupid, pointless tears burned her eyes, and she pushed, tried to shove away. He didn't give way, arms pinioning her to him.

"You can't make me believe it." Challenge hung in the low murmur of his voice. "Because you don't."

"Stop it." Her voice came out a husky rasp, like she'd been on a three-day smoking binge. Raw and angry, her throat hurt, and it had to be the cold air because it wasn't anything to do with him. It couldn't be. She pressed at his chest again. "Let go."

"Do you really want me to?"

She pinned him with her dirtiest look. "Yes."

The arms were gone immediately, as was the warm wall of his torso, the caressing heat of his hands. A step or so away, he watched her.

The chilliness rushed in, swamping her. She crossed her arms over her chest and rubbed at her arms. With her throat closing over a knot, she lifted her chin to stare him down. "See? You're nothing."

"Yeah." He lifted a hand to rub his thumb across her cheek, taking the wetness. "I see that."

She brushed shaking fingertips over her face, stared at the dampness glittering on her skin. Horror slammed into her. She didn't cry. Ever. Not since she'd left home. She hadn't cried over the disappointments of her life, over the sure-as-hell loss of her career. She hadn't even cried over her father's death. Over Jack's death.

And she certainly didn't cry over a man.

Silent sobs shook her shoulders. With one step forward, he folded her close.

"Come on, Mad," he murmured next to her ear. "Let it out, baby."

"Told you not to call me that." The words fought against the sobbing, lost beneath the pain.

"I know." He rubbed a palm over her hair, tucked her face into the curve between his throat and shoulder. "I know you did."

"I don't do this." She curled her hands into his jacket. She was going to push away. She was. In a second, she'd step away, pull herself together, show him how strong Madeline Holton was, how she didn't need *anyone*...

Silently, he wrapped her closer and brushed his mouth over her temple, then again. She swallowed a breathy sob and tried to suck back the tears trickling over her lashes. Letting her lashes fall, she pressed her face into the shadowy sanctuary of his neck, a harsh breath shuddering through her.

"I don't do this," she whispered. "I don't cry."

"I know." He dropped another kiss on her temple. "And I don't mean anything."

God, what was she supposed to do with this man, the one who refused to let her lie, the one who didn't push or pull at her, the one who simply seemed to accept who and what she was without question?

"It's cold." He said the words matter-of-factly and rubbed a hand down her back. "I know someplace we can get something warm to drink."

She finally pulled free of his embrace. "I'm not—"

"Your choice." He shrugged, an easy roll of broad shoulders, and gestured toward the driveway. "I'm headed that way. You can follow or not, no pressure from me. If you want to be with me, fine. If not, I can deal too."

Pulling his keys free, he strode along the walkway, across the driveway to his truck. Madeline stared after him as he fired the engine and reverse lights flared. Follow him? What did he think, that she wanted to be with him that much?

Headlamps swept the yard, the battered pea-green Ford rumbling through a three-point turn to ease down the driveway toward the road. Keys in hand, she walked to her car. She'd head home. Tomorrow, she and Tick would go talk to Kelly's mother, begin running down the possibility that Kelly might be their Jane Doe.

When she turned onto the rural highway, the tilted red glow of Ash's taillights hovered a good distance before her. At the Flint crossroads, he turned left, toward 19. Rather than taking the right to return to her mother's, she took the same left. She'd run into town, swing by the department, maybe start a search for any records having to do with Kelly's current whereabouts.

The taillights stayed ahead of her all the way into Coney. However, at the first stoplight, where she should turn right if she intended to go to the sheriff's department, Ash stayed straight.

Madeline shrugged as the light flared green and the sparse traffic moved forward. No problem if she satisfied her curiosity about his "someplace to get something warm to drink".

He pulled in at the timeworn roadside diner, in front of the restored railway depot that served as headquarters for the chamber of commerce. If she was smart, she'd go on, head to the station. She'd give up this weird back-and-forth non-relationship with Ash Hardison.

She turned into the parking lot.

When he stepped from the truck, a small smile creased his face. Not a smile of triumph or pride, but one of genuine pleasure. The expression warmed her more than it should.

"I don't get you, Hardison."

His eyebrows winged upward. "Why is that?"

"You know what I did and you're still here."

"So you threw yourself at Tick." He held out a hand. "I've known him a long time. You're not the first woman to do so, and I doubt you'll be the last, wedding ring on his finger or not."

Refusing to take his hand after that comment, she swept by him to the door. "I did not throw myself at him."

"That's not the way I heard it." He reached over her shoulder to tug the glass-framed door open. "Maybe you'll have to give me your version of events."

She pinned him with a look. "Nice try."

A warm, amused sound tickled her ear. Inside, the heat rolled over her, taking away the sting from the frigid air. The place was nearly deserted, a drowsy trucker sipping coffee and filling out his logbook in one booth, a teenager leaning over the counter and talking to the young waitress. Patsy Cline drifted from the jukebox.

Madeline chose the booth farthest from the door and slid in, wrestling out of her jacket and scarf. "He did not tell you I threw myself at him."

She couldn't imagine Tick describing it that way.

A roguish grin revealed Ash's white teeth. "No, he didn't put it that way. So why did you do it?"

The directness took her breath, rattled her. To cover, she reached for the menu.

"The mulled cider is great," he said, folding his hands on the faded Formica tabletop. "Or the hot chocolate."

She dropped her gaze to the menu. She really did not get this guy. The hell of it was she wanted to. And he knew. He *knew* and he was still here.

"Know what you want?" His deep voice tugged her free of the same old reverie. She lifted her gaze to find the teenage waitress standing by their booth, order pad open, pen poised.

"I—" She floundered, stared at the menu again. She'd not taken in any of it.

"How about two ciders and a couple of slices of cheesecake?" Ash reached for the laminated folder. "All right with you?"

"Yes." Flustered, she let him take it. She wouldn't be able to choke down a bite, though.

Once the girl had walked away, he took her hand. "You have to stop this."

Keenly aware of the warm weight of his fingers around hers, she brushed back her hair with her free hand. "Stop what?"

"Being cagey with me. Listen to me." He drew her hand toward him and leaned forward at the same time. "I'm here because I want to be. I'm interested in you, and I want to get to know you."

"You know too much." The words were out before she could stop them.

His mouth drew into a tight line, and he watched her a long moment.

"When I was twenty, I met my wife Suzanne." He rubbed his palm over her knuckles. "My dad tried to talk me out of seeing her, said she was a gold digger, that she was a lying conniver, not to mention

105

unstable. I didn't listen."

Madeline stared, taking shallow breaths between her lips. Why was he telling her this?

"We got married five weeks after we met."

She flexed her fingers about his. "What happened?"

"My dad was right. She turned out to be everything he said she was. She went through my bank account in two months, ran up close to a hundred grand in credit card bills." He laughed, a rough sound. "Even tried to take out my dad so I'd come into my inheritance early. When that didn't work and I tossed her out, she tried getting her hooks into my younger brother."

"Oh, no." She tightened her hold on him. "I'm sorry."

"I'm not looking for sympathy, Mad. It was twenty-odd years ago, and I'm over it, believe me. At the time, I swore I'd never get married again. That lasted almost ten years."

"So did you? Get married again, I mean?"

"No." His lips twitching, he shook his head. "Suzanne made me realize I had to be really sure the next time that I had found the right woman. I'm still looking."

With a nervous laugh, she pulled free. "You make it sound like you really want to get married."

The waitress arrived to set steaming mugs of cider, along with two thick slices of rich cheesecake, before them, the spicy scent wafting over Madeline's senses. He waited until the girl had departed again to speak.

"I'm not checking out every woman I meet as potential wife material, Madeline, but I'm forty-two years old. I'm a little beyond the singles bar and one-night-stand scene. Besides, after seeing Stanton settled with your sister and watching what Tick and Caitlin have together, yeah, I wouldn't mind having something like that in my life."

"Why are you telling me this?" She reached for her cider and took a gulping sip, realizing too late what a painful error that was. She grimaced at the harsh, stinging burn on her tongue.

"Because I want you to see that I made a really shitty mistake when I was a dumbass kid and I didn't let it rule my entire life."

Stilling, she narrowed her eyes at him. "Is that what you think I've done?"

"Honestly? Yes." He forked up a bite of cheesecake. "You let that night stop your life cold, didn't you, honey? I mean, you had a law-enforcement career, obviously, but what about personally?"

She refused to rub her arms against the chill his words brought with them. "You don't know me. What makes you think you can—"

"How many real romantic relationships have you had in the last eighteen years?"

She opened her mouth on a denial, but the words wouldn't come.

"How many, baby?"

"Didn't I tell you not to call me that?"

"None, right?"

"That doesn't prove anything."

"Except you're still punishing yourself for a rash decision you made when you were a confused kid."

Pain wrapped around her heart, pride demanding she force a light mockery. "Did I miss something? I thought you were a chicken farmer, Hardison, not a psychiatrist."

"Stop it." He grabbed her hand again, his pale eyes intent as he leaned forward. "Enough hiding behind the smartass front, Madeline. I see right through it, remember? I scare the hell out of you, just like you do me, because it feels too damn real too damn soon. That's what this morning was all about, when you couldn't get away from me fast enough."

She tried to tug free; he refused to let go.

With a shaky breath, she moistened her lips. "I don't want this."

"I know, but I think you need it. I think we both do."

A hand over her eyes, she slumped in the booth. "I don't know what to do with you."

"I could give you some ideas. There was that little thing with your tongue you did last night..." He passed his thumb over her knuckles. "I can handle not knowing if a venture will pay off, Madeline."

"Considering you're a farmer, I guess so."

A half-smile quirked up one corner of his mouth. "I'm willing to take a risk on this if you are."

"What is *this* exactly?"

"What do you want it to be?"

"You know, you do that a lot." She scowled. "I hate it."

"Do what?"

"Answer a question with a question."

His gaze glinting with intensity once more, he leaned toward her. "So what do you want, Mad?"

"Right now, I want to finish this cider before it gets any colder."

Laughter puffed from between his lips. "And Tick thought he had it tough."

She froze with her cup halfway to her mouth. "*What* are you talking about?"

"Stop looking at me like that and finish your cider." He cut off another bite of cheesecake. "Cait gave him a fit. You're obviously going to give her a run for the money."

"Somehow, I doubt Ms. Perfect-Society-Fed and I have anything in common."

"Oh, you'd probably be surprised. Just for the record, I hate when you do that too."

She reached for her own fork. "Do what?"

"Change the subject when things get sticky." He ran a blunt fingertip around the edge of his cup, then turned his piercing gaze on her. "I can't give you what you want, Madeline, if you don't tell me what that is."

"Maybe because I don't know."

"So we're going to make this up as we go along." He looked less-than-pleased with the prospect, and she laughed.

"Thought you could handle not knowing if a venture would pay off."

"Yeah, but that's with a business plan in place."

"So maybe we do this one day at a time and see what happens."

"Maybe. If you can promise not to run at the first sign of something that scares you."

"Well, you ask a lot, don't you, Hardison?"

"I don't do things in half-measures, Mad. You need to know that upfront."

Oh, yeah. Madeline lifted her cider and buried her nose in the warm scent. Like that didn't scare her enough to make her want to run.

Chapter Ten

"Lee's asleep."

Tick didn't glance up from the Krakauer book, but made a noncommittal sound in his throat in reply. Caitlin sank onto the bed beside him, adjusted her pillow and sifted her fingers through the hair at his nape. He reread the sentence he'd just completed.

She continued the slow stroke of her fingertips through his hair. "Tick?"

"Hmm?"

"It bothers you, doesn't it? That I don't see what happened with Madeline the way you do."

"That you don't agree with me? No, that doesn't bother me." He gave up on reading about Chris McCandless's journey into the Alaskan wilderness, placed the bookmark on the page and laid the tome aside. Frowning over her question, he folded his arms behind his head. "It does bother me that you can just excuse her."

"I'm not." She propped her head on one elbow and traced a finger along his abdominals. "You said she never did anything without a reason?"

"Yeah. So?"

"Did you ever wonder why?"

Eyes trained on the ceiling, he swallowed. "Honestly, I tried not to think about it at all."

She circled his navel, nerves jumping under the gentle caress. "So you never asked her?"

"Precious, I haven't spoken to the woman in eighteen years, not until Stanton hired her and I had to."

A small silence stretched between them. He knew better than to think the subject was closed. Instead, he counted ridges on the crown molding. She outlined his abs below his bellybutton.

"So why do you think she did it?"

"Cait." He closed his eyes, keeping the exasperated huff in his throat. "I know what you're trying to do and it's not going to work."

"Sure it is. You can't stand unanswered questions."

"Well, I can stand this one." He opened his eyes. "Can we drop it?"

"Of course." She twisted sideways to click off her bedside lamp. He reached for his, though why he bothered was beyond him. That had been too easy.

With the darkness hanging around them, broken by the soft illumination of the kitchen light, she settled at his side, her cheek on his chest. She rested a hand on his stomach, rubbing her thumb over his rib cage.

Arms behind his head again, he waited. He wasn't the only one who couldn't stand unanswered questions, an unfinished puzzle.

"Do you want to know what I think?"

Unable to resist a smile, he closed his eyes on a long exhale. "Sure. Why not?"

Her lamp clicked on, the warm glow flooding the room. She sat up, legs crossed, hair spilling about her shoulders. "It had nothing to do with you."

"Really?" He hefted against the pillow to a half-sitting position. "You could have fooled me, since I woke up with her kissing me and her hand in my jeans, wrapped around my balls—"

"Tick."

"What?"

"Do you want to tell me what happened?"

"You mean, do I want to sit in our bed and lay out the gory details of having Madeline Holton feel me up while I was drunk off my ass?" He elbowed his pillow. "Not no, but hell, no."

"Maybe you need to."

"Yeah. I need to talk about that." Like he needed another hole in his head. He folded his arms behind his head again, the muscles so taut they ached. "You wanted to have this conversation, precious. I was trying to read my—"

"Tick."

"What?"

"I understand you're angry. You have reason to feel violated and working closely with her can't be helping." She reached out to touch his jaw. "But talking about it may be the only way for you to end it."

End it? If she wanted it over, why did she keep pushing? "Nothing to talk about. She copped a feel, I made it awful plain I wasn't interested, and about the time Madeline started to pull away, Allison walked in."

"She's obviously impulsive, but you said she never acts without a reason." Caitlin's elegant eyebrows dipped in a frown of concentration.

"Let me know when you figure her out." He lifted his book and turned on his light again. "I sure as hell couldn't."

Caitlin removed the book from his hand. "She didn't want you."

"No, she didn't."

"But she was willing to have sex...to initiate sex...with you." Still frowning, Caitlin tucked her hair behind her ear. "Except your girlfriend walks in and...that's it."

He shook his head. "What's it?"

"It wasn't *you*. It's the girlfriend, Allison Whatever-her-name-is." She moved a shoulder in the easy shrug he knew so well. "Madeline was out to hurt her, to get even with her maybe, and you were the means to an end."

"Glad you figured that out." He gestured at the volume lying next to her. "Can I have my book back now?"

She picked it up and held it to her chest. "We need to finish this."

A grin hitched at his lips. "I can think of better ways to spend our time in bed, precious."

Leaning in, he kissed her, exploring her mouth with lazy flicks of his tongue. He cupped the back of her head, deepening the kiss. An arm about his neck, she pulled him down and fumbled the book toward her nightstand. It hit the floor with a soft thud. He slid the strap of her camisole aside, following the line of her shoulder with his mouth. Hell yeah, this was much better than talking about Madeline Holton, trying to figure out why she'd done what she'd done.

She trailed a fingernail along his spine, and he shivered under the easy contact, growling a little and nipping at her collarbone. Not that he really cared *why* Madeline had done it. The reason didn't matter because if he could just wait out the next few weeks—

"I wonder what she had against Allison." The words emerged on a breathy note.

"Caitlin." Tick sagged.

"Now you're using sex as an avoidance tactic." She outlined his pectorals with a fingertip. "You're not going to tell me you're not curious."

He opened his mouth on a denial and sighed. "Maybe."

"You could ask her."

"Yeah, and you could not bitch your brother out when he takes off on one of those mountaineering expeditions of his. Not happening, sweetheart."

Except, shit, now she had him thinking about it again, damn it. He didn't want to think about it, didn't want Madeline Holton in his head, let alone his marital bed.

Caitlin walked her fingers up his chest to the tip of his chin. "Deal with it, Tick. Don't let it have this much power over you."

"I'm not." He made to pull away.

She tugged him back. "Yes, you are, ever since she came back. You're doing the same thing she's done—let it take over your life."

"I have not." He frowned. "You're the one pushing the point tonight, Cait. You and Ash both. He can't leave well enough alone either. All I was trying to do was read—"

"You're avoiding it because you don't want to deal with it. Blaming her is easier."

"Hell." He did push away then, moving to sit on the edge of the bed, tension gathering in a tight knot at the base of his neck. "There's nothing to avoid. There's nothing to deal with it. It happened a long time ago and it's over and done with, all right?"

"All right." Something about her soft agreement made the strain in his muscles worse.

He shoved up and turned to face her, hands outspread. "Fine. What do you want to me to deal with?"

She watched him, her eyes soft. "How about the anger? The sense of betrayal?"

"Ah, sweet Jesus." Irritation trembled in him and he thrust his fingers through his hair. "There you go, with all the psychology stuff. I swear, you can be worse than Tori. Yeah, fine, whatever, what she did pisses me off. Does that count as dealing with it?"

"I really didn't mean your anger or sense of betrayal with Madeline."

He gaped for a full second before he snapped his mouth shut. "Then what are we arguing about?"

She looped her arms about her knees and rested her chin on them, still watching him. "Your anger at yourself."

"That's the craziest thing I've ever heard." He let the heavy sarcasm coat his words. "Why would I be angry at myself?"

"Because you took the easy route and let her father manipulate you into staying quiet. Because you hate what she did, but you hate that you let her get away with it worse." Caitlin tilted her head. "Because keeping quiet about it is a form of lying, and it goes against everything you believe."

"Don't you dare, Cait." The words came out gritty, from between clenched teeth. His irritation flared into something hotter, more virulent. He lifted a hand and chopped it between them. "Don't you dare do the profiling thing on me."

"Then find a way to deal with this and stop bringing it into our home and our bed." She tilted her chin, voice cool. "Because I'm not sharing you with another woman, not even like this."

He stared and swallowed hard. "I'm not—"

"Yes?" She quirked one eyebrow at him.

He released a pent-up breath. Damn it, he hated when she did this, when she figured out what was going on in his head before he did. "And what, exactly, do you suggest I do?"

"Talk to her."

"I tried. The first day she came back."

"Oh, sure." Caitlin's husky laugh shivered over him. "I'll bet you were very approachable."

"I was not that bad."

"Of course not." A small smile tilted the corners of her full mouth. She rose to her knees, knelt at the edge of the bed, reached for the waistband of his pajama pants and tugged him to her, belly to belly, chest to chest, her lips a breath away from his. "Come on, sweet thing, I've never known you to dodge the hard stuff just because it's hard."

He narrowed his eyes. "You think you've won, don't you?"

She linked her arms about his neck and kissed his jaw. "Yes."

"Just like that." He slipped his hands down her back, over her cute little rear, to the backs of her thighs. "I'm going to come to heel and talk it out with her."

"Not just like that," she conceded, moving her lips to the corner of his. She tightened her hold on his neck, pressing to him. "But you're thinking about talking to her."

He nodded, flexing his arms, lifting her a little. "Falconetti, you're insufferable when you think you're right."

"Maybe you shouldn't make it so easy for me, Calvert." She tipped her head back to look at him, hair falling over her shoulders. Damn, she was a tease *and* insufferable. A chuckle lodged itself in his throat.

"Making it easy for you wasn't what I had in mind." He lifted her higher, pulling her knees forward, sending her backward on the mattress. He came down over her, between her thighs, laughing at the flare of surprise in her green eyes. Sometimes a guy had to get the upper hand however he could get it. He caught her chin and kissed her, hard. He rubbed a thumb over her shoulder and grinned. "I win."

"Really?" With a wicked smile, she pulled his mouth down to hers, hugging his hips with her thighs. "We'll have to see about that,

Calvert."

After several moments, he lifted his mouth from hers and rested his forehead on her shoulder. "Wickedly brilliant and objective sheriff's investigator, huh?"

Her quiet laugh puffed against his temple and she threaded her fingers through his hair. "That's the one I love."

He rolled away to stare at the ceiling. "I don't get it, Cait. If she wanted to use me to get back at Allison, there were other ways. Better ways. That doesn't explain that whole mess at Mama's."

"Teenage girl. Unstable family life. Highly distressed." Caitlin lifted a hand and ticked off the points. "Drunk. Maybe some conditioning."

"Conditioning?"

"Tori says your mother didn't like Allison."

He harrumphed and let his eyes slide closed. "That's putting it mildly."

"Tick, sweet thing, you were raised in a conservative home where sex was equated with commitment. We're talking about the girl who seduced your mother's firstborn son in a football equipment room. I'm not surprised Lenora didn't like her."

"Wait a minute." He turned his head. "How do you know I didn't do the seducing?"

She only gazed back at him.

"All right, fine. It was Allison's idea."

"Okay, so tell me why you were drawn to Allison in the first place?"

"I..." He closed his mouth and frowned. "I don't remember."

"Then let's rephrase the question." She rolled to lever up on an elbow. "Who made the first move in the relationship?"

"I asked her out."

Caitlin arched one eyebrow. "Why?"

"Because..." He frowned, casting back in his memory for long-forgotten details. A flirtatious smile as Allison passed his locker in the hall. Little notes tucked under his windshield wiper.

"She pursued you, didn't she?"

"Yeah." He rolled so they faced one another. "How did you guess?"

"Because. I know you." She trailed a fingertip along his chest. "You're quite capable of—and good at—pursuit and seduction when it suits you. When you want something, you go after it, and you're unshakeable until you succeed. If you couldn't tell me why you were drawn to her, then you weren't the pursuer."

"All right." He tangled their feet together. "So explain to me what

114

this has to do with Madeline's 'conditioning'."

"Remember, I'm only theorizing." She met his gaze, her own serious, and he nodded. "She expected you to respond to her despite the earlier animosity between you two. You were sexually active with Allison. Madeline was probably already active as well—"

"Uh, yeah. With more than one boy. She didn't hide it and that made her daddy crazy."

"Like conquests, then? Situations where she was the one in control, making the moves."

"Maybe." He frowned. "Yeah, probably."

"This is a girl who's used to boys responding to sexual overtures. Her focus was not on you and..." She sighed. "Tick, sweet thing, you were a vehicle, a means. At that point, it probably never even occurred to her to think of you as a person, to think about what she was doing until it all blew up in her face. Then it was too late and all she had left, all she still has left, was the guilt and the shame."

Humming a quiet made-up tune, Madeline settled into her squeaky desk chair and flipped open the phone book. She skimmed a fingernail over the "C" listings...Calvert, Charles; Calvert, Delbert; Calvert, Lamar—*my God, how many of them were there, anyway?*— Carden, Childers, Chitwood, Clark...Coker, Lorraine.

Yes, that was her, Kelly's mama. They'd called her Miss Lorraine, just as her own mama had been Miss Miranda. Way back when, Lorraine Coker had been a hardworking single mother, with two jobs, a sweet no-nonsense heart and a headstrong teenage daughter. Madeline frowned over the address. 1335 Poison Ivy Way. She didn't recognize that street name.

"Hey."

At Tick's deep drawl, she glanced up. He paused at the counter, pouring a cup of coffee. Replacing the carafe, he jerked his chin in the general direction of the phone book. "Mrs. Coker lives out at Poison Ivy Way."

How did he...? "I see that. I don't remember that road, though."

"I wouldn't call it a road, per se." Mug in hand, he dropped into the chair at Cook's desk. The edges of his hair still seemed damp, what looked like a shaving nick marring the shadowy area below his chin. Madeline narrowed her eyes—no, not a nick. A tiny love bite.

Ick.

She forced her attention back to the conversation. "What would you call it, if it's not a road?"

"A long-ass driveway." He grinned over the rim of his mug. "She bought one of the acreages along Stagecoach Road a year or so back. Calls the department every time one of Drew Barron's cows gets on her land."

"I'd like to talk with her. If she has Kelly's dental records, or knows how we could get them..."

Tick set his mug down and rubbed both thumbs over its side. "You realize this is a long shot?"

She lifted her eyebrows at him. "You got a better lead?"

He pinned her with a long-suffering look. "So, if it's her, who would she have seen if she'd come back?"

Me. The syllable flitted through Madeline's brain and brought a little snag of pain with it. She'd have thought that, long years ago, but obviously, she'd have been wrong.

"Madeline?"

At the quiet prod, she looked up and shrugged. "I would have thought she'd come see me, but I guess not. Donna and Stacy, maybe."

His brows dipped in a frown. "Not Allison? She was in that photo you had last night."

Irritation spiked in her. How could he even ask that? Oh, of course. He'd never even been aware of what had happened, and that simple lack of perception pissed her off. She smothered the irrational anger.

"No, not Allison."

He nodded but didn't ask further questions. "After we talk to her mother, we should interview her friends and acquaintances, anyone with whom she might have made contact in the last... Hell, that's a lot of time."

"I know." The possible time span stretched before her, and Madeline tapped her fingers on the desk. "But Ford said this girl was still young—late teens. If it *is* Kelly, that means we're looking at...a shorter time span. Fifteen to eighteen years ago."

"Three years." A pained grin quirked at the corner of his mouth. "Still a hell of a lot of time."

"We can narrow it." She slapped the phone book closed and dropped it back in the drawer. "Let's go talk to Lorraine Coker."

Tick shot her a half-amused look over his mug. "Are you always this eager?"

"Well, yeah." She was a homicide detective. She lived for this stuff. "Why?"

His shoulders rolled in an offhand shrug. "I like it."

Now, *that* was scary.

Even scarier was the warm flush of acceptance his mild approval engendered. An awkward pause descended. He cleared his throat, coughed into a fist. "We can ride out that way, see if she's home, if you like."

"Sounds good." She rose and grabbed her jacket, fishing the unit keys from her pocket.

He rose and drained his cup. "Let me grab my coat, and I'll meet you out front."

Early-morning traffic was next to nothing, and soon they left the city limits behind. Farmland, pecan groves and pieces of hunting plantations spread out on either side of the rural highway. Madeline noted even the smallest changes in the landscape—the old Bullington place had been razed, the Garret house stood empty, a couple of new doublewides had replaced two old shotgun shacks along the way.

Tick tapped his thumb on his knee in what she now recognized as his "thinking" gesture. Silent, he cast periodic glances in her direction, strange, speculative looks that made her skin creep with nerves.

She glared at him as she slowed to turn left on Tuton Road. "What?"

He'd been gazing out the window at the broken-down feed store then, and he jumped at her voice. "What?"

An almost immediate four-way intersection required her to stop. She pinned him with a glower. "You keep looking at me like I've sprouted...I don't know, extra body parts or something."

He lifted both hands in a clear what-the-hell gesture. "I was thinking."

She didn't take her foot off the brake, despite the lack of oncoming traffic from any direction. "About?"

Eyes narrowed, he opened his mouth and snapped it shut again. "I was just...thinking."

Annoyance shivered through her. "You're beyond strange, Calvert."

With a roll of his dark eyes, he waved toward the intersection. "Are we going to do this interview or not, Holton?"

Brushing off the frustrating exchange, she accelerated through the intersection, hooking the first right on Stagecoach. It didn't take her long to find the long, rutted dirt drive labeled Poison Ivy Way, which traveled through overgrown underbrush along a couple of twists and curves before opening up to a small cleared patch of land, heavily landscaped with every plant known to a Lowe's garden center. A small

117

grayish blue doublewide sat between old oak trees, an early-model Toyota parked by the side.

Madeline pulled to a stop behind the car and killed the engine. Nerves sparked under her skin. What if she was wrong? What if it wasn't Kelly? She was about to put every parent's worst nightmare in front of Lorraine Coker. The idea was daunting, and from Tick's terse expression, she knew he was thinking about that too.

The glass storm door swung open as they walked up the dirt path to the steps.

"Madeline Holton, is that you?"

It was Miss Lorraine, but time had not been kind to her. The hair that had once upon a time been dyed a glossy black now lay in tight too-permed, too-bleached curls close to her head. Heavy smoker's lines creased her face, the thin skin making her appear closer to seventy than the almost-sixty Madeline knew she was. Beneath her thin cotton housedress, blue spidery veins marred skinny legs.

Madeline smiled. "It's me, Miss Lorraine. How are you?"

"Better now that I've seen you." The painfully raspy voice was the same. Miss Lorraine waved her up the steps. "Get up here and give me a hug, girl."

Still smiling, but with her heart already aching, Madeline obeyed. The steps rattled beneath her feet. Lorraine wrapped her in a cloud of stale cigarette smoke and Jean Nate. She rubbed a hand over Madeline's back.

"Oh, it is so good to see you," she whispered into Madeline's hair. She held on a moment longer, until Madeline's eyes stung, then released her and stepped back. "Let me look at you. My Lord, aren't you beautiful?"

"I don't know about that—"

"There you go." Lorraine shook her head. "Same old Maddie, won't take a compliment to save your life. Never did understand that about you, girl, as sweet, smart and pretty as you are."

Madeline was ready for the floor to open and swallow her at any moment, with Tick standing behind her, listening and silent. She could only imagine what he had to say about Lorraine's description of her as "sweet".

"Is that a sheriff's department badge? Why, honey, are you home for good? Your mama must be so pleased."

Pleased probably wasn't the word Mama would use. Madeline kept that to herself and shifted from one foot to the other, uncomfortable, but not willing to jump into the real reason for this visit. She disentangled herself as gracefully as she could. "I'm working with the department temporarily."

"Well, come on in out of the cold." Lorraine held the door and waved her inside. She glanced over Madeline's shoulder. "Come on, Lamar, your mama wouldn't want you out in the damp either, especially as sick as you were last fall."

"Thank you, ma'am, I'm sure not." A slight ironic smile played around Tick's mouth as he followed the women into the small home. Madeline slanted an inquisitive look at him. Sick?

"Sit down, sit down." Lorraine fussed around the tiny neat living area, seating the two of them on the couch while she settled into the recliner covered with a brightly colored afghan. She reached for the remote and muted the *Today* show, sending Matt Lauer into silence. "Lamar, I saw your mama in the grocery store just last week. She said the baby's doing well."

"Yes, ma'am, he is." Tick's white teeth flashed in a brief, genuine smile.

"So are you here about Drew's cows again? I swear, those animals—"

"Actually, no, Miss Lorraine, that's not why we're here." Madeline darted a quick, uncomfortable look at Tick. He seemed content to let her talk, his demeanor one of hey-this-is-your-idea-that-makes-it-your-show. She cleared her throat against the knot there. "We...earlier this week, the remains of a young girl were discovered. The time period indicates...well, that is—"

"You think it's Kelly." With one foot, Lorraine set the recliner rocking. Her expression didn't change.

Madeline swallowed. "I think it's a possibility."

With a silent nod, Lorraine looked away, gazing out the window over their heads. She rocked a moment longer, her pushes harder. "I always thought that, you know, that she might be dead."

"Mrs. Coker, we don't know for sure that it's Kelly," Tick said, quiet reassurance in his tone. "We would need to make an identification—"

"How would you do that?"

Madeline leaned forward, pitching her own voice to a soft, even tone. "We could use her dental records."

"Maybe." Lorraine shook her head. "She didn't never see a dentist but once, and that was Dr. Weeks over in Tifton."

"He's retired, but his son runs the practice now. I can call over and get her records." Tick rested his elbows on his knees.

Madeline swung her attention back to Lorraine. "Do you have anything of Kelly's, a diary or her letters?"

Lorraine shrugged, her rheumy blue eyes dark with pain. "I don't rightly know what I have, but you're welcome to all of it, if you'll think it helps. I boxed up her things, what was left of them, brought them with me."

She pushed up from the chair, knees creaking, and shuffled to the short hallway. Madeline caught Tick's eye and tilted her head. They trailed Lorraine to the back bedroom, as neat and clean and spare as the rest of the house. She fumbled in the closet for a moment, pulling free a lime green storage container.

"Here it is." She settled it on the bed, caressing a palm over the lid, much the way Madeline had seen Jack's mother do his coffin just after his funeral. She wanted to see what lay within that plastic rectangle, but opening it, pawing through the contents in front of Miss Lorraine seemed obscene somehow. They were already bringing her pain and worry, reopening her grief, when really they were working on Madeline's conjecture.

Her impulses...and everyone knew where those tended to get her.

Lorraine made another swipe across the lid, her mouth trembling. "You can take it with you."

"Thank you." Tick inclined his head, eyes solemn. He tugged a small pad free from his jacket's interior pocket. "I'm going to write you a receipt for this, and just as soon as we're done, I'll return it to you personally."

Because Madeline wouldn't be here to do it. The underlying message wasn't lost on her.

"That's fine." She took the slip and folded it, sliding it into the pocket of her housedress.

Tick hefted the box. "I'll put this in the car."

Madeline waited for him to clear the room before she took Miss Lorraine's hand and led her back to the living area. "Other than the postcard Kelly sent me, did you hear from her at all after she left? Through other friends? Did she call, write, anything?"

"No." Seated in the rocking recliner once more, Lorraine focused on a spot beyond Madeline's shoulder, as though that space on the floral-paneled wall would reveal the secrets shrouded by the past. "Just that card you shown me...nothing else."

"I'm so sorry we brought this up for you again." Madeline covered the wrinkled hand, sympathy flooding her. Brought this up? She was pretty sure something brought up Kelly's loss every single day. "As soon as we know something, I promise I'll be in touch."

Miss Lorraine wrapped her fingers around Madeline's in a grip surprising in its strength. "You be in touch, anyway. I've missed you,

Maddie girl, and I'm sure your mama has as well."

Madeline leaned down to hug her and brush a swift kiss over her cheek. "I will."

She slipped outside, meeting Tick on his way back up the path from the driveway. "Ready?"

He stopped, hands shoved in his jacket pockets. "Did you interview her already?"

"I asked her about other contact with Kelly, if she knew of anyone else who'd heard from her."

He waited and finally spread his hands. "And?"

She shook her head. "Nothing."

A grimace twisted his strong features. "Damn, this case will be a bitch even if it does turn out to be her."

Anger flashed through her. "Well hey, you can file it in your cold-case file and quit worrying about it, huh?"

An answering ire flared in his dark eyes. "What the hell is that supposed to mean?"

"You're the one complaining about it being too hard, Calvert."

"I'm not the one with a history of cutting out when the going gets tough, now am I, Holton?"

"Why do I even bother trying with you?" With a look that should have left him dead on the spot, she sidestepped him and stalked to the car. She didn't look at him as he sank into the passenger seat and slammed the door. Gaze on the rearview mirror, she backed up enough to let her turn around and head out the thin, rutted track. His thumb bounced off his knee again.

He lifted a hand between them but didn't look at her. "I'm sorry, all right? I had no intention of getting into this crap with you today."

She shot him a narrow-eyed glare. "You think we might be able to agree just to focus on what we have to do?"

"I'd like to think so. My wife doesn't agree."

Her foot hit the brake too hard at the stop sign. "What is that supposed to mean?"

"She thinks I have 'unresolved issues' where you're concerned." He made air quotes with his fingers.

She turned right onto Stagecoach. "So what do you think?"

The expression he slid sideways at her simmered with pure irritation. "Oh, she's right."

And he hated it. An irresistible smile curled Madeline's mouth. "Can't stand it, can you?"

He exhaled a breath that was half-huff, half-laugh. "You have no idea."

Rolling her shoulders in an effort to relieve the tension sitting there, she flexed her hands on the wheel. "We should probably stop dancing around the whole damn thing and just deal with it."

"Yeah." Another long exhale. "Probably."

Silence descended between them, rural scenery flashing by as the patrol unit ate the miles back to Coney. The smothering quiet itched over Madeline's skin, setting her nerves on edge. The town opened around them—auto-parts store, Pizza Hut, the peanut plant. The jingle of a Gary Allan song split the uncomfortable stillness as she pulled into the parking lot at the sheriff's department.

Tick tugged his phone from his belt. "Calvert. Hey. Actually, yeah, she's right here." He darted a look at Madeline and extended his cell, a sardonic twist to his lips. "It's for you."

Frowning, she accepted it. He swung out of the car, opening the trunk, ostensibly to retrieve the plastic container holding Kelly's belongings. Madeline lifted the phone to her ear. "Hello?"

"Hey, babe." Ash's voice, and pleasure shimmered through her entire body. She tamped it down.

"Hardison, 'babe' is worse than baby," she parried. "You can't call me that either."

"You know, you're a hard woman to please." Good humor saturated his words, and she melted a little against the car seat. Simply talking to him shouldn't be this satisfying, not since she'd seen him, kissed him, only the night before. Memories of that good-night kiss flowed through her, bringing back each shivering, delightful sensation. She'd been hard put to go home to her own bed.

The trunk slammed, shuddering the vehicle and thumping her back to reality. "Why are you calling? And why on Tick's phone?"

"Maybe I just wanted to hear your voice." His tone dropped with the words, sending another frisson of awareness over her. My God, the man's voice was sexy. "I had to track you down best I could, since you haven't given me your cell number yet. Figured if I found him, you wouldn't be far away."

"Well, you found me." She winced at the inane words, but she'd never been very good at flirtatious small talk. Outright sex? No problem. Carrying on a conversation? Not in her repertoire.

"Yeah, you sound awful enthused about that." His amusement reverberated over the connection. "Listen, I have a load of stuff to do today, but I thought I'd see if you wanted to do something tonight."

Do something? The possibilities shimmered before her, memories of that night in his bed, the taste and feel of him, the way he seemed to burn her alive.

"...I can cook or we can go out. There's always the movie thing, although I'm not sure what's playing in Albany." He was talking, and shit damn fuck, she'd missed most of it, probably, fantasizing about making love with him again...

Wait one holy-frikkin-second. Making love? Uh-uh. Sex. That was all. "Making love" indicated a level of emotion, a type of commitment that she simply didn't—

"Madeline?"

Oh Lord. She frantically tried to recall what he'd said and drew a blank. "Um, yeah?"

His sigh hung between them. "You missed all of that, didn't you?"

Should she lie? She slumped. "Yes, I did."

Another wry chuckle. "All right, it's obvious you're focused on work. Call me later and let me know what you want to do, okay?"

Focused on work? If he only knew. She swallowed. "Sure. Bye."

"Later, honey." The phone beeped with the dropped connection, and she closed it slowly. She rubbed the silver rectangle on her jeans, wiping her fingerprints from the shiny surface, and stared at the sheriff's department. Tick had taken the storage box inside, and she knew what waited for her there once she climbed those steps.

The past with all its ugliness.

Facing those unresolved issues.

Great. So she had one man she didn't know what to do with and another she didn't want to deal with. Avoiding the hard stuff had never gotten her anywhere in the past except alone and unhappy. Yanking the keys from the ignition, she shoved open the car door.

Maybe it was time to start taking things on the chin.

Chapter Eleven

Madeline found Tick in the shabby little conference area off the squad room. The bright plastic box stood in the middle of the table; he slumped in a chair and stared at it, a frown on his face, thumb bumping off his knee again.

She slid his phone across the table. "Why didn't you open it?"

"Thought you'd want to do it." He shrugged. "She was your friend."

"Thanks." She approached the long scarred table and ran her hand around the edge of the container, much as Lorraine had caressed it earlier. As badly as she wanted to know, at the same time, she didn't. Didn't want to open this box, didn't want those bones to turn out to be all that was left of Kelly. She wanted to go on believing Kelly was someplace else, living somewhere sunny and sandy, happy and free.

"Why'd you do it?"

The abrupt inquiry, the way his dark gaze sharpened on her face, set her back, stealing her breath and ability to speak. Ignoring the way her chest hurt, the way her fingers trembled, she reached for the lid. "Calvert, you—"

"You said it, Holton." His voice went hard. "Time to stop dancing and just deal with it."

"I think finding out if those remains are Kelly's might be more important—"

"Madeline, damn it, quit running from what you did and tell me why."

"For her, okay?" Her vision blurring, ears buzzing with a rapid rise in blood pressure, she smacked her palm on the box lid. "I did it for her."

"What?" Confusion twisted his features and he shook his head. "You're not making sense, Holton."

"I can't...I can't explain this to you." A blend of nerves and nausea roiled in her belly, burning her chest, pushing into her throat. "You'll never understand."

He leaned forward, gaze focused on hers. "Try me."

She turned, pushing her hair away from her face. "It's over, okay? I screwed up, I did it, but it's in the past. It happened and I can't change that. Why are we digging this up? It doesn't fix anything."

"Holy hell," he breathed. "You are so like her it's freakin' scary."

"What are you talking about?" She snapped the words out and spun when he didn't answer. He remained seated, staring at her with a stunned expression. If she hadn't been on the verge of throwing up from mingled anger and tension, the poleaxed look on his face might have been funny.

With a harsh laugh, he slumped back in his chair and rubbed his hands down his face. "Damn, it makes sense now, in a sick sort of way."

"Calvert, what the fuck are you rambling about? What do you mean, 'like her'?"

"Cait." He lowered his hands to meet her eyes. "Don't know why I didn't see it before."

She hitched one eyebrow at him. "You're comparing me to your *wife*?"

"Yeah."

"Sure, that makes sense since she and I have so much in common. She actually *likes* you." Ignoring the fact that Ash had made the same association, glad that Tick seemed to have let go of the past for a moment, she popped the box's latches free. She was like Caitlin Falconetti? Hardly.

"Maybe you don't have much in common with her now." Eyes narrowed, he rested his elbows on the table, his attention on her face. She shifted under his scrutiny but didn't look up. "But a few years ago? Oh, yeah. I see it now."

She glared. "See what?"

"Avoidance. Fronting. Hiding. Holding people off as a form of self-protection. Want me to keep going?"

"I want you to shut the hell up and let me get to work."

He pushed up and came around to stand across the table from her. He lifted the lid free and laid it aside. "You said you did it for her."

Oh God, he was never going to let it go now. Madeline blinked away a blur of tears as the scents of old paper and old memories wafted from the container. She couldn't look at him, couldn't look into the box to save her life. "I also said it didn't *matter*."

He rested a hand at either end of the carton. "Cait seems to think it wasn't about me at all. She thinks you were out to get back at Allison."

Madeline closed her eyes. She wanted to leave, wanted out, but where was there to go? She pulled on the bitchiness like a cloak, forced free a scornful laugh.

"Listen to you. 'Cait thinks.' Can't you think for yourself, Calvert?"

She could feel his steady regard. "We make a good team. I respect what she has to say, and usually, she's right when we're talking about people."

Madeline lifted her lashes. With her head bent, she didn't have to meet his gaze. Instead, lime green plastic framed what was left of Kelly's life, bracketed by his hands.

"Madeline, keeping secrets...that's never a good thing. The person it hurts most is the one keeping them."

"Thanks for the concern, Calvert." She lifted her eyes then, narrowed in her best fuck-you expression. The sudden sadness in his expression shook her. She injected mockery into her voice. "Where did that inestimable wisdom come from? Your mama?"

"No." He didn't react, merely continued to watch her, an old sorrow glinting in the dark depths of his serious gaze. "From helping Cait put our lives back together after she'd destroyed what we had by doing the same damn thing you are. Avoiding, fronting, hiding, holding people at a distance. Keeping secrets. She was wrong, and so are you."

"You are so—"

"What purpose is it serving, not telling me? We don't get along anyway. You hate my ass, so it's not like I can react in a way that will make you dislike me more, right? Hell, maybe putting it out there will make you feel better."

"Oh, sure. Confession being good for the soul and all that bullshit." She lifted the first layer of paper out of the box—sheets of notebook paper so old it had yellowed slightly, the ink fading. "We're talking about crap that happened almost two decades ago. Do you see my life suffering because of it?"

He laid a long-fingered hand atop the yearbook she'd been ready to lift. "Yes."

"Fuck you, Tick." She shoved his hand aside.

"You're not going to tell me that what happened that night didn't lead to you running off, to not talking to your father for years, Madeline. What about your relationship with your mama, with your sister? Your daddy died, for God's sake, and you hadn't spoken to him in what? Sixteen years?"

She froze with the yearbook halfway out of the box. "Don't you dare mention my father. Do you hear me? Don't you *dare.*"

"Why not?" He leaned in, intent on her face. "It's not like he meant anything to you, at least not the way you acted—"

She swung at him and found her wrist caught in a firm grip, their gazes locked in intense battle.

"No," he gritted and shook his head. "We're not going there, not now, not ever. Do you understand?"

Horrified, she swallowed. She'd never lost control enough to strike out physically—not at a suspect, not at her father, not at Allison or...not at anyone.

Oh, *God*, and Ash thought she was worth something. Only because he didn't know her, didn't see the real her—

"Madeline." Tick gave her a gentle shake. Stunned, she stared at him, thoughts bumping through her head in a wild chase. "It stops now. We're moving on. You're telling me. Everything."

"She loved you." The words were out, spilling free before she could think, before she could call them back.

"What?" Surprise flared in his eyes. "Who? Allison?"

"Kelly." With a twist, she extricated her wrist from his grasp.

His brows lowered. "What do you... I didn't know her, Madeline."

"You didn't have to." She rubbed at her arm, a chill running over her. "You just had to be you, that was enough for her."

He pulled out a chair and sat down, still frowning. "I don't think I understand."

With the weary movements of an old lady, Madeline did the same. She folded her hands on the tabletop and focused on the surface of her skin, rather than look at him. "I don't mean she loved you the way your wife does. She loved you the way a teenage girl worships the boy she can't have."

She reached into the box for the smaller shoebox she'd glimpsed earlier. With infinite care, she unfolded the thin news clippings and laid them out on the table. "See?"

"It's our football season my senior year." He sifted through them. "And baseball, graduation notices."

"Not *our* season," Madeline corrected, tapping a finger against his name, circled in one article. "*Your* season. *Your* graduation notice."

He flipped through the snippets, the skin around his mouth paling.

Tired, Madeline brushed her hair behind her ears and sighed. "She lived in a trailer park. Her daddy abandoned them when she was a baby. There was never enough money, she never felt like she was enough. She struggled with school, stayed on the fringes a lot. And you were...you. Smart, athletic, good-looking, from a good family. She loved the idea of you, of what being the girl who walked through those halls with you would be like."

"A crush." He speared his fingers through his hair. "I don't get how that leads to what happened with us."

"The crush didn't lead to what happened, Tick." Madeline smiled, a sardonic twist of her lips. "Allison did."

"I think maybe you better start at the beginning."

"God, she is such a bitch."

Ash lifted his eyebrows at Dale Jenkins as the virulent whisper floated to them across the processing desk at McGee's. The other farmer shook his head, a half-grimace, half-smile curving his mouth. Stacy Cheek had a mouth like a Teamster and a filthy little temper on her; it wasn't the first time the two men had been privy to her insights on other women, her ex-husband and life in general.

Dale leaned a hip against the chest-high counter and grinned. "So how 'bout those Braves?"

Ash chuckled. He'd missed the preseason game in which his beloved Astros had been completely routed by Atlanta. Instead, he'd been wrapped up in having cider and cheesecake with the woman who seemed destined to tie him in the biggest knots he'd ever seen. "We'll get you next time."

"Not if that boy keeps pitching like he does."

"Did you hear her?" Stacy's tone lifted above a whisper, real anger swirling through the words. "Miss High and Mighty."

"She always was." The second female voice was oddly familiar, and Ash raised his chin, tilting his head to get a better look. Yep, that was Tick's Miss High School Sweetheart. Entering data into the computer, she stabbed at the keys, her expression sour. "Don't you remember? Total snob, thinks she's better than everyone else."

Ash shook his head. What the hell had Tick seen in this woman, even as a teenager? It had to have been the sex. Ten to one, she'd been his first. Those were the ones a guy always lost his perspective over.

Stacy laid a sheaf of papers aside with a smack and grabbed the next stack. His, Ash realized with a wave of relief. Thank God. He'd be out of here fairly quickly and wouldn't have to listen to much more of this bullshit.

"She's working over at the sheriff's department," Stacy said, long nails clicking on the keyboard. "Donna said she's been in a car with Tick Calvert the last couple of days. Wouldn't you like to be a fly on the wall there?"

Fuck. They were bashing Madeline, while he'd been standing there. Anger washed over him, his neck burning.

"Like he has the time of day for her." Allison flicked her shiny hair over one shoulder. A hint of possessiveness lingered in her tone. "Like he ever did."

"Ladies." His voice came out louder than he intended. Holy God, for a second he sounded like his father, booming in the Texas State Senate. Ol' Clayton would have been proud. Two pairs of eyes swung to him, surprise in Stacy's, shocked recognition in Allison's. He leaned forward. "You think you could save your completely inappropriate bitchiness for another place and time and get my goddamn paperwork done?"

Stacy gaped. Deep scarlet flushed Allison's face. Dale muffled a laugh behind his hand.

"Well?" Ash spread his hands. "Do I need to get a supervisor in here?"

"No, sir." Stacy snapped her mouth shut and spun back to the computer. Allison pinned him with a killing look. He matched her glare for glare, staring her down. As much time as he'd spent in the rarified jungle of Houston society, this malevolent little bitch and her displeasure were nothing.

He flicked a finger at her keyboard. "I'm pretty sure Mr. Jenkins has better things to do than listen to your bullshit too. How about getting his stuff done as well?"

Still glowering, she shifted her gaze to the screen, letting him know in no uncertain terms she was doing so on her own impetus and not because of him. Yeah, sure, whatever made her happy as long as she shut her damn mouth and stopped running Madeline down.

Dale caught his eye, still chuckling. Ash crossed his arms over his chest. "Now, what about those Braves?"

With complete silence other than the clicking of keys and shuffling of paper coming from the other side of the desk, he and Dale indulged in an ambling conversation about baseball and the looming spring season. He let the inanity soothe his raging temper. Hell, he hated being angry. It pissed him off worse that he'd let them under his skin.

A few seconds later, Stacy slapped his printouts down on the counter without a word. Yeah, he was intimidated by that, too. What was she going to do? Flay him with her bad attitude?

"Thanks." He picked them up and leaned forward. "You and your little friend really should remember this is a small town. You never know who might be royally ticked off when you go around slandering people without reason. Think about it."

Papers rolled into his fist, he nodded at Dale and strode out.

The edgy resentment stayed with him all the way to his truck and as he drove off the premises. At the traffic light where the plant's long entryway joined the highway, he turned left instead of taking the right that would send him in the direction of home.

He needed to see Madeline. He didn't question or fight the impulse. She was busy and distracted, he knew that, didn't expect much, but damn it, he needed a few seconds in her presence to settle the jangling irritation.

The area around the courthouse square vibrated with construction crews and people doing business in the downtown area. He jockeyed the truck into a spot beyond the park and walked up the block to the sheriff's department. He took the wide concrete steps at a jog, two at a time.

Dry, overheated air slammed into him in the tiny lobby. He nodded at the kid working the desk. "Hey, Roger. Ms. Holton around?"

Roger tilted his head toward the hallway behind him. "In the conference room with Investigator Calvert."

"All right if I go back?"

Waving him on, Roger reached for the ringing telephone. Ash strode down the empty hallway to the squad room. Muted voices carried up the stairs from the radio room. The conference room door stood open.

"I think maybe you better start at the beginning." Tension coated Tick's voice.

Ash stopped in the doorway and rapped a knuckle on the frame. "Hey."

"Hey." Frustration gleamed in Tick's dark gaze. Madeline didn't look around. "What are you doing here?"

Ash studied the awful strain apparent in the hunched line of Madeline's shoulders. "Came by to see Mad for a moment."

She brushed her hair behind her ear but still didn't turn. Tick closed his eyes briefly on a harsh exhale. "Ash, we're busy. Can it wait?"

Protectiveness rose in him, and he lifted a couple of fingers. "Two minutes."

For a moment, Tick stared him down before giving in. He pushed up from his chair. "Fine. I'll be right back."

Ash waited until Tick's footsteps faded. "Madeline?"

She slumped back in her chair, fingers pressed to her brow.

"Yes?"

He went down on his haunches next to her. "You all right?"

"Yeah. Sure. I'm fine." She blew out a long breath and turned to look at him, her big hazel eyes sad and mournful. "Why are you here? I thought you had things to do."

"Just left McGee's. Needed to see you for a sec." He trailed the back of one finger down her cheek. She didn't smile, and sudden tears glittered in her eyes. He cupped the back of her head and pulled her into a loose embrace.

"Hey," he whispered, "don't do that. It can't be that bad."

To his surprise, she wrapped her arms around his neck, hard.

"I don't want to be here," she whispered into the curve of his shoulder. A palpable tremor moved through her slender body. "I don't want to do this."

He stroked her back. Whatever "this" was, as much as he wanted to shield her from pain, maybe, just maybe, facing it would act as a catharsis, free her from some of the old fear and hurt holding her back. Maybe it would be what she needed to get her beyond still being sick with shame over the past.

She deserved that. He turned his head, pressed a fierce kiss to her cheek. "I should go and let you get back to work."

With a trembling sigh, she nodded and released him. He rocked back on his heels and smiled at her, caressing the curve of her jaw. Renewed anger at Stacy and Allison burned in him. The absolute gall infuriated him.

"What is it?" Her eyes narrowed on his face.

"Nothing." He shook his head. "I was just thinking about all the good things you deserve—"

"Good things?" Her voice cracked on a harsh, ugly note. "You're insane if you think—"

He stopped the words with a kiss. "Yes," he murmured against her mouth. "Good ones, great ones even."

"This is—"

"Very right." He laid a finger across her lips. "Now, I'm going to get out of here before Tick tries to throw me out and I completely destroy his ego by showing him that it doesn't matter he's five years younger than I am. You are going to get through whatever 'this' is, and later you're going to give me a call and let me know what you want to do tonight. All right?"

She eased her head back so his finger fell away. "I don't get you, Ash."

"Honey, you've already got me." He smiled. "On the hook anyway."

"That's not what I—"

"I know what you meant." He leaned forward and kissed her once more. "Call me. I mean it."

He rose and exited before she could argue. In the hallway beyond the squad room, Tick leaned against the wall, arms folded over his chest. Clearly unhappy at being kicked out, he straightened as Ash entered the hall.

Ash shook his head. "Don't start."

Tick lifted both hands in a gesture of surrender, and a grin quirked at Ash's mouth. He shoved his hands in his pockets and cast a glance back at the conference room. "Tick, take it easy with her. She's...vulnerable."

"Yeah." Tick shot a look in the same direction. "I noticed."

"I have to get out of here." Ash tagged his arm. "Chickens don't feed themselves."

"The houses are automated, Ash."

"Yeah, but someone has to check the software."

"Later."

Ash headed out the side door. His day was looking better already.

Madeline stared at the door where Ash had disappeared moments before. How did having him show up for a couple of minutes make her feel so much more capable of dealing? She should be annoyed that he'd dropped in and interrupted her day, not filled with the warm and fuzzies because he'd wanted to see her, wanted to make sure she called him later.

Because he thought she deserved good things.

The man was downright dangerous.

"Brought you something to drink." Tick held a canned soda aloft as he strolled through the door. He set it on the edge of the table, other hand curled around his coffee mug. Madeline stared at the green soda can. It had taken Jack four months to realize she didn't drink coffee.

"Um, thanks." She reached for the icy can, condensation already gathering on the sides. The whole world had gone Twilight Zone, with a really great guy looking at her the way Ash Hardison did, with Tick Calvert treating her like a human being... Well, whatever good karma she'd earned lately, she was definitely going to fuck it up. Soon. That was her MO. Just look at what had happened with Jack. That had been her fault, and nothing would ever zero out that karma.

Tick peered into the storage container, lifting layers with careful hands. "I don't see a hairbrush or anything else we could use for a DNA match in here. Some letters and things, some posters, dried flowers, spirit ribbons, stuff like that."

"What about the letters?" She moved closer, afraid to disturb the balance of things too much. The last thing she wanted was for him to go back to the whole start-at-the-beginning idea. "That was before self-stick stamps. If she licked them, licked the envelopes, there's the chance that—"

"Nope." He shook his head, flipping through the small stack of pastel envelopes. "They're not from her. Looks like...they're from you. Letters to her over a summer, maybe, from the postmarks."

"The summer Autry and I spent with our aunt in Tampa." The words hurt, the memories of that fear-filled summer hurting even more. Nate had gone to their grandmother's, and her mama had spent the entire season at Greenleaf, after she'd... Madeline shook off the remembrance.

Tick laid the bundle aside and gave her an odd look. "I don't see anything helpful in here."

Madeline lifted her hair into a knot at her nape and rolled the can over her neck, trying to relieve the tension sitting there. "I'll start trying to track down the dental records from Dr. Weeks's office."

He nodded, gazing at the articles they'd laid out earlier. "So why did she run away?"

Madeline didn't look at him. The envelopes stared at her like so many accusations. Kelly had kept those, after everything? Her throat constricted, and she swallowed. "Because we broke her heart."

"We?"

"Me and Allison." She shrugged, an irritable motion, feeling like the room kept closing in on her. "Look, Calvert, do we have to get into this? What does it matter why she left, if we're focused on whether or not she came back? I don't want to talk about the whys."

"I need you to be a damn cop, Madeline. That means putting the personal stuff aside. If she came back, if this body is her, we're going to have to take her past apart, and I'll find out anyway. Just tell me."

"It's ugly. Would you want to drag out the worst thing you'd ever done and dissect it?"

"Whatever you did and what happened with me...would you do it again?"

"No." Horrified, she jerked her gaze to his. "God, no."

"Okay, then you're a different person. We're all different people."

He obviously hadn't spent a lot of one-on-one time with her high school friends lately. Allison, Donna, Stacy...they didn't seem to have moved past age eighteen, with all its pettiness and immaturity and selfishness.

"Holton." Exasperation dripped from his voice. "Out with it."

She stared, mute. She simply couldn't open her mouth and force the words out.

"Fine." He snagged his cell phone from the table. "I'll call Allison and ask her."

"You wouldn't."

"Try me." He flipped the phone open and pointed at it. "Got McGee's programmed in my farm contacts, right here."

"All right." She lifted her hands before tugging a chair from the table. She rubbed her eyes. "Kelly was younger, a sophomore when we were all juniors and you were a senior."

Nodding, he spun a chair and straddled it, folding his arms on the back and resting his chin upon them.

She feathered a hand through her hair. "God, it all sounds so stupid and childish now."

"Because we were kids," he said, his voice quiet.

"Kelly was so *into* you. It was almost scary. Allison too. Part of the reason they wanted me in their little group was because I had access to you, since our fathers were friends. After a while, the hero worship wasn't enough for Kelly. She wanted you to notice her. You didn't seem to really date any one girl."

The corner of his mouth hitched up. "Because Daddy was smart and kept all of us in sports and church activities and kept us working on the farm in what spare time we had. He had four boys in high school; it was probably the only way he could survive."

"Anyway, she wanted to be that one girl. The problem was, so did Allison Barnett, except Allison was smart enough not to talk about it." Her stomach trembled with nerves, and she sucked in a breath to settle them. "Not to mention smart enough to sabotage Kelly."

His brows canted downward. "Sabotage?"

"Oh, they both had a plan, Calvert."

"You make it sound like a freakin' battle engagement."

She laughed, the harsh sound making her throat hurt. "You don't know a lot about teenage girls and how they operate, do you?"

"Obviously not. Enlighten me."

"Kelly was actually the one who figured out that the way to get close to you was through sports. Only Allison...twisted that. Convinced her that seeing other guys on the baseball team, having them talk about her, would make you notice her. She was just naïve enough, just desperate enough to believe that."

Understanding dawned in his dark eyes. "She's not the one who...in the dugout—"

"Yes." She didn't want to hear him voice that. She'd sat with Kelly in the aftermath, helped her clean up, dried her near-hysterical tears, not able to understand why Kelly had done what she'd done, any more than Kelly had ever been able to get why Madeline had skipped classes to blow Bobby Wentworth behind the athletic building. "She's the one."

He looked shaken, a pinched whiteness about his mouth. "Because of me."

She wouldn't lay that blame on him, wouldn't wish that on anyone. "No. You might have been the motive, but the catalyst...that was Allison. The whole damn thing was her idea, right down to having Davy Terrell recruit the other boys."

"Holy hell." He pinched the bridge of his nose and blew out a breath. "She ran after that?"

"Yeah, later. After everyone at school made her life a living hell."

"I can see why. That shit was all over—"

"I remember, Calvert, believe me."

He dropped his hand and fixed her with an inquisitive stare. "You said 'we' broke her heart."

"I'm the one who convinced Kelly to go out with Davy when he asked. I thought...I thought maybe if she found someone else, she'd get over that fixation with you. I knew Allison, should have known she was up to something, and I never saw it coming, didn't do anything to stop it, and then it was too late."

"Madeline." He shook his head. "That wasn't your fault. No way should you have blamed yourself for that all this time. You didn't do anything."

"Exactly. I let this happen to her."

"That's like Cait thinking... I'll never understand women." He straightened, rolled his shoulders. "So the thing with you and me and Allison, that was payback, then, for what Allison did to Kelly."

"Payback?" Madeline crossed one leg over the other and folded her arms over her midriff. Her stomach ached. "I wouldn't call it that, not really. Allison was up to her old tricks again, and I was damned if she was going to get what she wanted, after what she'd done to Kelly."

"I don't understand."

"She wanted *you.*"

The totally male confusion twisted his brow once more. "She had me. We were dating."

How come the smart ones were always so dense?

"Dating wasn't what she had in mind," Madeline said, as though explaining some particularly difficult concept to a first-grader. "She wanted you the way Falconetti has you."

135

"What?" The horrified look in his eyes would have been funny if she hadn't been delving into her own private hell. "There was never any possibility that... I was a little infatuated, but it wouldn't have gone any farther. My mother couldn't stand her."

Madeline bit off the perfect mama's-boy joke and sighed. "Your brother had just gotten Barbara Blake pregnant, it was common knowledge they were going to get married because of that, and Allison thought she had the ideal way to snag you."

He moved his head in a slow side-to-side movement, more trying to take it in than negate the idea. "We weren't even... I mean, it's not like we were having sex all that often—"

"It only takes once, Calvert, especially when you're a dumbass nineteen-year-old and your girlfriend is lying about being on the pill."

Appalled realization dawned on his face. "Holy hell."

"I'm sure being trapped into a shotgun marriage with that bitch would have been hell, but not a holy one."

"Funny." He shot her a dark look. "So you figured if she caught us together, that would be it, huh?"

"I thought even if I had to go all the way through with it, screwing you once would be a small price to pay." She pressed her arms tighter over her aching stomach. "In my experience, boys didn't turn down a free piece, and it wasn't like I had to worry about losing your friendship or respect."

"Yeah." He frowned. "So I get everything up to that point. What I don't get is why you showed up at my mama's insisting I'd gotten you pregnant. Why do that if Allison had already seen us?"

"She stormed off. You left with Del. I thought everything was good, you know? Then she came back to the party." Madeline smoothed her hair behind her ear, remembering the virulence in Allison's voice, the spiteful triumph in her eyes. "I hadn't counted on her being able to put everything together, which she had. She was pretty smug about the whole thing. I wanted to smack that grin right off her face. I couldn't let her win. It was all mixed up in my head. It wasn't ever really about you, but what she'd done to Kelly, how she was going to get what she wanted..."

The words trailed off and she sighed, massaging her temple. "I'd had a few beers, which with my family history is *not* a good idea at all. I decided I'd talk to your mama, tell her everything, and she'd know what to do. She was always so calm and capable and everything my mother wasn't. I took Trevor's bottle of Southern Comfort, drank part of that on the way over to your house. Again, not a good idea.

"How I managed to get to your house without wrapping the truck around a tree, I have no idea. So I wake your mother up, and somewhere I got the bright idea that even better than telling her the truth, if I told her we had slept together and I was probably pregnant, that she'd make you do the right thing and then that would really fuck Allison over—"

"Oh shit, Madeline." He rubbed a hand over his eyes.

"Hey, I didn't say it was the smartest idea I ever had. Your mama, of course, didn't believe a word of it. She called Daddy, and then you and Del showed up and that was all she wrote. I was the biggest disgrace to the Holton name, ever, and...I don't know. Allison had won, she still had you, and Kelly was still gone. I'd torn it with Daddy in a way I never had before. I couldn't stand being at Mercer, and I couldn't stand being at home. Leaving just seemed the thing to do, so I did it."

"And looked back every damn day of your life," he murmured.

Shocked, she stared at him. She wouldn't have expected him to get that. "Well, yeah. Basically. I always thought, somehow, I'd get the chance to make up with Daddy, you know? Except he was killed so suddenly, and then it was too late. My mama is...well, my mama. She's never going to change. I don't know my sister, I sure as hell don't know my brother. I had being a cop, though, at least until I fucked that up by getting Jack killed and now...hell, now I don't have anything."

"Sweet Jesus, Maddie." Those long fingers pinched his nose again. "What a freakin' waste."

"You're telling me." A completely inappropriate laugh broke free, bubbling into the room with a faint note of hysteria. "Know what makes it okay, though? Allison's bitterly divorced and works at the damn chicken plant, and you're married to a woman who's everything she could never be. It's fucking priceless."

"It's not okay." His gaze turned fierce. "Nothing about this is okay. You shouldn't have been carrying this around so long, letting it cripple your life, and you wouldn't have if I'd...damn it."

She bristled. "I do not need your pity, Calvert."

"It's not pity, Holton. It's culpability. If I hadn't let your daddy guilt me into keeping quiet, I assure you Mama would have gotten to the bottom of things. I kept telling her it was okay, that it was just you being crazy, because Virgil didn't want me to say anything, didn't want your mother to know."

"No telling what he wanted." Sadness shivered over her, for the father she'd never really understood, who'd never really understood her.

"You know what, though?" A muscle ticked in his jaw, as if he was biting the inside of his cheek.

She knew she was wiped out and wanted to sleep for a week, but she doubted that's what he was getting at. "What?"

"Having all this out in the open is fine and dandy, Madeline, but it doesn't explain why Kelly came back, if she came back. If those bones are hers, it also doesn't explain how she got under that house."

Chapter Twelve

His cell phone didn't ring.

Shit, she wasn't going to call him. Ash tossed the little rectangle on the table next to the rocking chair. He shouldn't be surprised. It wasn't like he hadn't had to do all the pursuing so far. He'd just thought...

He shook his head and picked up his guitar, rested his feet on the porch railing. If she didn't want to see him, he couldn't make her want it. He played with the strings a moment, a chilly wind sweeping in across the yard and stinging his ears. Toying with the tuning, he settled more deeply into the rocker.

Maybe it was a good thing she hadn't called. He was fast on his way to getting in over his head with her. Maybe Tick was right, and he did his thinking about women with the wrong head.

He strummed the opening riff to an old George Strait tune. An engine purred on the highway beyond the tree line, slowed, brakes whining a little. Somebody turning into his driveway. He frowned. Not Tick's truck, and it didn't sound like Stanton's SUV, either.

Probably somebody else lost, looking for Long Lonely Road. He got a lot of those out here. Except the vehicle appearing around the bend in the drive didn't belong to a lost stranger. His pulse kicked up a notch. The sensible little Honda was Madeline's.

He set the guitar aside and went down the steps to meet her in the yard. She stepped from the car, her thick brown hair disheveled as though she'd tousled it often during the day. Her shoulders slumped, the entire line of her body crying dejection.

"Hey." He caught a flash of glittering hazel eyes before she surprised the hell out of him by walking into his arms, burrowing against his chest. He wrapped her close, rubbing his hands down her spine. Nose buried in her hair, he inhaled. "Rough day?"

She shuddered. "Oh God, you have no idea."

For several moments, he simply held on, absorbing whatever tension wracked her. She sighed and turned her face into his throat. "I should have called first. Just turning up like this...that was rude. You could have been—"

"No." He rubbed his cheek against her hair. "This is good."

She folded her arms about his waist, returning the embrace for the first time. Pleasure rumbled through him, shaking him to the core.

Shit, he was in over his head. Already. How fucking scary was that?

Almost as scary as knowing he didn't care, that even realizing she was more dangerous to him than Suzanne had ever been wasn't going to deter him from getting closer to her.

He slid a palm up to her shoulders, rubbed his thumb over her nape. "Hungry?"

Her hair brushed his chin as she shook her head. "Wiped out."

"Come on." He turned them toward the house, led her toward the steps. "You can lie down for a little bit while I finish up some paperwork."

Holding on to him, she rested her head against his chest. "You're a good guy, Hardison."

"I've been told that a time or two, but I like hearing it from you, Mad."

Twilight dimmed his bedroom, but enough light filtered in to let him see the emotion glimmering in her eyes as she turned into him. She tiptoed up to brush a kiss across his chin.

"Don't leave me," she murmured. "Stay and lie down with me."

Lying down with her would involve more than her resting, and they both knew it. He sifted his fingers through her hair, the strands cool and smooth on his skin. "Are you sure?"

She framed his face with both hands. "Yes."

He lowered his head, nuzzling the soft skin along her jaw. Her trembling sigh moved through him, and she lifted her hands to unbutton his shirt and push it from his shoulders. Sensation flowed out from the first touch of her fingertips on him, and his knees weakened at the impact. He laced his fingers through her hair, holding her head in place, and took her mouth, need and hunger flaring in him.

Her tongue tangling with his, she pressed nearer, palms sliding over his chest, across his rib cage, along his sides. A groan worked itself up through his throat, and he massaged the tense tendons in her neck.

The kiss morphed, from a devouring to a deluge of gentle nips and soothing sips. She slipped away long enough to yank her sweater over her head and toss it aside before curling into him once more.

"Ash," she whispered into the depths of his mouth, "touch me. I need you to."

The plea reached inside him and twisted everything together into a knot of wanting and desire and an emotion he wasn't ready to name. He curved his hands over her shoulders, slid his palms along her arms. The warm smoothness of her skin tried to steal his ability to breathe and damn near succeeded.

Her fingers traced his features, her eyes fixed on his in the fading light. "Make me forget, for a little while."

He wanted her to forget, wanted her to have only enough room to think of him. He eased his hands up to the curves of her breasts, encased in lavender silk, and chafed his thumbs across nipples already hardening under his caress.

Her appreciative moan speared through him. He wanted to have only enough room to think of her too and was fast getting there. With one arm wrapped around her waist, he bent and captured a swollen peak in his mouth, dampening the silk, closing his teeth around her, tugging, teasing.

"Oh." She dug short nails into his scalp. "Yes."

With his thumb and forefinger, he caught the other silk-covered nipple and rolled it, pinching a little. Her impassioned gasp tore through him, sending a flood of hot excitement straight to his groin.

Arching further in his embrace, she dipped a hand between them, finding the growing bulge between his thighs, cupping him through oft-washed denim. His turn to moan and he thrust forward, rubbing into her palm.

Hooking a finger into the tiny gap between her bra cups, he tugged the fabric up, baring her to his gaze and mouth. He dragged his tongue over the hardened tips. "Beautiful."

She released her hold on him to reach behind her and undo the clasp, shrugging free of the thin garment. He took one step back, drinking her in, and went down on his knees before her, trailing his fingertips along her belly, dispatching the hook and zipper of her slacks, sliding them down her legs, lifting first one foot, then the other free, discarding her loafers as he did so.

Letting his hands roam up her legs, over calves and the hollows of her knees, to the back of her thighs, he pressed his cheek just below the slight jut of her hipbone. A hint of soap and woman blended with the subtle tang of arousal and infiltrated his senses. A scrap of silk separated them. He slid his hands higher, cupping the rounded cheeks of her ass, and nuzzled her intimately. She rewarded him with a hissed indrawn breath. With her fingers digging into his bare shoulders, she leaned into him as she spread her thighs.

Through the thin fabric, he tongued her, wringing another gasp from her lips, her knees bumping into his arms. Finding the tiny swollen bud of her clit, he ran his teeth over it, sucked her into his mouth.

"Oh God." Her head fell back on the sultry moan, the picture she made—outthrust breasts, mouth open in abandon, eyes closed in pleasure—firing his craving to a deeper level. He drew her deeper between his lips and nails scored his skin. "I'll fall."

"I'll catch you," he muttered against her.

Tangling her hands in his hair, she slid down his chest, winding her thighs around his. Her eyes dilated with desire, she cradled his face. "I don't deserve you."

Remnants of his earlier anger flickered to life, licking at his chest. Damn, she deserved so much, deserved everything, and it pissed him off that she didn't see that. He caught her chin, kissed her hard. "Don't say that. Ever again."

He lifted her to him and came to his feet in one smooth motion. She wrapped arms about his neck, legs about his waist as he carried her to the bed. He curled his fingers in the tiny panties and stripped them away. She watched him, eyes shimmering in the last vestiges of evening, while he fumbled with his belt and fly, shoved jeans and boxers down.

Fuck, he'd forgotten his boots. He stumbled to sit on the bed beside her, hauling one free and tossing it across the room. She rose to half-sit and reached between his thighs, curling a hand around his hard-as-freaking-nails erection, sliding her palm along the length, base to tip and back again.

An inhale strangled in his throat. "Mad...damn, baby."

Her thumb swiped away the moisture at the head of his dick. "Hurry."

He heaved the other boot halfway off, kicked it away with his jeans, and groped through the nightstand for a condom. Finally, he twisted sideways, pushing her across the bed. She wound her legs about his hips and pulled him down, her hold strong and desperate.

Resting on one arm, he positioned himself with the other hand. She tilted her hips up to his, taking the first couple inches of him. Heat exploded around him, and he ground his teeth, catching his breath before driving home.

"Yes." She linked her hands behind his neck and tilted her head back, bowing into him, meeting his strokes with hungry pelvic thrusts of her own.

Giving herself to him. Taking him. Owning him.

The pleasure was too much, the emotional sensation too strong. On his elbows, he caught her face between his hands, forcing her to meet his eyes.

"Don't you ever"—he gritted his teeth against a wave of desire so powerful it made him ache—"give me that bullshit about what you don't deserve again. Do you hear me?"

She tried to shake her head, and he refused to allow it.

"You deserve everything, Mad. *Everything*. Do you hear me?"

"Ash..." Her face contorted with a wash of pleasure.

"You deserve this, deserve everything good. Say it, baby. I want to hear you own it." The same way she was possessing him. He gasped, sweat breaking over his brow, his thrusts deeper, harder, more desperate now.

"I can't."

"You can." He caught her mouth, desire and need coiling in him, higher and deeper, a spinning wheel of firecrackers waiting to go off. "Say it, baby. You deserve everything."

She arched harder into him. "Everything...oh, Ash, please..."

The firework explosion went off in her first, a string of bursting fire and contractions, one after the other, singeing him, setting off his own surge of heat and light and gratification so white-hot it hurt.

Her arms slack around him, he collapsed, barely able to keep his weight shifted off her. His eyes blurred, a stinging blend of sweat and something he didn't want to acknowledge, and he blinked, nuzzling her temple. "Hell, Mad."

She laughed once and pressed her cheek to his throat. He concentrated on catching his breath, scattering tiny kisses over her face and neck. Beneath him, he felt her slow glide into deeper relaxation, tension seeping from her body. Gathering his strength, he rolled to his side and took her with him, wrapping her close. She murmured, grasping at his torso, and he lifted his head, a laugh building at the sight of her, naked and beautiful and well loved.

And absolutely, completely, totally fast asleep in his arms.

The incensed wail built to another crescendo, and Caitlin cringed. She tucked Lee closer against her chest, shifted his position and eased up from the rocker. This tactic hadn't worked, so maybe walking would. Not that she held out much hope—they'd been blessed with two really good days and she'd known this was coming. She hated these periods, hated the helplessness that came with the interludes of crying that seemed to have no reason, other than Lamar Eugene Calvert III was furious with the whole damn world and wanted everyone to know it.

"Lee, please." She rested her lips on his damp brow. "Come on, sweetheart. Don't do this."

He cried harder, scrunching himself into a tight ball against her. She rubbed his back, to no avail. Nothing was working today—not nursing or changing or bathing or swaddling or swinging or singing or talking. At least she knew it wasn't about pain. Their pediatrician had assured her there was nothing amiss with the baby once the crying jags had started, and she'd learned early on that his "something hurts" cry sounded vastly different from his "I'm infuriated with everything" wail.

She couldn't even blame this particular personality trait on the strong streak of stubbornness that ran through the entire Calvert clan.

No, this was a legendary Falconetti temper manifesting itself early. Dear Holy Mother of God, forget the terrible twos—they were doomed when this kid reached his teens.

"It's all right, baby. Hush now." Resting her cheek against his head, she wrapped him a little closer and rocked side to side. He paused mid-cry, snuffling as he caught his breath, and she held her own, eyes closed, knowing what was next. Tension coiled in her, the waiting only drawing things out, making it worse.

He stretched, kicking and flailing, and the sobs swelled once more. She sighed and puffed out a half-laugh, patting him. At least it couldn't last forever. He usually wore himself out after a couple of hours, but slept fitfully on those nights, waking to grumble and fuss every hour or so.

"Lee, darling." She kissed him again, feathering her fingers over his soft dark hair. Fat tears rolled down his cheeks. The vulnerability settled like a lump in her chest. Why couldn't she figure out what made him so unhappy on these days? "This cannot be making you feel better."

A truck engine rumbled to a stop outside, and she closed her eyes on a whispered prayer of thanks. Sometimes he responded to Tick's deep voice and settled down. Maybe that would work this evening.

Footsteps thudded on the wooden steps and the back door swung open, emitting both Tick and a burst of cold air into the kitchen.

"Hey." He rubbed his hands together and stripped off his jacket. A frown of concern drew his brows together. "Sweet Jesus, you can hear him all the way outside."

"Really." She resisted the urge to point out one could hear him *inside* as well.

"Yeah." Tick dropped his keys and the mail on the island and crossed to her. "How long has he been like this?"

She glanced at the clock atop the entertainment armoire and huffed a tight laugh. "You really don't want to know."

"That bad, huh?" He slid his long-fingered hands around their son's torso and lifted him. "Come here, Leebo. What's the matter, son?"

Lee rubbed his face on Tick's chest, pulled in a deep shuddering breath and started all over again. With a sigh, Tick jiggled him, patting him and murmuring soothing nonsense.

Caitlin gazed at the misery on Lee's face, swallowed and promptly burst into tears. Horrified, she covered her eyes with one hand and tried to pull it together. "Oh my God."

"Hey, don't do that." Tick curved an arm around her shoulders and pulled her close. An image flared in her head, both she and Lee crying their eyes out against Tick's chest, and a giggle rose in her throat. Tick pressed a fierce kiss to her forehead. "Come on, precious, it's all right."

"No, it's not." She clutched at his shirt, trying to stem the tears. "I know he's unhappy and I can't figure out what's wrong or how to help him and nothing I try seems to work—"

"Sshh." He held her closer. "Hush. He's just showing us that he has a healthy dose of that famous temper of yours."

She half-laughed, half-sobbed into the warmth of his polo shirt. "That's his Uncle Vince's temper. I can control mine."

Tick's chuckle rumbled under her cheek. He pulled back and brushed the tears from her face. "Wait here. I'll be right back."

Keeping up a steady stream of one-sided conversation with Lee, he disappeared into his study and returned moments later, rolling two pieces of fluorescent orange foam in his palm. "Here."

"Ear plugs?" She fixed him with a look. "That's your answer?"

"Yes." He pressed them into her hand and spun her toward their bedroom with a tiny push. "Go get in the tub and soak. Put those in. I've got him."

She looked at him and the baby, thought about arguing for all of a nanosecond and obeyed.

How long she floated in silence and hot water in their clawfoot tub, letting the strain and insecurities flow from her body, she wasn't sure. Eyes closed, she relaxed into the sudsy indulgence.

Familiar hands settled on her shoulders, and she smiled as he trailed a gentle touch up to pop the plugs free.

"Hey, precious," he murmured, nuzzling behind her ear, his deep voice doing the same wicked thing it always did. He massaged a thumb over her shoulder. "Feel better?"

"Mmm." She pressed into his touch. "Much."

The silence sank in, and she turned her head to look at him where he knelt behind the tub. "How did you do that?"

"Do what?" His fingers dipped below the suds to caress the side of her breast. He smiled, following the curve of her ear with his mouth.

"Get him to stop crying."

"Magic." His other hand appeared before her, one of their crystal flutes filled with white wine in his easy grip.

Somehow she knew it was her favorite pinot grigio, the one her brother Vince always brought her from Europe. "Tick, I can't drink that."

"Yes, you can." He curved his palm around her breast in a touch both soothing and arousing. "I called Dr. Harper. Only stays in the breast milk for two hours or so after you drink it. Lee takes a bottle tonight, and you express the milk and discard it."

He lifted the flute and swallowed, then pressed the spot where his lips had been to her mouth. She took the glass and sipped, letting the tart fruitiness explode on her tongue. His other hand joined the first beneath the water, caressing, stroking, calming.

And exciting beyond belief.

She gave herself up to the magical seduction of his touch. "Tick?"

"Hmm?"

"What...oh, that feels good." She sighed and he laughed, the deep sound that kicked off a little thrill of yearning low in her stomach. "What kind of magic?"

He nipped at her earlobe, a slow, tantalizing scrape of teeth on sensitive skin. "Promise you won't get mad."

She straightened, suds sloshing, and met his dark mirthful eyes. "What did you do to my child?"

"*Our* child." He leaned in to kiss her, and she ducked her head back. "I'm offended, precious. What do you think I did?"

"Tick."

He reached for the wine flute and took another sip. "I called Mama to come get him."

"Oh Tick, no. You didn't. Not tonight, while he's raising hell." She slumped, a hand over her eyes. "Now she's going to think—"

"She thinks he's the best thing since sliced bread, which he is, and that you're an excellent mother, which you are." He pulled her hand away from her eyes. "She's been dying to have him to herself, and you need a break. Actually, after the day I've had, I could use one too. He was already calming down when she got here, he'll be asleep before she even gets back home and he's in great hands. So relax, drink your wine and let me win this one, all right, Falconetti?"

How was she supposed to argue with that? She tangled a hand in his collar and tugged him to her, to take his mouth in a slow, all-out-sex kiss. "Why don't you come in here and help me relax, Calvert?"

"Oh no, you don't." He eased back, grinning. "It's been months since I got to take my wife out. I'm going to shower while you make yourself beautiful, which doesn't require much effort on your part. Troy Lee's band is playing over at Henry's tonight. Wear the hooker dress, and we'll go dancing, the kind that would scandalize my Aunt Maureen."

"A waltz would scandalize your Aunt Maureen. Besides, I can't wear the hooker dress right now, Lamar Eugene." She gestured at the curve of her cleavage above the water. "Your son has greatly blessed me, and my cups would runneth over."

"I don't care what you wear." He kissed her. "You'd be sexy as hell in a gunny sack."

She sipped her wine as he pulled away and stripped off his shirt before reaching inside the shower stall to start the water. "What did you mean, the day you had?"

He shucked his slacks and boxer briefs, affording her a view of leanly muscled thighs and calves. She shivered despite the warmth of the water. Amazing how simply seeing him naked still made her all tingly and ready. Maybe Lee spending the night with his grandmother had been a very good idea.

He glanced at her over his shoulder. "I finally got the whole story out of Madeline."

"Really?" She arched an eyebrow at him.

"Yeah." He dumped his clothes in the hamper. "And you're not going to believe this. I'll fill you in later. Let me tell you, Cait, I did not like figuring out how much you two have in common. Made my skin crawl."

"Poor baby." She smiled and crooked a finger at him. "Come here and I'll make it better."

"No way. Like I don't know what's going to happen if I get that close. Now haul your cute little butt out that tub and get dressed. I skipped lunch and I'm starved."

"Madeline?"

Feeling like she was wrapped in layers of warm gossamer, she lifted heavy lids. The bedside lamp cast a golden glow in the room, gilding Ash's sandy hair as he leaned over her. An irresistible smile curved her mouth. "Hey."

He cupped her cheek in one work-roughened hand, his eyes full of affection. "Rested?"

"Um, yes." She flopped over to her back, blinking. Dark hovered outside. "What time is it?"

"About eight." He trailed a fingertip down her bare shoulder. "You've been asleep a couple of hours."

She stretched, intimate areas protesting with a most feminine ache. She felt rested and very well loved. Loved? Scratch that. Very well-made-love-to. Yeah, that would work.

She would not think about that exchange there near the end, what he'd made her admit aloud. Wouldn't think about the way he'd made her feel, cherished and special and—

"Those wheels are turning already." He ran a teasing finger down her nose. "What are you thinking about so hard?"

"Nothing." She pulled the duvet higher and struggled to sit up, keenly aware she was naked and he was dressed, freshly showered and shaved. God, he smelled as good as he looked.

He covered her hand where it rested atop the duvet with his and rubbed his thumb across her wrist. "Hungry?"

Surprisingly, she was. She'd thought, sitting in that conference room, spilling everything to Tick, then reliving those moments over and over throughout the day, that she'd never be able to face food again. But now, her stomach grumbled with real hunger.

She leaned forward. "Are you offering to cook for me again?"

"Actually, I was thinking we might go out." His lashes lifted, revealing eyes the color of the sea under storm clouds. "Tick called earlier. He and Cait are going over to Henry's for dinner and a little music. Sound like fun?"

Dinner with Calvert, who'd suddenly decided he had epic assholery to make up for? God help her. His cautious solicitousness during the day had threatened to drive her insane, until she'd wanted to beg him to go back to his ornery old self. See him socially?

"Madeline." Ash's quiet voice brought her out of the reverie. He regarded her with a serious expression. "He's one of my best friends, and he's my business partner. It's going to be kind of hard for you to take me and leave him."

She puffed out a breath and grabbed for the first, most logical excuse. "I don't have anything to wear without going all the way home to change."

He shrugged, eyes narrowed. "My sister leaves some stuff here for when she visits. Y'all are close to the same size, if you don't mind wearing her things."

Well, there went the wind out of her sails. This was the man who believed she deserved everything good. Hell, she could make an effort for him, simply because he believed. She curved her mouth into a smile that made her face hurt. "Sounds like a plan."

Dinner out with Calvert and the perfect Fed.

Shit damn fuck.

She couldn't wait.

Chapter Thirteen

"Did I mention how gorgeous you look?" An arm hooked around her neck, Ash murmured the words near her ear as they crossed the parking lot. The unassuming storefront establishment had dark windows, the name Henry's embellished on both glasses in swanky silver lettering. White lights surrounded the door and lit matching globular topiaries there.

"Only about thirteen times." Her laugh sounded shaky even to her, as she tried not to show how affected she was by his nearness, the force of his attention, and how nervous she was at the prospect of the evening stretching before her.

"Babe, it bears repeating, believe me." He kissed the side of her neck and let his arm fall away.

"What did I tell you about that endearment, Hardison?" The loss of his long, warm form sank in immediately. God, the man was addicting.

"There's just no satisfying you."

She bumped his hip with hers. "Oh, now I don't know about that. You did it very thoroughly earlier."

Laughing, he took her hand as they reached the doorway. He pulled it open, and a wave of music and chatter washed over them. Still holding her hand, he guided her through the considerable crowd, winding among tables and seating areas, skirting the dance floor, to an elevated area overlooking the empty bandstand. Along the way, she got the impression of intimate shadows, pulsing dance music, gyrating bodies, flares of neon, and cushioned chairs and couches scattered among gleaming black tables.

He jerked his chin toward the far corner, fingers tightening on hers. "There's Tick and Cait."

"Great." Oh, her joy knew no bounds.

Pasting on a bright smile, she let him draw her along to the corner semicircular booth where the others waited. She was with Ash and being with him made her feel good. She'd just keep her focus on that.

"Hey." Tick rose at their approach, and he and Ash exchanged one of those weird back-slapping pseudo-hugs she'd never gotten.

"Good to see you." Ash leaned over to brush his mouth over Caitlin's cheek. "Hello, beautiful. Cait, you remember Madeline, right?"

"Of course." A genuine smile flashed over Caitlin's face. "Hello, Madeline."

"Hi." Slipping out of her jacket, she slid along the leather bench.

"Oh, that's an Alexa Radley top, one of her new line." Caitlin's smile widened. "It looks fabulous on you."

"Um, thanks." She glanced down at the red silk, split to her navel and held together between her breasts with a single large gold ring. She caught Ash's eye. "It's new."

"Here we go," Tick said, easing back into his seat, a hint of indulgence she'd never heard in his voice before. "The fashion conversation is on."

"Don't start." Caitlin nudged his side, although she was so close to him Madeline wasn't sure how she managed.

"Have y'all ordered?" Ash stretched an arm along the back of the seat, and Madeline found herself enveloped in his clean scent and the warmth from his body. Awareness flashed over her.

Tick's dark gaze scanned the crowd, and he shook his head. "We were waiting for you."

Caitlin arched an eyebrow. "He couldn't wait to eat, though, and stopped at the Big Dawg on the way over here for a burger."

"I skipped lunch." He waved across the table. "Madeline, tell her how insane the day was."

She froze, but his face betrayed nothing more than good humor and cheerful camaraderie. Swallowing hard, she shrugged. "It was insane."

The server, a bubbly little brunette, approached to take beverage and appetizer orders and moments later returned with drinks.

Sheltered by Ash's arm, Madeline let the conversation—which consisted of a ton of genial ribbing between Ash and Tick—flow over her, along with a sense of the surreal. She'd never done this before. For the most part, she'd led a solitary life, not getting too close to one person, limiting her social existence to the occasional beer with her colleagues, an every-so-often date with a guy more interested in sex than her conversational skills. There'd been none of this, hanging out with friends, the easy give-and-take Ash and Tick engaged in.

It was nice, mostly, even with the weird feeling she kept getting

151

that Caitlin was profiling her silently, or that the other shoe was going to drop any minute. The conversation lulled as their food arrived, and she took a sip of her sparkling water, which she'd noticed was Caitlin's drink of choice as well, and watched as several young men set up speakers and equipment on the stage. At the edge of the bandstand, Troy Lee fiddled with a guitar. For once, he wasn't running his mouth.

She brushed back her hair. "So Troy Lee's in a band?"

"Yeah." Tick glanced that way. "It's his hobby. He's been out on medical leave so this is his first weekend in a while doing this. He plays with some local boys, country and rock covers. They're pretty good at it."

Ash forked up a bite of steak. "They'll do a couple of sets then the DJ picks back up."

"So do you bring in more on the nights there's live music?" Caitlin asked.

"Hell if I know." Ash lifted his beer. "Rob does the numbers."

"Smart guy," Tick deadpanned. "He's obviously already been exposed to your accounting skills."

"Kiss my ass, Tick."

Madeline glanced up at Ash. "This is yours?"

"My brother and I co-own three properties. This one, two others in Texas and Florida."

He was just full of surprises. "Are they all named Henry's?"

"No, the one in Texas is Emerson's—that's Rob's middle name. The Florida one is The Crow's Nest. Believe it or not, this one is named for a dog Rob and I had when we were kids."

"Yeah." A devilish grin lurked around Tick's mouth. "The one his ex knocked off."

"She didn't... You have a sick sense of humor, Lamar." Ash shook his head with a long-suffering sigh.

"Let's go, sweet thing." Caitlin nudged Tick from his seat. "You promised me a dance that would scandalize your maiden aunt."

She tugged him toward the stairs. Madeline watched them absently. The Fed had good taste in clothes, even if her choice of husbands sucked. Her white halter-top was just snazzy enough to balance the dark denim of her snug jeans, and if those slightly worn red cowboy boots weren't custom-made, Madeline would give up her probably final paycheck from the Jacksonville PD.

Reaching for her water once more, Madeline looked up at Ash. "Did she really kill your dog?"

"Not on purpose, at least I don't think so. That's how I met her actually. She hit him with her car, then came to the house to apologize."

Madeline lapsed into silence. What was she supposed to say? I'm sorry?

"She is giving him hell." Ash laughed, sliding his arm behind her again and gesturing toward the dance floor.

"Who?" She followed the direction of his finger, spotted Caitlin and Tick on the dance floor. "Oh. How can you tell?"

"His face."

Looked like they were dancing to her, not arguing. She shrugged and observed them a moment longer. Unlike many of the other couples, they danced facing one another, without the overt sexual movements, although something about the easy rhythm they shared seemed sexier than the grinding going on around them.

She could see dancing with Ash like that.

She wouldn't mind having him look at her like that, either, as though she were the only other person in the world and he couldn't wait to be alone with her. Heat flushed through her. God help her, she probably already looked at him that way. She sat back and turned, finding his face near and those storm-green eyes watching her.

Like no one else existed.

Like he couldn't wait to be alone with her again.

He fiddled with her hair where it fell over her shoulder, his gaze dropping to her mouth. Something fluttered to life low in her stomach, and she leaned in, aching for that kiss. Lips met, clung, and she tasted beer and salt on his mouth. She laid a hand on his thigh, slid it up to his hip, denim soft under her palm.

Drawing back, he nudged her nose with the tip of his and smiled, eyes gleaming in the dimness. He glanced sideways and straightened, making a regretful noise in his throat.

Reality intruded as Tick ushered Caitlin back to the table, a fresh Southern Comfort over ice in his hand.

"You two are tame. I don't think any maiden aunts would be scandalized by the way you dance." Pure devil glinted in Ash's gaze. "Here, anyway."

Tick grimaced. "What are you talking about?"

"I don't know." Ash saluted them with his half-empty beer. "Maybe...what happens in Texas stays in Texas?"

"Oh God." Caitlin hid an obvious smile behind her fingers.

Tick lifted both hands, palms out. "I don't know what you're talking about."

Ash rubbed his fingertips down Madeline's bare arm, leaving thrills in his wake. He tilted his longneck in Caitlin's direction. "Your brother is right…finishing school was wasted on you."

Madeline waved a hand. "I'm lost."

Tick's eyebrows rose. "Good."

Ignoring him, Madeline turned to Caitlin. "You went to finishing school. For real?"

"Unfortunately, yes." She gave an exaggerated shudder. "Even being in Switzerland for a year didn't make up for it."

"Swiss finishing school." Madeline shook her head. "And you married *him*?"

"Hey!" Tick straightened. "What is that supposed to mean?"

"Married him…" Ash grinned and took a long pull from his beer. "And promptly corrupted him. Shame on you, Caitlin Marie, taking this good Baptist boy and—"

"I'm nondenominational. How many times do I have to explain that—"

"And turning him into a reprobate." He slanted a wicked smile in Madeline's direction. "She completely debauched him, you know, dragged him out to the wild Texas society scene, took him to a strip joint—"

"Oh shit." Tick slumped, covering his eyes.

Beside him, Caitlin dissolved into laughter. "It's a gentlemen's club. I'll have you know there's a difference."

Madeline rested her chin on her hand. "So did you buy him a lap dance?"

"Buy him one?" Ash slapped the table, tears of mirth leaking from his eyes. Every molecule in Tick's body stiffened, and he sputtered on the sip of Southern Comfort he'd just taken. "Babe, she rented a private room in the club and *gave* him one. Although my understanding is that is not all that happened."

"Holy fuck." Tick's head whipped in Caitlin's direction. "You *told* him?"

She held up a hand, laughing too hard to answer.

"Holy fuck is right." Madeline stared at Tick and let a slow grin creep over her face. "Oh my God, they would put you *under* the church if they knew about that."

"I think we should call his Aunt Maureen." Ash managed to keep a straight face for two whole seconds.

Tick was shaking his head. "I cannot believe you told him."

Caitlin wiped her eyes, holding her stomach with one arm. "Ashleigh, you're a dead man."

Ash lifted his hands skyward. "See? Finishing school was a waste of money for you."

"Tick, sweet thing." She nudged him. "Ask your friend over there who owns that particular...what did you call it, Ashleigh? A strip joint?"

"Thanks a lot, Cait."

Madeline gaped at him. "You own a strip club too?"

"It's Daddy's money. I'm just the figurehead. He didn't want his name on the paperwork. Looks bad with the voters."

"Wow." She considered it a moment then turned an impish smile on him. "So will you take me some time?"

He laughed. "That depends... Am I getting a lap dance out of the deal?"

"Cait can give you lessons." Tick lifted his glass. "She's damn good at it."

"Hey, Hardison!" Troy Lee's eager voice cut through the chatter. He balanced on the other side of the railing, a few feet above the dance floor, his handsome face open and earnest. "Come play with us."

"No, man, not tonight."

Troy Lee waved toward the stage. "Come on."

Ash stretched, removing his arm from around Madeline's shoulders, and flicked a hand in Tick's direction. "Tell you what. If choir boy over there will sing, I'll play."

"Hey, yeah." Troy Lee grinned. "Come on, Calvert. One song. Maybe two."

Caitlin gave him a little shove. "Go on. Thrill me."

Tick rose. "You gonna play groupie later?"

"Playing stripper isn't enough for you?"

He laughed and waited for Ash to extricate himself from the booth.

Surprised, Madeline watched them go. She turned to Caitlin, who gazed after Tick with a soft smile. "Do they do this often?"

Caitlin shifted her hair away from her face. "This is the first time with Troy Lee, although they've done it with the regular group here before. Usually you can't get them up there until after three beers each. They're good, though. All that time Tick spent in the church choir as a kid and Ash had music lessons all his life, I think."

"Huh." Madeline's gaze settled on Ash as the two men threaded through the crowd to the stage. A little ripple of excitement moved over the audience. They wanted to see this as much as she did, obviously.

Following Troy Lee, they vaulted onto the low platform. Ash picked up a guitar, fiddling with the tuning, and they talked to the other band members in what looked like a small football huddle. Madeline grinned. Next thing you knew, they'd be slapping each other's butts.

"You are really having a good time tonight, aren't you?" Caitlin's soft question jerked her head around.

"Yeah." She considered the oddity of that for a moment. Hell, she didn't remember the last time she'd had this much fun and laughter in her life, and she sure hadn't expected it tonight. Her gaze strayed back to Ash. "I am."

"Good." Caitlin twisted sideways in the booth for a better vantage point. "You realize our responsibility here is to hoot, holler and thoroughly embarrass them."

A surge of warmth flowed through Madeline and bubbled out in a laugh. "Of course."

Lights flashed around the dance floor, highlighting for one second a head with shiny blonde hair. The laughter and everything good froze in Madeline's throat. Allison Barnett.

And not too far behind, Stacy and Donna.

Madeline squinted, focusing in on Allison's face in the shifting crowd. Troy Lee was talking into a handheld mike, making introductions, and his words washed over Madeline in a dull rush. Tick laughed, adjusting the height on a microphone stand. Allison hung on every move he made, an old hunger in her face that turned Madeline's stomach.

"Madeline." Caitlin touched her hand, and Madeline swung her gaze away from Allison, meeting Caitlin's concern dead on. "What's wrong?"

Below them, Ash strummed an opening riff. A cheer went up at what must be a favored song. Above it, Tick's voice joined in, with lyrics about lost love and rain and yearning, his raw tone suited to the song's pained angst.

Madeline tilted her chin toward the crowd. "The blonde, next to the redhead?"

"Yes?" Eyes narrowed, Caitlin scanned the heads. "Her? The one in the turquoise tube top?"

"Yeah. Her." Madeline swallowed. "That's Allison Barnett."

"What? Her?" Lips parted, Caitlin regarded Allison, obvious surprise on her face. "Oh my God, he lost his virginity with *her*?"

Madeline laughed before she could stop it. Caitlin slanted a rueful look at her. "That came out really bitchy and snobbish, didn't it?"

"No. Well, kind of, but it's okay." Madeline's attention tracked back to Allison, who'd edged closer to the stage. "He was probably thinking the same thing earlier today."

The band had segued into a new tune, a thumping rhythm with lyrics describing a gorgeous woman taking a man's life apart. Caitlin, eyes narrowed to glittering slits, watched Allison, who gradually eased her way toward the stage and the steps leading to it.

"Oh, I don't think so." Tossing her hair back, Caitlin slid from the bench. "There's no way in hell that's happening, honey. He's mine."

Madeline scrambled to follow. "What are you going to do?"

"Something I didn't learn in Swiss finishing school." Caitlin's boots thumped on the carpeted floor, soon lost in the pounding bass. Madeline caught a glimpse of the rhapsodic concentration on Ash's face as he played. He was good. Damn Allison for keeping her from enjoying this.

Traveling in Caitlin's wake, Madeline wound around a handful of customers. Close to the speakers, the beat thudded in her chest at a painful level. Caitlin paused on the steps and reached backward to tap Madeline's shoulder. She glanced up. "Hey, Madeline."

"Yeah?" At this point, she was screaming over the music.

Easing up a step, Caitlin cupped her hands to Madeline's ear. "Look at that."

Onstage, Tick and Ash shared a mike, belting out the chorus while Ash pounded through the chords. She couldn't see Ash's expression, but fun and passion and sheer joy lit Tick's face. She felt rather than heard Caitlin's soft laugh. "That's why I married him."

Caitlin continued down the steps. Madeline stayed where she was, her gaze trained on the two singing. Yeah, she could see wanting that emotion in your life every day. Ash swung away, fingers strumming softer as the song faded, the same elements reflected in his expression, and a realization she didn't want to look at too hard slammed into her chest.

Whistles and clapping blended with hollers and protests as the pair prepared to leave the stage.

"One more." Troy Lee held up a finger, grinning over the mike. "Come on, boys. Just one."

Laughing, Ash waved him off, and Troy Lee shrugged, soon charming the audience with his easy smile and good-natured prattle. A few patrons leaving the dance floor brushed by Madeline as they climbed the stairs. She ignored them, wanting to watch Ash, compelled instead to keep her gaze on Allison.

Ash made it off the stage first, and Caitlin smiled, patting his chest as they passed. His mouth moved in a laughing comment, and he jerked his head behind him in Tick's direction.

Caitlin met her husband as he descended. Madeline caught the flash of Tick's grin before Caitlin pulled him into a bedroom-only kiss that was the sheer staking of a claim, carnal and possessing. He faltered one step under the onslaught but recovered rapidly, lifting her against him and kissing her back. Caitlin tangled her hands in his hair. Wolf whistles and whoops of approval rose, the two of them oblivious to all but one another.

Madeline caught a glimpse of Allison's face—narrowed eyes, pursed lips, absolute fury and disgust twisting her features into something ugly and frightening. Her chin lifted, and she backed up, her gaze tracking the club to land on Madeline. Hatred flared in those blue eyes, strong and malicious enough that Madeline fought down the urge to retreat, turn away.

"I think his Aunt Maureen would be scandalized." Ash's laughing voice pulled her from the nonverbal exchange. He jerked a thumb over his shoulder. "Hell, I'm scandalized."

Madeline smiled, the expression feeling forced. When she looked beyond him to the dance floor, Allison was gone.

"So do I rate one of those?"

He came up another tread, putting them at eye level. A teasing light gleamed in his eyes, clear and pure enough to dive into, and a thin sheen of sweat filmed his skin, a holdover from the hot stage lights. A wide grin creased his tanned face.

She stared into the sea-colored depths, that terrifying realization squeezing her chest again, stealing her ability to breathe.

The teasing glimmer faded, shifting into something deeper, a simmering burn that pulled all the oxygen from her lungs. He snaked an arm around her waist, and she grasped his shoulders, meeting his mouth in a kiss that was a raw tangle of teeth and lips and tongues, less finesse and more pure, unrefined need.

"Hey, you two, get a room if you're gonna act like that." Tick's ribbing broke through the isolated haze of desire surrounding them.

Ash lifted his mouth from hers, still looking at her like she was the only person in the world. One corner of his mouth hitched in a lazy smile, and he blew out a breath, thumb rubbing the silk at her waist. Heat spread through her system from that small, steady contact. "Look who's talking."

"Hey, I didn't do anything." Tick urged Caitlin up the steps before him. "She grabbed me. I just went with the moment."

"And enjoyed every second of it." Keeping their linked hands at the small of her back, Caitlin pulled him along, every inch a woman secure in the fact the man with her was hers and hers alone.

"Well, hell yeah. Ten months is a long dry spell, precious."

Precious? What the fuck kind of endearment was that? Madeline lifted her eyebrows and caught Ash's eye. "Don't even consider it, Hardison."

"Never even crossed my mind." He spun her and swatted her ass to get her moving toward the table. "Hey, Tick, that shade of lipstick you're wearing does nothing for your coloring, man."

Eyes sliding closed, Madeline let the noise and heat and Tick's smartass rejoinder swirl around her, let Ash guide her with warm hands on her waist, let herself wish she could have this moment, all the moments with him, forever.

Chapter Fourteen

"You mean, you've never done it in a pickup truck? Are you serious?" Madeline's relaxed laugh trilled over Ash. Her shoulder nudged his side, her thigh aligned with his in the diner booth, each movement sending a rush of heated sensation through him. "Everybody's done it in a truck."

"Well, I haven't." Caitlin smiled over the rim of her cup.

"I'd have figured..." Astonishment coloring her voice, Madeline pointed between Tick and Caitlin. "I'm stunned. You're from Texas. Trucks everywhere."

With a quiet laugh, Caitlin set her steaming tea aside. "You've never met my brother. I went to an all-girls boarding school, and when I was home, he made sure I wasn't alone with any boys with trucks. I had to leave the country to lose my virginity."

"Switzerland?" Ash trailed his fingers over Madeline's arm, drinking in the warm, smooth skin. Damn, she fit good against him. This genuine woman was the one he'd suspected lurked beneath the ballsy bravado, and he loved the way she softened as the night went on, unwinding further with each beautiful laugh and smile, with each easy caress between them. As much as he wanted to take her home and back to bed, he remained perfectly content to sit with her like this, hanging out in the nearly deserted diner at two in the morning after they'd already shut the club down.

"Greece. European tour with Grandmother when I was eighteen." She shuddered. "His name was Sandor, and it was the absolute worst sexual experience of my life. It hurt and I was so disappointed I cried, and then I didn't do it again for three years."

"Amazing you ever acquired enough experience to corrupt choir boy the way you have."

Caitlin stuck out her tongue at him, much as he'd witnessed her doing with her brother back when Ash had gone to military school with him. "Would you stop?"

"Why should I when giving you a hard time is so much fun?"

"I don't know." She tilted her head to one side with a distinctly fake winsome expression. "Maybe because I might suddenly recall a story involving you and the words 'colonel's office'?"

He stilled, frozen by the mischief in that look. "Caitlin. No."

"Sounds interesting." Madeline slanted a glance at him from beneath her lashes. "I think I want to hear this."

"No, you don't." He patted her arm, inevitability staring him in the face. "Trust me."

Her gaze swiveled between him and Caitlin, a slow smile spreading over very kissable lips. "Oh, I think I really do."

"It's nothing." Resigned, he wrapped his hands around his cider.

"Nothing?" The naughty mockery in Caitlin's tone almost made him smile. "A threesome with the colonel's daughter is nothing?"

Madeline clapped a hand over her squeal of surprised laughter. Tick's coffee mug hit the table with a thump. "Holy hell, you had a threesome? And you didn't tell me? That's wrong. You share crap like that with your best friend, believe me."

Gorgeous hazel eyes sparkled at him. "Did you really?" she asked, still muffled by her palm.

"She's exaggerating. There was no threesome." He sighed and held his thumb and forefinger a millimeter apart. "Well, there might have been a slight threesome involved."

He glanced from those laughing eyes to dark brown ones filled with a modicum of shock and a hefty dose of male curiosity. "Hey, I was eighteen. It seemed like a good idea at the time."

"I'm sure." Madeline giggled and wrapped her hand around his upper thigh. Heat shot out from the contact. He shifted and pulled his cell free. Flipping it open, he scrolled through the contacts list.

"It's after two in the morning," Tick said. "Who are you calling?"

"Vince. To bitch him out for opening his big mouth."

Tick's guffaw drew the waitress's frowning attention away from the Soap Network. "You had a threesome with *Vince*?"

The skin on Ash's spine literally crawled; there was no other description for the shuddering, creepy feeling. "You don't have to put it like that. You make it sound like he and I...ah, man." Tick would never let him live this one down. He slanted a half-amused glare at Caitlin. "See what you did?"

"You started it, outing me on the damn lap dance. Payback's a bitch, Ashleigh."

"I think we're going to have to tone it down before they throw us out," Madeline said, leaning into Ash. "The waitress is giving us the evil eye again."

Tick brushed his tousled hair off his forehead. "We need to head home anyway, get a few hours sleep before we pick up the baby from Mama in the morning."

After a flurry of goodbyes, Madeline spread her palm over his knee, rubbing in a soft circle. "They are not going home to sleep."

"Hell, no." Ash laughed and hugged her to him. "You about ready to get out of here? You don't have to work tomorrow, but my day still starts early."

On the quiet ride home, she cuddled into his side, tracing random designs on his leg, the soft meandering caresses burning into him. He wanted to hold on to this night, to the feelings wrapping around them. He wanted to hold on to her, so bad it scared him.

The Ford shuddered to a halt in the driveway, stars peeking down from a clear, cold sky. He climbed from the truck and held out a hand, helping her as she slid out the driver's side door also. Keeping his hold on her hand, he drew her close and slammed the door, the hinges creaking. "Did you have a good time?"

"I had a wonderful time." Her shoulder fit perfectly into his underarm as they headed up the walk.

"Tick and all?"

A little whispery laugh between them. "Tick and all."

On the porch, she rubbed her thumb over the strings of his guitar leaning against the wall by the door. The notes drifted into the quiet. "Play for me."

He'd give her anything, even if that meant playing a little at two thirty in the morning when he had to get up at four thirty. Lifting the instrument, he nudged the door open. "Let's go inside where it's warm."

"No." She picked up the quilt folded over the back of the porch swing. "Out here, where it's quiet and dark."

He settled next to her, guitar balanced on his knee, and she wrapped the faded quilt about her shoulders. "What do you want to hear?"

"Whatever you want to play."

With her knee against his thigh, aware of her gaze on his face, he picked out an old love ballad he'd picked up while bumming around Mexico. He crooned the Spanish lyrics in a near-whisper, using the ball of his foot to set the swing on a soft arc.

Tentative fingers sifted through his hair, stroked over his nape, drifted across his shoulder and down his arm, leaving a fiery sizzle behind. He allowed his lids to slide down, drowning in music and caresses and Madeline. Going under and not worrying if he ever came up.

He played through the song twice, soaking in the soft feel of her touching him.

When the last notes faded into the silence, the strings stilling beneath his fingertips, she moved, taking the instrument from him with careful hands and laying it aside, climbing over him to straddle his thighs. She framed his face with her hands and stared at him a long moment before dipping her mouth to take his in a kiss both sweet and fierce.

He splayed his hands on her spine, allowing the exchange to go on and on, building a flame inside him, between them, until he couldn't breathe, until he was drowning in her all over again.

Finally, he lifted her and carried her through to the bed, laying her down and stripping away clothes and barriers in a long, silent loving that left him shaking in her arms. He drew her close and brushed the tousled hair from her face. His fingertips came away damp and he kissed her cheek, smoothing the tears from her skin with his lips. After, he left her only long enough to discard the condom, and then, with her cradled in his arms, he settled them both against the pillows and pulled up the duvet to cover their naked bodies.

Without releasing her, he let sleep claim him, surrendering to the knowledge of how much he already needed her.

Tick killed the engine and rolled his stiff shoulders. It had been a long day and he was tired, but he felt good, relaxed in a way he hadn't been in months. Damn, he'd laughed so much tonight the muscles in his stomach protested. He rested a wrist on the wheel and gazed at the house, bright light spilling from the keeping room windows onto the back porch in golden pools.

"What are you thinking about over there?" Caitlin brushed the back of her hand down his neck, indulgent affection in her voice.

"How good things are." He caught her hand and hauled her toward him. "How absolutely blessed I am."

She hooked her fingers around his nape and drew his mouth down to hers. Arms around him, she pressed nearer and the absolute rightness of this engulfed him all over again. Like it had done all day, his mind kept winding around Madeline's revelations, how different his life would have been if Allison's machinations had succeeded so long ago.

If she'd gotten pregnant, he'd have married her.

And because he was his father's son, raised with old-fashioned values about marriage and commitment, about better or worse, until death-do-you-part, he'd probably still be married to her.

If he'd married her at nineteen, most likely there'd have been no Quantico, no FBI.

No Caitlin. No Lee.

The picture of what his life would have been, based on what he'd gleaned from Madeline's comments, wasn't a pretty one. It was enough to scare the devil out of a guy, like that James Joyce piece he'd read in freshman English at UGA, the one with the gleeful description of the horrors of hell.

"Tick." Caitlin shifted against him, palms pressed to his chest, over his thundering heart. "Too tight."

"Sorry." He grimaced and loosened his hold.

"Don't be." She murmured the words against his jaw and shifted to straddle his lap, her sexy laugh burbling between them as the steering column got in the way. "I love the way you want me."

"You mean relentlessly? All the time?" He reached for the tilt control and moved the wheel up, allowing her to settle firmly over his groin. He swallowed a groan at the tight fit, blood rushing south of his belt, stirring, filling. "So bad my teeth hurt?"

"All of the above." She rocked into him, her voice going soft and breathless. She yanked his shirt free of his waistband, worked at buttons until she parted the fabric and ran hot palms over his chest. "Because I want you the same way."

He gripped her hips, slid his hands down to cup her ass, slipped his fingers between her thighs. Even through denim, he could feel heat and excitement pulsing. "Let's take this inside, precious."

"Oh, come on, Lamar Eugene." On a breathy exhale, she pressed her legs together, trapping his hands. She nipped his earlobe, ran the tip of her tongue around the swirl of his ear, and he bucked under her at the harsh thrust of pleasure. Holy hell, she knew every button he had and tonight desperation tinged the wanting, lent it an edge of urgency. "Supposedly my sexual education has been severely limited since I've never done it in a truck. Don't you want to be my first?"

"The first?" He eased his hands to her hips, ground her down onto him. "I better be the only."

"No one else." She stopped teasing his ear long enough to slide out of her halter-top and toss it aside. The filmy bra she'd worn underneath followed. "Only you. Always you."

He cradled a breast in each hand, the flesh full and hot, warmer against his palms, and he feathered his fingers over her, aware that with Lee at his mother's, she'd be sensitive, almost sore, until she had a chance to express. He pressed open-mouthed kisses to the upper slope of one breast, smiling at her moan of aroused approval before licking the edge of her aureole, avoiding what would be a too-vulnerable nipple.

Knees digging into his thighs, she arched on another moan and dug her fingers into his hair, pulling. He repeated the caress again and again, on each breast, her responsiveness sending another rush of heat to his groin, until he was so hard it hurt.

"If I'd been your first, you wouldn't have cried," he muttered against her ribcage. "I'd have made it so good for you, Cait."

"You make everything good." She lowered on him, belly sliding on his, her intimate heat resting tight against him. She kissed him, whispering into his mouth. "Everything, every day. I love you, so much I can't stand it sometimes."

He took her mouth, desperate need and emotion making him rough, and she wriggled against him, reaching behind her, until he released her lips, his chest heaving. "What are you doing?"

"Getting rid of my boots." A thud on the floorboard, followed by another seconds later. Her fingers moved to her belt and he watched, sprawled in the seat, while she shimmied out of faded denim and a wisp of satin and lace. A wave of desire took his breath.

"You are the most beautiful thing." He ran his hands up bare thighs and over the indention of her waist to caress her breasts once more. She bowed into him, settling knees on his thighs, hitting the horn as she did so, and he laughed, sprinkling more kisses over her sternum. "Sexy as hell. And mine."

"So take me then," she breathed into his hair. Her hands went for his belt. "Prove it again."

He let one hand flow down her body, dipping between her legs, sliding across damp folds and plunging a pair of fingers inside her while he swept his thumb over her clit, abrading the little bundle of nerves. She cried out, and he grinned against skin dewed with a light sweat. They were fogging the freakin' windows, generating enough heat to keep them warm despite the chill beyond the cab.

"Oh, God." One hand braced on the roof, the other on his shoulder, she rotated into his hand, getting him out of his jeans obviously forgotten. He stroked her again. If the rhythm of her breathing and the soft sounds she made deep in her throat were anything to go by, much more and he'd bring her to climax, but he wanted that with him buried deep inside her, wanted her coming all over him.

She'd released his belt and the button at his fly. With his other hand, he managed to get his zipper down, keeping up the pace of pleasuring her while lifting his hips to shove, wriggle and tug his jeans far enough down to release his eager erection.

When he removed his caressing fingers, she mewed a protest, but he grasped her hips, rougher than he meant to, hard enough he'd probably leave little fingertip bruises, and pulled her down over him. He thrust up into her, the wet pleasure of her punching him in the gut, just like always. She rewarded him with another small cry, her head tilting back, hair spilling over her shoulders.

Moving on him, she caught her bottom lip between her teeth and dug her fingers into his shoulders. Tomorrow, he'd have small barely-there bruises as well. Marked as hers. He tilted his head forward enough to take her mouth, a series of nipping little kisses.

"Mine," he muttered against the corner of her lips.

"Yes." She lifted thick lashes, and he glimpsed the possessive fire he'd seen earlier, when she'd caught him coming off that stage and laid a kiss on him that had had him hard in seconds. "Always."

He tightened his grip on her hips, pushing up harder, needing her to shatter soon, because it was too much, the wet slide of her body on his, the mingled scents of their arousal, her mouth against his, tongue flicking between his teeth, and he was *not* going to be able to hold out much longer...

On a gasp, she tore her mouth from his, folding both arms along the back of his head. "My God, Tick, please."

"Come for me, precious." He rubbed his tongue along the edge of her puckered aureole again. "Let me watch you."

He pulled her tighter into him, and the first squeezing of her orgasm began around him, shivering over every inch of him. In response, his climax barreled through him, stopping his lungs. He held on to her, the ragged puff of her breathing along his shoulder matching his own. She trembled in his arms, and running his hands up her back, he smoothed tangled hair from her face, peppering light kisses over her cheek, jaw and brow.

"Love you," he murmured. "So damn much, Cait."

"I know." She stroked a palm over the back of his head, resting her cheek against his neck. "You too."

He shuddered under the aftershock of pleasure. "Damn, if it gets any better, I won't survive."

She laughed, quiet and husky. Pulling back, she held his gaze, her eyes glittering with love and satisfaction. She touched a finger to his mouth. "You're right. Things are very good."

Wrapping her close, he shifted sideways, stretching them out best he could on the bench seat. His knee hit the steering column. He rubbed his cheek on her hair. "Even when my son is screaming his lungs out for no good reason?"

"Even then." With a humming sigh, she swept a caress over his side. "I wouldn't trade him for anything and you know it. He's perfect." She was quiet a moment before her hushed laugh shimmered through his body. "The best thing since sliced bread."

He grunted his agreement and lapsed into silence, enjoying these few moments of freedom to hold and touch her, letting his fingers roam over her back and hip while his thoughts swirled all over again.

She tiptoed a fingertip along each of his ribs. "You feel pensive."

"Pensive." He drew her closer, tucking the open flap of his shirt around her. "There's a word you don't hear every day."

"Tick. You're brooding about something." She levered up on an elbow, the narrow truck seat not offering a large range of motion. With her this near, he was glad of the lack of light. That insightful gaze of hers saw too much. "What's wrong?"

"Just stupid bullshit." A harsh laugh swelled from his throat. She waited, silence stretching between them. He twirled a swath of her hair around his forefinger. "You ever think about what your life would have been like if you'd married that guy you were engaged to in college?"

"Um, no." She traced his jaw. "I don't. We were so wrong for each other on so many levels and it wasn't meant to be. You're thinking about what could have been with Allison Barnett, aren't you?"

"Yeah."

"Tick, don't. Please."

"It's hard not to, Cait." He tangled their legs together, his foot banging against the door. He couldn't get her near enough to him tonight. "I mean, damn. Do you know how easily that whole situation could have gone a different way?"

"But it didn't. Because it wasn't meant to be." She caught his chin in a firm grip. "This...us. We were meant to be. Now stop making yourself crazy. I told you—I'm not sharing you with another woman, and this counts as having to share."

"I'm trying, all right?" He threaded his fingers through the thick fall of her hair. "I can't imagine missing out on loving you."

"Oh. My. God." With an irritated huff, she flopped to her back and almost toppled off the seat. He grabbed her waist and held on. "Let's see, if I'd married Dennis, I could have been a society wife, you know, a political asset, with a couple of overachieving kids, a Mercedes and a social calendar. Yes, that would have made me dazzlingly happy."

Reverse psychology. Why wasn't he surprised? "Cait."

"Better yet, here's a scenario for you. What if I'd ended up with the Navy SEAL I spent a couple of weekends—"

"Caitlin." He sighed. "I get the point. I'll let it go."

"Good." She rolled into him and looped her arms about his neck. "Because she's going to be trouble, and I need you at the top of your game."

He propped up on his elbow. "Trouble?"

"Mmm." She traced his collarbone. "I saw the way she looks at you tonight, and I don't like it. She's already called you away from home with that bogus 'I need to get some things from the house' bit, publicly bought you lunch in a gossip-bed... That's trouble brewing, sweet thing."

"Maybe." He nipped at her lower lip. "But you said it, precious. Hard to mess with something that's meant to be."

Chapter Fifteen

He snored.

Sprawled on her stomach, Madeline surfaced to a soft rumble next to her ear. She rubbed her gritty eyes and rolled to her back. Bright sunlight flowed in the windows, hinting at midmorning. Ash stretched out beside her, asleep, fully dressed.

Right down to his boots.

She smiled, resisting the impulse to trace those strong features. He looked relaxed, peaceful, but more than likely he'd been up since before daylight and had already put in a solid day's work.

Somehow this was enough, lying in bed with him on a lazy weekend morning, intimate areas of her body still feeling the imprint of his strength. Shit, she wasn't supposed to feel like this, wasn't supposed to be so damn happy just from...

His eyes snapped open, no vestiges of slumber clouding the clear green. "Hey, babe."

"You scare the hell out of me." She clapped a hand over her mouth. Where the fuck had that come from? She swallowed a groan. God, when would she learn to think before she spoke?

"It's mutual." He slid a finger down her cheek. "But I like it."

She shifted up against the pillow, pushing her disheveled hair out of her eyes. "What have you been doing?"

"Working. I've checked the houses, stacked feed, refilled the bins." He muffled a yawn with a fist. "Now I'm waiting for Tick to get his sorry ass over here so we can patch a roof."

She prodded his side, testing for ticklishness. No reaction. "You fell asleep with your boots on."

"I was wasted." One corner of his mouth hitched in a grin. "Too much lovemaking, not enough sleep. Feel a hell of a lot better now that I've had a nap."

On a nod, she let silence fall between them. He stroked that single fingertip over her shoulder and down her arm. "Tell me about Florida...about why you're here, I mean."

Her gaze flew to his. She swallowed. Tell him that, of all things? She shook her head, a slow negation of the very idea. "Ash, please, I can't."

"All right." His thumb joined the soft brush of his finger against her skin, became a firmer caress. "I didn't mean to push, Mad."

"I know. It's okay. I just..." She moistened her lips, the image of Jack sprinting up those stairs flickering in her head. "I can't do it yet."

"I get that." He shifted, levering up on an elbow. "There are things from my army days I still don't talk about."

She closed her eyes, the silence settling between them once more. Most of the tension slipped out of her under the steady warmth of his hand on her skin.

Empty hours stretched before her. He had plans and it was her day off. She'd always worked extra shifts in Jacksonville, burying herself in the job. There wasn't much to do here, except wait on a dental-records match that could take forever. She didn't have a real caseload, nothing to dig into and lose herself.

Limited choices hung over her. Time with her mama, which always made her crazy. Time with Autry, which could be even worse, since she'd spend the minutes comparing herself to her little sister's perfection. Time driving over to Valdosta to visit her baby brother in prison, and no way in hell was she ready for that.

Her life was shit, and it was her own damn fault, for putting everything into being a detective and precious little else into making a real life.

"I've been thinking."

She jerked at Ash's quiet statement. He watched her with serious eyes and an ironic smile. Geez, how long had she spaced, anyway?

"About?"

"I know you're only planning on being around a few weeks." He rubbed his thumb over her knee in a hard caress.

"Yeah." Why did that single syllable hurt so much, pushing it out?

His lashes hid his eyes for a moment before he met her gaze head-on. "Why don't you move some of your things over here from your mama's?"

The guy really knew how to take a girl's breath. Madeline swallowed. "Um, why?"

He merely looked at her.

Nerves fluttered in her belly. Coming over here, spending the night, borrowing his sister's things...that was scary enough. Bring her stuff here?

"Madeline."

"My mama would have a fit."

"Has that bothered you in the past?"

Well, no, but...

"Ash, you don't—"

"Babe, there's a lot in life to be afraid of. Public speaking, Iraqi soldiers shooting at you, losing your ass in a business venture. But being afraid of living? No way. You've got to get beyond that."

"You're afraid of public speaking?"

His deep laugh hung between them. "Stop dodging the subject."

Bringing her things here smacked of a relationship, of something semipermanent. Besides, she was leaving in a few weeks, as soon as the review board finished the inquiry into Jack's...into the shooting...and cleared her return to the PD.

"Mad, I'm not asking you to marry me here." Seriousness lurked beneath the sardonic humor. "We said we were going to take this one day at a time, but I like having you in my bed as much as you like being there. It's just easier if you have some stuff here for the nights we're together."

He made it sound so logical, so easy. Like the Devil and that slippery slope she'd been warned about so often in Sunday School while she was growing up.

A distinctive truck rumbled outside. Ash swung to a seated position on the side of the bed.

"That's Tick. I have to go fix a roof." He leaned over and kissed her, a quick featherweight brush of his lips that left her wanting more. "Think about it, will you, babe?"

"I'll think about it." With an irritated huff, she gave him a tiny shove toward the door. "And quit calling me babe."

He *sauntered* out, damn him, on an amused laugh, leaving her still facing an empty day and his too-seductive suggestion.

Shit. Now what was she supposed to do?

"You asked her to move in?" Tick's voice rose on a surprised note. "For real?"

Ash hammered in another nail. "I didn't ask her to move in. I suggested she bring some of her stuff over here."

"I think that constitutes moving in." Tick grinned around the roofing nail clenched in his teeth. Ash shook his head at that bad habit. He was going to swallow one of those things some day.

Ash gazed across the pasture. From his vantage point on the roof of chicken house number four, he could see the house. Madeline's car was still gone. She'd left a few minutes after Tick's arrival with no word on her plans. He was dying to know what she was up to, if she was over at her mama's, packing up.

"You are in sad shape." Tick laughed and adjusted a shingle. His hammer made short work of two nails. "You're whipped."

"Yeah? Go look in a mirror and say that." Ash stretched out for another handful of shingles, almost out of reach. His foot slipped off the batting board and a jolt of unease slammed into his gut. He scrabbled for purchase, knee banging into the board and popping to the side as his other foot slid uselessly over rough shingles.

He caught the one-by-four with the fingertips of one hand—damn it, his injured hand—and for a second relief hung before him, until his nails broke to the quick, stitches gave way, the injured muscles of his hand gave in and gravity pulled him over the edge. Hell, this was going to hurt.

His chin jammed on the metal edging. A glimpse of Tick's horrified surprise filled his vision before everything tunneled to the sick sensation of falling. Then hard earth slammed into his frame, and he couldn't breathe.

Pain, shock, a shout he wasn't sure was his or Tick's.

Nausea flooded his throat, his chest frozen, blue sky blurring.

Shit, this was bad.

Metal clanged over and over. Tick's white face appeared above him with a dismayed expression that would have been funny if he hadn't been absolutely fucking sure he was dying.

"Ash?" Tick's hoarse voice bordered on a squeak. "Don't move. I'm going to call for help."

Don't move? He couldn't fucking breathe and Tick was worried about him moving?

With excruciating slowness, his lungs decided to begin working. The problem was each inhale and exhale brought piercing, cringe-inducing pain. Hell, where didn't he hurt?

Metallic taste flooded his mouth, like he'd licked a flagpole. He concentrated on getting oxygen in and out, on not screaming, on the fact this was the dumbest-ass thing he'd ever done.

"Ash? Called for an ambulance. Don't move." Tick was back, breathing hard, hands roving over him, making darts of pain worse in places, sending shards of torture through his knee. "Can you feel that?"

Feel it? Shit, he was living it, wrapped up in nothing but friggin' agony. Tick looked down at him, eyes darker than usual with appalled concern.

"Holy hell, your face is a mess." Tick mopped around his chin and mouth with a handkerchief, and the flash of crimson staining the white fabric as Tick pulled it away turned his stomach further. What had he done?

Tick's face relaxed a little. "I think you just busted your mouth. Your lip is bleeding."

Strong, sure hands eased along his body once more, testing, assessing, sending rockets of pain over his nerves every so often. A touch at his torso took his breath all over again.

"Can you talk?"

"Never...getting..." his jaw felt like smashed glass, his tongue swollen and thick, and that metallic taste filled his nose, "...on a...fucking roof with you...again."

"Mama, I am thirty-six years old." Madeline pulled a stack of T-shirts from her dresser and dumped them on the bed. "I don't need your permission to do anything."

"I simply do not understand you," her mother said from the doorway. "What are you thinking, moving in with this man so fast?"

"I'm not moving in with him. I'm taking some stuff to his place for... Oh, forget it." Madeline opened her rolling case and tossed clothing into it in a haphazard jumble. She'd sort it out later. "I thought you liked him."

"I do. But, Madeline, spending nights at his house? What will people think?"

"Who cares? It's a small town, Mama. Everyone gets talked about, and if people don't know the gossip, they make it up. Lord knows you should be used to people talking about me by now."

"What would your father say?"

She froze in the act of transferring toiletries and straightened, a cold knot at the base of her throat. "Nothing. He's dead, and when he was alive, nothing I did was ever good enough, remember?"

"Your father loved you, Maddie."

"I think you're confusing me with Autry. She was Daddy's perfect little girl, the one who did everything right. I was..." Her throat closed, and she swallowed hard, blinking against a stinging rush of tears. "I was his biggest disappointment."

"I just think—"

"That's fine, think whatever you want, Mama. You're not going to change my mind."

"You know, that is the same stubbornness that broke your daddy's heart."

What about his stubbornness and her broken heart? The wave of pain and guilt shut her lungs down, the same old huge knot of remorse and separation settling in her chest, and she was right back where she'd been at eighteen. "Fine, whatever. I'm out of here, Mama."

"There you go, with that attitude."

Without a word, she lifted her bag and brushed by her mother. She refused to cry. Shedding tears never solved anything, never made a situation better. Her mama trailed her through the house to the front porch. "Madeline, please, would you stop and think about what people will say?"

God, that's all her father had ever been concerned with too. Didn't it ever stop? She tossed her bag on the backseat. "What are you going to do, Mama? Tell me if I go I can't come back?"

Those words echoed in her head, her father's anger bouncing around like it had for years. All she'd ever wanted was...

To get the hell away from here. To find acceptance, somewhere she could be herself without unreachable expectations hanging over her every single second. The Jacksonville PD couldn't call her back to work soon enough. She hoped Ash didn't mind having her around a few days. She was going to need that in order to calm down before facing her mother again.

Behind the wheel, she flexed fingers aching from being clenched too tight and backed around, finally pulling out to the highway and turning in the direction of Ash's. She fumed all the way to Long Lonesome Road.

An unmarked patrol car topped the hill behind her, blue lights and headlamps flashing. He flew around her, engine roaring. What was that all about? She frowned, trying to remember what all was on this road now.

She forced herself to relax, breathing through the hurt anger. She would not take this home to Ash. He didn't deserve the aftereffects of her crazy family dynamics.

The road straightened out from the double S-curve, blue lights still visible ahead of her. He was moving, though, almost at pursuit speed. Brake lights flared as the cop swung a turn.

Into Ash's driveway.

Fear surged into her bloodstream. She pressed harder on the accelerator, seconds stretched into dreamlike forever even as she closed the distance. Her pulse pounded in her ears, laid over by the cool calm instilled by years on the job.

Her little car jounced over a couple of ruts in the drive. The patrol car continued across the pasture before the chicken houses.

That was not good.

No way would her low-slung car handle that rutted field. Leaving it before the house, she took off at a run, fear pounding with every step. She reached the clearing around the chicken houses just after the unit came to a stop and a sturdy dark-haired man stepped out.

Beyond the unit, what she saw stopped everything.

Ash, lying on the ground, not moving. Tick crouched beside him. The cop grabbed a portable medical kit from his trunk and jogged toward them. Swallowing against a wave of fear, she ran the final few yards.

"What happened?" the cop asked, kneeling next to them and slanting a look at Tick as she finally skidded to a stop just behind him, transfixed by Ash's face, bloody, eyes closed, twisted in pain. "You push him?"

"Shut up, Cookie. That's not funny." Tick had Ash's wrist in hand, fingers pressed to his pulse point. "Where's the damn ambulance?"

"They're both out on other calls—heart attack in Rayford and a wreck at the Greenough crossroads. Roger's dispatching us one from Albany."

"That's twenty minutes away." With tentative movements, Madeline went down beside them. The amount of blood on his face, the ragged way he breathed, the absolute stillness frightened her. The naked anxiety on Tick's pale face made it worse.

"I'm a certified First Responder." The cop shot a curious look in her direction, running assessing hands over Ash.

"Not...you, Cookie. God...help me." Trying to grin, Ash opened one eye on a pained grunt. "Don't...touch my...*fuck*!"

The agonized cry shattered through Madeline, bringing a wash of tears to her eyes. Ash's chest heaved, his eyes scrunched closed. She laid a firm hand on the cop's wrist. "Don't touch him again."

Thick brows dipped in a glower over sharp gray eyes. "Lady, I—"

"Cookie." Tick's firm voice stopped him. "I've already checked him out. I think he's good until the ambulance gets here." His dark eyes caught Madeline's gaze, and the smile he attempted tried to be reassuring. "I don't think anything's broken. Ribs are tender, and he's messed up his knee. No numbness, he can move fingers and toes, but the way he fell...I want him on a backboard before he's moved anywhere."

Madeline's eyes jerked to the chicken house behind them—and the nearly twenty-foot drop to the ground. "You fell off the *roof*?" She turned on Tick, glaring. "You let him fall off the fucking roof? Don't y'all know what a safety harness is?"

"Sure they do," Cookie offered. "They just don't use 'em. Tick-boy won't wear a bulletproof vest either."

Did she *ask* him anything? Madeline narrowed her eyes. "Shut up."

"I know you from somewhere." Unperturbed, he shook a finger between them and looked sideways at Tick. "Where do I know her from?"

"She's Autry's sister." Fingers still on Ash's wrist, Tick checked his watch. "And our interim investigator. Madeline, this is Mark Cook. Cookie, Madeline Holton."

Ash grimaced. "Y'all...have to hush. Head hurts...like a mother."

At a distance, a high-pitched siren wailed. Cookie's handheld radio crackled, and he lifted it to his mouth, offering specific directions to the ambulance, which turned out to be from Chandler County EMS after all. The bus bounced over ruts in the field, coming to a stop beside Cookie's unit. The driver, a lanky rusty-haired man, hauled equipment out of the back while the second medic, a woman with big dark eyes and short black hair, hurried to the small group huddled on the ground.

"Ash Hardison, what have you done?" Bent on one knee, she ran gentle hands over him, her eyes concerned. "Hey, Tick, Cookie. Jim, get the neck brace and the backboard. Ash, darlin', can you talk to me?"

"Layla." His lashes fluttered up. She grasped his lid and held one open, checking his pupil with a penlight, then the other.

"That's me, sweetheart, filling in for Clark." She smiled, gaze flicking over his face while she continued prodding. "Seeing me for stitches wasn't enough this week? Did you miss me that much?"

His reply was a *mmphf* of amusement soon swallowed by a hiss of pain as she palpated his upper abdomen. Madeline cringed, wanting to wrap him close and absorb that pain. Her eyes burned, and she blinked to clear suddenly blurry vision.

"Oh yeah, that's probably a bruised kidney. You're going to be horribly sore. Tick, honey, get out of my way, would you? I need to get his pulse while Jim checks his blood pressure, and I can't do that while you're holding his hand." She leaned forward, one eye on her watch, and lowered her voice to a conspirator's whisper. "Feels guilty for pushing you off the roof, doesn't he?"

Tick huffed, an exasperated sound. Ash mumbled and caught his breath. "Shit...can't laugh, Lay. Hurts."

"I know, darlin'. But it's a good thing that you're alert enough to want to." She gave him a saucy wink. "Next time you want to see me, though, an invite to dinner would suffice. I'm flattered, but this is too much."

"No dinner." He flicked the fingers on one hand. "Mad."

"Mad?" She did that head-tilt thing once more, watching his face while she moved down to assess his legs. "Are you angry with me?"

"Watch his knee, Layla," Tick whispered. "He almost came out of his skin when we touched it earlier."

"Not angry." He moved those fingers again. "Mad?"

Madeline leaned forward, afraid to touch him. "I'm right here."

"Oh, I see. That's why I'm not getting any more dinner invites." Layla grinned, carefully cutting away his jeans so she could see his knee. Madeline hissed in a breath as the bruised, swollen mess came into view. Layla gave her an encouraging nod. "You can hold his hand, hon. Probably make both of you feel better. Ash? We're almost done here, and then Jim and I are going to take you to the ER and let them torture you for a while."

"Can't...wait." His fingers moved in Madeline's easy hold, and she stroked her thumb over his knuckles. God, she hated this, seeing him hurt, not being able to do anything. She'd worked a ton of medical calls in her career, but this was horrible. This was Ash.

"Yeah, there's that sense of humor we know and love. Listen, Jim's going to put the brace on your neck and I need you to be really, really still while he does that. Tick's going to help by holding and lifting your head, all right? Let him do it, and you just lie there."

The two men made short work of getting the plastic support in place.

"All right, almost there, honey. Backboard next, then on a stretcher and you're out of here." With professional ease, Layla guided the men through transferring Ash to the board and strapping him with a minimum of jostling. Madeline held his hand as long as she could, not even bothering to tell herself it was ridiculous to be this wound up over a guy she'd known four days.

Because it was Ash and that changed everything. He had changed everything.

"Here's the deal," Layla said as they loaded the stretcher into the back of the ambulance. "He's going to the ER. Stitches, CAT scan, ultrasound, the whole shebang. Tick, do you want to ride along—"

"No." Ash's hoarse voice cut her off. "Want Mad."

Madeline looked around at Tick, expecting to see resentment and censure on his face and finding neither. He jerked his chin toward the bus. "Go on. I'll follow."

She clambered aboard, snatches of Tick and Cookie's conversation floating to her.

"Hey, Tick, who's Allison Barnett anyway?"

Tick's groan was laden with disgust. "Why?"

"She's called looking for you three times today." A patrol car door swished open. "Didn't like hearing you were off all three times, either."

Layla slammed the ambulance doors and settled into the jump seat at the end of the stretcher. Madeline rubbed stinging eyes. God, what was Allison up to now? Couldn't she simply leave well enough alone?

"Mad." Ash pulled her back. She leaned forward, stroking the back of his wrist. His eyes clouded with pain. "Gonna stay? Want you with me."

"Of course." She caressed his hand once more, a hard rush of emotion she didn't want to identify curling through her. "I'll be here."

Chapter Sixteen

This was a bitch.

Ash blinked the fuzziness away from his vision, focusing on the white acoustic tiles of the hospital ceiling. Whatever painkillers dripped into him from the IV line kept the agony to a dull roar in his body but kept pulling him in and out of consciousness, so he didn't know how long he'd been here or exactly what damage he'd done to himself.

He was out of the ER and into a room. Fluorescent light gleamed over his head; he turned to the left. The dark of night hovered outside. He flexed his fingers. All right, he could move his arms, although the sensation was sluggish and dull. Someone had rebandaged his hand. He lifted fingertips and touched his face. More stitches below his mouth; his lip seemed swollen.

His right foot twitched when he told it to. His left leg...he couldn't move. Panic slithered through him. Why couldn't he move that leg?

Refusing to succumb to the dread, he scanned the room. He was alone, and a twinge of another kind of pain joined the alarm. Where was Madeline? She'd told him she'd be here.

Maybe she'd changed her mind. Maybe he'd expected too much.

A click and the door swished open. He glanced to his right, hope and anticipation rising in him, only to be dashed.

"Ash?"

His brother Rob stood just inside the doorway, his face set in lines of anxiety. Shit, now why had Tick called Rob? His presence wasn't a good sign. For Rob to come all the way from Houston... Hell, how bad was he injured? He closed his eyes, fear slinking over his nerves again.

When he tried to pull in a deep breath, pain exploded in his chest, cutting off his oxygen. His eyes snapped open as he struggled to get air into his lungs.

"Hey, easy." Rob's warm hand steadied his shoulder. "You're all right. Calm down."

Calm down. Sure. Easy for him to say.

"You look like shit." Another deep male voice, cultured, familiar. What was *he* doing here?

Finally able to pull in a shallow breath without hurting, Ash flicked a glare over Rob's shoulder at Vince Falconetti. "Thanks."

Vince's even white teeth flared in his predatory grin. "Anytime."

"What're you...doing here?" He stared at the ceiling again. He hated this, being flat on his back, being helpless.

"You took a twenty-foot fall, Ash. They were worried you'd broken your back." A wry note tempered the concern in Rob's voice. "Did you think none of us would come?"

Ash flicked a hand in Vince's direction. "What about him?"

"Daddy has the Lear in Alaska, hunting. I needed someone with a private jet and enough clout to get me in the air as soon as possible."

Vince smiled again, inspected his nails, buffed them on his shoulder. Ash would have rolled his eyes at the smug bastard if he hadn't felt like day-old cow shit.

"What'd doctor say?" Rob would have cornered the medical professionals first, would have the whole picture. He'd give it to Ash straight.

"You're lucky to be alive." Mouth tight, Rob looked truly shaken. "Bruised your kidneys, broke a couple of ribs, tore the hell out of the tendons on your knee. You're going to have to have surgery to repair it, but the swelling has to go down first. They've immobilized it."

Relief ripped through him. That didn't sound so bad.

"Messed up that pretty face of yours." Vince narrowed his eyes, studying him. "Nothing a good plastic surgeon can't fix."

"Fuck...you, Vince."

A rich chuckle rumbled from Vince's throat, and he tagged Rob's arm. "He's fine."

"You cut your chin open," Rob said, ignoring their friend and business associate. "Eight stitches. Another three or four inside, where you probably bit your lip."

On a nod, Ash closed his eyes. He was good. Not so much right this second, but he'd be okay. Obviously not working his farm for a while, but Tick would already have that covered. The weird half-sleep sucked at him, and he jerked to awareness, with a wild glance around.

"Time is it?"

"Almost eight. Why don't you get some sleep—"

"Where's Madeline?"

"Who?" Rob lifted his eyebrows and looked across the bed at

Vince.

Then she wasn't here. A different hurt settled over him. He shouldn't be surprised, probably. Not like he hadn't known she ran from her emotions, from the tough stuff. This definitely counted as the tough stuff, at least on his end. But he'd thought, hoped even, from the look in her eyes when they'd loaded him in the ambulance that...well, he'd been wrong.

Damn it.

"Madeline."

At Tick's voice, she turned from the vending machine, carefully cradling a cup of scalding hot chocolate. Her neck and back had stiffened after hours of sitting, watching Ash's sleeping face, and she'd hoped a warm drink would settle the nervous worry jumping in her stomach. A fine film of what she suspected was marshmallow floated on top of the pale brown liquid. Maybe this had been the wrong beverage choice.

She frowned at the cell phone in Tick's hand. "Are you supposed to have that in here?"

He waved a dismissing hand between them. "Just talked to Ford."

"Well?" She resisted the urge to prod him physically, as she'd done Jack more than once when he'd teased with the same kind of gleeful reticence over a lead, with a well-placed jab to the chest. She wasn't in the mood for this tonight, not with her mind tumbling over and over the possible implications of Ash's fall. God, it could have been so much worse, but seeing him lying motionless in that hospital bed was bad enough. Almost as awful as seeing Jack, after.

"Our body?" Tick's voice pulled her back. "Dental records match to Kelly Coker."

"Oh, God." She covered her mouth with one hand, appalled at the rush of tears stinging her eyes. Shit damn fuck, what was wrong with her? Hot liquid splashed over her wrist, scorching pain over her skin, and she stared with sick realization at her shaking hands.

"Hey, be careful." Long fingers plucked the steaming cup from her hand and set it aside. He pulled her toward the water fountain and shoved her wrist under the stream of icy water.

Her palm still over her mouth, she blinked hard, the vision of those bones spinning through her head. Kelly, alone, under that house for years and years. "I didn't want it to be her, Tick, I didn't want it to be *her*."

"I know. I'm sorry." The quiet sympathy, combined with the horrors of the day, undid her.

Hot tears spilled over, dripping down her cheeks, a rough sob tearing at her chest. She covered her face, trying to stop the crying, each image her brain spun only making it worse. Ford's initial examination had indicated a horrible death—stab wounds, head trauma. And it was Kelly, who'd never willingly hurt anyone, who'd even made Madeline stop her Jeep once to hop out and scoot a turtle off the road.

"Madeline, please don't." Awkward arms enfolded her, her nose bumping a cotton shirt. She buried her wet eyes into the curve of that shoulder and sobbed while Tick patted her back in self-conscious comfort. Something about that discomfited touch only made her cry harder. What was wrong with her? She hadn't even cried when Daddy had been killed or when Jack had been shot, when Jack had *died*, and now she was bawling her eyes out over a girl she hadn't seen in almost twenty years.

Maybe she was crying for all three of them: Daddy, Kelly...and Jack.

"I didn't want it to be her. I wanted..." Shit, her nose was running, waves of tears assaulting her, sobs like little wails ripping up from her throat. She hadn't cried like this since...since...

"Madeline. Come on. Don't do this."

Since that night she'd so royally fucked up everything.

"You're going to make yourself sick." Desperation tinged Tick's words, and a laugh bubbled up, turning to bigger, gulping sobs. "Quit it, Holton. I mean it."

Her knees threatened to give way, and she wrapped her arms around him, holding on and leaning in before she ended up on the floor. Finally, Tick gave up on the soothing words and shut up, simply wrapping her close and letting her cry.

She wept, crying it all out, until the tears slowed to a trickle and the sobs faded to breathless hiccups. Beneath her nose, Tick's chest moved in a harsh sigh. She closed her eyes. Oh, God. She'd lost it for sure now.

His arms flexed, and he rested his chin atop her head. "Better?"

She nodded and sucked in a breath, tested her knees to make sure her shaky legs would stand alone. Breaking his hold, she stepped back, not looking at him. "I'm sorry, this is so weird—"

"Tell me about it." The dry rejoinder struck her as funny, and she laughed, the shaky sound too close to the sobs she'd finally gotten under control. She sniffled.

"Oh no, you don't. We're not doing this again." Tick stepped away and reached for his back pocket, a grimace contorting his face. "Hell, I don't have a handkerchief. I used it earlier on—"

"You carry a handkerchief?" Did anyone still do that? Her grandfather had always had one in his pocket, ready to dry tears or mop up an ice-cream sticky face, but that had been her eighty-year-old Papa. The idea of Tick carrying one around struck her as funny too, although she didn't know why.

"Yes, I carry a handkerchief." He snagged a box of tissues from a table near the door and offered a handful. "Monogrammed ones, for your information."

"Monogrammed?" With a helpless laugh, she mopped at her nose and face.

"Cait's idea. She has this thing for monograms, and I have a drawer full of handkerchiefs with mine now." A rueful grin lifted one corner of his mouth as he mopped at the damp spot on his shoulder, smeared with remnants of her mascara. "Surprised I haven't ended up with her initials tattooed on my ass."

"I wouldn't give her any ideas." Madeline blew out a shaky breath and swiped her wrist over her cheeks. "She's a tad possessive about you."

"Yeah, I know." His expression said he didn't mind. He gave up on trying to clean his shirt and tossed the wadded-up tissues in the waste can. "We've got a hell of a job in front of us with this one."

She nodded. Following the investigator's rule of twenty-four, delving into the periods of twenty-four hours before and after a death, would be wicked hard when they couldn't be sure exactly *when* Kelly had died.

She should be raring to jump into this investigation. She always had been in the past—ready to go as soon as the call came in, chasing the leads, losing herself in the challenge and adrenaline.

Instead, she couldn't shift her brain into gear, into cop mode. Too much of it was still focused on Ash, on willing him to be all right.

"Listen," Tick said, bringing her out of the momentary reverie, "I know I should be all gung-ho and ready to go on this case, but it's been one hell of a day and I'm running on something like three hours of sleep. I need some caffeine, a change of clothes and maybe some food before I can fire on all cylinders. Why don't you check on our boy and I'll bring you something to eat?"

She opened her mouth to correct that "our" boy, but who was she kidding? She nodded. "Sounds good."

"All right." He checked his watch. "Give me about forty-five minutes. I'll stop by the station and grab whatever we have on this case, too."

"Okay." As he walked away, she lifted what was left of her hot chocolate—now lukewarm chocolate—and downed it quickly, grimacing over the powdery taste. Her wrist stung, and she rubbed an absent circle over the red spot.

A decorative mirror hung in the middle of the waiting area, and she took a quick glance, recoiling. Damn, she looked awful—hair tousled, eyes and nose red, all makeup gone. She smoothed her hair best she could, wiped away a smudge of mascara from under her eye. Straightening the hem of her T-shirt, she headed for Ash's room. The hall was relatively deserted, a couple of nurses chatting over a chart, a man using the phone at the nurse's station.

"I just left him. He's fine, really." The man's voice wafted over her as she passed. "I don't think it's necessary for you to come..."

She slipped into Ash's room without knocking. The television played softly, and she frowned. It hadn't been on when she'd gone to the waiting area and—

He wasn't alone. Madeline stopped just inside the doorway, clutching the edge of the door, sudden nerves flipping in her stomach. Her gaze jumped to Ash, who appeared to be still sleeping, and then to the tall man with flawless black hair sitting in the vinyl chair by the window. He looked up from the magazine he was idly paging through, and a wolfish smile touched his full mouth.

"Well, hello." Gleaming eyes, a much darker shade of green than Ash's, trailed over her face, dipped to survey her body, pausing over the length of her legs and again over her breasts, until she felt like he'd touched her. "May I help you?"

"I—" She darted another look at the bed and swallowed, running her tongue over her bottom lip. Ash's brother, whom Tick had called earlier and was trying to get a plane out of Houston. He had to be. That explained why he looked familiar, despite the difference in coloring. She tucked her hands in the back pockets of her jeans. She looked a mess, not the first impression she wanted to give his family.

Shit, she was worried about impressing his family? She was in so much trouble.

"Yes?" The smooth voice was like honeyed velvet, with a hint of gravel underneath. Deep, a little raspy, a lot rich. She frowned. He didn't talk like Ash, didn't have the same cadence in his sentences, which didn't make sense if they were siblings. Even she and Autry phrased sentences the same way despite their years apart. But something about his speech was familiar. His speech and those eyes.

Unease prickled over her and to mask it, she straightened, throwing her shoulders back in what Jack had always called her "bitch-cop stance". She narrowed her eyes. "Who are you?"

One raven eyebrow winged upward, and the predatory smile widened. "Oh, I like you."

She didn't trust this one as far as she'd be able to throw him. "I asked you a question."

At her voice, Ash stirred, blinking. "Mad?"

Keeping Mr. Slick in her range of vision, she crossed to lean over Ash. "Hey."

He fumbled for her hand, pain and meds hazing his eyes. "Thought you left me."

"Only long enough to get a drink." She cradled his head, caressing his forehead. "How do you feel?"

"Like day-old cow shit." His lashes fell, casting shadows on his face. "Glad you're here."

"Me too." She slanted a look at Slick, who'd risen to his feet and watched with a spare-me expression. "Is this your brother?"

Ash glanced to the foot of the bed. "Him? Hell...no."

Perfect teeth flared in a broad smile. "Oh come now, Ashleigh, I'm offended. I happen to come from an excellent gene pool."

"Shallow one."

A rich baritone laugh rolled between them. Women probably fell at his feet all the time. She wasn't impressed, and after the day she'd had, she didn't feel like playing games. "Who the hell are you?"

"He's leaving," Ash rasped.

"That's nice." Slick laid a well-kept hand over his heart. "I left my grandfather on the golf course to come to your side in your time of need—"

"Get out before I..." Ash sucked in a breath, winced and tightened his fingers on Madeline's, "...remind you my best friend is...fucking your sister."

A dull flush tinged high cheekbones, and Madeline swallowed a laugh. She stroked the inside of Ash's wrist. "You are really doped up, aren't you, to say something like that."

"That is precisely the only reason I am not dragging you out of that bed and beating you to a bloody pulp." Deadly ice dripped from each word.

Ignoring him, Madeline gazed down at Ash. "Cait's brother?"

Closing his eyes on a grimace of pain, Ash nodded. "Vince."

"Oh, him." Madeline smoothed the lines from his face and leaned down to whisper in his ear, just for him. "Lucky colonel's daughter."

A wicked smile curved his damaged mouth. "Damn straight."

"You should be resting." She ran her fingers through his short hair, the strands crisp.

The door opened behind her, and she glanced over her shoulder at the newcomer. This had to be the brother—same sandy hair, eyes closer to hazel than green but the same shape, same line of the mouth. His gaze settled on Madeline with heavy curiosity, but he crossed to stand beside her and speak to Ash first.

"Just got off the phone with Daddy. He wanted to come but I told him right now you were okay. Unless anything changes with you, he's staying in Alaska to finish his hunting trip."

"Thank God."

Rob huffed a small laugh. "Yeah, I know. I thought he'd make me crazy when I broke my leg skiing. I know he drove the nursing staff insane."

"Mother hen."

"Yes." Rob patted Ash's uninjured knee. He darted another glance at Madeline and extended his hand, his handsome face open and friendly. "Rob Hardison, Ash's brother."

"Madeline Holton." She took his hand in a brief, warm handshake.

"Nice to meet you." Rob's amiable smile made his eyes glow.

"You too." She dropped her gaze to Ash's face, his eyes closed once more. God, her social skills were lacking. Obviously, she'd not practiced them enough the last few years.

"Vince," Rob said, smacking his hands together and rubbing them lightly. "We should get out of here, get a bite, check into that bed and breakfast downtown. Let him get some rest. Ash, I'll be back in the morning. Madeline, again, good to meet you."

The door clicked shut behind them, the room plunged into silence except for the soft prattle of a sitcom from the television.

"He likes you," Ash murmured, drowsily.

Madeline moved her fingers over his hand, a soft, circular caress. "What?"

"He's never that nice."

"I doubt that."

"He's a shark." The words slurred a little, his lids fluttering. "Makes Vince...look like pussycat. Ask Cait."

"I'll do that." She pushed the button to kill the television and reached up to turn off the bright light over the bed. The room plunged into semi-dimness. "Now go to sleep."

He made a soft noise in his throat and within moments, the sound of his breathing told her the drugs and pained exhaustion had pulled him into slumber. She stood over him, studying the lines of his face.

His brother liked her? That was...hard to believe. Likable wasn't a descriptive word she'd choose for herself.

She sighed. Did it matter, anyway, whether the brother liked her? They weren't a long-term deal.

Laying Ash's hand down with exquisite care, she crossed to the chair under the window. She picked up the magazine Vince had abandoned and flipped through it, not seeing the colorful ads or registering the headlines. After a moment, she slapped the magazine down on her lap and stared across at Ash's sleeping face.

He thought his brother liked her. With that came the weird flush of pleasure again, almost like the one she got when Tick acted like she was a normal human being. That reaction didn't make sense either.

She did *not* care what Tick Calvert thought of her. Rob Hardison either.

With the magazine discarded, she pulled her knees to her chin and wrapped her arms around them, resting her chin on top. Caring what people thought was another of those slippery slopes, and that particular slope she didn't plan to fall down.

Chapter Seventeen

"Holton, wake up."

The whisper finally registered in her consciousness and Madeline opened her eyes to find Tick standing over her. He crooked a finger and tilted his head toward the door. With a quick glance at Ash's sleeping face, she unfolded cramped legs and followed him.

"How is he?" Tick asked in a low voice as she met him in the hall.

"He seems to be resting. He's been asleep since his brother left." She checked her watch. "That was over an hour ago."

"Grabbed you a sub from the Big Dawg." He jerked a thumb over his shoulder in the direction of the waiting room. "And when I went by the office to get our files, the rental agency had faxed over the tenant list. Damn thing is more than ten pages long."

With the turnover that house always had, she wasn't surprised. She rubbed sleepy eyes, still feeling like she was slogging through swamp mud, and followed him to the deserted waiting area.

Her sandwich and a soda waited on the low table before the vinyl couch and chairs. Tick dropped into the chair nearest the door; she took the couch. While she unwrapped her sub, he laid out the rental list, preliminary autopsy report and his initial notes on the crime scene at the Miller Court house.

The rich smell of ham and melted cheese made her stomach rumble with the realization it hadn't been fed all day. Lifting the bun, she picked off the lettuce. "Thanks for this."

"Huh?" He looked up from the rental list with a distracted expression. "Yeah, sure."

"So what are you looking for?" she asked around a bite of yeasty bread, spicy pepperoni and Italian dressing.

His gaze was back on the list. "Didn't your mama teach you not to talk with your mouth full?"

"Calvert."

"Trying to see who we might be able to eliminate." He paged through the list. "Maybe everybody in the last ten years? That gives us, what? Eight years in which she could have—"

"Less than that." She licked a bit of mayonnaise off the end of her thumb. "Ford said she was fifteen to eighteen. Kelly was sixteen, nearly seventeen when she ran away. That gives you the year, maybe two after I graduated from high school."

"Oh, hell yeah." He grinned, laying several sheets of paper aside. "That gives us...ten tenants. Shit, how can a house turn over that many times in a two year period?"

Madeline shrugged. "Maybe because it's the town rental whore? Kinda like your girlfriend."

"What are you talking about?" He pulled his pen from his pocket and drew a line across the paper.

"Do you really think just because Allison was your first that you were hers?"

"What makes you think she was my first?" He returned the pen to his pocket. "And stop referring to her as my girlfriend, would you?"

Madeline snorted and settled back with her sandwich. "Like everybody doesn't know she was your first. Girls talk, remember?"

He looked up at that. "I don't want to know."

She took a huge bite of the sub and mumbled around it, "Probably not."

"I wonder if any of these people are still local. I don't recognize any names. Take forever to run them all." His attention dropped to the paper, and she gave in to the devil of temptation.

"I'll let you take care of it. I heard once you were really fast."

Irritated dark eyes lifted to hers in slow motion. "Madeline, I swear to God—"

"It's a sin to swear or didn't you pay attention in Sunday School?"

"Are you done?"

She surveyed the half a sandwich she had left. "Almost."

"We need to run Kelly's Social Security number. If she ever used it during that year she was gone, it might narrow our timeline further."

"Sounds like a plan." The food was relaxing her. God, she'd been hungry. She reached for the soda. "So I heard Cook say your girlfriend had called the station looking for you, three times. What did she want?"

"She is *not* my girlfriend." The words sounded like they were pushed between gritted teeth. "I don't know what she wanted. It's not like I called her back."

"Wow. She snapped her fingers, and you didn't come running.

189

That's going to piss her off."

"You're obnoxious, you know that?"

"It's a gift." She tried to keep a straight face, the day's stress wanting to bubble into completely inappropriate laughter. "You know, it's a good thing your kid doesn't have a pet bunny. Allison's just the type to boil it."

An unwilling smile quirked at his mouth. "Yeah, and my wife would kick her ever-lovin' ass too."

Madeline laid a hand over her stomach. "You don't know how I would love to see that. Hell, I'd pay money."

He sobered, gaze tracking to the autopsy report. Leaning forward, he lifted it and frowned. "You don't think..."

"What?" Instincts honed by years on the job tingled to life. He had that look, the same one Jack used to get, when they were tossing around ideas. Weird how she could read Calvert after five days almost as well as she'd been able to read her partner after seven years together.

"Is she the type to do more than boil a bunny?" Tick's drawl pulled her away from the raw memory.

"Murder?" Madeline frowned. "Maybe? I mean, she could be ruthless. She didn't cringe at setting up that ballpark gangbang to get Kelly out of her way, but killing someone? I don't know."

He scratched his jaw, stubble rasping. "Wish I could put Cait in a room with her for a little while, let her run a preliminary profile on Allison's personality."

"Oh, that would be fun."

He ignored her, eyes narrowed, still rubbing his fingers across his jaw. "I wonder..."

"What?"

"Allison doesn't know we know it's Kelly. For all she knows that body could belong to any number of cold cases."

"Yeah. And?"

"Cait's got a couple of serials that went cold and were never solved. Hell, she worked a case here with multiple victims." A slow grin slid over his face. "Might make sense that she'd check out these remains, want to talk with the person who discovered them."

Madeline laughed. "That is...almost brilliant, Calvert."

Still grinning, he lifted his brows, eyes glittering. Heart pounding, Madeline grinned back. "I want to watch."

With the slow burn of investigative adrenaline burning in his gut, Tick took the stairs two at a time. The house was quiet and he'd checked all the downstairs room; Caitlin had to be in the nursery. He knew better than to call her name. If she'd gotten Lee down and he woke him up, there'd be hell to pay.

He paused in the doorway. Sure enough, she curled into the squashy armchair, nursing the baby. He sucked in a breath, a little winded. "Hey."

"How's Ash?"

"Resting. Doctor's hoping the swelling will be down enough tomorrow to repair his knee." He crossed to sit on the ottoman before the chair. Leaning forward, he brushed a kiss over Lee's brow, then dropped another on the slope of her breast.

She tangled her fingers in his hair and lifted his head to her mouth. "Behave."

He smiled against the corner of her lips. "You weren't saying that last night."

"Tick..."

"Did he have a better day?" He cupped the baby's head and watched heavy little lids lower.

"Much." She shifted to the side and patted the chair, which he'd picked out specifically because it was big enough for two. "Come sit with us."

He eased next to her and wrapped an arm around her. Her head brushed his chin, and he smiled against her hair. "I want you to do something for me."

Her quiet laugh trilled over him, and she laid her free hand on his thigh. "Where have I heard that before?"

"Get your mind out of the bedroom." He nuzzled her temple. "If I arranged for you to interview Allison Barnett, do you think you could get a read on her?"

She turned her head to meet his gaze. "I don't think you want me in a room alone with her."

"I'm serious."

"So am I."

"Listen." He took her hand. "I need to know if you think she's capable of murder."

"Sweet thing, after seeing the way she looked when I kissed you? I don't have to interview her. If she could have, she'd have killed me on the spot."

He kissed her knuckles. "That's not what I'm talking about."

"You think I'm joking? I'm absolutely serious. I've interviewed multiple murderers who looked less able to kill."

She rested her head against his shoulder. Lee bounced a foot,

191

jabbing Tick's abdomen. He caught the tiny foot in his palm.

"If I interview her before you have reason to suspect her, McMillian would have a fit. He wouldn't like that coming out in court."

He grimaced at the mention of the local DA. "True."

Quiet settled around them, broken only by Lee's soft snuffles and muffled gulps. Tick feathered his thumb over the small toes. Caitlin's fingers tapped his thigh in a soft rhythm.

"Did you know her first husband died?"

"What?" Surprise jolted him, and he looked down at her. "No. When it was over, it was over. I didn't keep up with her."

"Heart attack." She shifted, twining her foot around his calf. "He'd just turned twenty-one. She got the small life-insurance policy he had, twenty-five thousand dollars. Married husband number two within six months."

"Huh."

"Husband number two was a member of the Southern Brotherhood."

That caught his attention. During his days with the FBI's Organized Crime Division, he'd followed the activities of the fringe biker group, an offshoot of one of the four major outlaw motorcycle groups the Bureau monitored regularly. "Really."

"Yes." A small self-satisfied moue pursed her lips. "That twenty-five grand was gone in months. She's worked and supported the family—she has a daughter from both marriages. After the divorce, she got sole custody. Husband number two is in Reidsville, doing ten years for various nefarious activities."

"You've been busy today, haven't you?" He tucked her hair behind her ear. "You didn't use Bureau resources to check her out, did you?"

"Of course not. I used Falcon Security resources and convinced Tony he wanted to do this for me as quickly as possible. I don't trust her, and I wanted to know everything I could. I'm telling you, Tick, she's trouble."

"Good morning, sleepyhead." Madeline's soft touch drifted over his cheek, and Ash opened his eyes to a wash of early-morning sunlight. She smiled down at him, her eyes soft and clear.

His mouth felt weird, tasted worse, and he swallowed, muffled pain arching along his nerves with the action. "Hey."

"Should I even ask how you feel?"

"Sore all over." The agony lay beneath the drugs, just out of reach. Each muscle felt like pulled taffy, wound back around his body too tight. He let his eyes trail over her—tousled hair, wrinkled T-shirt. "Did you stay here all night?"

"I did." She stroked his jaw, avoiding the stitches below his lips. "Tick and I worked in the waiting area for a while last night, then I slept in the foldout chair."

Did she realize what that implied? He held her eyes. "Thank you."

The corners of her mouth hitched higher. "I told you I wouldn't leave."

A wave of almost-pain swept up his leg from his knee. He closed his eyes. Thank God for meds. "Rob here?"

"I haven't seen him yet." She stroked his hair, as if she realized he hurt and wanted to take it away. "But it's early."

He nodded and exhaled, the throbbing receding some.

"I am going to bail on you for a little while today." Her fingers continued their soothing rhythm. "We have a couple of leads to follow up."

Another nod as the nausea of pain settled deep in his gut, taking his breath for a moment. Man, he would be glad when this was all over. Hurting and being laid up had never been his idea of a good time.

"Um, Ash?" Her touch paused at his forehead. He looked up in time to see uncertainty flash over her face. "Do you mind if I go out to your place to shower and change? My things are there, and I kind of had it out with Mama yesterday. I don't think I want to go back home for a while."

The implications of her preferring his home to her own were staggering. He moved his hand, caught hers, and smiled. "Yeah, babe, that's good."

"There you go, thinking I'll let you call me babe just because you're laid up..."

He squeezed her fingers. "Go on. Do what you need to do. I'll see you later."

Leaning over, she whispered her lips across his. "Be good. I'll be back this afternoon."

Moments later the door clicked shut behind her. He stared at the ceiling. The empty hours of the day without her stretched before him.

Damn it, Tick was right. His ass was whipped already.

Tick slammed the door on his truck and jogged toward the steps. He'd forgotten his gloves, and his hands tingled in the icy breeze. Damn, he'd be ready when spring got here.

"Tick!"

The familiar voice brought him up short and sent a different type of ice down his spine in a weird frisson, a lot like the elemental shudder of running across a moccasin while trekking through the woods by the river. He tensed and turned. Couldn't avoid her forever. Tugging his cap lower over his eyes, he waited for Allison to join him. She smiled, arms wrapped around her, hands cupping her elbows.

"I'm glad I caught you," she breathed, still smiling. Something about that smile made his skin crawl. "I tried to call you yesterday."

"My day off." He couldn't quite keep the coldness out of his voice, and her smile faded. Like he gave a crap. Madeline's revelations, about Kelly, about Allison's machinations where he was concerned, kept beating in his head. "Did you want something?"

"I was hoping I could get back in the house."

He jerked a thumb over his shoulder. "I'll have a deputy meet you there while you get what you need. We should be able to release the house to you in a couple of days."

"Oh, I was hoping you'd go with me." With a little pout of disappointment that did absolutely nothing for him, she laid her hand on his wrist. "And we'd have another chance to catch up."

Disgust moved over him. He lifted her hand from his arm. "No thanks."

"What is wrong with you?" The question came off playful, but something dark lurked beneath her words.

"Allison, I'm not interested in 'catching up' with you, now or ever."

Shock moved across her delicate features, but an ugliness twisted her mouth. "This is not like you. I can't believe you're talking to me this way."

"I'll leave the keys at the front desk. Ask Lydia to get you a deputy to meet you at the house."

"That's it?" She grabbed his arm, nails digging in despite the thickness of his jacket, and spun him back to face her. "That's all you have to say?"

"Yeah."

Her entire face was twisted now. Had that ugliness been there when they'd been kids? Had he been infatuated enough to miss it back then?

"It's that bitch Madeline Holton, isn't it? God only knows what she's been telling you."

"What makes you think Madeline had anything to tell me?" He crossed his arms over his chest. "Better yet, what are you afraid she'd tell me?"

That set her back and she blinked. "I don't know what you're talking about."

"Sure. Not worried at all she'd tell me you lied about being on the pill? Or how you set up Kelly Coker—"

"Kelly didn't get anything she didn't want."

"You really believe that, don't you?" Un-freakin'-believable. "See Mrs. Lydia."

"Do you think that's it, Tick?" The ugliness invaded her voice now. "That you're just going to walk away from me like this?"

He snatched the front door open, irritation slithering over him. "Yeah, Allison, that's it."

"This isn't over."

She was delusional. He ignored her and continued inside. At the desk, he paused long enough to leave directions for someone to meet Allison to get her things. Edginess ran under his skin, blending with a simmering anger.

It wasn't over? The idea that she might be threatening him made the anger worse. Where did she get off?

She clearly didn't know who she was dealing with.

Madeline swung out of her car, head bent against the wind.

"You bitch!"

Allison Barnett stood before her on the sidewalk, her face red, entire body trembling with fury and hatred. Madeline stared at her a moment, expecting the deep-rooted shame and resentment to flood through her.

Nothing.

Somehow, it was all gone—all the old acid, just gone, swallowed up somehow. Because of Ash maybe? Because of his simple belief? Or maybe because she'd finally lanced the old wounds, let all the poison drain away in that slow confession to Tick.

For whatever reason, Allison held no power over her anymore.

"Bitch, huh?" Madeline smiled. "Yep, that would be me."

"I suppose you're satisfied with yourself now. I'm going to make you sorry you were ever born, Madeline Holton."

"I don't know what you're talking about, Allison, but I don't have time for this." Madeline brushed by her. "I don't have time for you."

She bounded up the department steps, feeling lighter than she had in...well, forever. That easily. She'd confronted and exorcised that ghost.

That demon.

Maybe there was hope. Maybe Ash was right. Just maybe, she did deserve good things in her life. Maybe she deserved him.

"Hey, Mrs. Lydia." She greeted the woman working the desk, who'd taught her Sunday School once upon a time. "Is Tick in yet?"

"His office."

"Thanks." Almost feeling like whistling, she stopped at Tick's door and knocked. At his quiet "it's open", she pushed the slab inward.

He glanced up, wearing irritation like a cloak. "Hey. Glad you're here. How's Ash?"

"Sore."

"I'll bet." Jaw tight, he dropped his gaze to the computer printout on his desk. "You plan on going back to the hospital today?"

"Later. I told him we had leads to follow up. What's up?"

"I just ran Kelly's Social Security number. She worked in a hot dog stand down in PC for about a year. Tried to call them, but they're obviously not open yet. I'm hoping we might be able to track down someone who knew her or who could give us an idea of where she went after she left there."

"Give me the number." Madeline held out her hand. "I'll keep trying. You have paperwork, right?"

He grimaced. "Yeah."

Taking the slip from him, she wandered to the squad room and spent some time doodling notes and thoughts in her notebook. She kept circling around to the idea of who Kelly would have come back to see. Her, maybe? And someone had hurt her before she made it that far.

Allison. Had Allison hurt her?

The memory of the hatred burning in Allison's eyes earlier flared. Maybe Allison was capable of murder.

An hour later, notes from her phone call in hand, Madeline returned to Tick's office. "How do you feel about a little trip to the beach?"

He looked up from the report he was reviewing, eyes gleaming, earlier annoyance gone. "Did you find something?"

She dropped into the chair before his desk and leaned forward, excitement bubbling in her. "The daughter of the original owners runs the place now. Not only does she remember Kelly, but they were friends. Kelly had a room in their house. The daughter kept some of the things Kelly left behind. Plus, she's going back through their employee records. Her dad is a major packrat, and she thinks she might be able to pinpoint pretty closely when Kelly left Florida."

He was on his feet, shrugging into his jacket. "Let's go."

Outside, she fell in beside him on the way to his truck. "If we can get—"

"Holy hell." His shocked intake of breath stopped her own voice. "Damn it!"

"What?" She followed the direction of his gaze and stared. The white paint on his hood had been gouged all the way to the metal.

His mouth tight, he ran a finger over the long gouges and smacked his palm on the hood, hard. "Son of a bitch."

"Who did you piss off, Calvert?"

He unlocked the truck and jerked the driver's door open. "Your friend Allison."

"She's no friend of mine."

He slammed the vehicle into reverse. "All right, Holton. Let's put this case together."

"Can I offer you something to drink?" Susan Blakely ushered them into the small, crowded office of Salty Sea Dogs.

"We're fine," Madeline said. Now that they were here, the anticipation began to wane. In its place was a melancholy sensation—this was one of the last places Kelly had been alive.

Susan sank into the chair behind the big metal desk and indicated the chairs on the far wall. "You're absolutely sure it's Kelly?"

"Unfortunately, yes," Tick replied. He balanced a small notebook on his knee, pen poised in hand.

Susan blinked hard, tears lending her eyes a wet shine. "I was afraid of something like this, when she didn't come back. I told myself, oh, she just decided to stay once she was back home."

Madeline met Tick's gaze, intrigue flaring between them. She pinned on her best interview smile. "Anything you tell us could prove important."

"I don't know where to start." Susan reached for a tissue and dabbed at her eyes. "Ridiculous, isn't it, being so upset over a girl I only knew a year, who I haven't seen in almost twenty years?"

"No," Madeline said. "Not ridiculous at all."

"Why don't you start at the beginning?" A gentle note filtered through Tick's voice.

Susan nodded and wiped her eyes once more. "She came in to eat one afternoon. I'd just gotten in from school. She was counting out change to pay for her food, and Daddy refused to take her money. He was like that, my dad. He sat her down and started talking to her. He figured out pretty quickly she wasn't as old as she said she was and that she didn't have any place to go. He put her to work on the register, set her up in the little apartment over the garage."

"How long did she stay?" Tick's pen scratched over his notebook.

"That was September and...let's see, I graduated the following May. She left sometime the next fall. I looked for the payroll records, but Daddy must have discarded them."

"That's okay." Tick looked up, a smile flashing over his face. "Your timeline gives us a starting point."

September to the next fall. A year. Madeline looked up to meet Susan's wet gaze. "Do you know why she came home? I mean, it had been over a year since she'd left. Why go back?"

"Because of me." Susan glanced toward the ceiling in the classic if-I-do-this-I-won't-cry move. "Because I convinced her she should."

"What do you mean?"

Susan ran a fingertip along her lashes. "We used to talk in the afternoons, after the early rush and before dinner. We talked about a lot of things—what she wanted to do with her life, what I was going to major in, what she'd major in if she went to community college here. Friends, boys. Eventually, she confided in me about why she ran away.

"There'd been...at first she told me she'd made this huge mistake over a boy." Anger tightened Susan's expression. Tick flicked a look in her direction, then focused on his shoes. Tension tightened his entire body; Madeline could feel it rolling off of him in waves.

Guilt.

God, did she recognize that emotion.

"But the more she told me," Susan continued, "the more I saw that it wasn't her mistake at all. There was this boy, one she wanted to impress, and one of her 'friends' convinced her she could do that by...by..."

"Participating in group sex." Madeline swallowed against a rise of bile.

"That's what Kelly called it, but it was obvious she hadn't wanted to do it. She felt coerced. It sounded more like rape to me."

A muscle flickered in Tick's taut jaw line.

"Kelly was filled with guilt over the incident. It took me months to convince her she should get some help, see a counselor. My aunt was a nurse; she set her up with the local women's shelter for some appointments with a counselor. Slowly Kelly started letting go of the guilt, began to see that what had happened hadn't been her fault."

"That she was a victim," Tick said softly.

Susan nodded. "Exactly."

"That still doesn't explain why she returned to Georgia."

"Her counselor suggested she begin taking control of her life by confronting the 'friend' who'd set her up in that situation...this...this..."

"Allison." The name left a bad taste in Madeline's mouth.

"That's right." Susan's gaze shifted, turned misty as if she were seeing the past once more. "I helped talk Kelly into it. Going to confront that girl, I mean."

Madeline's stomach knotted. The whole confronting-the-past seemed like a great idea, unless the past in question involved Allison. Had that single action gotten Kelly killed?

Susan tunneled her hand through her hair. "After I talked with her, Kelly decided to do it. She was going back to see this girl, to show her that despite what she'd done, Kelly was okay and was making something of her life. Then she left...and she never came back. Now you're telling me she's dead. She's dead, and it's all my fault."

Her voice broke on her final words.

"No." Tick lifted his head. "Nothing about this was your fault."

Something about the way he said it gave Madeline the feeling he addressed her as well.

After talking to Susan Blakely, they spent a few minutes going through the items Kelly had left behind. To Madeline's disappointment, doing so revealed nothing helpful for their investigation. Again, however, she found herself seized by bittersweet emotions as she touched Kelly's things.

Once back in the truck on the return trip, Madeline gazed out at the passing scenery after she'd called the hospital and peppered the nurses' station with questions on Ash's condition, only to be told he was sleeping. She ignored Tick's knowing grin and watched as the coastal view slowly gave way to the hills and pine trees of north Florida.

After miles of silence, she looked sideways at Tick. He drove, tapping his thumb on the wheel.

"What are you thinking about?"

He gave her a quick look as he steered into the left-hand turn onto Highway 91.

"That we need to find a way to put Allison and Kelly together during the days after she left Florida. Just knowing she planned to see Allison isn't enough. Too circumstantial."

"And one more thing..."

"Yeah?"

"Even if she went to see Allison, how the hell did she end up under that house? Allison wasn't living there then, and come on, Tick, if she knew what had happened to Kelly, if she knew that body was Kelly, do you really think she'd call the police? It doesn't make sense."

"Yeah." His mouth tightened. "I know."

"So what's next?"

"We start looking for the link between Allison and that house."

To her surprise the soft swish of tires on the highway and the crooning of Kenny Chesney from the radio lulled her to a doze despite the questions and possibilities tumbling through her head. Only minutes later it seemed, Tick's hand on her knee shook her to alertness. "Holton, we're back."

"What?" She blinked at him, the feeling of walking through mud back in full force. "Oh, okay."

He pulled the keys from the ignition. "Tell you what—let me check in with Lydia and then we'll grab some lunch and go by the hospital to see—"

The opening notes of a Gary Allan song cut him short. He lifted his cell phone and squinted at the display. "That's weird."

Did he think she was psychic? "What?"

"It's your mama's number." He flipped the phone opened and lifted it to his ear. "Hello?"

Unease shivered over Madeline. Her mama, calling Tick? God only knew why.

"Yes, ma'am, she's right here." He twisted in the seat, eyebrows lifted at her. "Have you been on the Internet this morning?"

Considering she'd gone straight from Ash's side to his place to shower then here to be accosted by Tick's crazy ex-girlfriend? "No."

He lifted the phone again. "Mama, how bad is it? All right, I think..." He pinched the bridge of his nose. "We'll come over there. Yes, ma'am, leave it off the hook. Until I get there. In about ten minutes."

His mama, calling from her mother's. Oh God. That couldn't be good. Visions danced through her head—alcohol poisoning, another of her mama's depressive "spells".

The suicide attempt that summer she and Autry had gone to Tampa.

"What's wrong?" she asked as he returned the cell to his belt. She winced at the cool note in her voice. He fired the engine and she frowned. "Why did you want to know if I'd been on the Internet?"

"You're getting calls at your mama's house."

"Calls." Something about his words filtered through, and she stared at him, horrified, as he steered them into the light traffic. "What kind of calls for me are coming into my mother's house?"

He braked for the red light but didn't look at her, his thumb bouncing on the steering wheel. "Obscene ones."

Chapter Eighteen

"Rob, if I don't do something, I'm going to go crazy." Ash thumped his fist on the mattress. This being flat on his back, staring at the ceiling, rankled. "Get Mackey in here. I should be able to sit up and work."

"You need to rest—"

"Get him in here."

"Fine." Rob lifted both hands in defeat. "I'll be right back."

The door swished shut behind him with a soft thump.

"You are a lousy patient," Vince said, his voice mild. His gaze tracked over the screen of his laptop.

"Yeah." Ash eyed the two hundred thirteen dots on the acoustic tile directly above him. He'd refused the last round of pain meds, so he hurt, but at least his mind was clear. "You try this for a while."

"Don't think so." A couple of keys clicked. "I'm smart enough not to get on a roof with Calvert."

Ash avoided the chuckle that he knew would only make his chest seize up. "It wasn't his fault."

"All right, then I'm smart enough to hire someone else to fix the damn roof."

True to his word, Rob returned in minutes, with Dr. Jay Mackey in tow. With minimal persuasion, Ash convinced the physician he could at least sit up and work. Once the doctor departed, Ash set about convincing Vince to loan him his laptop until he could send Rob for his own.

"I can check futures."

Brows arched, Vince placed the slim notebook on the rolling table.

"Hey, hand me a pad and the phone too. I want to check my voice mail."

Vince tossed the pad and a pen on the table, and the phone

landed next to them with a thud. "Would you like me to fluff your pillow?"

Ash reached for the receiver. "That won't be necessary, Jeeves."

Rob unfolded his newspaper with a snicker and met Vince's annoyed gaze over it. "He's feeling better."

With a glance at his watch, Vince leaned against the windowsill. "Maybe we'll actually get out of here before two."

"What's your hurry?" Receiver tucked between his chin and shoulder, Ash punched in the access number.

"I have a dinner date, whose company is quite preferable to that of the farmboy cop my sister married."

"You really have to..." Ash let the sentence trail away.

"What?" Rob looked up from his paper.

"I have twenty-three messages."

"Probably well-wishers." Rob folded over to the business section.

"I swear, if Tick put me on the prayer list at his church, I'll kill him." He lifted the receiver to his ear as the system signaled the first message. "Every little old lady—"

"Madeline..." The hissed whisper slid over the line. "Gonna make you spread that pretty little pussy for me...after I pound it a while, I'll slide my cock down your throat..."

The reality of what he was hearing, the male voice, the words, wormed their way into his consciousness. "What the hell?"

He deleted the message without thought, rage and nausea settling into his gut as the second message proved more of the same. The third, the fourth...

"Fuck." Anger firing through him, he slammed the table away from him. It careened over the floor, and the shiny black laptop tumbled to the tile.

"Ash." Rob was on his feet, newspaper forgotten. "What's wrong?"

Vince stared down at the ruined notebook and slowly lifted his glittering gaze. "Son of a bitch. I just bought that."

Ash rubbed a hand over his hair as Rob bent down to retrieve the phone. "Don't."

Rob ignored him, receiver at his ear. Frowning, he extended the instrument to Vince. His eyes widened, brows arched. He slanted a look at Ash. "All of them like that?"

Jaw clenched so hard the stitches inside his lip pulled painfully, Ash nodded. "Yeah. Looks that way."

"This doesn't make sense. Why would she give out your phone number for—"

"She wouldn't." Vince replaced the receiver in the cradle and picked up the remains of his laptop. "Not that one."

"You're right. Not her." Ash met Vince's shuttered gaze. "Someone else did this."

And he was pretty sure he wouldn't have to look far to find a logical culprit. He gestured at Vince. "Hand me the phone."

Brows lifted, Vince complied. Ash balanced it on his good leg and dialed for an outside line.

Rob jerked his chin at him. "Who are you calling?"

Ash flicked a glance in his brother's direction. "Tick."

At the mention of his brother-in-law, Vince grimaced. "Why him?"

"Because Madeline's with him." Ash waited through ring after ring. Damn it, Tick needed to answer the phone.

"And?" Confusion darkened Rob's eyes. Ash sighed. For a savvy businessman who handled millions daily, his little brother was slow. Hell if he was going to explain. Tick's voice mail picked up, and Ash ground his teeth, immediately regretting the action. Damn, his jaw hurt. "Tick, it's Ash and I need to talk to you or Madeline, ASAP."

He rattled off the hospital number and extension, and replaced the receiver. Now all he could do was wait. He closed his eyes.

Shit.

"Madeline Rachel Holton, how *could* you?"

Her mother's screech seared Madeline's eardrums, and she cringed. Seated at the kitchen table, hands over her face, Mama was in one of her full-fledged snits, full of screams, sobs and sniffles. A full-fledged *royal* snit induced by a combination of vodka and having a daughter who was, no doubt, the biggest slut in the state.

This was like high school all over again.

"Mama, I didn't do anything." Madeline strove for a peaceful tone, one she had no hope would actually work. "Please calm down—"

"Calm down?" Her mother lowered her hands, her face blotchy with tears and red with alcohol. "You have men calling here with that...that *filth* and you're telling me to calm down? Thank the good Lord your daddy is dead and not here to see this—"

"Miranda." In the adjacent chair Lenora Calvert laid a gentle palm on her shoulder. "Getting all upset is not helping. I really doubt Madeline is responsible for this."

Nice to have someone with a little faith in her. They were few and far between. Madeline let her lashes fall, closing out the accusation on her mother's face. She could just imagine what Tick was thinking, standing behind her with the kitchen phone in hand, silently jotting down numbers from the caller ID.

Nine obscene phone calls. Madeline shuddered. Nine men calling her mother's home, detailing in graphic *Penthouse Letters* detail what they wanted to do to her. What they wanted her to do to them. Her mother thought she'd encouraged this, instigated this.

She seriously wanted to throw up.

"Miranda, let's go wash your face, and you can lie down for a while." Chairs scraped on the tile. Madeline opened her eyes and caught Lenora's gaze, about to remind her that anything that posed a threat had to be removed from the bedroom. Lenora smiled on a wink and wrapped an arm around Mama's shoulders. "Don't worry. I know what to do."

As they left and silence descended, Madeline folded her arms over her midriff, as tight as she could get them. The cold lump of emptiness was back in her gut. Behind her, Tick's pen scratched on paper, grating against her raw nerves.

"Madeline?" His quiet voice ground over those same exposed synapses. "You okay?"

"I'm good." Just peachy, actually, since he'd witnessed her mother's drunken fit in all its glory, had taken the phone after Madeline had answered one of the calls and heard every gory detail as Bob from Nebraska described how he wanted to fist her. Hell, he was probably pissed off with her too, since his precious saintly mother had answered the phone and been exposed to everything earlier.

At least Ash wasn't here to witness this. The man who wanted her to believe she merited good things in her life.

She closed her eyes. Good things. Right. She was never going to have those, never going to deserve those, not really. There would always be shit like this coming up, coming back to haunt her, and what decent guy wanted to deal with that?

The sooner she went back to Jacksonville, went *anywhere*, the better.

She sucked in a breath, sucked the pain down and locked it away. A couple more deep breaths and she was good. Back in control. Yes, this was better. Not caring, not feeling, complete and total focus on the job at hand.

The only way Allison could win was if she cared. If she didn't, then nothing the little bitch did mattered. She couldn't ruin a life Madeline didn't have.

"Well, she's resting." Lenora set the water carafe and tumbler from Mama's bedside table on the countertop, placed the little box that held her medication beside it. She crossed to stand by Madeline and rub a comforting hand over her shoulders. "This will be all right, Maddie. I promise."

A tight smile made her face hurt. "I'm fine. Really."

She didn't miss the sharp look Tick directed at her. She met his gaze head on. Hell if she'd back down.

"Autry's coming to pick your mother up." Lenora continued sweeping little circles over Madeline's back, comforting caresses that made her want to scream. "Miranda's going to stay with her and Stanton a couple of days."

A shudder passed down Madeline's spine. Because when Tick had pulled up the website on his phone, her mama's address had been there in full. Because who knew what man would show up at the door, thinking to fulfill the sick little fantasies posted with her name. God, her mama would *never* forgive her for this. Autry and Stanton's lives disrupted by this... Yeah, that was good. Bet Stanton was thrilled to have hired her on now, even temporarily.

Tick shot her another of those assessing glances. "We'll go by and get your stuff from Ash's on the way back to town."

She nodded. Even he saw it, that the best thing she could do was just...just...

Damn it, she would not cry. She wouldn't. Throwing her shoulders back, she pulled in a deep, cleansing breath.

"Cait and I can take the guest room on the second floor, and you can have our room." He snapped his notebook shut and tucked it in his inside pocket. "That way Lee won't wake you. He's not really sleeping through the night yet."

What was he talking about? "I'll check in to the motel."

His brows dipped in a frown. "There's no need, and I'd feel better if—"

"Are we finished here?" She ducked out from under Lenora's easy touch.

His frown deepened. "Yeah, but—"

"Let's go. I need a cigarette, and Mama won't let me smoke in here."

"Okay, just wait a second." He leaned down, tugged up his pants leg and pulled a gleaming .22 semiautomatic from an ankle holster. As she watched from the door, he checked the slide and chambered a round before engaging the safety and handing it to his mother. "Lock up behind us."

Outside, she slid a crumpled pack of stale cigarettes from her pocket and lifted one to her lips. She patted her jacket. Damn it, no lighter. With the foulest curse she could think of, she tossed it into her mother's neat flowerbed.

One more transgression.

She stalked to his truck and waited for him to unlock it. He glanced at her as she fastened her seatbelt. "Madeline—"

"I don't want to talk about it."

"But—"

"Fuck, Calvert, do you not understand plain English? I do not want to talk about it."

With a rough sigh, he fired the engine. Once on the highway, she ignored the looks he kept darting her way. With a deliberate movement, she turned away, staring out at the passing fields without seeing anything.

A buzzing filled the silence, and he tugged his cell free to lift it to his ear. "Calvert. What? I had it on silent. I haven't checked it yet. I'm not...what?"

The truck swerved, and Madeline braced a hand on the dash. Shit, he was going to get them killed. Although...

She squashed the thought, but it tried to squirm free, taunting, tantalizing with the promise of escape. Was this how Jack had felt that last day as he'd headed up those stairs?

"You're not serious. Yeah, listen, we're about five minutes away. We're on our way." He tossed his phone on the dash.

Madeline released the dash now that her life was no longer in imminent danger. "Tell me that's a lead on Kelly's case."

"No." Mouth a tight line, he looked sideways at her. "That was Ash. We're going by the hospital."

"Drop me at the station." She wasn't going anywhere near the place. She focused on the scenery again. "I want to start looking at that rental list."

"Madeline, I think you should come with me." He cleared his throat, and foreboding flooded her. Oh, shit damn fuck, why did she *know* what was coming? "Ash called home to check his voice mail this morning and—"

"And I'm getting calls over there."

"Yeah. He's hot about it and—"

"I'm sure he is." What man wanted to deal with that? God, Allison was clever. Madeline would give her that. Fast too.

Tick's gaze darted her way once more. "I'll call over and start the process to get us a warrant for any computer Allison has access to, as well as for the website itself too. They can tell us which ISP posted to them."

"Sounds great." As he slowed for the fork coming into town, she flicked a hand to the left, toward the sheriff's department. "I mean it. Drop me by the station."

"Madeline. Come on."

"No. I have work to do." Tension crept up her nape. She forced it back into its dark little hole with a couple of controlled breaths. "It's not necessary for both of us to take Ash's complaint. If we split up, we can make better progress."

He slammed the brake for a red light, muttering something that sounded like, "Just freakin' like her."

A couple of minutes later, he pulled into a parking spot near the department entrance. "I can't change your mind? He wants to see you."

God, here they went again. She gave him a doleful look. "No, you can't. There's no reason for me to go. Just...deal with it."

"Sure." He stared across the parking lot, thumb beating the steering wheel in a maddening rhythm. She shrugged. His displeasure was no concern of hers. He was nothing.

All of it was nothing.

She slid from the truck and slammed the door behind her. She had a job to do. Some way or another, she would prove Allison's involvement in Kelly's death.

This time, Allison would pay for what she'd done.

"I need you to go by and talk to her. I already thought of that, precious. I can't send Tori because she'll just freeze her out. She knows you, and I think she'd be more open to you." Tick's voice preceded him from the hallway. "Yes. Please. I want you to be careful. I pissed her off this morning and who the hell knows what she's capable of."

Ash's eyes snapped open as the door swung inward. He fumbled for the remote to lift the head of the bed. Tick, his expression tense and harried, returned his cell to his belt and pushed the door shut behind him.

He was alone. Ash frowned. "Where's Madeline?"

If anything, the line of Tick's mouth tightened. "At the sheriff's office."

"Why?" Even as he uttered the question, the answer rooted in his brain. Damn it, she was running again. Hiding, putting up those protective barriers. Except this time he wasn't in any shape to go after her, force her to face anything. He rested his head against the pillow with a slow, deliberate motion and glared at the ceiling. "Fuck."

"Yeah." Tick rolled his shoulders in a strained shrug. "She's shaken up and trying to play it off. I asked Cait to go talk to her."

The sweet way she'd smiled at him replayed in his head, and he swallowed a groan of frustration. This had undone every bit of progress he'd made with her. Hell, had probably set him back a few steps farther than where he'd begun. The level at which that scared him was frightening in itself.

How the hell did a woman become indispensable, the center of everything, in less than a week?

"Where's Rob?" Tick's quiet question pulled him back from the brink. Ash blinked at him.

"He and Vince went to run an errand." Ash rubbed a hand over his eyes. Shit, he had to figure out what to do next, where to start. Choking Allison Barnett with his bare hands was probably out of the question. His buddy, local law enforcement's version of Captain America, would have issues with that plan.

Tick nodded. "You might want to call the phone company, have your number changed."

"So are you doing anything about this?" Ash fixed him with a hard look. "You know who's responsible."

A grimace twisted Tick's face. "Knowing it and proving it are two different things. I've started the warrant process—"

"You owe me three grand." Vince's smooth words cut across Tick's drawl. He flicked a receipt onto Ash's bed. "Who needs a warrant?"

Tick's eyebrows lifted. "Any cop worth his salt."

"Good thing I'm not a cop, isn't it?" Vince's eyes gleamed. "Took Tony less than an hour to find the ISP and the computer she used to access the 'net."

"Great for Tony. Doesn't help me any." Tick held both hands aloft as Vince opened his mouth. "Don't tell me. You tell me and I can't use any of it, even when I get a warrant."

None of this was helping Ash. He closed his eyes, trying to tune them out. Damn it, he needed to be out of this bed. Needed to be...

Focusing on that wasn't helping, either. He couldn't change anything. At this point, all he could do was hope she'd come to him on her own. She'd done it before. Maybe he'd get lucky this time too.

Fat fucking chance.

He clenched his teeth before remembering that was a really bad idea.

Tick's cell phone rang with that stupid Gary Allan song he played over and over in the truck. The jangling guitar notes danced over Ash's raw nerves.

"Are you supposed to have that on in here?" Vince asked as Tick lifted it to his ear and ignored him.

"Calvert...what? What do you mean, not there?" Tick's dark gaze darted to Ash's. "I just dropped her at the office"—he twisted his arm to look at his watch—"less than a half hour ago. She didn't tell Lydia where she was going? Yeah, do that. Call me."

His expression troubled, he returned the phone to his belt. Ash eased up on the bed. "What?"

"That was Cait. Madeline's not at the department. Obviously, she walked out without telling anyone where she was going."

Well, of course not. People running from the hard stuff never did.

Chapter Nineteen

Why was she here? Hunched against the cold, Madeline folded her arms and crunched up the gravel path. Good question. First had been the call from Autry, her sister's voice shaking with concern while she asked if Madeline was all right. Then, when Madeline had finally gotten her off the phone, her cell had rung again. She'd answered it without thought, only to have yet another male voice fill her ear, taunting her with all the down-and-dirty things he wanted to do with her.

She'd turned it off, tossed it in her drawer and walked out of the sheriff's department, not even telling Lydia where she was going. It was her day off, technically—she didn't have to answer to anyone.

Somehow, she'd found herself at Ash's and used the key he'd given her. Inside, his warm, clean scent seemed to permeate the air. She'd ignored it, ignored the memories, gathered her things, all of them.

While she'd been shoving her T-shirts back in her bag, the phone had rung. The answering machine picked up. The owner of that male voice, John from wherever, wanted to fuck her up the ass. She'd closed the door on his words, leaving the key on the hall table.

Now, she was here. Dead brown grass crinkled beneath her steps. She pulled a cigarette from the crumpled pack and lifted the lighter she'd rummaged from under her passenger seat. Resting her elbow on one folded arm, she took a long drag and blew out a stream of smoke.

It curled and dissipated above her daddy's tombstone.

"Guess you were right all along, weren't you, Daddy?" The loudness of her own voice in the silent cemetery startled her. She scuffed a toe along the marble slab covering his grave. "What was it you said...a disgrace? Not fit to carry the Holton name."

A rough laugh hurt her throat, and she sucked in another lungful of smoke to cover the sting. "Mama's right. It's a good thing you're dead. If you were here for this one...it would definitely kill you."

The wind rustled the few dead leaves still clinging to the oak limbs above her.

She glared at her father's name cut into the sparkling gray marble. "Well, you won, you old bastard. You were right all along. You told me if I left, I couldn't come back. I didn't get it back then, but believe me, I do now. There's no place for me here. Like there ever was."

Expelling another stream of smoke, she kicked at the slab once more and blinked hard. "Why, Daddy? What did you want from me? Why did it always have to be so hard? It never mattered what I did, if I tried or didn't try, nothing pleased you. Why couldn't you just love me for who I was?"

Angry at herself for even caring anymore, she flicked the butt to her feet and ground it out. Shit damn fuck. She was talking to a dead man, like he was going to give her answers from beyond the grave.

God, she hadn't even made it through a week here, let alone six.

Maybe she should just return to Jacksonville. Even if the PD didn't want her, even if they never cleared her, there were other jobs. That's all she needed anyway…something to pay the damn bills. She didn't have to stay here. Kelly's case would get solved. Calvert would see to that.

Quiet footsteps sounded behind her on the gravel, a light and graceful gait. Madeline closed her eyes. Did she even have to look?

"May I join you?" Caitlin stopped beside her.

Madeline waved in a silent it's-a-free-country gesture.

The wind whipped up around them. With a shiver, Caitlin tucked her hands in the back pockets of her jeans. "What, no 'how did you find me?'"

"You're a Fed." Madeline shrugged. "Tracking people is your job."

Caitlin nodded toward the gravestone. "Did you find what you were looking for?"

Madeline slanted a glare in her direction. "No."

"Me either."

That was Madeline's cue to ask what she was talking about, to play the "look how much we have in common" game. She was so tired of games it wasn't even funny.

"Have you eaten today?"

God. Madeline blew out a long breath. "No."

"It's cold out here." Caitlin rubbed at her arms. "Come on and let's go get some tea—"

"We're not friends." Madeline turned on her, tension buzzing up her neck, her face burning. "I'm not going to have tea with you and confide all my problems to you so you can find a way to make it all better. Got that? So just go away, back to your perfect little life and leave me the fuck alone."

"That's good." Caitlin arched one eyebrow. "Works every time, doesn't it?"

"Obviously not."

"Is that it? Are you just going to let him win?"

Him? Madeline glanced at her and scowled. "Don't you mean 'her'?"

"No." Caitlin shivered, rubbing her arms again. The wind played with the edges of her hair, brushing her face with a few stray strands. "Allison is the type to do herself in. Plus Tick's pissed off, so she doesn't really stand a chance. He's a bloodhound when he gets like this." Caitlin jerked her chin toward the headstone. "I mean him. Are you going to let him win?"

Cold fury washed through her, a slide and fall of ice that froze everything. "You don't know what you're talking about. You know nothing about my relationship with my father."

"True." Caitlin stamped her feet, an obvious attempt at keeping warm. "But don't you think it's telling that you're here of all places?"

Madeline closed her eyes. If she ignored the Fed, maybe she'd go away.

"*My* father screwed up my head so badly, it's a wonder I ever had any type of relationship with a man," Caitlin said, her tone so conversational she might have been commenting on the antique wrought iron surrounding the Holton family plot. "My mother died when I was six, and he promptly sent me to boarding school. Whenever I came home, the story was always different. One time he'd love me and be glad to see me, the next he barely spoke to me. I was perfect, then I was nothing. Over and over and over again, until I spent more time trying to figure out how to make him love me than I did on anything else. It didn't stop when he died, either. By then, I'd just expanded my repertoire, trying to be what everyone wanted me to be, their idea of perfect, because that's what made people love you."

"Looks like everything turned out okay." Madeline flipped her hair over one shoulder.

"Oh, yes. After I threw away everything that mattered because I couldn't believe in it, couldn't believe it might be real." Her soft laugh bubbled between them, a note of sadness in it. "Thank God Tick's as stubborn as he is."

"Is there a point to this?"

"Why are you out here?"

"I don't know." Madeline made a dismissive gesture. "Because there was...because..."

"Because you think there's nowhere else to go." Caitlin's gaze remained steady on hers. "Except maybe Jacksonville, right? As soon as you can hit the road."

Shaking her head, Madeline looked away.

"You can only hide so long, Madeline." Caitlin's voice gentled. "Sooner or later, you have to let go and let yourself believe."

Madeline lifted both hands and let them fall to smack her thighs. "Believe what, Caitlin? Tell me that. What the fuck am I supposed to let myself believe?"

"That someone can accept you as you are. That he can love you and it won't matter what happens because it's not about how perfect or imperfect you are. Because it's about you and him and what lies between you." She smiled, although her eyes remained serious. "That the whole world could fall down and he'd still be there. Because he's not your father and you don't have to prove anything to him."

"You don't—"

"Know what I'm talking about." She sighed. "Yes, I know. I'm wasting my breath because you can't see what's right in front of you. You're going to walk away, no, *run* away. You're going right back to the person you were the last time you ran because it's safe and it's easy and you don't have to risk yourself. In the process, you'll hurt yourself. And Ash. But you'll tell yourself he's better off and that he'll forget. Except he won't and neither will you. But that's what you're going to do, so why I'm even trying is beyond me."

"You're so wrong." Madeline shoved her hands in her pockets, to warm them, not to hide the trembling. Bad enough her voice was shaking. "If I leave, it's because...because..."

"Yes?"

"God, I *hate* you."

"Yes, well, it wouldn't be the first time I've heard that." Caitlin caught her gaze and held it. "We both know what you're throwing away if you go. What have you got to lose if you stay?"

With a hard swallow, Madeline stared at her.

"Madeline. If you leave, it's done. It's over. You've lost. Now answer me. What have you got to lose if you stay?"

"Everything." The whisper hurt. "Damn you, if I stay, I could lose everything."

"But isn't it worth fighting for? You're not even trying, though. You're just tossing it away, like it's nothing. Like he's nothing."

"I've known him six days. You talk about this like it's a done deal, forever and always and a fucking wedding ring."

Caitlin's lashes fell and she shook her head on a soft laugh that grated on Madeline's last nerve.

"What is so damn funny?"

"Six days, huh? I'd known Tick three. We were at Quantico. I'd shown him up twice during training, and he'd been so easygoing about it. On the third night, we were all studying for some horrifically important test. He was explaining something to me and looked up with that grin, and I just *knew*. God, he scared the hell out of me. The more I got to know him, the worse the fear was. Because I wanted to believe in him and I just couldn't." Something wistful colored her voice. "I fought it. That worked for about, oh, nine years. We wasted a lot of time, and I hurt him terribly before it was all over."

"That's all fine and dandy, but—"

"You can drop the world-weary persona." That knowing little smile, the one Madeline despised, curved Caitlin's lips again. "It really doesn't work with me."

In her pockets, Madeline curled her fingers inward, until they bit at her palms. "Why are you doing this?"

"I like you and adore Ash, and anyone with minimal insight can see the potential between the two of you." She flicked a glance at the headstone. "Maybe because you got the same raw deal I got when it came to father-daughter relationships. Maybe because at this point, you're even more unhappy than I was without Tick, and no one should have to go through that. I at least had my friends, my grandfather and even Vince to turn to. The way I see it right now, you have no one. Is that what you want for the rest of your life? I'm not saying you have to open up to Ash and make something out of what you two have been building. But you've got to open up to someone. You can only do this by yourself for so long."

Yeah, and "so long" seemed rapidly to be running out. God, she was tired. Tired of running, tired of holding herself away.

Madeline shot a hard look at her. "What did you mean, you hadn't found what you were looking for, *either*? Looks like you have everything you ever wanted."

"I never got the answers I wanted from my father. The whys of it all. I figured out later, thanks to a doctoral degree in psychology and well, being with Tick, that the whys really didn't have anything to do with me. They were all about him, and there wasn't anything I could have done to change him, to make him want me or love me the way I needed him to." This time her smile was more genuine. She dared to nudge Madeline's ribs with her elbow. "How do you think I knew where to look for you? Now how about that hot tea? I am freezing my ass off out here."

"No thanks. Maybe another time." What she was about to say made her want to throw up, the fear rising to choke her. "I need to go have a conversation with a man who can actually hear me."

The room lay quiet around him. If only his mind could be still as well. Everyone was gone—Tick off running down leads, Rob and Vince on their way to Texas. The silence and his immobility offered too much time to think, to wonder if she'd go for good.

He'd bet money on it.

Because anyone knew an injured animal ran for cover. He was aware of no other sanctuary Chandler County held for her, other than him. If she hadn't come to him, then he'd bet his next share of Henry's quarterly profits she'd go.

He closed his eyes and let the drugged half-sleep take him. As the day wore on, weariness and anxiety had lessened his ability to deal with the waves of pain radiating out from his knee, and finally he'd succumbed to the need to simply make it *stop*.

For long minutes he floated in and out on swells of slumber. Footsteps pulled him from the restless sleep. He lifted heavy lids to find Madeline gazing down at him with a hesitant expression. Was she real? Or a longed-for figment of his drugged imagination? Painkillers fuzzed his brain, and he tried to formulate words.

"I'm sorry," she whispered, fingers wrapped tight around the bed rail. "That you had to deal with this, to hear everything."

He laid his hand over hers and found warm skin under his fingers. She was real, thank God. "Did you ask her to put your name and information out there?"

"No." Her expression horrified, she shook her head. "Of course not."

"All right then." He blinked rapidly, to clear the drowsiness still pulling at him. "It's not your fault."

"Try telling my mother that." The wry mutter most likely wasn't meant for his ears. Her fingers fluttered beneath his. "You shouldn't have to deal with this. No man—"

"Mad, it's the same as your being with me after I got hurt. You help one another through the tough stuff."

"I'm not...I don't know how to believe in that, Ash."

Fighting off a wave of drowsiness, he let his gaze linger on her face. Awful tension dragged at her features and dulled hazel eyes. She looked like if she didn't rest soon, she'd fall out.

He tightened his hold on her fingers. "Know what I need?"

"What?"

"To hold you a little while."

"Really. You need to be resting." One corner of her mouth hitched in a half-hearted smile. Her gaze dropped to his knee. "Besides you're not supposed to be moving."

He patted the other side of the bed. "I'm not moving the knee, there's plenty of room and I need to be close to you. You look like you might need that too."

She was quiet a moment, then slid her hand from beneath his. As he watched, she came around to the other side of the bed and lowered the rail. He lifted his arm, giving her room to lie beside him. With ginger movements designed not to jostle him, she settled next to him and he wrapped his arm about her shoulders. She rested on his chest, one hand beneath her cheek.

"Hmm, feels good." He brushed a kiss over her hair. "I've missed you."

"I just saw you this morning," she murmured.

His lids fell, a combination of medication and weariness pulling at him. "It's been a long day."

"You're telling me."

He smoothed his hand up and down her arm in a slow, soothing sweep. Warmth from her body seeped into him. Slowly, the tension drained from her, and he sensed her slide into relaxation.

"Why don't you take a nap?" he whispered.

"I don't want to waste this time with you."

The lost note in her voice tore at him. She thought their time was limited, and why not? Obviously, everyone else's love came with limitations and expectations. Had she never had anyone care for her completely, without reserve?

And wait a minute...he wasn't really think in terms of love. Friendship, desire, caring...sure. But love? He wasn't thinking that.

Except he was. He opened his eyes, to find hers closed, lashes casting half-moon shadows on her cheek. He watched her, letting the realization make its way through him.

He could love her. Falling the rest of the way would be so easy.

Winning her mistrustful heart in return? That would be hard as hell.

He brushed another kiss over her hair. She relaxed further against him, lips parting, even breaths puffing warmth against his skin through the thin hospital gown. He tightened his arm, bringing her closer to him. She murmured once and stilled.

He closed his eyes, sleep pulling at him. For now, he was content to live in this moment.

Tick flipped to the next page of his printouts. In the kitchen behind him, Caitlin hummed a soft song, some Irish ditty she'd picked up long ago from her grandmother. Resting against his stomach, Lee gurgled around his pacifier and jiggled a foot, just brushing the papers Tick held. The warm, slight weight of his son tempered the frustration of not finding a single, freakin' lead anywhere.

Half the people on the rental list didn't even live in the state anymore, hadn't come from Chandler County to start with. If there was a link between Allison and this house, he didn't see it.

No. He narrowed his eyes at the list of background information on tenant number four. There was a link, he simply hadn't found it yet.

With a muffled coo, Lee kicked harder, rustling the papers. Tick folded his hand over the baby's middle. "What are you doing, boy?"

"Aggravating you, obviously." Caitlin closed the dishwasher and set it running. "Want me to take him?"

"He's fine." He moved the page out of reach of the wriggling little foot. Caitlin perched on the chair arm, rubbing her fingers down his nape. He gave an appreciative groan at the relaxing rhythm. With a quiet laugh, she nudged him forward to a straighter position offering her greater access to his shoulders. He shifted Lee on his lap and let his lids slide shut for a moment.

"Lord, you have the best hands." He rotated his head, working the muscles beneath her massaging fingers. "I think I'll keep you."

"Did you know no autopsy was performed on Allison's first husband?"

He made a negative sound in his throat.

"Don't you think that's odd? A healthy twenty-one-year-old dies of a sudden heart attack and there's no autopsy?"

"Was it a holiday weekend?"

"Yes." Her lips rested against his nape, sending shivers over him. "Labor Day."

"Figures." He opened his eyes. The background checks stared back with inexorable frustration. What if they couldn't make this case? The thought of Kelly Coker dying alone, being left to rot beneath that house, and never receiving justice for what had been done to her didn't sit well.

His reason insisted that there might be other explanations, that Allison might not be involved at all.

His instinct said otherwise.

The woman had keyed his truck over a minor slight. And what she'd done to Madeline, because she blamed her? Hell, if she possessed a molecule of human decency, he sure didn't see it.

"Nobody questioned the lack of an autopsy?" he asked, scanning the next renter's background information. Young marine, honorably discharged, who'd lived in the house for all of three months. He'd moved out before they thought Kelly returned to Georgia.

"Not that I could tell. Everything looked like it was an open-shut case. It was a small hospital, an even smaller town with a two-man police department."

"What town?"

"Cressley."

"Oh hell." He grimaced. "They've had the same chief for almost thirty years. He can't find his ass with both hands."

"I'd bet you it was antifreeze." Caitlin murmured the words against his hair. Lee's jiggling slowed, his little body relaxing under Tick's hand. "That would present as a heart attack and unless they ran the right tox screen, which they didn't..."

"Yeah, but I'm not sure you could get the Cressley PD to open an investigation into a death that was declared due to natural causes almost twenty years ago."

"Hmm." She rubbed her cheek on his hair. "I'm sure the insurance company that paid out on his policy would be interested."

"You have an evil mind, Agent Falconetti."

"Oh, and you love it, Investigator Calvert." She moved, easing up to bend over them. "He's asleep."

He lifted his palm so she could slide her hands under the baby and pick him up. She cradled their sleeping son under her chin, whispering her lips across his dark hair as she carried him upstairs to bed. Thankfulness slammed into Tick once more. He had everything, despite how close he'd come to losing it all, more than once, it seemed.

Hell, if he'd ended up married to Allison, he might be dead now. The certainty that she'd had something to do with Kelly's death coursed through his thoughts again.

The memory of Madeline's lost, defeated withdrawal rose, swirling with the questions and frustrations. She deserved justice as much as Kelly. He owed her that, for the part he'd played in stunting her life. Leaning forward, he rested his elbows on his knees, eyes closed on a prayer. He needed guidance. Needed a way to forgive himself for what he couldn't change.

Soft footsteps sounded on the stairs. On a long inhale, he opened his eyes and reached for his papers. There was an answer here. He just had to find it.

Barefoot, Caitlin padded across the room to pick up Lee's floor-time toys and drop them into their basket. "Finding anything?"

"No." He flipped to the next background check. "Just a bunch of really normal people."

"There's no such thing." A hint of laughter colored her voice.

"Well, these people are as close as it gets." He turned past the brief traffic record of the kindergarten teacher who'd lived in the house for two months after the marine moved out.

The phone rang, and he jumped. Caitlin reached for the cordless, lying on the coffee table.

"No." He leaned forward to snag the phone, the memory of Madeline's calls rising in his mind. He'd pissed Allison off as well, and at this point, he wouldn't put anything past her. "Let me answer it."

He punched the phone on and lifted it to his ear. "Hello?"

"Calvert, how the hell are you?" Agent Harrell Beecham's familiar voice filled his ear, and he relaxed.

"Hey, Beech." He tossed his feet up on the ottoman. Caitlin caught his eye and smiled. Beecham had been at Quantico with them, and over the years, both of them had worked FBI cases with him, Tick more so because he and Beecham had both been with the Bureau's Organized Crime Division. "What's up?"

"That's what I'm calling to ask you." On Beecham's end of the connection, paper rustled. "Want to tell me why you're running a background check on Nick Hall?"

"Nick Hall?" Tick flipped rapidly through the papers before him. If he'd triggered the OCD by checking up on the guy, he didn't qualify as normal.

"Yeah, Nick Hall."

"Am I stepping on the Bureau's toes?" Here it was—Nicholas Randall Hall. He'd been living in the house on Miller Court between August and November...and Kelly had left Florida, they believed, in September. Hot damn, this was it, he could feel it.

"Not stepping on our toes, per se. Let's just say we'd like to know what your interest is."

"Why don't you tell me what you know about Mr. Hall?" Tick skimmed the information he had. Couple of speeding tickets, arrest for drunk and disorderly, another for writing a bad check. What did the FBI want with this guy?

"Calvert."

Tick crossed one ankle over the other. "He might be connected to an old murder down here. What have you got?"

"Now, not much. The boy's gone and found religion, turned his life around." Cynicism lurked in Beecham's normally dry tone. "He's been clean for at least six months."

"Wow. Six whole months."

"Yeah. Imagine that."

"So why's the OCD interested in him?"

"Well, his brother *hasn't* found religion yet. He's still following the tenets of the Southern Brotherhood, even though Nicky left months ago. We're keeping tabs on Nicky, hoping it will give us some insight into Jake's activities."

The Southern Brotherhood. Holy hell. Sheer excitement sizzled through him. "Beech, you just made my damn *year*."

"Glad to help. Listen, anything you find on Nick, I want to know first, okay, man? Interdepartmental sharing and all that bullshit."

"Bullshit is right." A grin quirked at his mouth. If he could make this link, if it played out like he thought it would, Allison was on her way down. Hell, Madeline deserved to be the one slapping the cuffs on her. He'd make sure she got that chance. "Only reason you're calling me is because you think I might have something. Gotta go, Beech."

"Calvert, wait—"

He killed the connection and dropped the phone, flipping for the next page. There had to be a current address here. Had to be.

Caitlin laughed. "Did you just hang up on him?"

"Um, yeah." Shit, where was page six?

"Are you going to share what has you so wound up?"

"This guy...the one who lived in the house during the time we think Kelly came back from Florida." Damn it, he had page five, page seven...what had he done with page *six*? Ah, hell. Either it hadn't printed or he'd missed it somehow, and it was still on his desk. How bad would Caitlin bitch him out if he went back to the office?

"Yes?" Indulgent affection colored the syllable. Probably not too much bitching.

"He was in the Southern Brotherhood." He grabbed his shoes by the chair and tugged them on.

"Really." Intrigue flared in Caitlin's eyes. She perched on the edge of the coffee table. "Just like Allison's second husband."

"Right." He shuffled the papers he had back into their file.

Caitlin frowned. "Where are you going?"

"Left the paper I need at the office." On his feet, he leaned over and kissed her. "I want to go by the hospital, show this to Madeline."

"How do you know she's there?"

"Because." He couldn't resist leaning in for one more kiss. "You said you thought that's where she headed. You're hardly ever wrong about people, and I know Ash—once he got her there, he'd do everything in his power to keep her."

Chapter Twenty

Madeline drifted into awareness. Her arm, twisted beneath her, buzzed with sleeping nerves, and her neck protested its angle, sending twinges of discomfort down her nape. However, warmth pressed along her front, strong fingers cupped her rib cage and unaccustomed security wrapped around her. Her lashes fluttered up, and she lifted her head, the discomfort flaring into real pain. God, her neck hurt.

Quiet voices echoed in the still hallway beyond the door. Light from the security lamps in the parking lot cast a bluish glow in the room. She raised her arm, peering at her watch. Almost nine. Hell, the nurses had to have been in here at least five times in the last few hours. Had she slept through all that? Her cheeks burned with embarrassment. What would they think of her, sleeping in Ash's hospital bed?

"I made them leave you alone," he murmured, eyes closed. "You needed the rest."

She hadn't spoken aloud, so how did he...? She propped up on her elbow, awakening nerves sending tingles up and down her skin. "How did you—"

"I've figured out how you think." Humor lurked beneath the pain and drugs slurring his voice. "Then you were worrying about what they would think, which really doesn't matter a damn. Next up is the whole 'I scare the hell out of you' thing again."

"You do," she said, her voice shaky. Actually, not so much him— but how he made her feel, like being drawn to the edge of a canyon, wanting to capture its wonders, yet being afraid of falling over the precipice at the same time.

He opened his eyes, the pale green depths dark with quiet emotion. "I don't want you to be afraid of me, ever. I wouldn't hurt you, Mad."

For a long moment, she stared into those eyes then slowly lowered her head to close the gap between them. She kissed him, his mouth warm and supple beneath hers. Making a low sound in his throat, he speared his left hand into her hair, deepening a kiss that was at once both hungry and tender.

He moved his hand, cradling her face, easing back to whisper his lips over her eyelids, one cheekbone, the corner of her mouth. Soft feathery kisses that made her chest hurt. Tears stung her eyes.

"Everything is so damn good with you," she murmured.

"If you say you don't deserve it"—he gripped her chin in a gentle hand and made her meet his gaze—"hell, if you even think it, I swear to God I'll spank you."

A tremulous smile shaped her mouth. "Is that a promise?"

His eyes flared, and a deep chuckle rumbled between them, at least until he cut it short, a hand over his chest. "Shit, babe, don't make me laugh. It hurts."

She touched her fingers to his jaw. "I'm sorry."

"Don't be." He turned his head to brush a kiss over her palm. The sense of rightness settled over her again, and she pressed her eyes closed. Walking away from him would be incredibly hard, but she had to go. She couldn't stay here, not here.

Could she?

His arm tightened about her, pulling her against him for a moment. He rested his mouth against her brow, and a shuddery breath moved through his strong frame.

"Mad," he whispered, warm breath shivering over her skin, "I love you."

She froze, her ability to breathe gone, just like that. He had not just said those words. She jerked back, her eyes snapping open.

He waited, watching her with a resigned expression. The hopelessness in his gaze made her want to cry. She would have, if the fear hadn't iced over everything within her.

"Ash, don't say that. Don't go there. Not with me. Please."

His mouth drew into a tight line, and he looked away. His silence only made the ice inside her that much worse.

She shook her head. "You don't understand. I'm not...I can't...I told you from the beginning, I'm not in the—"

"Don't give me that bullshit." A subdued anger trembled in his voice, although she felt the emotion was directed as much at himself as at her. "Just don't. I shouldn't have said anything. It was...I just shouldn't have."

He rubbed a hand down his face, and everything inside her seemed to fold in on itself. The sweetness and warmth and rightness evaporated, dissipating like dew under the onslaught of a summer sun. She shivered. The loss of those pure emotions left her empty and wanting them back.

But not enough to pretend to be something she wasn't. Easing away from him, she shifted to sit on the edge of the bed. She darted a quick look at the door and rubbed her hands down her arms. Old instincts tried to urge her toward the door, telling her to run.

Something new and quiet bade her stay, even with the tension thick and heavy in the room. She feathered a hand through her hair. "I don't know what to say."

He watched her, the bleakness gone from his eyes, replaced with a gleam of hope. "You don't have to say anything. The fact you're not already out the door is enough for now."

"You're so easy to please." She tried to laugh at her own dismal joke and failed.

"Not really." He didn't smile. "But the first thing I learned in military school was that each victory in a small battle is one step toward winning the whole damn war."

"Battle? Are you trying to conquer me?"

He didn't respond to her tiny attempt at wry humor. "Not you. That fear you wear like a Kevlar vest. I want you to live, Madeline, whether it's with me or not. You—"

"Deserve that?" A shaky smile hitched at the corner of her mouth.

"Yes. You do." Brows lowered, he watched her. "Don't let what I said...the way I feel about you...don't let that come between us, Madeline. I'm not rushing you, not expecting anything in return right how. I just want you."

Her eyes burned, a wash of tears casting the room in a shimmering haze. No one had ever wanted just her. Her body, yes. Her? No one.

He jerked his chin in a come-hither gesture. "Get over here."

Her breath caught. She hadn't lost him because of her extreme reaction to his declaration, because she couldn't return it yet. She turned into his embrace, resting her head carefully against his chest, the steady beat of his pulse under her ear spreading peace and warmth through her.

"I shouldn't have said it yet. It's way too soon for you to hear that from me," he murmured, sifting his fingers through her hair. "But I'm glad I did."

So was she. Even as much as they frightened her, she could cherish the words, cherish the man who'd given them to her so freely. She smoothed her fingers over his chest, the thin hospital gown slightly rough under her touch.

"So am I," she whispered.

Footsteps, with a familiar cadence, sounded in the hallway. She frowned, and Ash's fingers stilled in her hair.

"That's Tick," he said, just moments before a rap came at the door and it swung inward. Madeline jerked to sit on the mattress edge and swiped at her eyes, her back to him.

"Hey. Sorry to interrupt." A hint of sheepishness colored Tick's voice but didn't quite disguise the notes of excitement and adrenaline. Certainty speared through her. He had a lead. She rubbed at her damp eyes again and turned sideways to face him. Sure enough, he slapped a rolled up paper against his palm, the thrill of the chase gleaming in his dark gaze. "Madeline, can I talk to you a minute?"

With a nod, she laid her palm on Ash's stomach. His pulse beat there too, strong and sure, beneath her hand. "I'll be right back."

Uncaring of Tick's presence, she leaned down to brush her mouth over Ash's and caught the flare of what that meant to him in his eyes before she slid from the bed. She pointed toward the hallway. "Let's go to the waiting area."

Outside, she slanted a curious look at Tick. God, he practically vibrated with energy. "What's going on?"

He grinned. "I think I can tie Allison to the house."

A glimmer of his excitement flared in her. "Really?"

"Yeah. How do you feel about riding over to Moultrie?"

"Now?" She took a quick look at her watch.

"Well, tomorrow morning." A guilty grin curved his mouth but did little to diminish the glow in his dark eyes. "I think if I tried to take off tonight, Cait would have a fit. I told her I'd only be gone a half hour or so."

"So why are we going to Moultrie?"

She listened as he explained how their background checks on the former tenants of the Miller Court house had triggered a call from an old buddy with the FBI. "Anyway, this guy was a member of the Southern Brotherhood motorcycle club. Coincidentally enough, so was Allison's second husband."

"I don't believe in coincidences, Calvert."

"Yeah." He grinned again. "Me, neither. Listen, as soon as that warrant clears for Allison's computer, Cookie'll be all over it."

"Sure." She tousled hair that had to be a mess already. "Thanks."

He tilted his head toward the hallway. "I'm going to take off. Good night."

"Good night," she echoed. Once he was gone, she slipped back into Ash's room. He slept, lingering pain still dragging at his features. She curled into the stiff armchair, her gaze on his face. Arms tucked around her updrawn knees, she rested her head against the chair back. Going to her mother's for the night was out of the question, and she couldn't go to Ash's either. No sense in checking into a hotel.

Besides, he was here, and that made this the only place she really wanted to be.

The neat neighborhood made up of late-model mobile homes and landscaped yards lay far out in the country, closer to Adel than Moultrie. Tall woods rose on either side of the highway, the area familiar to Madeline from her childhood when her grandpa had taken her to Reed Bingham State Park for fishing expeditions. Tiny remnants of grief pinched at her heart. She'd been happy then, even at home, in the days before Mama's moods grew more and more unpredictable after Madeline's brother had been born.

She rubbed a thumb over the door handle, gazing out at pines and scrub oaks while Tick drove. Were there other good memories, times with her father and mother, that she'd buried away under the pain of separation and loss? If so, they were so far beneath the bad memories she couldn't find them any longer.

But the minutes and hours spent with her Grandpa Holton remained clear and strong in her head. She could almost feel what it had been like to be wrapped in one of his bear hugs, whiskers scratching her cheek, Old Spice and peach snuff surrounding her, while her entire being was blanketed by the assurance that she was loved, treasured.

Valued. Accepted. Wanted.

The way Ash made her feel. She scraped a fingernail across her lips. He said he loved her. God, she believed him.

That made her happy on a level that scared the cold living shit out of her.

What was she going to do about him?

"Do about who?" Tick's soft laugh pulled her from the reverie, and she stared at him. Shit damn fuck, had she said that *aloud*? He slanted an amused look in her direction. "You were mumbling."

She folded her arms. "I was thinking."

He was quiet a long moment. "So what are you going to do?"

Her gaze flew to his face. How did he...?

"I mean, are you still planning to go back to Jacksonville?"

She finally caught her breath and snapped her mouth closed. "I-I don't know. It's moot right now, anyway. They haven't cleared up Jack's...the shooting."

"I owe you an apology." He cleared his throat, a raw sound. "I was really hard on you about that when you came, and I shouldn't have been running my mouth."

That floored her about as much as Ash's declaration of love. She stared at him. Having him apologize would have been like having her daddy admit he'd been wrong—something she'd never expect to hear.

She swallowed. "Thank you."

He flashed a quick grin and swung into a right-hand turn, taking them into Nick Hall's neighborhood. "How was Ash this morning?"

"Good." She ran her thumbnail along the seam of her tweed slacks, remembering the sweet sleepy smile he'd graced her with when she leaned down to kiss him goodbye. "The swelling's down enough they can make the repair to his knee, according to Dr. Mackey. It's not supposed to be a major procedure."

Tick shook his head, squinting at numbers on mailboxes. "It's not. One of our deputies had it done last year after he twisted his knee during training. They did his as an outpatient procedure, and he was only off duty for two or three weeks afterward."

She nodded, the minor worry still twisting through her. Maybe she should have stayed with him, but he'd assured her he'd be fine. Besides, it wasn't like she was his wife or they had a real commitment between them anyway.

But he'd said he loved her. All of it kept tumbling through her head, including Tick's question about her intentions regarding Jacksonville. What would she do, if or when they called her back to duty?

Tick braked. "This is it."

Madeline looked across the wide yard at the white doublewide. A neat porch had been added on the front, providing a welcoming haven with wicker furniture and winter-hardy plants.

Tick pulled to a stop behind a beige Ford SUV. "Ready?"

To find out what had happened to Kelly, to give her justice? More than ready. "Let's go."

She strode with him up the stepping-stone walkway. The screen door squeaked as Tick pulled it open. Madeline reached forward to knock at the glass-paneled door. Moments later, a lean bald man appeared and swung the door open.

"Nick Hall?" Tick asked.

"Yes." The man frowned. "Can I help you?"

Tick held his credentials aloft. "Investigator Calvert, Chandler County Sheriff's Department. This is Investigator Holton."

Knowledge and recognition flared in Nick Hall's eyes. He knew. Madeline watched him, the way his slight body tensed before his shoulders fell. Intuitive realization trailed through her. This was the person who'd murdered Kelly.

Or he knew who had.

The knowledge flashed through her mind in mere seconds.

"We'd like to ask you a few questions," Tick said in a quiet voice.

Hall nodded. "I know why you're here."

Madeline sensed the jolt of surprise that ran through Tick's tall frame. She could relate. She'd never had a possible suspect come out with something like that.

"Why are we here, Mr. Hall?" Madeline asked.

"You're here because of the girl." Hall seemed to fold in on himself. "The one under the house."

Madeline lifted her eyebrows at Tick. His mouth tight, Tick held up a hand. "Please don't say anything else, Mr. Hall. I would like for you to come back to Chandler County with us to answer a few questions and possibly give us a statement, but first I need to apprise you of your rights."

Hall nodded, listening in silence while Tick rattled off the Miranda warning. Hall's expression of quiet acceptance never altered. Confusion twisted Madeline's brow into a frown. In her experience—and she'd had plenty—suspects didn't do this.

"Do you understand each of these rights as I've explained them to you?"

Hall's chin moved in a short nod and his Adam's apple bobbed in a hard swallow. "Yes."

"Bearing these rights in mind, would you like to talk to us now?"

Hall nodded once more, and this time, before his lashes fell, Madeline caught the glitter of tears in his blue eyes. "Yes, I want to talk to you." He pointed over his shoulder. "Should I get my keys or do I have to ride with you?"

"You're not under arrest," Madeline said. She met Tick's shuttered gaze, and he nodded. "You can drive if you like, and we'll follow."

Within minutes they were on the highway again. Tick's attention locked on Hall's SUV before them, traveling at a moderate speed. "Madeline, have you ever...?"

"No. Never."

"Me, either." He dragged a hand through his hair, the dark

strands falling on his forehead in disarray. He really needed a haircut. "It's too easy."

"He didn't mention a lawyer." Madeline brought up the point that niggled most with her. The guilty ones always screamed for a lawyer first. It was the ones who believed themselves innocent who often did not.

Back at the sheriff's department, they escorted Nick Hall inside. In the squad room, on their way to the small interview room, Tick paused. "What the hell?"

"Son of a bitch! You fucking asshole!"

Madeline frowned toward the stairs. A woman's voice screaming obscenities trailed up from the jail level.

A familiar female voice. Madeline caught Tick's eye. "That's—"

"Yeah." As Cookie's voice joined Allison's incensed screaming, a grin hitched up one corner of Tick's mouth. "That's from the booking area. Guess that warrant came through, and he turned up enough for an arrest. This way, Mr. Hall."

In the small room, Madeline reviewed the Miranda warning with Hall again and procured his signature on the release while Tick set up the video camera to record the interview. Madeline waited, impatience trembling through her. Finally, Tick settled into the chair farthest from the table and jerked his chin at her, tacit permission for her to take the lead in the small gesture.

She folded her hands on the table. "Mr. Hall, tell us about the girl under the house."

He buried his face in his hands, a rough sound—almost a sob— shaking his body. "I tried to forget about her. I knew this would happen some day, but I tried to forget. In the last few months, since I came to the Lord, I knew I should come forward, tell someone, but I was afraid."

"We're all afraid at times," Tick said in a soft, almost expressionless voice. "Were you afraid of someone? Was there someone else involved?"

"No. No." Shaking his head, Hall lowered his hands. "Just me. I did it."

Madeline caught Tick's eye again, read her own surprise reflected in his dark gaze. Just him? Had they been wrong?

She leaned forward. "Tell us what happened, please."

"I'd been at a party—"

"One second, please." Tick grimaced and scratched a note on his pad. "What month was this?"

"September. After Labor Day." Hall rubbed a hand over his eyes.

"I'd been at this party and I met this girl. Shoot, I never even knew her name. She'd been drinking or something, like she was high or something, right? Stumbling, slurring her words. I wasn't sober, neither. She was real cute and I thought... Well, she didn't fuss any when I kissed her. She even went to the car with me, and I took her home, back to my place."

"The house on Miller Court," Tick clarified.

"Yeah. That one." Hall paused, staring down at his hands splayed on the tabletop. "We came in the back door, into the kitchen. Once we were inside, we, um, I started to touch her. I thought she was into it, you know? Except then she starts crying, and she's trying to push me back. I grabbed her, shoved her into the counter and cussed at her for playing hard to get. I was a different person back then, you know?"

Tick scratched another note and flicked a glance at him. "Go on."

"So she picked up this knife I'd left out on the counter and tried to cut me. Like I said, she was drunk or high or something, and she barely scratched me, but it pissed me off. I took the knife away from her and...and..."

Eyes clenched shut, he bit down hard on his lip. His shoulders shook. Madeline stared, no sympathy stirring in her. But she had plenty of questions swirling around. Something about his story didn't sit right.

She leaned back in her chair. "And? What happened?"

Even she could hear the chill in her voice. Yes, bitch-cop, as Jack had so often called her, was back in full force.

"I just went crazy. I snatched the knife, and I stabbed her, over and over." Hall's voice broke. "And then it was done and she was lying there on the floor and there was so much blood...I panicked. I hid the body under the house and cleaned up and waited for the police to catch up with me. Sometimes I'd forget for days at a time, but then I'd dream of it and all of it would be right back in my head."

Madeline focused on his face. "Is that all?"

"Yeah." Hall nodded, a sick look twisting his features. "That's all."

Tick looked up. "You're sure?"

Obviously, he'd noticed the same thing she had.

"I'm sure."

Tick gave a slow nod. "I want to get your official statement. Investigator Holton and I will be right back."

In the hallway, Tick leaned an arm on the wall. Madeline gazed through the two-way glass. "Notice anything odd?"

"Like how he didn't mention anything about Allison?"

"Maybe she wasn't involved." As much as it pained her to

231

articulate it, the detective in her had to face the fact—it was entirely possible Allison hadn't been involved. "He didn't say anything about a head injury."

"Ford said she'd taken a hit to the skull hard enough to kill her."

"Know what else bugs me?" Madeline rested her shoulders against the wall and stared at the map of Chandler County hanging opposite. "He keeps talking about her being drunk or stoned...and Kelly didn't drink, ever. No drugs either."

"She'd been gone a long time, Madeline. People change."

"But she was moving forward with her life, Susan said so. Why would she have been drinking or using if she came up here to confront Allison?"

"False courage, maybe?"

"No." That much she was sure of. "I don't think so."

Tick frowned. "He said she was stumbling, slurring her words."

"Yes."

His eyes glinted. "So what else causes that?"

"You mean something like a slow subdural cerebral hemorrhage?" Madeline tilted her head. "From a head injury that she suffered at or before that party?"

Tick cleared his throat and passed a hand over his jaw. "We need a time frame."

"Yeah. Go call Ford. I'll take his statement, find out everything I can about the location of that party, who might have been there."

"Madeline...the guy confessed. He killed her. She was alive when she got to his house. That makes him the murderer."

"Yes, and I don't believe Kelly would have gone with him if she'd been in her right mind. I want to find out what happened to put her in that situation. She deserves the truth, Tick."

"Yeah. I know." His voice lowered, roughened. "I'll go call Ford."

"Man, you really know how to pick 'em."

At Cookie's dry remark, Tick looked up. He'd been on hold with the GBI lab longer than he wanted to think about. "What are you talking about?"

"At least your taste improved." Cookie dropped into the chair facing Tick's desk. A wicked grin curved his mouth. "I don't think Falconetti ever referred to me as a 'fucking asshole'."

Tick couldn't resist the answering grin. While Caitlin could curse with the best of them—more than a decade in law enforcement tended to enhance one's vocabulary—he was pretty sure those particular words had never left her lips joined together. Her taste in insults ran a little more highbrow. "I think she's referred to you as a cretin once or twice, though."

Cookie gave him the finger, and Tick laughed. He set the phone to speaker and returned the receiver before leaning back in his own chair.

"I'm assuming since you have her downstairs that the warrants turned up something."

"Yeah. She used the computer at Donna Martin's house, where she's staying while she's out of her own place. Tried to play it off, lay the blame on Donna, but Donna was clocked in at the chicken plant and the kids were at a friend's, so her story doesn't even begin to hold water. I don't think she's gonna be welcome at Donna's after she makes bail."

Tick pinched the bridge of his nose. "That's great. Wish she'd thought about that before she did something this stupid. What about her kids?"

"That woman reproduced?"

Tick held up two fingers. "Twice. One from each marriage."

"That bitch as somebody's mother is a scary thought."

"Yeah." A humorless laugh puffed from his lips. "Try imagining her as the mother of your kid."

"No thanks." A grimace twisted Cookie's mouth. "But it sounds like you've been there a time or two in your head."

"She lied to me about being on the pill back when we were dating. I checked the oldest daughter's date of birth, just to make sure."

With the background music provided courtesy of the GBI, Cookie laughed, damn him, deep guffaws that grated on Tick's already stretched nerves.

"What is so damn funny?"

"The idea of you"—Cookie pointed at him—"married to her." He gestured toward the hall and the stairs beyond. "She's the type to smother a guy in his sleep because he told her his steak was underdone. What the hell did you ever see in her?"

"I was a kid. What do you think I saw in her?"

A knowing gleam lit Cookie's gray eyes. He opened his mouth, and Tick cut him off. "Has she tried making bail?"

Cookie shrugged. "She called Larry over at Quick Bonds, but he hasn't done anything yet."

Tick steepled his fingers and tapped them against his mouth. "Wouldn't mind keeping her here as long as we could. Makes me feel better knowing where she is and that she can't do anything."

"I can charge her with assault or making terroristic threats."

"Yeah?"

"Cussed me out, told me I'd be sorry. Sounds like a threat to me."

"Me too." It was a technicality, and Tick struggled with the ethics for all of two seconds. "Charge her. We can drop it later. If Larry's willing to throw bail on both charges, hold him off as long as you can. I want some time to try to link her to Kelly Coker's death."

"Gotcha. Want me to—"

"Agent Ford." Sara Ford's deceptively sweet voice cut him off. Tick reached for the receiver.

"It's Calvert. I need to ask you a couple of questions about Kelly Coker's autopsy."

"Okay. Hang on one second while I find the report." Papers rustled on her end. "Got it. What do you need to know?"

"That skull fracture you mentioned. Could she have bled out from that head injury?"

"I believe so, yes. It's a radiating fracture, from blunt-force trauma."

"If she died from the stab wounds, what's the time frame for her receiving that blow to the head?"

"From the size of the fracture? Thirty minutes to an hour. Any longer and she'd have been unconscious."

"The brain bleed...would that present as drunkenness?"

"It could. She'd be disoriented, uncoordinated, probably displaying slurred speech."

Hell, yeah. He scratched notes on the conversation. "You said thirty minutes, maybe an hour?"

"Probably closer to the thirty-minute mark. It depends, but my money would be on a fast bleed."

He frowned and doodled his name across the bottom of the pad. "Any idea how she got the head injury? I mean, is it from an object striking her or her head hitting a hard surface?"

"I can't say for sure, Calvert—"

"But you have a theory, Ford. You always do."

"The fracture is to the back of her skull...like someone slammed her head against a wall or into the floor. Does that help?"

"More than you can imagine." He tapped his pen on the pad. "Thanks, Ford. I owe you one."

"You owe me several."

"Yeah. I'll make it up to you at some point, I promise. Later."

"Somehow, I think you've made that promise to me in the past. Goodbye, Calvert."

Replacing the receiver, he went looking for Madeline. He found her in the squad room, typing Nick Hall's statement. The subdued man sat in the hard wooden chair cater-corner to the desk, responding in a low voice to Madeline's periodic questions. Tick pulled up a chair at an angle. Madeline cast a quick look in his direction.

"The party then, you said it took place at the home of one Jon Williams?"

"Yes."

Madeline glanced at Tick again, obviously to see if the name got a reaction. He nodded at her. He knew Jon Williams, they both did—he'd been a year behind Tick in school, had graduated with Madeline—and if Tick remembered him correctly, had been the kind of kid neither of their parents would have wanted them hanging out with. Trouble from the word go.

"So, Kelly, the girl under the house...who invited her?"

Confusion twisting his face, Hall shrugged. "Nobody. It wasn't that kind of party. People just showed up."

Tick leaned forward, hands clasped before him in a loose grip. "Did you see her with anyone?"

Hall shook his head. "She stumbled out of the bathroom as I was coming down the hall, ran into my chest and put her arms around me." He fingered the tattoo on the inside of his wrist. "That's why I thought she was into us, you know?"

"How long was that before you left?"

"I dunno...maybe five minutes. I grabbed another beer and we left."

"How long did it take you to get back to your place? The Williams place is out in the country, right?" With each of Tick's easy questions, Madeline's fingers clicked over the laptop keys. He was grateful for that, as her transcription allowed him to watch Hall's face for reaction rather than split his attention taking notes.

"Ten, maybe fifteen minutes."

Approximately twenty minutes, which fit within Ford's timeline.

Only they still didn't know how she'd received the head injury. Or how she'd gotten to that party.

A frown tugging at his brows, Tick met Hall's miserable gaze. Hell, maybe he should go for broke. "Did you know a girl named Allison Barnett? She might have been going by the last name Turner."

"No. I don't remember an Allison anybody."

Tick didn't miss Madeline's did-you-really-think-it-would-be-that-easy look. He lifted his eyebrows in a one-could-hope expression before realization slammed into him. Holy hell, they were using the same nonverbal communication he and Cookie employed. Somewhere along the way, she'd become one of them.

He cleared his throat. "Mr. Hall, we're charging you in Miss Coker's death. I'm going to have a deputy escort you downstairs to intake, where you'll be fingerprinted and booked into custody."

After he'd called a jailer up to handle the booking and they were alone in the squad room, he expelled a rough sigh. "Damn it."

Madeline looked up from her laptop. "What?"

"Just facing an ugly fact." He shoved a hand through his hair.

A small frown drew her brows together. "Which fact is that?"

"The totally shitty one that says we may never be able to tie Allison to Kelly's death."

Chapter Twenty-One

"Don't throw in the towel just yet, Calvert." Madeline saved the file holding Hall's confession and sent it to the printer. "Just because Hall didn't place Allison there doesn't mean we don't have avenues. There were other people at that house."

"Well yeah, I know, but it's not like there was a guest list we can track down."

"True, but we're talking about the wicked witch of Chandler County here. Back then, she never went anywhere without her entourage. Ten bucks says either Donna or Stacy was with her. They might be loyal, but they're not stupid. If they think they might face charges of some sort for withholding information—"

"Donna's pissed off with her." A slow grin passed over Tick's face. "Allison tried to pawn the whole putting-your-name-on-the-Internet thing off on her."

"Then that's where we start." Madeline pushed up from the chair and reached for her jacket. "Because if Donna's in a mood, she'll turn on Allison in a heartbeat. Trust me, been there, done that."

"Tell me something," Tick said as she shrugged into her coat. "You said they wanted you because you had access to me. What the hell did you get out of the deal?"

She flipped her hair over her collar. "People who didn't expect more than I could give."

He shoved his hands in his pockets as they strode out the side door. "It was bad, even before what happened with us, wasn't it?"

"Yeah, but I'm not talking about it with you, Calvert."

"Never asked you to, Holton. It was one question."

"That's usually where it starts."

He laughed, and for once, the deep rumble didn't set her hair on end. Once in his truck, she held out a hand. "Let me borrow your cell. I want to call and check on Ash."

With a frown, he handed it over. "Where's yours?"

"In my desk. I'm still getting calls from men who want to do more than play footsie with me, remember?"

His mouth tight, he fired the engine. "Yeah. I remember."

Since he was in the driver's seat and she didn't have to worry about it for once, she slumped in the passenger seat and dialed through to the hospital and asked for the nurse's station on Ash's floor. Minutes later, she returned Tick's phone, smiling all the while.

He slanted a grin in her direction. "That looks like good news."

"He's out of surgery, and it went well. He's in recovery, and the nurse said he should be back in his room sometime after lunch. If everything looks good, he can go home tomorrow."

"That is good news." The grin continued to flirt about his mouth. "He's probably going to need someone to, um, take care of him for a couple of days until he's completely mobile. Monroe, our deputy who had the same surgery, did. You're not going back to your mama's yet, right?"

Madeline narrowed her eyes at him, but if he saw, he ignored it. That sounded suspiciously like...matchmaking...which was weird beyond belief.

Lips pursed, she folded her arms and didn't reply.

"What?" He half-chuckled and lifted his hands from the wheel for a split second. "I just made a suggestion. A pretty damn logical one."

She hitched one eyebrow.

"You're telling me you didn't already think of it?"

"No, I didn't. I've been a little busy, chasing down leads on a twenty-year-old murder case and dealing with the fallout from your crazy ex-girlfriend's idea of an Internet prank, remember?"

"At least you said 'ex' this time," he muttered.

"I suppose you're going to tell me Falconetti has waited on your ass hand and foot at some point while you recuperated?"

"I wouldn't call it 'hand and foot', exactly." He rolled his shoulders. "I had pretty major surgery the day after Lee was born, and she was on her feet before I was. I needed her those first few days at home, believe me." One corner of his mouth quirked in an affectionate smile. "There's something about having the woman who loves you take care of you. It's not the same having someone else do it."

"I'm not the..." She swallowed, hard, against a sudden lump in her throat, Ash's quiet "I love you" resounding in her ears. "I'm not the woman who loves him."

"Really?" Tick looked at her askance. "Could've fooled me."

"We're friends and we're dating casually while I'm here. That's all."

His disbelieving snort bordered on rude.

"You don't—"

"Know what I'm talking about, yeah, yeah, sure." He flicked a dismissive gesture between them and slowed for the turn into the chicken plant's long drive. "All I'm saying is that since you got here, if you haven't been working, you've pretty much been with him. Since the day he got hurt, if you haven't been working, you've been at the hospital, right at his side. Yeah, that looks like casual dating and friendship to me."

She opened her mouth on a smart rejoinder, but he stopped at the guard shack, forestalling her. He didn't know what he was talking about. Love? She didn't know the first thing about loving someone. She wouldn't even know where to start.

"Then there was the way you kissed him at Henry's the other night." He jockeyed the truck into a visitor's parking spot.

"Oh my God. So I kissed him. Big fucking deal." She unsnapped her seatbelt and slung the door open with a little more force than necessary. He really needed to shut up.

"Yeah. You kissed him, all right." He tucked his hands in his jacket pockets as they strode up the sidewalk. "The way Cait kisses me when we've been apart for more than a day."

She stopped short. "That doesn't mean anything. None of that means *anything*. I like him. We're friends. Yes, I kissed him, and yes, I've been worried about him but...it doesn't *mean* anything."

He halted where he'd continued a few steps ahead of her and simply looked at her, an expression of extreme patience on his face. He didn't say a word.

"It doesn't mean anything," she repeated. When he still didn't respond, she narrowed her eyes and swept by him. "Oh, shut up."

His quiet laugh only infuriated her more. She ignored him as he fell into step beside her again. In love with Ash Hardison? Ridiculous. Beyond ridiculous. It was...it was...

Absolutely true?

Tick held the door open for her, and she glared. "You're insane."

He shrugged. They crossed the lobby, and he punched the button at the elevator. She gave him an airy look. "You're crazy, Calvert, I mean it. Absolutely fucking nuts."

Eyebrows raised, he lifted both hands in a "whatever" gesture. The elevator arrived with a soft ding and inside, she leaned against the opposite wall, arms folded. He laughed and threw out his hands. "What?"

She glowered. "You and this...this...*love* idea of yours. You're crazy."

"I think you've covered that topic, ad nauseam, Holton." He crossed his arms over his chest. "You think about him at weird times, don't you? Like in the middle of the day, out of the blue, when you're supposed to be focused on the job."

"Uh, no." She rolled her eyes and waited for lightning to strike her.

He nodded, a slow bob of his chin, a knowing smirk lurking about his mouth. "And of course, you don't feel like you want to pounce on his ass when you finally do get to see him."

"That's just lust."

"Probably can't carry on a decent conversation with the guy outside of bed, either."

Just about books. Or music. Or life experiences and what was important.

God, how slow was this elevator, anyway? They were only going up two floors.

Tick's smirk widened to a grin. "And he doesn't make you laugh or just make life a hell of a lot of fun, either."

"You read women's magazines, don't you?"

"No. I wake up every day next to a woman I can't stop thinking about or keep my hands off of. We talk about everything, she makes me laugh when I don't want to, and my God, living with her is fun, even when we're fighting and I can't win to save my life. The hell of it is, she loves me too, and I thank the good Lord for that every damn day of my life because I came this close"—he held his thumb and forefinger a millimeter apart—"to losing her for good. When you find that, Holton, it's precious, and you hang on to it. You don't throw it away, and you sure as hell don't walk away like it's nothing."

The elevator shuddered to a stop. She finally managed to close her mouth as the doors slid open. He wrapped a hand in front of one and caught her gaze, his own dark and serious. "Think about it."

Think about it? Like he hadn't completely destroyed her concentration. Like she'd be able to think about anything else.

Tick whistled as they walked down the hallway to the offices. Madeline chewed on the inside of her cheek and tried to ignore his obnoxious ass.

Was that it? Did she love Ash? Surely it couldn't be that simple. Hell, she'd always envisioned love as this insurmountable expectation, more trouble than it could possibly be worth.

Well, she just wouldn't think about it now. They had this interview to do, and she'd focus on that. She could think about Tick's insane ideas later.

What if he was right? What if she did love Ash? That would change everything. She bit her thumbnail, tearing at her skin, welcoming the small pain as a distraction. She couldn't very well go—

"Holton?" On a weary sigh, Tick propped the office door open with one hip. She caught his eye and flushed, heat flooding her neck and face at the amused gleam in his dark eyes.

Oh, shit damn *fuck*, her focus was gone. She brushed by him. Donna looked up from the files she was putting away. Her gaze tangled with Madeline's, and her face twisted, annoyance and dislike flaring in her blue eyes. "What do you want?"

Madeline straightened her shoulders but put on a nonthreatening smile. "Just to talk."

Donna snorted. "We don't have anything to talk about. There's no way the *three* of us have anything to discuss."

"Donna, we need to ask you a few questions. About Kelly Coker."

With a small shake of her head, Donna rolled her eyes heavenward. "Why would you come asking about...oh." Her expression shifted and she bit her lip. "The body under Allison's house? That's *Kelly*?"

Madeline nodded.

"Oh my God." Donna felt for the nearest chair and sank into it. "I don't believe it. I always thought...she said she'd been in Florida and I thought she just went back..."

"She said she'd *been* in Florida?" Intensity hovered in Tick's voice.

Donna lifted her gaze to his, with a confused nod.

"You saw her after she ran away." Madeline leaned on the waist-high counter. She didn't miss Tick's hey-sometimes-it-is-this-easy expression.

"Yeah. At a party one weekend, about a year after we graduated. Hell, she showed up at my house, looking for Allison. I knew Allison would be at the party, and I told Kelly to come on. Thought it would be like old times."

"A party at Jon Williams's house?"

Donna nodded and looked between them, perplexed. "What is this about?"

Madeline sifted a hand through her hair. "You just left her there?"

"No. I went looking for her sometime around one in the morning. I was ready to go, but Allison said she'd already gone."

"Allison talked to her?" Tick rested his elbows on the counter, his gaze intent on Donna's face.

"Yeah, I guess you could call it that. Kelly was talking. Allison was yelling and bitching."

"Do you remember what they were arguing about?" Madeline asked.

Donna gave her a "duh" look. "No. That was twenty years ago almost, and I'd had two or three wine coolers. Besides, you know how Allison was, always going on about something."

"Yeah," Madeline said, voice soft. "You actually saw them together?"

"Didn't I just say that? They were fussing. Kelly got upset and she went in the bathroom. Allison followed her. That's the last I saw of her. Kelly, I mean."

The bathroom. Allison followed her in the bathroom, and at some point, Kelly stumbled out and into Nick Hall's life.

To be savagely murdered within an hour. Except, if Ford was to be believed, she'd already been on her way to bleeding out from a slow brain hemorrhage.

"Thank you for talking to us." Madeline pushed away from the counter. Catching Tick's eye, she tilted her head toward the door. "We'll let you get back to work."

In the hallway, she punched the elevator call button savagely. "Well, there's a circumstantial link. We know they were together, in that bathroom, before Kelly stumbled into Nick Hall and he took her home and killed her. You know that's the best we can do. She'll get away with it."

"Maybe." He pushed a hand through his hair and squinted up at the numbers. "I don't know what the precedence is. We can't charge her with murder because she didn't cause the death, but maybe we could do an aggravated assault charge. Maybe a contributing charge."

"It's not good enough." Madeline stalked into the elevator. "Kelly's dead, and without adequate medical attention, she'd have died from that head wound. We both know how she got it, even if we can't prove it. Again, Allison gets away with everything."

"Maybe not." Tick rubbed a hand over his jaw. "We'll run it by the DA, see what he has to say, and go from there."

Madeline pushed open the door to Ash's room and stopped, surprised. Ash rested on the edge of the bed, dressed casually in a T-shirt and sweats. An Ace bandage encased his knee. A pair of crutches leaned against the bed.

Warmth flashed in her while Tick's questions rolled through her head. She clutched the door handle, a tentative smile curving her lips.

"Hey."

He grinned, despite the lines of pain bracketing his mouth. "Hey."

"What are you doing?" She cringed at the inanity of the inquiry. "You're up."

"Yeah. I'm damn glad too."

"How do you feel?" *Did you mean it when you said you loved me?*

"Pretty good." One corner of his mouth quirked up. "I convinced Mackey to let me out of here today."

"Oh, that's great." Her voice emerged breathy and a little tremulous. "How are you getting home?"

"Well, I was going to call Stan, but now that you're here..." His fabulous grin flashed. "Want to give me a ride?"

Tick's suggestion that Ash would need someone to take care of him insinuated itself into her brain. The scary thing was she wanted to take care of him. Nurturing had never been part of her makeup, so it had to be him. Could she add "wants to take care of him" to Tick's definition of being in love?

She moistened her lips with the tip of her tongue. "Of course I'll take you."

If anything, his grin widened. "So get over here and kiss me."

Her stomach lifted and turned over in a nervous little roll. Releasing the door, she crossed to stand before him, in the vee of his legs, injured one canted to the side. He rested his hands at her hips. She wrapped her arms around his neck and leaned in to cover his mouth with her own. Beneath hers, his lips were warm and pliable, and his fingers flexed at her hips. Aware of his stitches, she kept the kiss light and teasing, gentle and loving. Curling closer, she laid a hand along his jaw, a hint of stubble abrading her palm. The sheer volume of emotion coursing through her, the absolute rightness of being with him, all swirled within her, coalescing into a solid core of emotion.

She pulled back, framing his face with hands that shook wildly. "I don't want to love you. It scares me to even think about it."

"Then don't think about it. We're not in a rush. We're just together." He rubbed his lips over her temple. "Take me home, Mad."

"All right." She managed to firm her lips enough to produce a tremulous smile. "Let's spring you, Hardison."

From the passenger seat, Ash studied Madeline while she drove. He was thrilled to be out of that hospital bed and on his way home. He was even more thrilled to have Madeline with him.

I don't want to love you.

Her shaky statement trickled through his consciousness. She hadn't said she *didn't* love him. She'd said she didn't *want* to love him—as in maybe she did.

It was enough to give him hope.

Relief washed through him when she turned into his driveway. Damn, he was glad to be home. Glad to have this woman with him at his side.

After she parked next to his truck, as close to the porch as she could get, she came around to open the door and assist him in extricating himself from the car. Once he was on his feet with the crutches keeping him steady, she didn't move away, the constant warmth of her palm on his back burning all the way through him.

She used his keys to open the front door. "You should go to bed and rest."

He canted an eyebrow at her. "I've been in bed long enough. I might sit my ass on the couch, but no way am I going straight to bed."

He hobbled into the foyer. In the dim light, the spare key gleamed on the hall table, tangible evidence that she'd planned to leave him because of Allison's stunt. He ignored the piece of metal and swung into the living room. She followed, hovering at the doorway.

"Are you hungry?" She fiddled with the hem of her jacket. "Should I get you something to drink?"

"All I want right now is you." A smile quirked his mouth. "Get over here so I can hold you for a while."

"Don't think I'm following orders," she said, crossing the room to settle beside him on the couch. He curved an arm around her shoulders and tucked her into his side. Contentment suffused him.

"Hmm, that feels good." He rested his cheek on her hair and drank in the way she relaxed into him. "I've missed this. Missed you."

She laughed. "I haven't been anywhere, Ash. Most days, I've been with you, remember?"

"But not like this." He smiled against the silk of her hair. He let his head fall back and closed his eyes.

He woke, not coming through layers of sleep, but jerking into a heart-pounding awareness, the way he sometimes did when he dreamed of Iraq. He stared at the ceiling, swallowing against the metallic taste of drug residue, fighting off a sudden wave of nausea. The angle of late-evening sunlight slanting in from the western-facing windows told him several hours had passed. He was alone, stretched out on the couch, his injured leg propped on two pillows from his bed.

"Hungry?" Madeline's soft voice drew his dulled attention to the kitchen doorway.

"You can't cook." The inane words popped free, and he grimaced. His brain was on the fritz.

She laughed. "No, but I make a mean sandwich, and I do know how to microwave soup."

"Sounds good." Maybe food would settle his stomach, kick-start his fuzzy thought processes. First though, he needed to take care of another, more pressing biological need. He pushed himself to a seated position and swung his legs to the floor.

Agony shot through him. Holy fuck, the drugs had worn off. Sweat beaded on his upper lip, and he breathed through the waves of nausea gripping his gut.

"Ash?" Concern filled her shaking voice and gentle hands smoothed his hair and over his nape. "What do you need? Let me—"

"Got to take a leak." Eyes clenched shut, he dragged in a couple more deep breaths. "Hand me my crutches, would you, babe?"

"When you are well, we're having one serious discussion about that endearment."

Aluminum clanked, and he opened his eyes to find her holding the crutches before him. Dreading the movement, he took hold of them and lurched to his feet, grateful for her steadying hands. "Thanks."

"Do you need me to—"

"No." He still had some pride. "I think I can manage."

She nodded, hazel gaze calling him a liar. She motioned over her shoulder. "I'm going to fix you something to eat and get you a couple of those painkillers. Holler if you need help."

It was slow going, taking him long minutes, but he made it down the hallway to the bathroom and back under his own power.

In the living room, she waited, the coffee table laid out with plates and bowls for two. Steam wafted lazily from tomato soup and what looked like thick Reuben sandwiches waited alongside. His mouth watered. Damn, he was hungrier than he'd thought.

She came forward to assist him on his way to the couch, one palm pressed to his chest, the other to his back.

"See?" The teasing note in her voice didn't quite cover a strain that set the hair at his nape on end. "I'm not completely useless in the kitchen."

"Looks great." He let her help him settle on the couch. She handed him a glass and two white tablets. He tossed them off and hoped they were fast-acting. Hell, Mackey had said the surgery would make his knee feel better, not worse. Right now, it hurt like a son of a bitch.

She folded her legs to sit on the floor across from him. They ate in silence, although he didn't miss the inscrutable looks she kept darting in his direction. Foreboding settled over him. Was she getting ready to run again? Talking herself out of loving him before they'd even begun?

Finally, when he'd devoured everything on his plate, and she'd pushed half her sandwich in his direction, she stopped fiddling with her napkin and looked up to focus her shuttered gaze on his.

"If I did love you...I don't know how to do that, Ash. I mean, I don't even know what that entails, what I'm supposed to do. I've never loved a man before."

He caught his breath, staring at her, trying to get his damn brain in the right gear so he didn't screw this to hell.

"You don't have to do anything." He cleared his throat because, damn, his voice wanted to come out as a shaky whisper. "You just have to be you and be with me."

She puffed out an exasperated sigh and rolled her eyes. "You make it sound so simple. It can't be like that. There have to be rules, things you'd expect—"

"No." He shook his head, afraid even to take his eyes off her. "You're already more than I ever expected to find."

Tears washed her eyes with a crystalline sheen. "You can't say that. I'm not—"

"You're everything I want, just as you are." He swallowed against the lump that had taken up residence in the back of his throat and went for broke. "I love you, Madeline. I know it's too damn soon, I know you don't know what to do with that, but God help me, I do."

She brushed at the tears spilling off her lashes. "I'm scared, Ash."

"I know, baby. So am I."

Her face crumpled, tears falling harder. "I can't love you and then fuck this up, and I always do that."

"I think the only way you could mess this up now is by walking away, going back to that life you don't live. I want you to live with me, Mad. Live with me and be my love."

She laughed through her tears and swiped the back of her wrist across her nose. "You're quoting poetry at me."

"Marlowe." His own eyes burned, nothing to do with his pain, everything to do with hers. "But that's all I want you to do, Madeline, all I expect from you. 'Come live with me and be my love'."

She blinked hard, looked away, then turned wet, fierce eyes in his direction. She bit her lip and Ash's stomach plummeted.

"I don't know if I can." A tremor hovered in the words, enough to give him hope.

He moistened dry lips and pushed out a single syllable.

"Try."

Chapter Twenty-Two

Rousing from a half-remembered nightmare, Tick rolled over and flung an arm across Caitlin's side of the bed. His hand encountered cool sheets and he cracked one eyelid. Darkness hovered outside and he was alone in bed. He rubbed his face and sat up with a quick glance at the clock. Three forty-three.

With the quilt tossed aside, he rose and padded into the keeping room. The kitchen light cast soft illumination over the area, and he found Lee asleep in the portable crib and Caitlin in the armchair, laptop open, a legal pad balanced next to it.

"What are you doing up?" he whispered.

"I nursed Lee and couldn't go back to sleep. I've been doing some research."

"It's not even four and it's cold." He dropped a kiss on the side of her neck. "Come back to bed."

She rubbed a palm down his bare arm. "Look at this."

His cheek close to hers, he blinked still-bleary eyes and focused on the laptop screen. An earnest young man grinned at him, a driver's license shot, faintly familiar. "Who's that?"

"Jamie Turner, Allison Barnett's first husband."

"Really." He frowned and took a closer look. "He seems familiar."

Caitlin turned her head and graced him with her I-don't-believe-this look. "He looks like you."

"No, he doesn't." The scoffing words trailed away. Yeah, the long-dead young man had dark hair and eyes like his own, but... "You think?"

"I think. This"—she opened a new tab and a prison-intake photo popped onto the screen—"is the second husband, Mike Brinson."

"Mr. Southern Brotherhood." Tick squinted at the photo. No resemblance here, except maybe another set of brown eyes. Brinson, bald and brawny, stared into the lenses with a coldness Tick had seen more than once on any number of suspects.

"That would be him."

Tick rested his hand on her shoulder and rubbed the edges of her hair between his fingers. "Why, exactly, are you researching Allison's former husbands in the middle of the night?"

"Probably the same reason you've been having trouble sleeping for the past week." She lifted her shoulder to capture his hand against her cheek. "Because it looks like she's going to get away with the part she played in Kelly Coker's death and it makes me crazy."

"I've looked at this thing six ways to Sunday and nothing I can come up with is enough to charge her yet." He moved to sit on the ottoman before her. "You think she killed him?"

"I'd lay money on it." She closed the laptop and set it aside. "Only a few problems with that. One, as you pointed out, it's a closed case with a natural-causes death."

"Two, the FBI doesn't investigate murder, and FBI profilers on maternity leave don't do lone gunman investigations." He reached for her legal pad.

"And three, it's not in your jurisdiction, either." Caitlin wiggled deeper into the chair.

He tapped his finger against her notes. "You think she's a sociopath?"

"Narcissistic at the least. Just long-distance diagnosing based on what I know."

He flapped the pad against his leg. "Why kill him?"

"Money. Maybe to get him out of the way if she was already involved with Brinson. You could even theorize, if that resemblance between you and Turner isn't a coincidence, that in killing him, she was exorcising you, although that's really stretching it, I think." She rested her chin on her hand. "Maybe just to get out of the marriage because she was tired of it."

Nodding, he traced his thumb over the dark question mark she'd written behind the word "sociopath". "You know, I went to high school with the investigator over at Cressley. I could talk to him... What could it hurt?"

She smiled and nudged his thigh with her toe. "Is there anyone you didn't go to high school with?"

"It's southwest Georgia. Not too many people around here I don't know, precious." He caught her ankle and tugged her toward him, leaning in to kiss her. Pulling back, he sobered. "But if she did kill him and someone can make that case, then maybe that's another way to get justice for Kelly."

⬦

Slumped in her desk chair, Madeline pressed a finger to her aching temple and tried to ignore the sounds of seven a.m. shift change drifting up the stairs.

"Hey, Chris, I brought breakfast. You want the grilled PBJ, or egg and cheese biscuit?" Troy Lee's raised voice competed with slamming doors and jailers doing head counts.

Madeline scratched a note in the margin of the incident report she was reviewing. Geez, he was loud. Parker's reply, muffled and indistinct, followed. At her elbow, her cell phone buzzed. She stiffened and cast a cautious glance at the screen before opening it. "Hey."

"Hey, yourself." Ash's drowsy voice flowed over her, warm and appealing. "What time did you leave?"

"About five." She rubbed the bridge of her nose and yawned. "I couldn't sleep and didn't want to bother you, so I came on in. You were still sleeping the sleep of the drugged."

His harrumph came clearly across the connection. "I'm not taking any more of those things at night."

"You will if it makes you feel better." She leaned back in her chair. In the past week, she'd discovered he was a horrible patient, and while she understood his caution with the painkillers, hurting just because he was stubborn didn't make much sense either. "I should be home a little after five. Promise me you won't do anything stupid around the farm while I'm gone."

"Define stupid."

She ground her teeth. The man was incorrigible, and if she didn't lo—*like*—him so much, she'd kill him. "Like work. I don't want you doing anything more strenuous than sitting in the office, working on that 'system' of yours."

"Have I ever mentioned I like it when you're bossy?"

"Your knee needs time to heal. I want you to take it easy." She swallowed hard. "Please?"

Silence trembled between them. He cleared his throat. "Whatever you want, babe."

"I'll, um..." She pushed her hair away from her face, her own throat tight for some God-only-knew reason. "I'll see you later."

After his quiet goodbye, she closed the phone and laid it aside. With a quiet exhale, she rested her face in her hands for a moment.

"Looks like deep thought." Tick dropped into the chair next to her desk.

She lifted her head. "You're early."

"So are you." He traced a scar on the chair's wooden arm. "Trouble sleeping?"

"Yeah." She tapped a restless tattoo atop the desk. "I always turn into an insomniac when a case isn't going well."

He tossed a photograph on the blotter. "How would you feel about taking a little ride over to Cressley?"

"Why?" She lifted the picture of the young dark-eyed, dark-haired man. "Who is this?"

"Allison's first husband. He died of a sudden heart attack at age twenty-one. Cait thinks"—one corner of his mouth hitched in a self-derisive smile—"if we follow up on that, we might find out it wasn't a heart attack."

A little flutter of excitement came to life at Madeline's pulse. "I really like the way Cait thinks. But why go over there? Why not just phone?"

"I know the investigator. I'm thinking an in-person visit might make it harder for him to blow us off."

She pushed up from the chair and shrugged into her jacket. "Let's go then."

A slow smile crossed his face. "There's that enthusiasm I like."

Flipping her hair over her collar, she gave him a look. "Listen, having you treat me like a human being is weird enough. No being nice to me on a regular basis, Calvert."

He pulled his keys from his pocket. "All right. I can handle that."

Early-morning traffic surrounding Moultrie slowed them, so they approached Cressley's city limits just before nine. Madeline stretched stiff legs, pointing her toes. "Where do you know the investigator from?"

"High school." He checked his rearview mirror as the four-lane narrowed to single-lane traffic. "Football, baseball. That kind of stuff."

"So who is it? If you know him, I might as well."

"Bobby Wentworth."

The name dropped between them like a bomb. Madeline gaped at him a moment, then snapped her mouth shut. A harsh laugh bubbled in her throat and she covered her eyes. "Fuck, no."

The words came out louder, slightly more hysterical than she meant them to. The truck swerved slightly and Tick glanced at her. "What?"

"I don't believe this." She laughed at a situation far from funny. Damn karma. Just her fucking luck. "You're kidding me."

"*What?*" Tick looked at her again and slowed for a stoplight. "Holton, what is wrong?"

"Bobby Wentworth is the investigator we're going to see."

"Yeah. He went through the academy the year after I did." The light turned green and a horn beeped behind them. He hit the accelerator. "What is the big deal?"

She sighed. "When I was a junior, I cut class and blew him behind the weight room because Allison dared me to."

"Holy hell..." He shook his head. "Well, this is going to be awkward."

"You're telling me."

He laughed, damn him, his shoulders shaking with quiet guffaws. "Shit, Madeline, that was a stupid-ass thing to do on a dare."

"Hey." She resisted the urge to punch him in the arm to shut him up, the way she would have with Jack. "At least I was only stupid with him once. How many times were you stupid with your psycho girlfriend?"

"That is not nice." He took a right off the main drag.

She did cuff his arm then. "You're *laughing* at me."

"Well, it's funny." He draped his wrists on the steering wheel and spread his hands. "This wouldn't happen to anybody but you."

"Oh, thank you very much." Her mouth twitched. Shit, he was right. Who else would this happen to?

"If it makes you feel any better, Cait once jumped me on the couch while I was still wearing my gear. We managed to key my radio and treat half the department to about thirty seconds of us hot and heavy." He pulled into the gravel lot fronting the small Cressley city hall.

"Nope, sorry, not the same thing, Calvert." She released her seatbelt and pushed the door open. No sense in dragging her feet. The reality wasn't going away anytime soon.

As they walked up the sidewalk to the neat brick building that housed both the city offices and the small police department, she threw back her shoulders and envisioned for a moment relating this whole story to Ash. He'd probably laugh his ass off. Oh hell, maybe she'd laugh with him, once this was over and done.

Tick held the door and they entered a tiny foyer. The young blonde at the city clerk's desk looked up and smiled. "Good morning. May I help you?"

"Investigator Calvert, Chandler County Sheriff's Department." Tick held his ID aloft. "Is Investigator Wentworth available?"

She pointed down the hall to the left. "Third office on the right."

"Thank you." He ushered Madeline before him. Her stomach twisted and she sucked in a couple of deep breaths. At the partially open door, Madeline rapped sharply.

"Come in." The voice was no longer familiar, not that she'd known him that well to begin with.

With Tick on her heels, she pushed the door open. Bobby looked up from the file on his desk, but recognition didn't light his eyes until he caught sight of Tick. He rose to proffer a hand. "Well, hey, boy, what are you doing down here?"

"Need to talk to you about an old death." Tick took his hand in a hard shake. "Good to see you, Bobby."

Bobby's blue gaze tracked to Madeline with polite expectation. Tick cleared his throat. "You remember Madeline Holton. She's serving as our interim investigator."

Recollection dawned on his face and he stuck out his hand. "Madeline Holton? Well, I swear. Good to see you, girl."

"You too." She found her own hand engulfed in a firm grip and then he stepped back, gesturing.

"Y'all come sit down. You said something about a death?" Bobby settled behind his desk again.

"The coroner called it a heart attack, but an autopsy was never completed." Tick handed over the manila folder he'd brought with them. "We've uncovered some unrelated information concerning a cold case in our jurisdiction that makes us think maybe his death wasn't so natural."

"A heart attack, huh? At twenty-one?" Bobby glanced up, askance. "I mean, it happens, but a lot of times it don't happen, right?"

"Right." Tick dragged out the monosyllable.

Bobby lifted a couple of papers, his gaze on the folder's contents. "Any family left?"

"Nope, not locally. His parents both died a few years ago; he was an only child. An aunt who used to live in Alabama, but no recent address."

"Wait. His wife was Allison Barnett." Bobby lifted his eyebrows. "That's some shit. You thinking she might have had something to do with his 'heart attack'?"

"We do."

"Huh." Bobby paged through the rest of the file. "She always was a little off. No offense, Tick."

"None taken." He rested his elbow on the chair arm and rubbed his jaw. "She's a lot off now."

"Tell you what...I can't make you any promises, but I'll talk to the chief, see if he'll let me take a run at this. I'll start by tracking down the aunt, maybe contact the insurance company that paid out on the death." Bobby flipped the folder shut. "We'll see where it goes."

"We appreciate it." Tick rose and the two men shook hands again over the desk.

Bobby slanted a smile in Madeline's direction. "Again, good to see you, Madeline."

Another round of handshakes and Tick shepherded her into the hall and through the lobby. Outside, she squinted across the hood as he unlocked the truck. "That was...not as weird as I'd thought it would be."

He slid behind the wheel. "What'd you expect, for him to ask you for another go right there? C'mon, Madeline, it had to be an awkward moment for him too, but you're both professionals and it happened twenty-freakin'-years ago. You gotta learn to let things go."

"Did you just refer to me as a professional?" She fastened her seatbelt. "Are you sure you're feeling all right?"

He gave her a look and shifted into reverse. "I mean it, Holton, you have to learn to let some stuff go. You carry it around until it cripples you—"

"I owe you an apology." The words were out before they'd completely formed in her mind.

He braked harder than necessary. When he glanced at her, surprise glinted in his eyes. "For what?"

"For..." She swallowed hard. "For what I did. I never even thought about you as a person, as someone that my actions might hurt—"

"Don't." Remorse twisted his expression. "You don't have to, and there's more than enough blame to go around."

She brushed her hair away from her face with shaking hands and made herself look him in the eye. "I am sorry."

He nodded once, and his throat moved. "So am I."

Silence fell. He rubbed his palm over the steering wheel. "You know what? I skipped breakfast. Let's hit El Toreo's before we head back."

"Yeah, let's do." She smiled and glanced away. "Sounds like a great idea."

Just as she'd expected, Ash laughed.

"It's not funny." She wrapped her arms about his waist and buried her face against his chest.

"It's not, but it is." He rested more of their weight against the counter behind them and rubbed the small of her back. His mouth danced across her temple. "Kinda like looking back at Suzanne's crazy shit."

"Yeah." She lifted her head to look at him. Tiny lines of weary pain still bracketed his mouth and eyes. "Are you sure you want to go to Calvert's for dinner? You look tired."

"I'm also going stir-crazy. Being cooped up in the house for a week is making me nuts. So yeah, I'm sure I want to go." He spun her toward the living room. "Now get your coat so we can get moving."

She drove them the few miles to Calvert and Falconetti's home. With the swelling receding on his knee, Ash had eschewed his crutches and instead leaned on a cane as they went up the walk. She tucked her hand under his arm, simply pleased to be in his presence.

Tick met them at the back door. "Hey, y'all, come on in."

Warmth enveloped them inside, and spicy scents lingered in the air as Tick took their coats. "Let me get you a drink. Madeline, water, beer, tea?"

"Water's fine."

"Cait's upstairs with the baby." Tick pulled a beer from the refrigerator and filled a goblet with ice and water from the pitcher on the island. He extended it in Madeline's direction. "She'll be down shortly."

Ash accepted his beer. "Is that her alfredo I smell?"

"It is."

"Fantastic." Ash hugged Madeline to his side. "Babe, wait until you experience this. The woman makes the best alfredo sauce I've ever tasted."

His enthusiasm was darn near infectious. She patted his arm. "I can't wait."

Tick tagged Ash's chest. "I have those proposals I was telling you about in the study. If Madeline doesn't mind, I can show them to you quickly."

Madeline waved an airy hand. "Be my guest."

Ash leaned in to brush his mouth over her cheek. "I'll be right back."

Once they disappeared down the short hallway, Madeline wandered along the interior wall, studying the array of photographs displayed there. As on Ash's shelves, studio or posed images shared space with spur-of-the-moment snapshots. She touched a fingertip to Ash's grinning face in one. Maybe, just maybe, she could get used to this live-with-me, be-my-love idea of his.

She'd pulled off a solid week without fucking it up yet. That had to count for something.

"I'm sorry to keep you waiting." Caitlin's quiet voice startled her. Madeline spun to find the other woman at the foot of the stairs. "Did they abandon you to retreat into farm-talk again?"

"Something like that."

"You look good." An enigmatic smile played about Caitlin's mouth.

Narrowing her eyes, Madeline tucked her hair behind her ear. "What is that all about?"

If anything, Caitlin's smile widened. "What do you mean?"

"You and your damn subtext, Falconetti." She sketched a gesture between them. "I look good?"

"You're different than when you first came back, Madeline. More relaxed, more real. So yes, you look good." Caitlin turned toward the kitchen. "I'm going to get some tea while I toss this salad. Want some?"

"There you go again, with your tea-and-friendship routine." Madeline waved her goblet. Ice tinkled against the glass.

"Can a girl ever have too many friends?"

"Do you really want me to answer that?" She perched on a stool at the island. "You've seen my taste in friends."

"Former friends." With the kettle on, Caitlin pulled a cellophane-covered bowl from the refrigerator. "Lifetime-ago, not-the-same-person-anymore friends. Maybe it's time you cultivated some new ones."

"Yeah. Maybe." Madeline rolled the stem of her goblet between her hands. "Dinner smells good. Thanks for having us."

"I've been looking forward to it." Caitlin added chopped tomato and green pepper to the greens, then followed up with a drizzle of vinaigrette. "I adore Lee, but sometimes I need some adult company after spending all day with him. Tick tells me you went to see Cressley's investigator about Allison's first husband's death today."

Madeline darted a glance at her, but found nothing but polite curiosity in her expression. "We did. He said he'd look into it."

"Sometimes, as hard as it is to accept, that's the best you can hope for." With the salad tossed, Caitlin lifted the kettle and poured steaming water into her mug. "How's your second week been? Better than the first?"

"Are you kidding? Armageddon would be better than last week." Madeline faked a shudder, and Caitlin laughed, husky and soft. "Is this where I'm supposed to spill all my issues and you tell me how to fix them over your hot tea there?"

"I thought you said we weren't going to have tea and bond."

"I know." Madeline feathered a hand through her hair. "I'm not good at bonding, period. I did make an entire lunch with Autry the other day, just me and her. My mother isn't speaking to me yet, but at least I can spend an hour with my sister without the same old sniping."

"Well, that's an improvement." A winsome smile curved Caitlin's mouth. "My brother and I can't go five minutes without sniping."

"It's weird. She's probably the one person I should have the most in common with, and I can't get past the polite niceties with her. Maybe it's been too long."

Caitlin shrugged. "Sometimes, it's easier to forge bonds with people outside our families. Look at Tick. He and his brothers are pretty close, but he's probably more closely bonded to Ash or even Reed or Cookie. Believe me, as much as I love Vince, I have old friends with whom I share a closer tie. Considering the length of your estrangement, it doesn't surprise me that you don't feel close to her yet. But give it time."

Time. She could do that. She'd never thought she'd be able to stay longer than ten minutes in the same room with Tick Calvert without coming apart with sick nerves, and hell, they were settling into a working ease as if they'd been doing it for years.

Perhaps fixing her relationship with her sister wasn't impossible.

Minutes later, the men rejoined them, and as laughter and conversation unfolded over the table, Madeline slowly relaxed further. The sense of comfort wrapped around her, lingering even on the drive back to Ash's.

"Tonight was fun." She rubbed at her arms while he unlocked the door.

"It was." He ushered her inside, but she didn't miss the wince that crossed his face.

She tapped his chest on her way to put her cell on charge. "You need to take a painkiller and get some sleep..."

Her voice trailed away. She stared at the display on her phone, the familiar number under the words "missed call".

"What is it?" Tension coated his voice.

"I don't know yet. I must have missed a call while we were in the dead zone." She dialed her voice mail and lifted the phone to her ear, letting the familiar voice, the words both hoped for and dreaded wash over her. Her chest fluttered, tightened, fluttered again. With shaking fingers, she closed the phone.

"Madeline? What is it?"

She put the phone down and turned to face him. "I have to go back."

"Back?"

"To Jacksonville." She blew out a breath. "The message was from Blaine Railey, one of the detectives investigating Jack's shooting. They want me to meet with the chief of the division."

"Mad." He took a step toward her. "Are you all right?"

"I'm...I'm good." Her hands still shook and she rubbed them down her thighs. "I didn't expect it to be this soon."

Nerves twisted in her belly. Were they taking her back or was her career in Jacksonville over? And if they were taking her back, what did that mean for her and Ash?

He was thinking the same thing—she could see it in the sudden wariness tightening his face.

"I have to...I'm supposed to meet with them at nine tomorrow morning." She shoved a hand through her hair. "I should call Tick and then I'm going to head out—"

"Tonight?"

She nodded. "I can spend the night at my place and not have to fight the outlying traffic on the way in."

He passed a hand over his nape, a stunned look on his face. "Are you coming back?"

Startled, she stared at him. "I...I don't know yet."

"I see." He leaned on the opposite wall.

"Ash, I just..." Desperation bit at her. "I don't even know how this is going to go. I don't know what I'm doing yet."

"I understand." He cleared his throat. "You have to do what's best for you."

"I don't want to hurt you." The words tore free of her constricted throat. "That's the last thing I ever wanted—"

"Babe." A half-smiled hitched one corner of his mouth, although his eyes remained serious. "You're not gonna hurt me. Jacksonville is four hours away by car, half that if I fly. If that's where you want to be, we'll find a way to make it work."

No ultimatums? No my-way-or-the-highway? She pulled herself short. He wasn't her father; making negative expectations based on her interactions with Virgil Holton wasn't fair to the man standing before her, who'd been nothing but steady and patient, who never expected more than she could give.

"You're great, did you know that?" She reached for him with trembling hands and wrapped her arms about him. She sighed into his throat. "I love you, Hardison."

They froze. She felt every muscle in Ash's body go still. Shit damn fuck, had she just said that?

She pulled back, afraid to meet his eyes, and when she did, found them glowing with joy. She shook her head. "I didn't say that. I didn't."

He laughed and tugged her closer. "Yes, you did, and babe, I've never heard sweeter words in my life."

She wagged a finger. "Don't go getting ideas—"

"I wouldn't dare." He ducked his head to kiss her. "If you're set on going to Jacksonville tonight, you'd better call Tick."

With an odd sense of reluctance dragging at her, she slipped from his easy embrace. "I guess."

"Want some company for the ride?" He cleared his throat. "Or some moral support for tomorrow?"

She cast him a sidelong glance. "You'd do that?"

He simply looked at her and she sighed. "I'd like to have you with me, but I know you have stuff to do here."

"Like what? Stare at the walls and go nuts?" His expression gentled. "C'mon, Mad. Part of this deal is we do the hard stuff together. You walked me through mine. Now it's my turn to walk you through yours."

Her eyes prickled. "Thank you."

"Go make your call. I'll start packing a bag."

When they got to Jacksonville long after midnight, her neighborhood was dark. Pulling into her tiny spot felt familiar but held no sense of homecoming. After killing the engine, she rubbed damp palms over her knees. "Well, this is it."

"It's nice." He released his seatbelt and eased from the car, testing his knee. Moving gingerly, he shouldered his bag and she grabbed hers from the backseat as well.

"Come on." She slipped an arm about his waist to offer support as they went up the walk. On the narrow stairs leading to the garage apartment she'd rented forever, she preceded him, taking quick glances back to check on his progress.

The lock stuck, just like always, and she jiggled the key. The door swung open and she fumbled for the switch. Light flooded the one-room space. Suddenly nervous and intensely aware of Ash behind her at the doorway, she tried to view her home through his eyes.

The neat space seemed impersonal, filled with furniture that came with the apartment. A couple of photos graced the surface of the refrigerator, but beyond the tiny stuffed red devil on one end of the sofa, the room contained no authentic personal touches.

She dropped her bag next to the sofa. "Like I said, this is it."

He set his own bag down and shut the door. His gaze fell on the devil. "He's cute."

"It's nothing." She shrugged and turned away, her throat tight. "Jack's idea of a joke."

"He was your friend."

A shuddery breath tore free of her frozen lungs. "Yes. He was."

Ash watched her a moment. "I'm sorry, Madeline."

Sudden tears spilled down her face, and a sob scratched her throat. "So am I."

"Ah, babe." He limped across the room to her. "Come here."

She let him enfold her and didn't bother to deny the tears. She turned her face into his neck and wept.

"Let it out, baby," he whispered against her hair. "Let it out."

Harsh sobs wracked her and he fumbled them onto the couch, his harsh intake of breath close to her ear.

"I'm sorry." She held him closer. "Your knee."

"It's okay." He rested his mouth at her temple. "You're what's important. It's okay to cry, baby. Sometimes you just need to."

She nodded, her hitching sob cut off by a wide yawn. Ash rubbed a hand down her back. "You're wiped out. You need some rest."

"My bed isn't as big as yours." She murmured the words into the curve of his throat. "It's only a double."

"I think we'll fit. Besides, I like being close to you." He smoothed damp hair away from her cheek. "Come on. I'm tired too."

Amber illumination from the security light outside filtered into her bedroom. She flipped back the covers then shed her clothing while Ash stripped off his shirt and struggled out of his jeans. She snagged his shirt and pulled it over her head to serve as a nightgown, the soft cotton wrapping her in his remaining warmth and scent.

With a shaky sigh, she crawled into bed and into his arms. Exhaustion suffused her, but her grief for Jack and the apprehension about what morning would hold kept her eyes wide open. She huddled closer to Ash and tried to regulate her breathing. He needed to rest, even if she couldn't.

Long minutes passed in silence. Ash feathered his hand over her shoulder. "Mad?"

"Yes?" Her voice came out small and too sad for her liking.

"Would talking about it help?"

"I'm frightened." She pressed her cheek closer to his chest, warm skin doing little to alleviate the chill holding her prisoner. She aligned her fingertips to his ribs, his pulse bumping under her palm with soothing steadiness. "This is almost as bad as waiting at the hospital. I was sure he was gone. I'd seen his chest and... Oh God, I'm scared, Ash."

He wrapped his finger in her hair. "What happened, baby?"

"I didn't stop him. That's what happened." She sucked in a breath that felt like ground glass. "It had been a...a bad year. Jack had always been impulsive. Yeah, imagine me saying that about someone else, but our impulses...they were different. I get a hunch and I act on it, but the hunches come from the investigation, you know? Jack just acted, then he'd sort things out later. I still don't get it, but we were a good team. Our case closure rate was one of the highest in the department. But last year, after his marriage went to hell, things weren't good."

Ash didn't speak, but slid his palm up to cup her nape, working at the tight muscles there.

Madeline squeezed her eyes closed against what came next, but the images lingered, seared into her memory. "We went out on one of my hunches, to reinterview a witness linked to a drug-deal shooting. I was sure the guy was lying to us because the suspect was his cousin and I wanted one more go at him, especially. He lived in a rat-hole duplex, one of those with the stairways straight up the middle. As we get there, Jack thinks he sees the suspect go in the house. Before I could call for backup, he went sprinting in, up those stairs. He didn't even kill the engine."

She caught her breath on a choked sob, and Ash tucked her closer against him.

"I shut off the car, grabbed the keys and my handheld and went after him. The shots started before I even made it up the front steps. By the time I got inside, it was over and the suspect was out the back door. Jack was...he'd taken a blast to the chest from a sawed-off shotgun." Tears leaked from beneath her closed lids. "I should have stopped him or insisted we take the other pair of detectives from our hot squad with us. My impulses put us there and Jack's ended up getting him shot."

"Babe, I don't see how you can think that's your fault. He made the choice to get out of that car, to go in without even you with him for backup."

"I kept telling myself that, but I couldn't let myself believe it. Blaming myself was easier than facing what I first thought when they told me he was dead... Do you want to hear the worst part?" she whispered.

"I'll listen to anything you need to tell me."

"For a second, I thought, 'He did this on purpose.' He'd talked about it, after Paula left, about eating his gun, and I told him that was the coward's way out. We fought about it. He said...he said it was better than the way I lived, that he'd rather be dead than not living at all, and being without Paula made him feel that way. He couldn't stand it. "

"You can't know for sure if he did or not, Madeline." Ash swept a soothing caress down the length of her spine. "I do know this, though. You spent a lifetime punishing yourself, burying yourself in guilt for what happened with Tick, and I'll be damned if I'll let you spend another doing the same over this. Get mad at me if you want, darlin', but he made those choices. Not you. No matter what happens tomorrow, I'm going to make sure you stay alive. Do you hear me?"

"I do." She twisted to look at him in the gloom. She laid her hand along his jaw. "Thank you."

He turned his head to press a kiss to her palm. "For?"

"Showing me how to live again." Her voice broke, and he leaned in to kiss her.

"I didn't do anything but love you." He shifted, canting his injured leg to one side. "Go to sleep now, baby. Tomorrow could be a long day."

Madeline stepped out of the station house into the cool winter sunlight. A bite of sea hung in the air, and she drank in a lungful as she hurried down the steps and to the small parking lot. She spotted Ash instantly, leaning against the hood of her car, arms folded over his chest.

He straightened as she approached. "How did it go?"

She smoothed her hair behind her ears, a new nervousness assaulting her. "I'm cleared for duty."

His grin flashed. "That's wonderful. I'm glad for you, babe."

"Me too." She scuffed her loafer against the asphalt. "Did you mean it, Ash?"

"Mean what?"

"That if I needed to be here, we'd find a way to make it work."

"Of course I did. I mean, damn, I'd love to have you with me all the time, but I know how important what you do is." He jerked his chin at her. "Get over here. We'll work it out. I promise."

Going into his easy embrace, she lifted her mouth to his. Their lips clung, the sweetness of the soft exchange leaving her breathless. She touched his chin. "If I stay here, that makes that whole 'live with me and be my love' kind of hard, doesn't it?"

"Babe, life's hard. You know that, but some things are worth working for." He brushed a kiss over her wrist and she felt rather than saw his smile. "Besides, you'll be my love no matter where you are."

She held him tighter. "I'm very...blessed...to have you in my life."

A laugh rumbled up from his chest. "We're making progress, then."

"What are you talking about, Hardison?" She leaned back to meet his gleaming eyes.

"You didn't try to tell me you don't deserve me."

"You." She rolled her eyes and he laughed again before he kissed her.

"We'll be fine, Mad. We will. I'm pretty sure you're gonna give me a hard time whenever you can. You'll get scared and you'll want to run, but you won't."

"How do you know?"

"Because you're not the same old Madeline anymore, are you?"

Her breath caught. The same old Madeline would have been gone long ago. "No, I'm not."

"That's what I thought."

With relief and joy burbling through her, she cast a teasing look up at him. "So, Hardison, do you like the new me?"

"Oh, babe." Despite his slow grin, his eyes remained serious. "I love the new you."

Epilogue

"I don't think I can do this." Madeline raked a hand through her hair, nails rasping on her scalp. Fear and an all-out urge to throw up mingled in her. "I really don't think so, Ash."

"Yes, you can." Infinite patience colored his voice. She loved that about him, loved how he took everything in stride and never let it push him toward the deep end.

That was her territory.

She swallowed and swiped at her damp eyes. "What if—"

"Mad. Babe." He swung the bathroom door open and leaned against the doorjamb, a long-suffering expression on his face. "Stop torturing both of us and just pee on the damn stick already."

He made it sound so easy, like they weren't talking about a life-altering event here. Puffing her cheeks with a long exhale, she shoved him toward the bedroom. "Fine. Get out."

Long moments later, she opened the door to wave him back in. They leaned over together, attention fixed on the home pregnancy test lying atop the vanity. God, it took forever.

Madeline brushed back her hair and eyed the wash of pale pink moving through the indicator window. "How long is this supposed to take?"

Ash sighed, and she sensed him rolling his eyes. "Three minutes."

"I can't watch anymore." She squeezed her eyes shut. "Tell me when it's over."

She counted to one hundred and fifty and cracked one eye. "Is it positive?"

"Look for yourself."

Nibbling her lip, she opened her eyes and stared down at the test. One pink line.

"It's negative." She took a step back, a crushing sensation seizing her chest. Surely that wasn't disappointment. Hell, she'd been freaking out for the last two days, since she'd skipped her period. What would she have done with a baby anyway? She should be relieved. Only the emotion coursing through her felt a lot like letdown. She threw back her shoulders and met Ash's gaze. "That's good, then."

He crossed his arms over his chest and looked back at her.

"You're not disappointed, are you?" She tucked her thumbs in the back pockets of her jeans. Finally, she caught her breath again, the smothering sensation receding.

He lifted one eyebrow. "Aren't you?"

"Ash, come on. Us, with a baby? *Me*, with a baby? Be serious."

"I am."

She stared then lifted both hands, palms forward, as though warding off some evil force. "Oh, no. No. Definitely not."

The fabulous grin she loved lifted the corners of his mouth. "I didn't say a word."

"Exactly. Just like you didn't say a word about marriage and somehow I ended up married to you anyway."

If possible, his eyebrow rose higher. "Are you complaining?"

"No, but—"

He smothered the protest, hooking a hand around her nape and pulling her in for a slow kiss, a smooth tangle of tongues and passion. She slipped her arms about his waist and leaned in. Oh, kissing this man was the best part of her day.

Loving this man, being his wife—which she'd been sure she couldn't do—was the best part of her life.

He lifted his head to murmur near her ear. "You'd make an excellent mother."

"Ash." She rested her face against his shoulder. "Don't do this. Don't make me want it."

"You already want it." His deep chuckle rumbled beneath her cheek. "It's all over your face, every time you're with Lee or your nieces."

She thumped a fist against his chest. "I hate when you're insightful."

"I know." He kissed the curve of her neck. "Come on, Mad. Let's give it six months with no precautions and see what happens."

On a rough sigh, she let her head fall back. "Oh, all right."

"Speaking of Lee"—Ash took advantage of her posture to nibble his way down her throat—"his daddy will be over here in a little while. We're haying the north pasture today."

"Sounds exciting." She tiptoed her fingers down his chest.

"Sounds hot and sweaty," he corrected, pulling her closer.

She leaned in to kiss the corner of his mouth, licking a little at his upper lip. "You like hot and sweaty."

"I like hot and sweaty with you." He dipped his hands to cup her ass and lift her into him. "Not Tick."

Desire clenched low in her belly, trembling in a wet pulse between her thighs. "Do we have time for hot and sweaty?"

He backed up, pulling her toward their bed. "I'll make time."

Sitting on the side of the bed, Ash finished buttoning his shirt then leaned over to brush his lips across Madeline's shoulder. Clutching the sheet to her bare breasts, she rolled to watch him. The sense of connection settled in her once more, bringing with it the precious certainty that this was the man she'd been destined to find, to love.

She reached for him, rubbed her thumb across his wrist. "I love you."

The words didn't come easily—they never did—but the sweet curve of his joyful smile made the effort worthwhile.

"I love you too, Mad." He planted a hand on either side of her and kissed her, dipping his tongue between her lips in teasing strokes before pulling back with a rueful laugh. "I've got to get moving."

She'd love nothing more but to keep him here with her, but the wish was impractical. Hay didn't cut and bale itself. With a sigh, she slid from the bed and gathered her clothes while he stamped first one, then the other foot, into his boots. An engine purred to a stop outside as she tugged her T-shirt over her head. Slipping on her jeans, she frowned at Ash. "That doesn't sound like Tick's truck."

He shook his head. "No, it doesn't."

Barefoot, she padded with him down the hall to the living room to see who their unexpected caller might be. On the porch, she halted and stared, surprise slithering through her.

Donna Martin walked up the narrow path to the front steps, sunlight shining off her red hair, a tentative smile trembling on her mouth. She stopped at the bottom of the steps and tucked her hands in her back pockets. "Hey, Maddie."

"Donna." She darted a quick look at Ash. He shrugged, brows lifted in a don't-ask-me expression. "Hey."

"I was wondering if maybe I could talk to you for a few minutes?" Donna worried at her bottom lip with her teeth.

"Sure." Madeline half-turned and gestured toward the door. "Ash was just headed out to the pasture. Would you like some lemonade or tea or something?"

Donna came up one step, then another. "Tea would be good."

Ash wrapped an arm around Madeline's waist and leaned in for a quick kiss. "I'll be back in a while."

As he walked away, Madeline waved Donna up the steps. "Come on in."

In the kitchen, she filled glasses with ice and tea, added lemon wedges. What was Donna doing here? They hadn't spoken in months, since that day back in February, when Madeline and Tick had interviewed her about Kelly's attendance at the party the night of her death.

She placed a glass before Donna at the kitchen island. "Here you go."

Still biting her lip, Donna wrapped both hands around the glass. Madeline took the other stool and waited. Donna rubbed a finger in the trail of a condensation drop. "So I hear you're working for the GBI now."

"I am." She loved it too, although when Tick had first broached the idea of her applying for the agent's position, she'd thought he was crazy. She sipped her tea. "Donna, you didn't come here to talk about my new job."

Donna shook her head, glanced away, then turned fierce eyes in Madeline's direction. "I don't really know why I'm here except...except I keep having these dreams. About all of us. About Kelly."

Madeline nodded and waited. Outside, a truck engine rumbled to a halt.

A shuddery sigh shook Donna's shoulders, and tears glittered in her eyes. "I can't stop thinking about that party. I knew leaving her with Allison was a bad idea. I knew it and I did it anyway because I didn't want to be the one on Allison's bad side. If I'd...if I'd done something, maybe Kelly wouldn't have died, you know? I have this dream, that she's under that house, but I helped put her there and—"

"Donna, don't." Madeline reached for her former friend's hand. "What happened wasn't your fault. It was Allison's and it was Nick Hall's. They're paying for that." After pleading guilty to murder, Hall was serving twenty-five years to life at Reidsville's state prison, and Allison remained incarcerated in Lowndes County, awaiting trial on murder charges stemming from her first husband's death. Madeline patted Donna's wrist. "You can't live your life blaming yourself, Donna. Doing that...it poisons things. It poisons you to the point that you might as well not live at all. You deserve better than that."

Donna blinked tears away from the fringe of her lashes. "You've changed a lot, you know that, Maddie?"

"I don't know if I've changed, Donna, or if my outlook changed." Madeline shrugged. Through the window, she could see Ash in the field behind the house. Tick approached him with a grin and a handshake. Funny how things had come so far since she'd arrived in the winter. She'd wanted to be anywhere else then; now, she couldn't imagine her life in any other setting.

Or perhaps, she couldn't imagine her life with anyone else.

"Your outlook?" Donna drew in a shivery breath and dashed at a stray tear. "Like how you live your life?"

"Yeah." Madeline smiled, pulling her gaze from the sunlight glinting off Ash's sandy hair, a rush of love and acceptance washing through her. She squeezed Donna's shaky fingers. "I finally learned how to forgive myself, how to live. Even more important, I learned how to love."

"I knew I smelled something good." Ash smiled at her from the doorway. The screen door vibrated to a close behind him, and he hopped on one foot, tugging off his sock. Dust and seeds covered his shirt and jeans, and a hay stem stuck straight up from his hair.

Madeline shook her head. "Soup and sandwiches. Nothing special."

On his way to the laundry room, he dropped a kiss on her nape. "It's always special when you cook, babe."

Because she rarely did it. She swallowed the retort and cut the steaming grilled cheese in half. "What did I tell you about calling me 'babe'?"

Chest bare, he stuck his head around the doorjamb. Devilment twinkled in the sea-green depths of his eyes. "I forget."

"Keep it up. I'll forget to make you a sandwich."

He reappeared, clad in only his boxers. "So what did your friend Donna want?"

"I'm not sure I'd call her my friend, Ash." Madeline laid the knife aside. What was Donna now? Maybe just another memory, something faded and frayed around the edges, a reminder of the desperate girl she no longer was?

He wrapped both arms around her waist and buried his nose in the curve where her shoulder met her neck. Smells of sunshine and hay and clean male sweat surrounded her. Heat from the line of his chest permeated her back. "What did she want?"

"Just to talk. About Kelly. About the past." Leaning into him, she laid her palms over his wrists. An "I love you" lodged in her throat, and she swallowed. He deserved more, deserved everything she had to give him. "Ash?"

"Hmm?" He hugged her tighter and kissed the side of her neck.

"While we were talking, I looked out the window, and I could see you working. It hit me all over again, then, how special and...perfect...you are." Tears burned behind her eyes, and she blinked hard. A tiny sob shuddered up from her chest. "How I wouldn't have anything if it weren't for you."

"Hey, don't do that. Don't get upset." He turned her in his arms and tugged her closer, so near she could see the fine pores of his skin, the even coating of dust on his face and neck. He lifted a hand to brush her hair behind her ear as her tears spilled over. "You'd have found your way, Mad, even without me."

"No, I wouldn't." Gulping back a bigger sob, she bracketed his beloved face with her palms. "I don't think you know how much I needed you, how much I needed that awesome patience of yours, so I could learn how to live. Without you, I didn't even realize I wasn't living my life, Ash."

She lifted her mouth to his, kissing him, the sharp tang of dust and sweat mingling with the salt of her own tears. Breaking the kiss, he spread a hand over her back, urging her against him, holding her as if she was a treasure of great value. She folded her arms about his neck and clung.

"I love you," she murmured, face pressed to his throat. Against her cheek, his pulse throbbed strong and sure, a steady thrumming she knew was meant solely for her, just as she knew her own beat only for him. "I know I don't say it often enough or—"

"You don't have to." He whispered the words against her hair. "All I need you to do is live with me and be my love."

Madeline smiled. "And all I need is you."

About the Author

How does a high school English teacher end up plotting murders? She uses her experiences as a cop's wife to become a writer of romantic suspense! Linda Winfree lives in a quintessential small Georgia town with her husband and two children. By day, she teaches American Literature, advises the student government and coaches the drama team; by night she pens sultry books full of murder and mayhem.

To learn more about Linda and her books, visit her website at www.lindawinfree.com or join her Yahoo newsletter group at http://groups.yahoo.com/group/linda_winfree. Linda loves hearing from readers. Feel free to drop her an email at linda_winfree@yahoo.com.

GREAT
CHEAP
FUN

Discover eBooks!

THE FASTEST WAY TO GET THE HOTTEST NAMES

Get your favorite authors on your favorite reader, long before they're
out in print! Ebooks from Samhain go wherever you go, and work with
whatever you carry—Palm, PDF, Mobi, and more.

Samhain
Publishing
ltd

WWW.SAMHAINPUBLISHING.COM

LaVergne, TN USA
08 August 2010
192562LV00002B/87/P